FAIRLIGHT

KEVIN PROVANCE

This is a work of fiction. While certain historical figures, locations, and events are used to provide a historical setting, the characters, dialogue, and incidents are the author's own creations. Any resemblance to actual persons, living or dead (outside of the historical record), is entirely coincidental.

Thank you for respecting this author's hard work and for your support. We also appreciate positive reviews.

First published in 2026 by SVL Studios.

OTHER TITLES BY KEVIN PROVANCE

The Displaced Series
Displaced I: Conundrum
Displaced II: The Exchange
Displaced III: Endgame
Displaced IV: Holding On

The Ryan Thomas Series
Scarecrow
Scorpion

Historical Fiction
Fairlight

Standalone Novels
Prisoner of the Game
Without A Word

CONNECT WITH ME ONLINE

Facebook: facebook.com/kevinprovance
X: x.com/KevinProvance
Instagram: instagram.com/kevinprovance
YouTube: youtube.com/@kevinprovance
Blog/Mailing List: kevinprovance.com

FOR BOOK CLUBS

Download the free Fairlight Book Club Guide at:
www.kevinprovance.com/fairlight

For the Historical Society of Carroll County, Maryland — and for the stewards of its history.

You keep the world that holds.

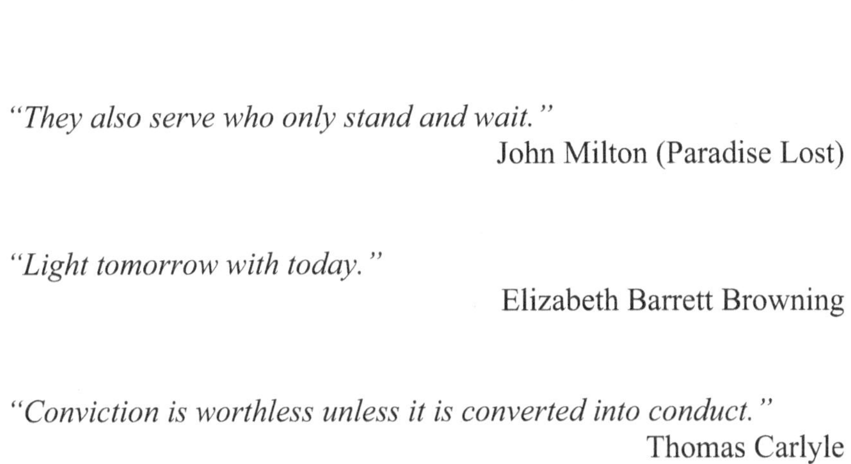

"They also serve who only stand and wait."

John Milton (Paradise Lost)

"Light tomorrow with today."

Elizabeth Barrett Browning

"Conviction is worthless unless it is converted into conduct."

Thomas Carlyle

PREFACE

A few things before we begin.

Writing about Carroll County, Maryland—Westminster, Taneytown, Bruceville—between 1857 and 1860 required a blend of research and imagination.

George, Maggie, and Frederick Mehring; William W. Dallas; Sheriff William Segafoose; Joseph Shaw; William H. Grammer; and Charles W. Webster were all residents of the time. Houses such as Myrtle Hill and Trevanion are documented homes that still stand today (and are privately owned—please respect their privacy).

The Marlowe family, Hannah Mehring, and their journey are fictional. The Marlowe farm and Fairlight are also fictional, though they rest upon real ground at the outskirts of Taneytown.

For readers interested in the historical record behind the story, I explore those details in the Author Notes at the end.

Because much of this novel unfolds in the years immediately preceding the Civil War, racially insensitive language appears in these pages, implied or spoken outright, but never gratuitously. It reflects the period and the character who uses it.

To remain faithful to that era, I adjusted my prose for those chapters, adopting a nineteenth-century cadence. It required careful study of how people wrote and spoke at the time: direct, deliberate, and sparing. Also, many of the characters were shaped by Brethren and Methodist traditions that valued humility, restraint, and emotional reserve, particularly in matters of courtship and conduct.

This story unfolds within my shared literary universe, specifically alongside the Ryan Thomas series (*Scarecrow* and *Scorpion*) and the Marlowe family, first introduced *in Prisoner of the Game*, all set in the nineties. None of those novels are required reading. Although Ryan and his friends appear in the novel, *Fairlight* stands on its own. Any relevant details from earlier works are woven into the narrative. Chronologically, this story takes place after *Scorpion* and before the forthcoming *Black Widow*. I mention this only to clarify why the present-day timeline is 1997.

Now, we turn toward the forests of northern Carroll County, where the remains of a long-vanished house draw a small group of friends into a story buried for more than a century—a story of love, fracture, and a name that refused to disappear.

Welcome to *Fairlight*.

K.P.

A PLAYLIST FOR FAIRLIGHT

This book has a soundtrack—a collection of songs that accompanied me through the writing, the revisions, and the long nights in between. These tracks aren't tied to specific scenes, but they helped shape the mood, the rhythm, and the emotional pulse of *Fairlight*.

If the land had a voice, this might be it.

www.kevinprovance.com/fairlight

Some songs remind me of the woods at dusk. Others carry the weight of memory or quiet resolve. A few pulled me through the hard-to-write chapters. If you listen while you read, I hope they bring something more to your journey into Fairlight's world.

CONTENTS

Prologue 1
Act I - The World That Holds 7
Chapter I 9
Chapter II 16
Chapter III 32
Chapter IV 47
Chapter V 50
Chapter VI 63
Chapter VII 68
Chapter VIII 82
Chapter IX 88
Chapter X 100
Act II - The World That Burns 105
Chapter I 107
Chapter II 123
Chapter III 127
Chapter IV 146
Chapter V 150
Chapter VI 164
Chapter VII 166
Chapter VIII 186
Chapter IX 191
Chapter X 224
Chapter XI 228
Chapter XII 267
Act III - The World That Continues 271
Chapter I 273

Chapter II 288
Chapter III 309
Chapter IV 316
Chapter V 321
Chapter VI 329
Chapter VII 338
Epilogue 348

PROLOGUE

Friday, August 14, 1987

I

The rumor of a haunted house in the woods was how it started. Whispers placed it south of Taneytown, Maryland, somewhere in the stretch of land separating the old antebellum gristmill estate, Trevanion, from the twentieth-century Otterdale Mill.

A recently graduated student from Westminster High School, Victor Merrick, heard it from a friend at Francis Scott Key High, who claimed to have heard it from Old Man Marlowe's eldest son, Ephraim. That alone was enough to give the story weight, given the landholdings and longevity of the Marlowe family in Carroll County. Supposedly, the house stood on Marlowe land, hidden deep within dense woods. No matter the route taken, at least a mile lay between the road and the destination.

Victor shared the story with his two closest friends: Martin Wexler and Walter DuMont.

Martin was the loudest of the three, exuding a calm confidence and speaking without a filter. Fresh out of high school and already bored with settling into local work, he approached life as something to be conquered, indulging in pleasures one by one. He had the looks to support his attitude—short black hair and sharp blue eyes—and never missed an opportunity to remind others of his appearance.

Walter was Martin's opposite. Quiet, cautious, and uncomfortable with confrontation, he preferred predictability and disliked surprises. He wasn't unattractive, just unremarkable; brown hair, brown eyes, and an expression that often suggested he had already reconsidered whatever was happening. Trouble rarely began with Walter, yet he frequently found himself right in the middle of it.

Victor fell somewhere in between the two. He embraced his identity as a geek with unapologetic pride and didn't give a damn what others thought of him. He listened more than he spoke, asked questions that others didn't consider, and sometimes showed enthusiasm that exceeded common sense.

Given all that, it was no surprise that Martin was immediately in favor of exploring the woods at night in search of a haunted house. Walter wasn't. Victor was enthusiastic at first, until the reality of distance, darkness, and isolation began to sink in.

By then, it was already too late to back out.

II

At nine p.m., after the mall closed, Martin, Walter, and Victor emerged from the doors near the Glenmar movie theater and the Dream Machine arcade of the newly opened Cranberry Mall.

The sun had already slipped below the horizon, leaving the sky washed in deep blue with the first faint stars beginning to show.

They crowded into Walter's white 1982 Chevette and headed north on Route 140 toward Taneytown. Martin took the passenger seat; Victor sat in the middle of the back, unfolding a hand-drawn map and holding it up to the passing streetlights. His friend at FSK High, Matt, had dictated the directions over the phone.

Martin shifted in the stiff vinyl seat and glanced back. "So where are we going, exactly?"

Victor squinted at the paper. "Nusbaum Road."

Walter snorted. "Where the fuck is that?"

"Off Trevanion Road."

Martin reached back for the map. Victor handed it over.

"What's this dip here?" Martin asked, pointing to a crude bend drawn as a backward checkmark circled in red.

"That's where we park," Victor said. "From there, we walk."

Walter leaned over the center console. "How far?"

"A quarter-mile. Maybe a little more."

"And the creek?" Walter asked, pronouncing it *crick*.

"Matt says it's low."

Walter exhaled sharply. "Matt says. Great."

Martin studied the map again, already reorganizing it in his head. "Walt, here's a shortcut," he said. "Bang a left on 31. Take Uniontown Road instead of going through Taneytown."

Walter followed the suggestion after passing Western Maryland College, its lights fading behind them.

"I know that area," Martin added, grinning. "I banged a girl out there in Middleburg a couple of months ago. There's a quicker way to Nusbaum."

"Of course you did," Victor muttered, rolling his eyes.

"After Trevanion Road, Otterdale Mill is the second right. Big Pipe Creek is a couple miles up. Nusbaum comes right after."

Walter nodded. "And then?"

"Then we find the V in the road," Martin said, tapping the map, "park, and walk."

No one spoke after that. The farther they drove, the darker the road became, the last traces of town thinning behind them as the land opened into fields and shadow.

III

With their shoes and socks far wetter than anticipated after crossing the creek, the boys found themselves less than a thousand feet into the field beyond it. Victor felt a sudden, sinking certainty that he'd misjudged the scope of the trip.

There was no moon. The sky was pitch black. Against the faint glow on the horizon from Taneytown, the forest rose ahead of them as a solid, imposing wall.

Victor cleared his throat. "You know…maybe this wasn't the best idea."

"Pussy," Martin whispered.

Walter shook his head. "Marty, I didn't want to do this at all. It's too fucking dark out here. Did anyone bring a flashlight?"

Martin stopped. The other two halted as he turned. "I didn't. You didn't either?" Walter shook his head. "Vic?"

"Nope."

Martin dragged a hand down his face. "This was your idea, bitch! That includes the prep!"

"I brought the compass," Victor said, the defensive tone unmistakable.

Walter snorted. "Great. At least we'll know which direction we're running when we hit a tree."

Martin turned back toward the woods, studying the darkness. The forest stretched wide. Hundreds of feet from the creek to their left and running more than a mile to the right. "I don't see how we're supposed to find anything in there."

"Matt said it's toward the middle," Victor said, pointing vaguely.

"How far in?" Martin asked.

Victor looked down. "He didn't say."

Walter peered at him, letting out a short laugh. "Shocking."

Victor returned the look. "Dude! Just…shut up!"

Martin checked his watch; the faint green glow briefly lit his face. "It's after ten. We'll look around for a bit. If we don't find anything in an hour, we're done."

IV

Within fifteen minutes of entering the darkened forest, the boys cautiously navigated the trees, their eyes darting in all directions in search of an old house. The ground beneath their feet was a thick carpet of decaying leaves from autumns past. They made a crunching, shifting sound with each step. Frogs croaked, and crickets chirped. The noises wove a dense tapestry throughout the entire woods. The deep hoot of an owl echoed through the forest at steady intervals.

The growing psychological hysteria between them remained unchecked, no matter what they tried. Sounds that weren't there. Glimmers of movement at the edges of their sight, gone the instant they turned their heads.

When it happened, they were primed to believe the worst.

A faint cracking sound from afar interrupted the quiet. It stopped all three in their tracks.

"What the fuck was that?" Walter asked in a petrified whisper, his head snapping back and forth, looking for the source.

The sound escalated from a crack to a deep groan, its source indistinguishable in the suffocating blackness.

Victor shut his eyes tightly, a futile attempt to make the unfolding events disappear. "Oh, my God," he whispered sheepishly. "I don't wanna die. Jesus, I'm so sorry I did this. Yea, though I walk through the valley of the shadow of death—"

"Shut up, Vic!" Martin snapped in a harsh whisper, his gaze fixed on the impenetrable darkness within the trees.

A profound stillness settled over the woods, as if everything had suddenly held its breath. Even the crickets had ceased chirping. Slowly, the boys' gazes shifted to one another, their expressions mirroring a chilling sense of impending disaster.

That's when the sound came again.

Not a crack this time, but a deep, tearing report. Wood splitting under its own weight. Branches snapped in rapid succession, the noise rushing toward them through the dark.

Martin's eyes went wide. "Oh, shit! *RUN!*"

They spun and bolted.

Leaves slid under their feet. Walter stumbled first, catching himself with a sharp grunt before scrambling upright again. Victor's breath came in panicked bursts, his arms flailing as he fought to keep his footing. Behind them, something groaned, low and strained. The sound of breaking limbs followed, close enough to feel.

They burst from the trees into the open field and didn't slow.

Martin glanced over his shoulder once. He saw nothing. That didn't help.

They reached Big Pipe Creek at a reckless sprint, splashing straight through it, water soaking their legs as they clawed up the far bank. Walter yanked open the driver's door and dove inside. Victor followed. Martin slammed the passenger door shut as Walter twisted the key.

The engine roared to life. Gravel sprayed as the Chevette fishtailed onto the road and tore away into the dark.

None of them spoke.

Something had moved through those woods. Something heavy enough to break branches and fast enough to chase them.

They didn't go back to check.

Victor told Matt what had happened that night. About the woods, the sound, the way something had come at them through the trees. By the end of the month, the story had already moved on without him.

At Francis Scott Key High, it gained details.

At Westminster High, it gained teeth.

By 1989, the tale had settled into something closer to legend. A group of kids wandering into the woods in search of a house no one was meant to find. If they came too close, something would rise to meet them: a guardian, a presence, a thing that lived among the trees. It announced itself with a roar and the sound of breaking limbs that would drive intruders back the way they came.

The details shifted, the shape changed, and the truth thinned.

What never changed was this: no one ever reached the house.

For years, teenagers went looking. Some came back with stories. Some came back silent. Some claimed they'd been chased. Others swore the woods themselves had turned against them.

No one ever saw the house.

Not until Ernest Marlowe took Todd Metheny, Ryan Thomas, Carrie Beck, and Deborah Hall into the woods in the spring of 1997.

ACT I

THE WORLD THAT HOLDS

CHAPTER I

Wednesday, May 21, 1997

I

Ryan Thomas stepped out from beneath the pale stone archway of Hill Hall and into the late afternoon sun, the warmth catching him off guard.

It had felt cooler that morning. Spring was still undecided. But now the air carried the scent of freshly cut grass and something close to relief. He began rolling up the sleeves of the green, blue, and white flannel.

Three days. After that, his days as a student at Western Maryland College would finally be behind him. Again.

By autumn, his part-time instructor schedule would begin.

Todd Metheny ducked through the arch behind him, his gray "Green Terror" T-shirt riding up as he walked. He tugged it down without thinking, the fabric still sitting wrong even after a dozen washes. "Ryan, I'd never have survived these criminal justice courses without you as a study partner," he said, his voice echoing faintly off the stone as they started up the ramp toward the quad.

Ryan ran his fingers through his short blonde hair, adjusted the strap of his backpack, and slapped the absurdly seven-foot-tall Todd on the back. "Sure, you would've. It's like I've told you a million times, dude; studying this material is no different from studying a script from one of the many plays you were in."

Todd let out a quiet laugh, brushing chestnut brown hair from his eyes as they stepped into the open. "Yeah. And I wasn't very good at that either. Deborah always kept me honest there."

Ryan chuckled at the methods twenty-three-year-old Deborah Hall employed to motivate Todd. They usually involved pulling him backstage for some out-of-sight alone time. What that entailed, Ryan was sure he couldn't say.

"Deborah is the best thing that ever happened to you, brother," Ryan declared, looking up at Todd, his gaze deep blue and determined, despite their height difference. "I'm glad you two finally decided to move in together." A sly grin crept across Ryan's face. "Now, all you have to do is make an honest woman of her."

With a flicker of unease, Todd laughed a little too loudly at Ryan. "Like you did with Carrie? What was it? Two days ago?"

Ryan smiled fondly at the mental image of twenty-two-year-old Carrie Beck, with her silver-blue eyes, standing a mere five-foot-one, her sunflower-yellow hair flowing past her shoulders. "You left out the part where I bought the house she's always wanted."

Todd tossed Ryan a doubtful glance as they left the quad, the air thick with the scent of freshly cut grass as they approached Lewis Hall. "The old house on Uniontown Road with the wraparound porch. I'm amazed it's still standing, with the condition it's in. How long has it been abandoned?"

"A couple of years. It looks worse than it is." Ryan's eyes drifted toward the Victorian house on the south side of Lewis Hall, where the current WMC president lived. "Are you on duty tonight?"

"No, I'm working four twelve-hour shifts over the next week. Friday, Sunday, Monday, and Wednesday," Todd said. It was part of his demanding rookie schedule as a trooper with the Maryland State Police. "My patrol car is in the shop. Deborah had to drive me this morning."

Ryan scanned the parking lot to his right, past Baker Memorial Chapel, and said, "I don't see her."

A sheepish smile crept across Todd's face. "She's at work. I may have possibly suggested to her I'd grab a ride home with you."

Ryan stopped walking and, with a smirk, tilted his head up at Todd. "I live at the top of East Main. You live in the Greens. You're noting the opposite directions here, right, future detective?"

Todd laughed. "Blow me, smartass! I thought maybe you'd give me a quick tour of your old spooky house."

Ryan shrugged with indifference, resuming his walk past the President's House. "Sure, why not? Carrie will be pissed I didn't let her do it. That's her thing now, apparently."

"Mum's the word. Where are you parked?"

Ryan pointed past the President's House. "On 39th, behind Alumni Hall."

"Alumni Hall," Todd whispered, deliberately chuckling under his breath.

Ryan rolled his eyes, a silent gesture unseen by Todd, who was walking one pace ahead. He knew where this was going. They'd danced these steps many times.

Todd purposefully cleared his throat. "I'm still assuming after all these years, you still don't believe Alumni Hall was haunted."

Ryan sighed, his voice making a deliberate humph. "It's only been two years, dude. And no, I remain unconvinced."

Todd huffed a quiet laugh. "You say that like we didn't live through it."

"We did," Ryan said. "That's exactly my point."

Todd glanced down at him. "You're telling me before everything went to hell with Scarecrow that the lower level didn't feel off to you?"

Ryan adjusted the strap of his backpack. "It felt like a guy hiding in a basement who didn't want to get caught."

"That's not all it was."

"That's all it needed to be," Ryan shot back. "Everything else? The cold spots, noises, people tripping over nothing? That's what happens when you've got a killer climbing around backstage and ten people's worth of paranoia floating through the building."

Todd smirked and shook his head in resignation. "You've got an explanation for everything, dude."

"I've got the *correct* explanation," Ryan said. "We know what happened in there. We proved it. You were there. You saw it with your own eyes."

Todd didn't argue right away. His eyes lingered on Alumni Hall a second longer.

"Yeah," he said. "We proved most of it."

Ryan let out a breath, somewhere between a sigh and a laugh. "Two years later, and you're still on that. I might buy restless spirits who were wronged in this life. But ghosts that haunt buildings? No." Ryan looked up at Todd and grinned, a playful glint in his eyes. "You'd have to explain why they can't leave the house or why they don't move on to whatever's next."

"Watch Beetlejuice."

"Ha!" Ryan barked, trailing off with a laugh. "Great movie, but…no."

Todd shrugged. "I'm just saying…not everything we felt in there had some messed-up guy behind it."

Ryan finally glanced toward the building, then back ahead. "Like always, we'll have to agree to disagree."

They continued walking.

II

After a short drive down Uniontown Road and directly across Route 31, Ryan slowed his Lexus and turned into the driveway on his left without using a turn signal. No one was behind him. \

Todd stared at the old Colonial house with the wraparound porch surrounding the ell. From a hundred feet away, the porch still looked dignified. As Ryan pulled up beside the house, his gaze fell upon the basement entrance, a dark opening carved directly into the gentle slope of the hill. Todd took a thorough look around at the home's condition.

"I've never seen this house this up close before," Todd whispered. "The porch is in awful shape."

"It's seen better days."

They exited the Lexus and walked through the wet spring grass up the hill to the porch entrance. Todd stood a half-step behind while Ryan pointed out what needed fixing. The old house sat square and stubborn on its foundation, stone walls thick as bookends, shutters missing, porch sinking toward the yard.

"I paid a hundred and twenty for it. That includes the barn, outbuildings, and ninety-six acres," Ryan said, running his hand along the faded white paint of the porch column. "Closed on it two days ago."

Todd whistled softly, the sound barely audible as they reached the porch's edge and turned left. Now, they were looking down one story to the ground, with the smell of damp, uncut grass rising, since the house was built into the hill. He grinned at Ryan. "Carrie's gonna make it pretty for you."

"That's the idea." Ryan pointed to the door behind them. "I proposed to her in the front room, right there." He nodded at one of the boarded-up windows. "The rest, you know."

The wood smelled damp; the plaster inside sweeter, like wet paper left in sunlight. Vines were working their way up the stone pillars of the porch, young and bright and green in the May warmth.

"Do you know who built this house…and when?" Todd asked.

"Lydia Royer, our realtor, knew a bit about the history," Ryan said, feeling the rough texture of the gray stucco wall. "She says she's related to the wife of the man who built it. A grandmother five times removed. His name was Mehring. The best they've been able to pinpoint the exact year is in or around 1855."

"Mehring?" Todd asked casually.

"Yeah. Jacob Mehring. Lydia said the name like I was supposed to know it."

Todd didn't answer right away. The surname stirred something familiar: an antebellum home called Myrtle Hill from Ernest Marlowe's father's stories. A man named George Mehring lived there when the area was called the town of Bruceville. Back then, there was only one Mehring line in the county. It didn't take a genealogist to make the leap.

Todd smiled. The house wasn't important, not really. But the name was.

As Ryan spoke of the decaying roof, Todd abruptly interrupted with a question about ghosts. "You don't think an old house like this that predates the Civil War isn't haunted? All I'm saying is, places remember things. Like Alumni Hall does."

"Places remember mildew," Ryan said. "And maybe termites."

Todd snorted with laughter as they retraced their steps on the porch, the soft boards yielding with each step, the damp plaster's scent filling the air. He brushed a flake of paint from his hand, chalk-white against his jeans.

"Have you ever heard about the so-called haunted woods of Taneytown?" Todd asked.

Ryan glanced up. "Which one? They've got a ghost story for every cornfield out there."

"The woods south of town off Otterdale Mill," Todd said. "Kids say it's haunted. They say there's...something out there. A house nobody can get close to. Supposedly, if you start walking toward it, you'll hear a noise in the trees, like a whole damn herd coming at you. They run before they ever get close enough to see anything."

Ryan snorted. "That's adrenaline, not ghosts. And probably a raccoon."

Todd's eyebrow arched, a silent question forming in the space above his eye. "Raccoons don't crash through the woods like linebackers, dude."

"Deer, then. Or teenagers. Teenagers make most hauntings happen anyways."

Todd didn't push. That wasn't the point. Skeptics needed curiosity, not answers.

"You guys got plans Friday? Say, around seven?"

Ryan contemplated it as they stepped off the porch, feeling the rough texture of the broken concrete under their shoes, heading toward the overgrown grass. "Nothing, as far as I know."

"I'd like to show you."

"Show me what? Deer in your haunted woods?"

"The house. The spot the kids claim they can't approach. I've been there. It's on Marlowe land. There's a story there. I think you'd enjoy it. Or at the most...appreciate."

Ryan paused, making eye contact with Todd. He could see the moment Ryan took the bait. Not because he believed, but because he didn't.

"What's really out there?" Ryan asked, peering at Todd with uncertainty.

Todd smiled. "An old house. Or what's left of one. You'll like it. I'll bring Deborah. We'll build a fire and wait for the sun to set."

"Don't you have a twelve-hour shift on Friday?"

"Six a.m. to six p.m.," Todd replied. "Meet us at my house around seven."

Ryan gave a heavy sigh, shoulders slumping as he finally agreed to Todd's request. "If it were *anyone* else, I'd say no. So, I'll give you the benefit of the doubt. We'll come. But I'm not promising I'll get scared."

Todd grinned. "I wouldn't want that. I just want you to see something."

"And no having one of the Marlowe boys hiding in the woods to come crashing through the trees."

Todd laughed out loud, but then sobered, nodding in agreement. "No tricks. No gimmicks. Only truth."

CHAPTER II

Friday, May 24, 1997

I

"Are we there yet, Uncle Todd?" Carrie Beck said, purposefully sounding like a young child complaining about the unending car trip.

The hum of the engine was barely audible as she and Deborah Hall sat in the backseat of Deborah's 1995 Honda Prelude. Todd drove because he knew the way.

Ryan snickered from his place in the passenger seat. "It's only been ten minutes, Scout," he said, referring to Carrie by the nickname he'd given her two years ago after they'd begun dating. The name was a reference to Scout Finch of "To Kill a Mockingbird," as Ryan thought she symbolized the mockingbird's innocence and beauty.

From her seat behind Ryan, Carrie watched Trevanion Road pass, becoming a colorful, fleeting streak outside the car window as Uniontown Road quietly gave way to Middleburg.

Todd sped up, the engine roaring in response. Forty miles per hour became fifty since the empty road stretched out before him. "Now we'll make better time."

"Alive, if you don't mind, babe," Deborah said, her shoulder-length blonde hair bouncing as she leaned forward, her breath warm on his neck as she rubbed Todd's shoulder from behind.

"Where exactly are we going?" Ryan asked, scanning the area ahead. "Judging by our direction, we'll end up in Middleburg or Keymar." He turned and smirked at Todd. "Not exactly south of Taneytown."

Todd nodded in confirmation. "I keep forgetting you think like an investigating journalist. We're taking a quick side quest before we reach the woods. I want you all to see a piece of the bigger picture first."

"I don't understand," Carrie said. "What does your totally out-of-the-way side quest have to do with the haunted Taneytown woods?"

A grin played on Todd's face, as if he held a delightful secret. "You'll see. We'll be there in less than ten minutes."

II

Eight minutes and seven miles later, Todd slowed to take a right onto Francis Scott Key Highway, heading north into Keymar.

"Alright," Ryan whispered. "My curiosity is officially piqued."

"I know this area," Carrie said, glancing at Todd, then at Deborah. "Francis Scott Key was born around here. The Terra Rubra estate."

"You know your history. Very good," Todd said, quoting the character Biff from Back to the Future II, approximating Biff's gruff voice.

Ryan leaned his head back and laughed. "1989 called, dude. It wants its lacking sequel back."

Todd glanced at Ryan as if he might not have agreed with that assessment, but let it pass.

"This is it," Todd said as he slowed to turn right onto the paved but not well-maintained Bruceville Road, while the FSK highway curved off to the left. Ryan watched the road as they drove slowly down its slant, the trees' shadows stretching long in the setting sun. The dense green shrubbery transformed into a shadowy forest in a matter of moments. "The town of Bruceville that was."

The road's asphalt appeared uneven, as if the country merely wanted to claim it had paved a road. There were no shoulders. Only the rough edge of the pavement blended into the grass. In some areas, the road was so narrow that drivers would have to yield to oncoming traffic, much like on a one-way street. As if sculpted by time itself, the path plunged through the hill, a channel so old it seemed to predate any recorded history. The slope became so steep that the car could easily roll away if left in neutral.

Nineteenth-century houses lined the road, stone foundations half-swallowed by grass. These were the kind of homes that didn't bother announcing how old they were. They didn't need to.

Carrie gazed at them, spotting the ground-level ones to her right and the elevated ones to her left, which needed stone or concrete steps to meet the road—window-mounted AC units protruding from the front windows like metallic tongues panting for relief. The numerous satellite dishes implied that cable TV was not a luxury in that area. However, the road was lined on both sides with wooden poles humming faintly with the unseen power of electricity and communication.

"This is the land that time forgot," Ryan whispered as he watched the two-story, weathered stone house slowly float by. The front of the wall had two imposing doors, each firmly embedded in the structure. "That house there looks like it might've been a general store."

"It was. It was also an ad hoc post office." Todd replied, driving slowly, one hand loose on the wheel, eyes forward as the lane dipped deeper into the countryside, as if it were leading somewhere secret.

Ryan turned to look at Todd. "How would you know that?"

A mischievous smile spread across Todd's face as he remained silent.

"At least tell me where this road goes," Ryan said, not growing impatient per se, but eager to learn more.

"To the end," Todd said.

Carrie belted out a laugh from the back. "Could you be any more enigmatic, Toddster?"

"Great word, hon," Deborah said, bobbing her head with a smile.

Todd slowly drove down the last stretch. Everyone in the car stopped talking. It felt as though conversation didn't belong there in that moment.

The road ended abruptly, much like some stories do: suddenly and without warning. Myrtle Hill was at this dead end, with a red house perched against the green of the hill. Its porch sagged under the weight of old shade trees. The home appeared cared for, yet weary, as if someone had only maintained the parts visible from the outside. Below the hill, Big Pipe Creek flowed past in the shade of the old Virginia pine trees. Though the creek was hidden from view, its gentle murmur was perceptible to a keen ear.

With nowhere else for them to go, Todd braked and idled for a moment. The four of them sat looking at the house without speaking, as though it were deciding whether they could come any closer.

"Does this place belong to someone?" Carrie asked.

"It always has," Todd whispered.

He eased the Honda off to the right, tires crunching gravel. They climbed out. The air was warm and close; the only sounds were insects and the slow ticking of cooling metal under the hood.

"Pretty spot," Carrie murmured.

"Built in seventeen-ninety-something," Todd said, mostly to himself. "It was an old mill seat. The water's steady here."

Ryan glanced at him. "Mill?"

Todd nodded toward the shade beneath the trees, where the creek lay hidden beyond the grass and pines. "A long time ago. Before the war. Before the house, even. The creek powered the stones that crushed the grain, or corn, or whatever else the farmers brought over."

"Who owned it?" Ryan asked.

Todd took a moment before answering. "The Mehrings. Things started here."

Carrie raised her hand, a gesture that immediately hushed the chatter. She turned her ear toward the creek, listening. The water caught on rock somewhere below, the sound patient and insistent.

"Mehring," Ryan repeated. "Any relation to Jacob Mehring?"

"The guy who built our house?" Carrie asked.

"I think so," Todd replied. "Before the night's over, we'll know."

Ryan's hearty laugh filled the air. "And hopefully your cryptic streak will end."

Todd continued to smile without replying.

Carrie turned away from the property, the gravel crunching under her feet, and faced her friends. "In all seriousness, Todd, this is a beautiful piece of land. Quiet. Serene. I could totally fall asleep to the sound of the water."

"Hannah liked it," Todd added quietly.

Ryan opened his mouth to ask more, but Todd had already turned back toward the Honda. “Come on,” he said. “We’ve got ground to cover, and we’re losing light.”

III

Todd backtracked halfway down Middleburg Road and turned left onto Clear View Road. They’d end up higher on Trevanion Road via the shortcut, bypassing the Uniontown Road intersection, saving ten minutes. With the time nearing 7:50 p.m., there were now a scant thirty-one minutes before the sun dipped below the horizon.

Todd turned left onto Trevanion Road, now heading north toward Taneytown.

“How much farther?” Ryan asked Todd. He casually glanced over his shoulder, not expecting a clear and concise answer.

“Three and a half miles, give or take,” Todd replied, his eyes scanning the empty road and the endless green alfalfa fields across the occasional rolling hill. “We should be there in five to ten minutes.”

With a giggle, Carrie reached across, her fingers brushing Ryan’s flannel as she gripped his shoulders. “The legendary haunted woods of Taneytown! I can’t wait!”

Carrie’s jesting words, which carried a subtle, humorous undertone, piqued Deborah’s attention. “Do you believe in ghosts, Carrie?”

“Not really,” she replied, meeting Deborah’s gaze. “But unlike my faithful fiancée up there, I *am* open to having my mind changed.”

Todd’s eyes flickered to her in the rearview mirror. “How so?”

“Show me a ghost. I’ll believe it,” Carrie stated.

With a slight shake of his head, Ryan chuckled under his breath. “Carrie has a talent for simplifying things.”

Todd slowed the Honda as he rounded the left bend in the road. As the line of trees guarding the field on the left receded, it exposed a red brick Gothic-style house, its many chimneys reaching toward the sky. He crossed the road and parked on the soft green grass.

“Whoa,” Carrie whispered, her voice tinged with wonder, leaning forward to peer across Deborah and through her window at the massive house.

“Yeah,” Deborah whispered. “It still takes my breath away every time I see it."

Ryan asked. "Are we there? That was the shortest five minutes I've ever heard of."

Todd shook his head, smirked, and looked at Ryan. "That's what she said, brother."

"Ha!" Carrie barked, trailing off with a laugh. "Not even close!"

Todd continued, "This is Trevanion. Another piece of the bigger picture I wanted you to see. It's a private home, so this is as close as we can get."

Ryan felt as though Trevanion announced itself before they even reached it. A low stone wall didn't feature iron gates; instead, it had two square pillars set far enough apart to allow a carriage to pass through. Between them, a narrow drive curved uphill, worn pale by wheels and weather, as if the land itself had been trained to yield to its owners.

Mowed close on either side of the property, the lawn sloped down to tall, watchful trees. The house stood in the distance, blending into the landscaping, its red brick blending with the grassy surroundings. The façade appeared formal and deliberately designed. Trevanion was tall rather than wide, with a central tower rising above the roofline, proclaiming its permanence. White trim highlighted every edge—window frames, cornices, and the shallow balcony above the entry. Even the porch arches exuded a sense of measured restraint, offering an ornate welcome.

The house didn't sit within the land so much as command it. Offering no shelter as one approached, the broad, exposed lawn created no sense of intimacy. The trees were kept at a respectful distance from the house, as though growth itself was tolerated only on Trevanion's terms. From the drive, the windows appeared watchful rather than inviting; their symmetry exact, their height slightly aloof.

"It's an impressive old house," Ryan said. "I'm eager to hear how Myrtle Hill and Trevanion tie into your haunted woods."

Before merging back onto the road, Todd checked for oncoming traffic, then sped north. "We're almost there."

IV

A minute later, Todd turned left off Trevanion Road onto Nusbaum Road, a narrow, unmarked road with a gritty asphalt surface. Unlike the road in Bruceville, the county had kept this one in better condition, which was a collective relief. Nusbaum Road veered away almost as if it forked off Trevanion.

"You're about to see some real Carroll County countryside," Todd said, carefully navigating the turns of the narrow road.

The road straightened, offering a clear view of the sporadically spaced line of sixties-era homes stretching along the left. On the other side, the verdant farmland and trees stretched out, creating a sea of green.

From offside, Todd quickly glimpsed Ryan, the green of the field reflecting in his eyes. "Carrie said she would believe in ghosts if she saw one. If you were to see one too, would *you* change *your* mind?"

"Depends on how we define ghosts," Ryan replied. "There are no bedsheets with holes cut out of them, or apparitions floating around like the opening of Ghostbusters. And even if you could prove those things, it doesn't answer the question of why there are ghosts to begin with. Why didn't they move on to whatever's next, whether it's Heaven or the next life?"

"Debs? Wanna take that one?" Todd asked.

"Those spirits are unaware they've died," Deborah explained. "Some have strong attachments, like family, home, or possessions. Others experienced sudden or traumatic deaths. And some are trapped by unresolved issues or earthly desires."

With his lips pursed, Ryan's gaze lingered on Deborah. "You pretty much just said everything Tangina from Poltergeist said."

Todd couldn't contain the laughter that bubbled up inside him.

Ryan focused his eyes, studying Todd's face intently. "Laugh it up, fuzzball."

"Oh, my God," Carrie whispered, her voice tinged with mock exasperation as she rolled her eyes. "The pop culture references are totally out of control tonight."

"It doesn't make Tangina wrong," Deborah replied. "With that in mind, this next part won't surprise you. Citing Hebrews 9:27: *'And just as it is appointed for mortals to die once, and after that the judgment.'*"

Carrie jumped in. “Meaning people only have one life and then face God.”

“Exactly,” Deborah said. “Some say that what we think of as ghosts are deceptive spirits, or demons, impersonating the dead, and aren’t human.”

Carrie frowned. “Hmm. One of those I’d prefer *not* to see, thanks!”

Todd continued, “Ghosts could also be what we think of as purgatory. Souls awaiting divine judgment.”

Ryan turned to face forward, watching Todd navigate a hard left curve. The path wound through green fields, past silent trees, and over rolling hills. “By that logic, John Myers haunted Alumni Hall because of his sudden and traumatic death? Because in 1970, the ten members of Scarecrow accidentally killed him and dumped his body in the Alumni Hall sub-basement?”

“Yes,” Todd replied cleanly and plainly.

“Wouldn’t there be ghosts or spirits all over the place then?” Ryan asked.

“There very well could be.”

Less than a minute later, Todd made a complete forty-five-degree turn in the road with still no house in sight.

“Are we on Old Man Marlowe’s land?” Ryan asked. “Someone is keeping these crops well-maintained.”

“Not on this side of Big Pipe Creek,” Todd replied. “Well, not anymore. Not since the early twenties.”

Carrie leaned forward. “This was an old farm road once, wasn’t it?”

“Indeed, it was,” Todd said, his voice laced with satisfaction as he watched Carrie in the rearview. “It stretched from Trevanion to Otterdale Mill Road, although it wasn’t called that originally. There are lots of old farm roads scattered around Carroll. Some became actual roads. Some faded in the mists of time and no longer exist.”

Ryan almost uttered a quip about spirits, the words right there, but let the moment fade.

Silence reigned in the car until the road curved into the trees, with the slow, steady creek following alongside. A sharp, barely navigable V-turn into a deeper forest was required just as the creek became visible from the road.

“What the hell is this devilry?” Carrie asked, her eyes crinkling at the corners in a grin. "That was a weird turn."

"There used to be a dam there," Todd replied. "Now it's further down at Otterdale."

A minute later, they emerged from the forest into a field, passing an old, overgrown farm road on their left. Todd motioned toward it. "There's an old one, Carrie."

As they drove by, Carrie watched the old path, covered in weeds and worn with time. They arrived at the intersection of Otterdale Mill Road shortly thereafter.

After turning left and driving a half-mile, they crossed a bridge over Big Pipe Creek and arrived at their destination.

The middle of nowhere.

Todd turned left onto a dirt road amidst a cornfield, the dust rising around his tires as it disappeared over the hill. "Now we're on Marlowe land."

A cloud of dust kicked up behind the Honda, the only sound the engine's hum as silent anticipation filled the vehicle. Ryan glanced at the odometer as the half-mile mark ticked by. He moved his gaze to Todd. "Kids actually walk all the way back here to explore the woods?"

Todd and Deborah exchanged a secret glance, their laughter ringing out in the car. "After we stop, we'll still have three-quarters of a mile to go. On foot."

Carrie snapped her head around at Deborah, jaw dropped. She smiled and nodded silently in confirmation.

"This is actually the easiest way there," Todd added. "There are shorter ways, but then you'd have to find a way to cross the creek and more woods."

Todd brought the car to a stop at the treeline beside an old white Ford pickup, kicking back dust that lightly coated the vehicles. Behind them, farm outbuildings stood silhouetted against the setting sun. A man of Todd's age exited the pickup and approached.

"How many farms does Old Man Marlowe own?" Ryan asked. "I thought he just owned the one with the Victorian house off Old Taneytown Road."

"This is a sharecrop farm," Todd replied, exiting the Honda. The rest of their party followed. "Marlowe owns five or six of them. And speaking of Marlowe."

Ryan instantly recognized the man as he approached. Ernest

Marlowe, Old Man Marlowe's youngest son, stood dressed in beat-up brown-and-blue flannel, faded blue jeans, and a green John Deere baseball cap.

"How's it hangin', Metheny?" Ernest said, with a slight Maryland accent.

"Long and low, brother," Todd replied as they shook hands in an arm-wrestling grip. Todd turned, letting Ernest's hand go. "Deb and Ryan, you know. The little blonde pipsqueak there is Carrie Beck. Ryan's fiancée."

"Pipsqueak?" Carrie asked, peering up at Todd from beneath her furrowed brow. "Okay, Gigantor. You know about dynamite and small packages, right?"

Deborah snickered under her breath, letting out a snorting noise.

Ryan shook Ernest's hand firmly and then clapped Todd playfully on the arm. "You should've seen that coming, dude. Carrie doesn't play."

"Spicy!" Ernest said with a healthy grin, carefully extending his hand to Carrie. "Nice to meet you, ma'am. Anyone who gives Todd the business like that is A-OK in my book."

"We met once, a long time ago, at the Farm Museum," Carrie replied, firmly shaking Ernest's hand. He gave Carrie an uncertain look, his mouth slightly agape as if the meeting was lost to him. "You were there with your brother and dad, displaying some antique tractors. I wanna say it was 1992? I was a junior in high school. It was the Fourth of July. I went with my two best friends, Tiffany and Lauren."

"Oh, yeah," Ernest said, his face lighting up as the memory snapped into place. "They were blonde, too. Weren't they?" Carrie's eyes sparkled as she nodded excitedly. "One of them sounded like a damn valley girl, always using the word 'like.'"

"Tiffany," Carrie said, glancing at Ryan, who also smiled at the memory of their mutual and lost friend. "That was totally her."

"Tiffany…Cutter?" Ernest asked.

Carrie smiled and nodded.

Ernest removed his cap and held it between his hands. "I was sorry to hear about her. The whole Scarecrow thing."

Carrie, her smile faltering only by a degree, nodded. "Thanks. It wasn't the first time, sorry to say." Ernest stared at her, waiting for more. "We lost Lauren a year and a half before Tiffany. Bad car accident."

Ernest realized then, with a jolt, that Carrie had suffered the loss of two of her dearest friends within two years. "That's truly awful. I'm so sorry. You seem to be handling it well enough."

Carrie turned back to Ryan, a playful glint in her eye as she winked. "Two years ago, I reconnected with someone who helped me to see I could still trust people and let them in."

Ryan's smile was a warm beam as he gently took her hand. "And I reconnected with someone who helped me learn to love again after losing Tiffany, too."

Ernest glanced at Todd, slipping the cap back onto his head, covering his shaggy hair. "Ryan was dating Tiffany?"

Todd nodded. "More or less."

"So…I assume they're talking about each other?"

"They are," Todd stated flatly, his eyes flicking towards them, implying their overly affectionate behavior should wane some. He deliberately cleared his throat, a loud, purposeful sound to get their attention. "Anyways, I've asked Ernest to come along as a tour guide. Putting to one side that it would probably take me all night to find the spot where the house was, this is Ernest's story to tell."

Ryan glanced at Ernest. "There's a story that explains why the kids think these woods are haunted?"

Ernest pulled his lips together, a subtle whistling sound escaping as he thought. "I don't know," he said after several seconds. "I think so. But you'll have to judge for yourself."

Todd pointed the key fob at the Honda and, with a subtle click, popped the trunk open. Inside, four backpacks sat in a pile, just as they'd left them before leaving Westminster.

Ernest opened the passenger door of his truck. With deliberate care, he picked up an overstuffed backpack from the seat. "Lock and load, guys."

He turned, watching the sun inch toward the horizon, its orange glow intensifying. "We'll have to hurry if we want to get there before we lose the light. Figure we'll be walking about fifteen, maybe twenty minutes. We'll find the makings for a campfire there." He smiled openly as Ryan and Carrie looked up from the trunk, putting on their backpacks. "We're gonna be out there a while. Hope y'all brought snacks."

V

Ryan checked his watch when they crested the hill in the woods. It was nearly 8:20 p.m. The sun was about to set completely, its last rays painting the sky in hues of orange, yellow, and white.

As they walked, they passed a field, the ghosts of golden grain still whispering in the wind, before entering the adjoining woods again. The acres were scattered with brush and wild green shrubbery, the remnants of time's slow, steady reclamation.

Carrie stood atop the large rolling hill surrounded by old-growth trees, barely able to make out the steady shimmer of Big Pipe Creek below. To her left, and slightly down the hill, the ghostly outline of a partial stone wall was barely visible amongst the overgrown weeds.

Ryan came up behind her, his arms encircling her waist in a sudden embrace. "Not very scary, is it?"

"It's sad for me to see the ruins of something that used to be so important to someone. Now there's nothing left."

"Ashes to ashes, dust to dust."

Carrie turned within Ryan's warm embrace to look at him.

"That doesn't make me feel any better, MacGyver," she said, using the nickname she'd given him because of his impressive ability to improvise solutions.

"Sorry, Scout," he whispered, tenderly kissing her lips.

"What's everyone else doing?"

"Todd wanted me to come get you. Ernest is putting together a makeshift fire pit with a circle of stones. He's insisting on doing it by himself while Todd and I drag over a couple of downed trees to sit on. He's asked if you and Deborah could gather up some firewood."

"Sounds fair," Carrie whispered. Twilight cast a new light in her eyes as she looked at Ryan, revealing a silver aura he'd not seen there before. "There's something about these woods, Ryan. I don't know."

"As in…they're haunted?"

"Maybe. But not like 'ghosts' haunted," Carrie said, looking around at the layers of leaves on the ground. "There's memory here. I can…feel it…somehow."

Ryan kept watching Carrie until her gaze finally met his. "Let's see where the night takes us. Agreed?"

Carrie pulled Ryan close, feeling his warmth against her. "Agreed. I love you, MacGyver."

"I love you, Scout."

VI

Ryan and Todd dragged two suitable sections of old, fallen trees across the ground, the wood smelling of damp earth. They arranged them around the level space Ernest had cleared, where the sounds of the creek were faint in the distance as the ground sloped downward.

Ernest, panting from the exertion, had carried over several armfuls of old, thin, blue shale stones, forming a circle the size of an average tractor tire. The girls began placing kindling inside the circle and stacking larger branches nearby to feed the fire.

Ryan sat on the rough bark of the old maple tree, the smell of wood decay prevalent. Carrie sat beside him, followed by Deborah, with Todd bringing up the rear. Ernest positioned himself on a smaller log angled away from the rest of the group, his backpack resting against it. He methodically stuffed dry grass and weeds into the kindling, inhaling deeply as the earthy scent of the forest filled his lungs.

With the sun on the verge of setting, Carrie cautiously surveyed the surrounding forest, the trees' shadows stretching out as dusk approached, and the ethereal orange, red, and yellow of twilight setting in around them.

"These are maples and sycamores, aren't they?" Carrie asked.

"Yes, ma'am," Ernest said, retrieving a Marlboro Red, flicking open his silver Zippo, the flame momentarily illuminating his face as he lit the cigarette. He inhaled deeply, sending the smoke curling upward. "Red and silver maples, with the occasional cottonwood and oak."

Carrie's wandering gaze stopped at a single, tall pine tree nearby, standing as if it were foreign, yet somehow belonging. "And still a single pine tree grew and survived."

Ernest casually glanced over his shoulder at the pine. "It did."

Todd slapped his faded green WMC backpack and announced, "I brought hot dogs! Light the fire, Marlowe!"

Ernest dragged his cigarette, plucked it from his mouth, and pushed the cherry end into the dry kindling. Smoke slowly billowed above his hand, the fire finally catching with a slight whomp sound. The flames crackled, gradually intensifying, casting dancing shadows on their faces as they rose.

The fire was small by design. A mere flicker against the encroaching shadows, never daring to defy the night.

The woods settled into their night sounds. Crickets sawed the air, a distant owl let the world know he was there, and the low hush of leaves rubbed together overhead. An old foundation, where Ernest had pulled stones for the fire pit, sat a few yards away, half-swallowed by moss and time. If one didn't know they were there, they'd think it was just another rise in the earth.

Carrie sat with her knees drawn up, jacket zipped high. Ryan leaned forward, elbows on his thighs. Deborah nudged a stick into the fire, sending a scatter of sparks upward. They rose, stalled, and vanished.

Ernest didn't speak right away.

He let the quiet stretch until it became uncomfortable, until everyone realized they were waiting on him. The firelight danced across his face. He looked past them, not at them.

"My grandfather, Henry, used to bring my dad here as a boy, then my brother and me," he finally said, his voice steady and unhurried. "Not to scare us or to tell ghost stories. But just so we could sit."

He gestured with his chin toward the stones of the foundation behind him.

"There was more left back then. You could still see where the house was more clearly, and there was a bigger spot where the barn had fallen. The millrace was easier to trace. The water still remembers where it used to run."

Ernest paused again, seeming to weigh something, then continued.

"Grandpa Henry used to say, 'There are places that hold memory like heat. You don't see it. You don't always feel it right away. But it's there.' This land—" He tapped the ground lightly with the toe of his boot. "—never forgot."

The fire popped. Ryan shifted, finally unable to keep still. "You said there were people who lived here."

"Yes, sir," Ernest said, smiling faintly, not unkindly. He looked up at the trees. "They built something good here. Something that mattered."

Ernest drew a slow breath. No one interrupted him now. "What I'm about to tell you isn't a ghost story. Not in the way people usually mean. It's a story about love, work, and envy. It's about a house that meant more than it should have, and about a man who couldn't take that." He looked at each of them. "When I'm done, you can decide for yourselves whether these woods are haunted."

Ernest turned back toward the stones and the single pine tree beyond them, barely visible in the last wisps of the day's light. "Once you hear it, you won't ever walk through these woods the same way again."

The fire crackled. Ernest looked back at it. "Todd, did you show them Myrtle Hill and Trevanion?"

"Yes, sir."

Ernest's nod conveyed satisfaction. "Have y'all ever seen my Pa's house on Old Taneytown?"

Everyone answered yes, except for Carrie, who shook her head. "I've not, but I've heard about it. A big white Victorian with a red barn behind it."

"It was built in 1838 by my—" Ernest began counting on his fingers. "—my great-great-great-great-great-grandfather, Christian Marlowe, and his wife, Mary, although my family has been here way longer than that. Hezekiah Marlowe came over from England sometime in the mid-eighteenth century. He bought one of the original land patents before Carroll County existed, right alongside Edward Diggs and Raphael Taney, the guys who formed Taneytown. Our land was called 'Marlowe's Stewardship.' Hezekiah believed he never owned the land, that he was only the steward, passing it down from generation to generation, who would then take their turn watching it. My father, Everett, is the current steward. When he passes, the responsibility becomes mine and Ephraim's, my older brother."

"That's humble," Carrie whispered. Todd, his face illuminated by the blazing fire, nodded and passed a raw hot dog on a stick to Carrie, who was to give it to Ryan.

"It's how we respect the land," Ernest continued. "We take care of it; it takes care of us. Neither owns the other."

"That's beautiful," Carrie said.

Ernest gestured toward the rustling leaves of the shadowed trees, bushes, and lone old pine tree behind him. "Welcome to Fairlight. The home of Josephus and Hannah Marlowe."

CHAPTER III

Thursday, April 9, 1857

I

They were still in the lower field as the sun dipped into the west, resetting the fence where the heifer had pushed through in the night, when Jacob Marlowe straightened and wiped his hands on his trousers.

"Race you to the barn," he said, too quickly. "Last one sharpens the sickles."

Josephus didn't look up right away. He was threading wire back through a post, fingers steady. There was more fence to mend yet. More daylight to spend wisely.

"That's not a race worth running," Josephus said. "They need doing either way."

Jacob grinned and stepped back, already preparing to sprint. "You say that like you don't care who does the work."

"I care that it's done," Josephus replied. He gave the wire a final twist and set his hammer down. "We're already behind."

Jacob's grin widened, a glint in his eyes. "Afraid you'll lose, Joskin?"

The name landed where it always did—half jest, half goad. Josephus let out a deep breath and pushed himself upright. "I don't want to compete with you," he said, calm as ever. "There's more fence—"

But Jacob was already running.

He took off across the field, laughing over his shoulder. “Come on! Eighteen today, isn’t it? We don’t want you overexerting yourself. Old men pull muscles!”

Josephus muttered under his breath as he followed, not so much pursuing Jacob as refusing to let the moment go unanswered. His stride was long and steady, built for endurance rather than quick bursts of speed. He knew the reason the sickles hadn’t been sharpened the night before. Westminster. Joseph Shaw, editor of the *Carroll County Democrat*. Rumors of a Southern Confederacy. The Dred Scott decision. It was one of those meetings that left Jacob wired with secondhand certainty and no patience for dull tasks.

He also knew what would happen if their father, Christian, learned where Jacob had been.

Jacob glanced back mid-run, saw him gaining, and grinned like a jester. “Keep up, Joskin!”

Josephus didn’t answer. He rarely did. The play on his name was meant as a jab.

The barn rose ahead of them, doors open, tools stacked just inside. Jacob lunged through first, skidding on loose straw, chest heaving as he spun around in triumph.

“Looks like you’re on sharpening duty,” he said, breathless and pleased.

Josephus crossed the threshold a moment later, slowed to a walk, and set the hammer down on the wooden workbench. He bent forward, hands braced on his knees, not from exhaustion but habit, then straightened. “Aye, alright.”

Jacob blinked. Just once. “That’s it?”

Josephus shrugged and rolled up his sleeves. “You’ve got other work to do. Take care of it.”

Jacob hesitated, something like suspicion flickering across his face, then relief. He nodded and turned away without another word.

Josephus waited until he was gone before reaching for the whetstone.

II

Jacob Marlowe was leaner than his brother and two years his

junior. His body was drawn tight as if always braced for motion. Where Josephus was balanced, Jacob was coiled. He moved quickly and often—pacing, shifting his weight, riding hard—and carried himself with a restless forward tilt, as though still deciding whether to stay or flee.

His hair was darker, nearly black in certain light, worn longer than his brother's and often falling into his eyes. He didn't bother to brush it back unless it interfered with what he was doing. His features were sharper than Josephus's: high cheekbones, a narrow nose, and a mouth that seemed perpetually on the verge of saying something he'd already rehearsed in his head. His jaw often tightened, even at rest.

Jacob's eyes were striking: dark, intent, and quick to fix on others. There was a heat to them, not unkind by default but watchful, constantly measuring. He looked at people as though trying to determine where he stood in relation to them, and whether that position was acceptable. When anger came, it arrived suddenly, flashing across his face before he could temper it. When he smiled, it was fleeting and rarely reached his eyes.

His hands were capable but careless. He gripped too tightly, worked too fast, leaving behind minor signs of impatience—a nick where there needn't be one, a tool set down too hard. Even standing still, he appeared in motion, as if the world hadn't yet permitted him to rest.

Jacob looked like a man already braced for the ground to give way at any moment, and was already set to strike if it did.

Josephus Marlowe had the build that comes from steady, unremarkable labor. Tall without being imposing, broad enough in the shoulders to carry weight, but never bulky. His strength looked earned rather than asserted. He stood easily, as if he'd learned where his body belonged in a room and didn't feel the need to claim more space than that.

His hair was a warm brown, worn short and kept that way out of habit rather than vanity, with a tendency to curl slightly at the nape of his neck when it grew out between trims. His face was open and plain in a way that became handsome only after one spent time with him: a straight nose, a firm but gentle jaw, and eyes the color of river water; gray-blue, steady, and attentive. When he listened, he did so with his entire face, as if the world had his full permission to speak.

Josephus's hands were his most telling feature. They were large, scarred, and permanently marked by work. Split knuckles, callused palms, faint burns that never quite faded, but careful in their movements. He handled tools with confidence and people with restraint. When he smiled, it was unguarded and rare enough to matter; when he didn't, there was no hardness in its absence.

He looked like a man who expected to remain where he'd been planted and intended to tend it well.

The sickle rang softly against the whetstone, a steady, patient sound. Josephus kept his eyes on the blade, turning it just enough to catch the light, just enough to hear the change in pitch when the edge began to take.

Footsteps crossed the barn floor behind him. He didn't look up.

"Enjoy the view while it lasts," Josephus said. "You already won."

The steps stopped. Josephus glanced over his shoulder and straightened.

Christian Marlowe, the family patriarch, stood just inside the doorway, hat in his hands. He wasn't a man who spoke often, but when he did, people listened. His voice carried the steadiness of someone who'd worked the same land long enough to know what it would yield—and what it wouldn't. Order was important to him, from fixing fences before winter to returning tools to their proper locations. He was in his mid-forties but carried the years like an older man: shoulders set from decades of labor, hair already gone to iron at the temples, his face lined not by worry but by weather and sun. He looked first at the sickles laid out in order, then at the whetstone, already damp with use.

"I thought Jacob was sharpening those," Christian said.

"Aye, he was," Josephus replied carefully. He turned the blade again. "That was the plan."

"Yesterday."

Josephus nodded once. "We were fixing the fence this evening. The heifer did more damage than we expected."

"That doesn't answer my question."

The whetstone slowed. Josephus wiped the blade on his sleeve and set it aside before answering. "Jacob went out yesterday afternoon. He said he would be back before supper."

Christian's mouth tightened—not in surprise, but recognition.

"Westminster."

"Aye, sir."

Christian stepped farther into the barn. "I had a notion."

Josephus's eyes met his, holding his attention with an unspoken intensity. He didn't soften it now. "He stayed later than he meant to."

"And the work was not completed."

"No, sir."

"I asked him about it this morning."

"I know."

"He told me he forgot."

Josephus nodded. "Aye, sir."

Christian was quiet for a long moment. The barn creaked around them, wood settling in the heat. At last, he said, "You didn't forget."

"No."

"And you didn't tell me."

"I saw no need," Josephus said. "You already knew."

Christian watched him—really watched him now. The son who never raised his voice. The one who didn't run from work or consequence, even when it wasn't his.

"I would have come down hard on him," Christian said.

"I know."

"And you chose to take it on yourself," he said. Josephus didn't argue. He picked up the next sickle and set it to the stone. Christian turned toward the door. "Finish up. Then come wash up for supper."

"Aye, sir."

When Christian's footsteps faded, the barn felt quieter than before. Josephus continued working, the whetstone singing steadily beneath his hands, doing the work that needed doing, the truth already spoken and left where it belonged.

III

Mary Marlowe sat at the head of the table with her back straight and her hands folded, her black hair pinned tight and already touched with gray.

She was thinner than most women her age, though softened now by years of work and childbearing, her body shaped less by time than by use. Her blue eyes were keen and unblinking, quick to catch a look held too long, or a tone turned careless. The work had roughened her hands, voice, even her patience, but it had not dulled her, and there was a firmness to the way she held herself that made clear this was not a table where foolishness went unanswered. When the air shifted and words sharpened, Mary felt it first, and her silence carried warning enough.

While Christian exuded strength, she also possessed a quieter yet equally powerful presence. Where Christian measured time by harvests and weather, Mary measured it by people—by who was ill, who was grieving, who had gone too long without being asked how they were holding up. She kept the household running with a quiet competence that never announced itself. Bread appeared when it was needed. Lamps were filled before dusk. Words of comfort were offered without spectacle.

Christian and Mary were a matched pair, not by romance alone, but by shared restraint. Neither of them believed love needed constant declarations. It showed itself in small things: Christian splitting extra firewood before Mary thought to ask; Mary setting aside the choicest apples for Christian's long days in the field. Their faith was much the same: deep, private, unquestioned.

One of the domestic servants named Molly laid supper on the dining room table when the men came in from the barn, the table set plain but full in the way of early spring; salt pork, boiled potatoes, stewed greens still bright with vinegar, a loaf broken open and wrapped in cloth to keep warm. The windows were open to the evening, the smell of damp earth and new grass drifting in from the fields.

Jacob took his seat quickly, settling back with the loose confidence of a man who believed the day had ended in his favor.

He didn't reach for anything. Instead, he folded his hands and waited.

Molly, a heavyset black woman in her early thirties, moved between the kitchen and the table with practiced ease, her skirts brushed clean, her presence so habitual it rarely drew comment. She carried a serving bowl toward Jacob's place and set it on the table.

"Am I not to be served? Why else do we have slaves?" Jacob said lightly, not looking at Molly. "Seems a waste not to use them."

The room stopped.

Mary's hand froze on the edge of the table. "Jacob!" she said sharply. "Don't be vulgar! Serve yourself."

Jacob blinked, surprised more by the rebuke than by the words themselves. "Aye, ma'am," he whispered, contrite enough to pass. He reached for the bowl. Josephus intercepted it.

Meeting Jacob's gaze and never breaking it, he took the serving spoon, filled Jacob's plate with deliberate care, and set it down in front of him.

"There you are, brother," Josephus said mildly. "You're welcome."

Jacob stared at the plate, then up at Josephus. Something like irritation flickered across his face, but it passed. He gave Josephus a thin smile and picked up his fork.

Christian watched the exchange without comment. He waited until everyone had served themselves and said grace before he replied. "This is not a plantation, Jacob," he said, his voice level. "And it never will be."

Jacob swallowed. "I didn't say it was."

"You implied it," Christian replied. "And implication has a way of hardening into habit if it goes unchallenged." He set his fork down. "The people who work here are paid. They live on this land because they choose to. They leave when they have grown, with wages saved and tools enough to start somewhere else. That has always been the understanding."

Jacob leaned back slightly. "And they stay because they're treated well."

"They stay because they are free to go," Christian said. "Don't confuse the two."

The table was quiet now, except for the soft scrape of cutlery. Josephus kept his eyes on his plate. Mary watched Jacob closely, as if bracing for something she already expected.

Jacob's smile returned, unfolding more deliberately this time. "You're different, Father. I've always said that."

"Praise is rendered insincere if it's followed by 'but,'" Christian said.

Jacob hesitated just a moment too long. "But that's not how it works everywhere," he said at last. "Westminster's full of men who'd tell you the world's changing whether you like it or not."

Christian's gaze sharpened. "Is that so?"

Jacob felt it then. The shift. He straightened, too late to retreat. "I'm only saying—"

"I know what you're saying," Christian said. "The question is why you needed to hear it from someone else."

Silence pressed in around the table, heavier than before.

Josephus lifted his head.

"Westminster," Christian said, repeating Jacob's declaration. "That's where you were yesterday."

Jacob didn't deny it. He sat straighter, as if the truth, now spoken, could be owned.

"There was a meeting," he said. "You know that Shaw—"

Christian nodded. "I know the *Carroll County Democrat* prints more ink than sense when he's stirred."

Jacob bristled. "He's not stirred. He's *awake*. There's talk now…real talk. Not rumors. Men organizing. A confederacy of states that won't be told what to do by courts in Washington."

Mary's fork paused halfway to her mouth.

Christian's voice remained steady and quiet as he spoke. "What courts?"

After a moment of thought, Jacob blurted it out. "The Supreme Court has made it plain enough. A man's property is his property. Dred Scott settled that."

Josephus felt the words land like a dropped plate. His gaze fell upon his father, catching the quiet intensity in his expression.

"Settled," Christian repeated. "An interesting word for a thing that strips a man of standing altogether."

Jacob waved his hand with a scoff. "That's not what it does. It just recognizes reality. Negroes aren't—"

"Careful," Mary said.

Jacob ignored her. "—aren't citizens. The Court said so. Shaw says this was always coming. That the North's been pretending otherwise."

Christian leaned back slightly in his chair. "And you believe him?"

"I believe my eyes," Jacob said. "I believe what every man with land and sense already knows. The South will not kneel to abolitionists and the Know-Nothings—"

A grim determination set Christian's jaw. "You mean the Know-Nothings that Shaw was so eager to bolt from?"

Jacob flushed. "Aye. They're fools. Hiding behind lanterns and passwords like boys playing soldier. Shaw's done with them."

"And where has he led you?" Christian asked.

Jacob leaned forward now, voice gaining heat. "Toward the truth. Toward men who aren't afraid to say what this country runs on. Toward a South that won't be ruled by the *American Sentinel,* calling every farmer a tyrant and every man a sinner."

Silence pressed down on the table.

Christian folded his hands. "You confuse noise for courage," he said. "And ownership for righteousness."

Jacob let out a single, sharp bark of laughter. "You pay wages. You let them leave. Fine. But don't pretend that makes you different in kind. It only makes you different in degree."

Josephus felt a pang of dread in his gut.

Christian looked steadily at his younger son. "It makes all the difference," he said. "Because the moment you decide a man cannot leave, you decide you may do anything to keep him." Jacob opened his mouth. "And don't tell me it stops at labor. I've seen what happens to men who try to run. I've seen how quickly 'property' becomes punishment."

Jacob's voice rose. "That's not *our* way—"

"No," Christian said. "It is not. And it shan't become so while I have breath."

The words landed final, immovable.

Jacob pushed back from the table, then caught himself. He felt his jaw tighten, working with unspoken emotion. He glanced once at Mary, then at Josephus—searching, perhaps, for reinforcement.

Josephus stared at his brother and said nothing.

At last, Jacob sat back down. He lowered his eyes to his plate. "Aye, sir," he whispered.

"Jacob, I will not tolerate skipped labor," Christian added, laying down the law as he always had, expecting compliance. "If you want ideas, you must first prove discipline. If this behavior continues, I *will* send you to work elsewhere."

"Aye, sir."

It was Christian who would have the last word. "If this is the road you choose, you shan't walk it under my roof forever."

The meal continued after that, but the air never quite returned to the room. Jacob ate quickly, mechanically; his fire banked, but not extinguished. Christian finished in silence. Mary's hands moved with a jerky energy as she cleared the table.

Josephus stayed where he was, hands folded, watching his brother retreat inward. Not repentant, only constrained.

IV

Christian waited until Molly had cleared the dishes and Mary had stepped back into the kitchen before he spoke.

"Josephus," he said. "Stay a moment."

Jacob paused, too, halfway to the door, then settled back into his chair as if invited. Christian didn't tell him to leave.

"This is not how I meant to give it," Christian said, and for the first time that evening, there was something like regret in his voice. "But today is still today."

Josephus looked up. "Sir?"

Christian reached into the inside pocket of his coat and drew out a folded sheet of paper, worn thin at the creases. He set it on the table, then laid his hand over it—not possessive, but steady.

"There are forty acres west of Brick Mills along Big Pipe Creek," he said. "Good water. Enough fall for a wheel, if a man were inclined to build one."

Josephus looked at his father. "Brick Mills?"

Christian nodded once. "Dallas calls it Trevanion now." Josephus didn't speak. "I've held the note. Family money. Enough to get the work started, if you choose. The land is yours, regardless. What you do with it is your decision."

Jacob released a soft exhale. "A mill," he whispered. "You're giving him a mill."

"I'm giving him land," Christian replied. "And the means to decide."

Josephus found his voice at last. "Father, I didn't ask for this."

"No," Christian said. "You earned it."

The words hung there. Quiet. Final.

Christian pushed the paper toward Josephus. "Tomorrow," he said, "I shall take you to see it. You don't have to answer now. A man should look at his ground before he promises himself to it."

Josephus nodded, still dazed. "Aye, sir."

Christian stood. "Happy birthday, son."

He left the room without another word.

Jacob watched the door close as Christian went outside. Then he looked back at the paper, at Josephus's hand resting just beside it. "Forty acres," he whispered. "That's quite a future."

Josephus didn't rise to it. "I'm unsure as yet what I shall do."

Jacob managed a thin, guarded smile. "You will."

V

The Marlowe farm was set back from the road as if it had chosen distance on purpose—not out of secrecy, but patience. The land rose gently before it, fields laid out in long, honest sweeps, bordered by split-rail fences silvered by years of weather. Nothing here was decorative. Everything earned its place.

The house was sturdy rather than handsome: whitewashed clapboard over a stone foundation, two stories tall, its windows evenly spaced and unpretentious. With posts worn smooth where hands have rested while waiting, the porch spanned the front of the house, roofed and shaded, having served as a spot for children called in at dusk, neighbors arriving by wagon, and a father standing alone to think. The door opened straight into a vast central hall that smelled faintly of soap, wood smoke, and apples stored too long in the cellar.

Behind the house, the farm's working heart fanned outward. A red-painted barn anchored the yard, its doors tall enough for wagons and teams, its loft heavy with hay. Nearby stood the corncrib, the smokehouse, and the shed where tools hung in careful order—nothing fancy, but nothing neglected. The animals knew the rhythms here. Chickens scattered freely. Cows moved at their own deliberate pace. Horses were spoken to as partners, not as property.

Down a slight slope, half-hidden by trees, sat the springhouse. Stone-walled and cool even in summer, it breathed water steadily, the sound a quiet constant that never quite leaves the mind once you've noticed it. Milk crocks lined the shelves. Butter firmed in shallow pans. It is a place of work, yes, but also of stillness. If someone needed to think, or write, or simply listen, this is where they would come.

The orchard lay beyond: apple trees planted years earlier, their trunks thick and reliable, branches trained more by use than by design. In good seasons, the ground beneath them was littered with windfalls, sweet and bruised, drawing wasps and children alike. Even in times of scarcity, the trees remained steadfast and patient.

From the rise behind the barn, one could see the land as it genuinely is: fields carefully worked, but not exhaustively; woods left standing where they serve the soil better, untouched; fences mended rather than replaced. It wasn't a wealthy farm, but it was secure. No part of it felt temporary.

The Marlowe farm didn't impress at first glance. It endured. And once that was understood, it became difficult to imagine it ever failing—until, of course, the world decided otherwise.

Josephus and Jacob stopped at the fence where the field thinned; the grass was worn low by years of passage. The boards there were polished smooth by hands that lingered, men deciding whether to stay or go.

Josephus rested his forearms on the top rail. Jacob stood beside him now, not behind him. Equal ground for the moment.

"Do you really want it, Jos?" Jacob asked.

Josephus didn't feign ignorance. "I want to do it right."

Jacob let out a quiet huff. "That was *not* an answer."

"'Tis the only one I have, brother."

They stood in silence. The land sloped away beyond the fence, darkening as it dipped. Somewhere behind them, Christian's figure moved near the barn, small at this distance but unmistakable.

"He's already decided," Jacob said. "You know that."

Josephus shook his head. "He left it to me."

"That's the same thing," Jacob replied. "He just wrapped it kinder."

Josephus's attention then shifted to him. "This doesn't mean there's no place for you."

Jacob laughed once, without humor. "Doesn't it?"

Josephus opened his mouth, a silent sigh escaping, then quickly shut it.

"I hear Trevanion has work," Jacob said.

"You don't have to leave," Josephus insisted, turning to face his brother.

Jacob laughed softly with a dash of bitterness. "Don't I?"

"No. Not right now. Not today. You're still sixteen. Trevanion would not take you without father's blessing. He surely will not give it right now," Josephus gestured toward the direction of Trevanion and the land past it, the fields already claimed, the future already spoken for. "All Father has given me is debt."

Jacob didn't answer right away. He glanced once toward the barn, toward the land, the house, and the life that had already begun to tilt away from him.

They stood there a moment longer, neither willing to say what that would mean if spoken aloud.

Jacob turned south, where the ground dropped, and the light faded faster.

Josephus remained at the fence and faced north, his hand resting on the rail, the paper folded carefully in his pocket like a promise that already carried weight.

Neither looked back.

VI

Jacob didn't go back to the house.

He walked until the fence lines thinned and the ground dipped, until the air cooled and the sounds of the farm fell away. He didn't have his horse. Trying for Trevanion on foot wasn't an option for him tonight, not in this state.

That irritated him more than it should have.

He stopped where the land sloped south, where the path bent out of sight. From here, Trevanion was only a direction, not a place. A thought one could walk toward without arriving.

Jacob kicked at a stone, sending it skittering across the grass.

Forty acres. A note. A future spoken as if it were already shaped.

He pressed his hands into his pockets and leaned forward, breathing harder than the walk deserved. He told himself he was angry. It was easier than naming the other thing—that sense of being edged out without being pushed.

All Father has given me is debt.

The words came back to him uninvited. He didn't test them or soften them. He let them sit.

Christian didn't tell him to leave. That was the worst of it.

Christian never did. He waited. He let things settle until they looked like choices.

Josephus would accept. Of course, he would. Josephus always did what fit the land that was already measured for him.

Jacob straightened and looked south again. Not because he was going there now, but because someday he would.

He turned back before the dark thickened, steps quickening as the farm came back into view. Jacob knew the rules. He knew the years still standing between him and any real leaving.

But now he knew the shape of the road.

And that was enough to keep him awake.

VII

Josephus waited until the house had settled before he went back outside.

Mary had banked the fire, leaving a soft, warm glow. Christian had said goodnight, saying nothing else. The farm lay in its familiar hush, the kind that allowed rest.

Josephus took the folded paper from his pocket and turned it over once in his hands before putting it back. He didn't read it again. He already knew what it said.

Outside, the night air was cool and damp. He walked past the barn, past the tools set neatly where they belonged, and down toward Bear Branch. The frogs had already started up along the water, their sound steady and unhurried. He stopped where the ground fell away just enough to hear the creek before he saw it.

Forty acres.

He let himself picture it, but not grandly. No wheel was turning yet. No building had been raised. Just land. Trees. Water moving where it always had. Something that would need clearing before it could give anything back.

The thought didn't thrill him. It steadied him.

Josephus sat on a low stone and rested his hands on his knees. He thought of Jacob. Not with anger, not with disappointment, but with the dull ache of recognition. They'd always stood in the same places and seen different things. Tonight had only made it plain.

All Father has given me is debt.

He turned the words over once, like a tool left out of place.

Christian gave him land, aye. A note. A future. But also time. Expectation. The certainty that whatever he built would be watched. By neighbors, by family, by the man who taught him to work without cruelty.

Josephus exhaled slowly, knowing debt came in many forms.

He stood at last and walked the edge of the creek, measuring the fall with his eyes, the way his father once taught him. Big Pipe Creek would certainly be wider than Bear Branch, the flow stronger. He wasn't planning yet; only imagining what lay ahead.

When he turned back toward the house, the lamps were out. The farm was dark, intact, waiting.

Josephus paused once and looked south, where the land dipped and the night deepened. He knew where Jacob would stand if he were here. He knew why he wasn't.

"I'll keep it," Josephus said softly—not to the land, not to his father, but to the work itself. "As long as I can."

Then he headed back inside, already carrying tomorrow with him.

CHAPTER IV

Friday, May 24, 1997

I

Ernest Marlowe stopped talking.

Not abruptly. Just enough that the silence drew attention to itself. The fire popped once, then settled. He scanned the circle, his gaze flicking from one face to another, observing the subtle shifts in expression that had already formed.

Surprise, mostly. A few exchanged glances.

Deborah shifted on the log.

Todd's eyes darted between Carrie and Ryan.

Carrie didn’t move.

She sat still, eyes lowered, hands folded in her lap. There was no shock in her expression, only recognition. As if something she’d been waiting for had finally named itself.

Ryan cleared his throat. He did it gently, the way one does when interrupting a prayer. “I don’t mean this disrespectfully,” he said. “But how can you possibly know all of this? I mean, this all happened a hundred and forty years ago.”

Ernest nodded. He’d expected the question.

“The story’s been passed down,” he said. “Four generations, at least. Told and retold, corrected when it drifted. The Marlowes are careful that way.” He reached for his backpack and drew it closer. The zipper sounded loud in the quiet. “But that’s not all.”

He reached inside and brought out two books, one at a time. Thick. Leather-bound. The covers worn smooth at the edges, darkened by hands that had opened them for decades. The spines were cracked but intact; the pages inside were dense with tight, slanted writing—an ornate, almost Gothic cursive that looked more drawn than written.

Carrie leaned forward without realizing she had.

"These belonged to Christian and Mary," Ernest said. "A farm register and a household journal. They kept them their whole lives."

Ernest held them carefully, as if the weight counted. Then he set one back into the pack and placed the other on the log beside him, but away from the fire, deliberately, on the far side, where no stray ember could reach it.

"They don't get passed around," he added, not unkindly. "They're family."

No one argued.

Ernest opened the first journal, then glanced up once more at the group before reading. "This is Christian's entry from the same evening," he said. "After supper.

"Worked fence in the lower field where the heifer broke through overnight. Damage greater than first thought. Repaired by noon. Sickles sharpened late.

"Gave Josephus notice of the west tract on Big Pipe Creek, past Brick Mills, forty acres, with water sufficient for a wheel, should he choose to build. I have held the family note these past years and now place it in his keeping. I told him to see the land before answering.

"Supper unsettled. Jacob spoke out of turn and repeated arguments he had heard elsewhere. Corrected him. He did not persist.

"Josephus bore the weight of the day as he always has. I am mindful of this.

"Weather fair. Creek running steady."

The words settled into the firelight with a different weight than they had on the page—measured, spare—set down as if the facts would be enough.

When Ernest finished, he closed the book and let the silence return. Then he opened Mary's household journal.

Mary's handwriting was finer and more urgent. Ernest read more slowly this time, as if mindful of how much feeling Mary had pressed into the margins.

"Tonight the table felt smaller than it has in years.

"Jacob spoke carelessly, as if words were things that could be set down and forgotten. I corrected him, though I do not know whether it mattered. There is a sharpness in him now that was not there before, or perhaps I did not wish to see it.

"Christian gave Josephus his birthday news at last. Land. A future spoken aloud. I watched Josephus listen, and my heart ached for both of them, for what was given and for what was not.

"Jacob sat very still after that. Too still.

"I do not fear that he is wicked. I fear he is certain.

"When the men left the table, the house felt hollow, though nothing in it had moved."

When Ernest reached the last line, his voice softened unintentionally. "I pray this passes. I pray we have not crossed a line we cannot step back over."

He closed the journal.

No one spoke for a long moment.

The fire crackled. An insect hummed somewhere beyond the circle of light.

"That's where it starts," Carrie whispered, lifting her head.

Ernest met her eyes. "Yes."

"That's where the fracture started," she said without accusation or surprise. Just certainty. "It only spreads from there."

Ernest nodded once.

CHAPTER V

Friday, April 10, 1857

I

Christian Marlowe and his two sons left the Marlowe farm before the sun had decided to rise.

The road was familiar enough that no one spoke of it. Elder took it at a steady walk, Christian's reins loose in his hands, the gelding moving as though the path were something long agreed upon between them. Atlas, with Josephus at the reins, followed without urging, compact and sure-footed, his breath slow and even in the cool air. Brimstone came last, restless despite the hour, head lifting and lowering as if the dark itself offended him.

The dew lay thick on the grass. Hooves passed through it without sound.

They rode in silence. Not the strained sort that waits to be filled, but the kind that settles naturally among men who have worked together long enough to know when words are unnecessary. Christian rode upright but at ease, weight balanced, hands quiet. Josephus matched him instinctively, his posture learned not from instruction but from observation. Jacob shifted in the saddle more than he needed to, adjusting reins that didn't yet require it.

Trevanion lay off to one side of the road, unseen but present all the same. No one turned their head toward it, although Jacob's eyes shifted to see its silhouette from the corner of his eye. The lane curved softly ahead, a familiar sight that remained unchanged over time.

The sky paled by degrees. First, a thinning of the dark, then a suggestion of color along the far edge of the fields. By the time they reached the rise, the world had taken on enough shape to be trusted.

Christian reined in at the crest.

Elder stopped as if he had been waiting for the thought to arrive. Atlas halted behind him, lowering his head briefly, blowing out a long breath. Brimstone checked a half-step late, stamping once before Jacob gathered him back.

Below them, the land opened.

Big Pipe Creek cut a quiet line through the low ground, its banks marked by sycamore and maple, their pale trunks lifting out of the mist. Tulip poplars rose farther back, straight and tall, already claiming the upper air. The fields sloped gently toward the water, furrows softened by seasons of use, their edges blurred by dew. Along the bend where the earth dipped, water gathered—not yet a stream, only a darkened hollow where the ground refused to stay dry.

Mist hung low among the trees, drifting as the light reached it. When the sun broke the horizon, it did so without hurry. As the vapor captured the first light, it became pale and golden, mimicking the land's breath.

No one spoke at the sight laid out before them.

Josephus studied the slope, the way the ground faced the morning. He took in the sound of the water, faint but steady, and the shelter offered by the rise. It wasn't the look of a man tallying acreage, but of one listening, as though the place were already speaking, and was careful not to interrupt.

Atlas stood quietly beneath him, weight shifting just enough to remain comfortable, ears flicking once toward the creek and then forward again. The horse didn't need to be tied. He didn't need reminding.

Behind them, Brimstone tossed his head and stamped again, unsettled by the stillness. Jacob's hand tightened on the reins in response with a pressure that spoke of restraint rather than trust. The horse yielded, but his energy remained, coiled and waiting.

Christian watched none of this directly. He had no need to.

At last, Josephus spoke. "The light is fair here."

His voice was low, almost tentative, as though he were offering the words to the land rather than claiming it. He didn't look at his father when he said it.

For a moment, nothing followed. Only the quiet shift of mist and the faint sound of water moving over stone. Atlas exhaled again, long and slow, as if the words had settled something in him.

Christian turned his head slightly, enough to look at his son. He didn't smile. Approval, when it came, didn't take that shape with him.

"I shall call this land Fairlight," Josephus continued, steadier now.

Christian considered this. His gaze moved once over the land, then stilled—simply acknowledging what stood before him. Elder didn't move beneath him. The horse stood square, patient, as if bearing witness were his only task.

"It's a fine name," Christian said at last. "Plain. And rightly chosen."

The words were simple, spoken without adornment. They carried weight all the same.

Josephus let out a breath he'd not known he was holding. He nodded once, accepting the judgment as much as the praise.

Jacob said nothing.

He sat a pace behind them, eyes fixed on the slope, the creek, the way the light lay across ground that would not be his. Brimstone shifted beneath him, eager to be gone, ears pinning briefly before flicking forward again. Jacob kept his hand firm on the reins, waiting for an opening, a moment sharp enough to speak into.

It did not come.

The mist thinned. The sun climbed. The land remained.

Christian rested his hands lightly on Elder's neck, a familiar gesture that asked nothing and received nothing in return. He didn't press forward. There would be time enough for that. For now, it was enough to let the land be seen, named, and left untroubled.

They stood there a while longer, three men and their horses, the future settling quietly into the ground beneath them.

II

Elder didn't move when Christian dismounted. Atlas lowered his head to graze. Brimstone danced once before Jacob tied him short, harder than necessary.

On foot, the land revealed itself differently.

Christian and Josephus walked ahead, their pace unhurried but purposeful, stopping where the slope changed, where the ground stayed dry longest, where water could be carried without strain. Christian spoke sparingly, pointing once or twice with an open hand. Josephus listened, nodding, storing each remark carefully.

Jacob followed behind.

He tried to keep pace at first, but his attention snagged again and again—on the curve of the creek, the width of the lower field, the way the morning light favored the rise. Each time he slowed to take it in, the distance between them grew. When he hurried to close it, the gap reopened elsewhere.

Christian noticed. He said nothing.

"The house ought to sit here," Josephus said at last, stopping near the upper edge of the slope. "High enough to keep dry. Close enough to hear the water."

Christian considered the ground beneath his boots. He pressed his heel once into the soil, testing it. "Aye. And the mill below, far enough that the noise won't carry. You'll want the outbuildings set back from both. Wind will matter."

Josephus smiled faintly. He was seeing it now, not as a dream, but as a sequence of choices that could be made well or poorly.

"If you mean to build proper," Christian continued, "you should speak with Elias Koontz in Westminster. He's a careful man. Knows how to lay a house that will stand. He seeks foreman work again."

Josephus looked up. "I thought he was settled."

"He was," Christian said. "The last place suffered a fire. Took most of it. He finished what he could and moved on."

A pause. The word lingered.

"He has men," Christian continued. "Good ones. If the weather holds, they could raise the house and outbuildings inside six months."

Josephus let out a breath, half awe, half relief. "That soon?"

"If you don't dither," Christian replied. "And if you plan before you build." He turned then, fixing Josephus with a look that was not unkind but carried expectation. "You may ride to Westminster this afternoon. You will find Koontz at the Anchor Hotel, west end of Main, near the forks. Speak plain. Tell him what you want, not what you think you ought to want."

"Aye, sir," Josephus said at once.

Christian paused, looking upslope toward where the creek bent out of sight.

"After your meeting, word will travel fast. William Dallas will hear of Fairlight soon enough."

Josephus glanced at him. "Trevanion?"

"Aye. Another mill changes a man's accounting," Christian replied. "Some take it as competition. Some take it as disorder."

"We aren't taking anything from him," Josephus said.

Christian nodded. "No. But men who rely on control rarely see the difference."

Behind them, Jacob stopped short. "Could I ride with Jos to Westminster?"

Christian didn't turn immediately. When he did, his expression was already decided. "No."

Jacob blinked, a slight tremor in his eyelids at his father's refusal. "Why not?"

"Because Josephus sharpened the sickles last night. You did not. *You* shall cover his chores. Clean the stalls. See to the rest."

Jacob flushed. "That's not—"

"You are to do it," Christian said, his tone firm but controlled. "That's the end of it, Jacob."

Jacob's jaw set in a firm line, betraying his inner turmoil. He took a breath, then another, heat rising fast and ill-contained. "There's other help. Why don't you just get the nigg—"

"Hold your tongue, Jacob!" Christian's voice cut clean through the word, stopping it where it stood. He stepped closer now, not threatening, but unmistakably present. "You shall *not* use such language where I or your mother can hear it. Nor anywhere else, if you know what's good for you. You shall complete the chore assigned. This discussion is finished."

The silence that followed was sharp enough to sting.

"Aye, sir," Jacob murmured, his voice barely audible as he glanced up at his father, his head still bowed.

The words were correct. The tone was not.

They walked on.

Josephus and Christian spoke quietly of costs—timber, stone, labor—careful not to speak over one another.

Jacob lagged again, his hands clenched, his thoughts running hotter by the minute. When he spoke, it was to interrupt. "Why not use slave labor? There's enough of it around. You would certainly save money."

Josephus answered before Christian could.

"No," he said, the word sharp with certainty. Josephus turned, eyes bright with something close to anger. "No slave labor. Ever. If Negroes wish to work at Fairlight, I will pay them a fair wage and treat them as men. As Father does."

Jacob scoffed. "That's *not* how the world works."

"It is how *this* place will," Josephus said. "Or I shan't build it."

Jacob let out a short, bitter laugh, the sound sharp in the quiet. "You think because Buchanan won, everything has been settled?" he asked, referring to the last presidential election. "The people voted. The country has spoken."

Christian stopped walking. "The people voted," he said calmly, "under a split ticket. Had the Know-Nothings not run Fillmore, Fremont would have beaten Buchanan outright."

Jacob turned toward him, eyes flashing. "That's speculation, Father."

"It's arithmetic," Christian replied. "And it matters which one you are using."

Jacob's breath came fast now. "The Republicans and the Know-Nothings will tear this country apart. Look what they've done to Baltimore. Gangs, riots, lawlessness. Mobtown!"

"You mistake disorder for democracy," Christian said. "They are not the same."

"And you mistake easing your conscience for changing the world," Jacob shot back.

Josephus shifted uncomfortably, glancing between them without speaking.

"They learn your land," Jacob pressed on. "Your habits. Your rules. And then you turn them loose with nothing but a name and a promise."

"They leave with skills," Christian said quietly.

"They leave with nothing that cannot be taken from them the next day."

Christian's jaw tightened. Just barely. "You think I don't know that?"

"I think you pretend it evens the scale."

A pause followed—long enough to hurt.

Christian folded his hands together, fingers interlacing slowly. When he spoke again, his voice was level, but something in it had hardened. "Your message is that you wish to keep them."

Jacob's breath hitched as a sudden tension coursed through him. "I'm saying the world does not reward good intentions. It rewards control."

Christian held his gaze. "And what does it do to the man who needs control to feel safe?"

"That's not—"

"No," Christian said, restraining the edge that threatened his voice. "That's exactly it."

The land lay quiet around them, the creek murmuring as it had all morning. Whatever utopia had existed there an hour earlier had not vanished, but it had been tested and found wanting of unanimity.

Christian turned away. "Return home, Jacob. Now. I shall speak with you later, when you have thought the matter through proper."

He didn't say, '*Calm down.*' He didn't need to.

Jacob stood rigid for a moment, breath tight in his chest. Then he nodded once—sharp, resentful—and turned back toward the rise.

Brimstone sensed it immediately. The horse tossed his head as Jacob reached for the reins, sidestepping, ears pinned flat. Jacob caught the bit hard, too hard. The leather snapped once in the quiet.

"Don't," he muttered, low and warning.

Brimstone stamped, neck arched, testing him. Jacob leaned in, voice close to the horse's ear now, not loud but edged with threat, the kind meant to be understood rather than heard. His heel pressed. His hand held fast.

The horse resisted for half a breath longer, then yielded.

Brimstone fell into line, muscles tight beneath the saddle, obedience earned rather than offered. Jacob swung up without ceremony and turned the horse toward the road, not looking back.

Christian watched until the sound of hooves thinned into the distance. He said nothing. Only when Jacob was out of earshot did he exhale.

Josephus waited, respectful and uncertain, not looking at his brother or Brimstone.

Turning, Christian looked once more over the land—Fairlight—and nodded, as if recommitting himself to something already chosen.

"Come," he said. "Let us finish walking it."

III

Josephus and Christian walked the lower stretch of the field, where the ground sloped gently toward the creek and the grass grew thicker.

The sun was higher now, the mist thinning to nothing. What remained of the morning's hush felt earned rather than accidental.

Josephus broke the silence first. "Father, who are the Know-Nothings? Jacob speaks of them as though everyone ought to know."

Christian's stride didn't change. "They call themselves the American Party. That should tell you enough already."

Josephus frowned slightly. "I've read Joseph Shaw railing against them. But I've never understood why."

Christian glanced toward the trees lining the creek, then back to the land underfoot. "They began as a secret order," he said. "Men meeting behind closed doors. When questioned, they were taught to say they know nothing. Hence the name."

"Secret politics," Josephus whispered.

"Aye. Dark lantern politics, some call it," Christian replied. "They fear what they don't understand. Irish. Germans. Catholics, most of all. They speak of loyalty, but what they mean is sameness."

Josephus absorbed this quietly. "What do they want?"

Christian didn't answer at once. "Longer roads to citizenship," he said finally. "Fewer voices allowed to speak. Restrictions made to look like order. They say it keeps the country safe."

"And Shaw?" Josephus asked.

"Shaw sees enemies where it suits him. He's been railing at the wrong paper for months now, chasing shadows someone else is casting."

Josephus frowned. “On purpose?”

Christian’s mouth tightened. “Some men prefer confusion. It gives them room to move.”

Josephus nodded. Politics, to him, had always seemed like something that happened elsewhere; in towns, in halls, in newspapers that arrived folded and already late. The farm didn’t care who spoke in Washington so long as the weather held and the creek ran steady.

“I don’t much care for it,” he admitted. “All of it feels distant. Loud.”

“That’s not a fault,” Christian said. “A man ought to know how to mind his ground first.”

“But if pressed,” Josephus added after a moment, “I suppose I would side where you do.”

Christian looked at him then. “Which is?”

“With keeping people from being owned,” Josephus said.

Christian nodded once. “That will do.”

They walked on, the sound of water steady beside them. Whatever banners men raised elsewhere, Fairlight lay quiet, unconcerned with parties or platforms. It asked only whether those who stood upon it would act with decency.

For now, that seemed enough.

IV

Jacob didn’t slow until the rise fell away behind him.

Brimstone took the road at a hard trot, hooves striking sharper than normal, breath coming quick beneath the saddle. Jacob let him have it for a time. Speed felt like agreement. Wind stripped the last of Christian’s words from his ears, though not from his thoughts.

The land slipped past, familiar and suddenly ill-fitting. Fields he’d worked. Fences he’d mended. Ground he knew better than most men his age, and yet would never own.

Brimstone tossed his head, testing the reins again.

“Enough!” Jacob snapped, tightening his grip.

The horse surged once more before settling, resentment passing cleanly between them. Jacob leaned forward, weight pressing down, heels firm. He didn’t strike. He didn’t need to. Brimstone yielded, muscles tight, obedience pulled taut like wire.

They passed Trevanion without stopping.

Jacob's eyes flickered toward it despite himself—the long slope, the outbuildings, the men already moving about their work. There, labor was ordered. Hierarchies understood. A man could rise if he proved himself willing to enforce the rules that kept everything running.

Not like Fairlight.

Fairlight would be built on patience. On talk. On the sort of goodness that waited and waited and called that strength.

They say they set men free, he thought, jaw clenching. *They call it justice and walk away clean.*

Brimstone shied at a shadow crossing the road. Jacob checked him hard, breath flaring. "Don't start, Brimstone!"

The horse steadied, ears flicking back, listening. Jacob felt the response—the way pressure brought order, uncertainty retreating when met head-on. The lesson settled deeper than any argument that morning: control worked.

By the time the Marlowe farm came into view, Jacob's anger had cooled into something more durable. He reined Brimstone down at last; the horse blowing hard, damp along the neck, compliance earned and complete.

Jacob dismounted and looped the reins without ceremony. The chores awaited. He would do them. He had no choice.

But as he turned toward the barn, his thoughts had already ridden elsewhere—toward men who spoke plainly about power, toward places where no one apologized for holding it.

The ride had ended.

The direction had not.

V

Josephus left the Marlowe farm in the early afternoon, the sun already warming the road.

Atlas set out at a leisurely, long, steady walk, carrying Josephus east along the Taneytown–Westminster turnpike, the road already stirring with wagons and riders. Josephus let the reins lie loose in his hands. There was no need to urge the horse; Atlas knew the way well enough, and if he didn't, he would learn it honestly.

The morning's arguments hadn't followed him. Not that Josephus had forgotten them, only that they'd not taken root. He'd listened, weighed, and then set them aside, as one does with matters that would keep. There would be time for all of that later. For now, there was a road, a destination, and the quiet satisfaction of having his father trust him with something that mattered.

The land looked different from the saddle at this hour. Light lay clean across the fields, unbroken by mist or doubt. Creeks flashed now and then through gaps in the trees, their sound a steady accompaniment rather than a presence. Farmers waved as he passed. One called his name. Josephus lifted a hand in reply, smiling without thinking about it.

Atlas shortened his stride near a shallow dip in the road, choosing firmer ground without being asked. Josephus rested his hand briefly against the horse's neck. Not in praise, exactly, but acknowledgment. The gesture felt natural, almost absent-minded.

He thought of Fairlight.

Not the house yet, nor the mill, nor even the labor it would require. He thought of the way the light had rested on the slope that morning, how the land had seemed to receive the name rather than resist it. He wondered what it might mean to build something that didn't need to prove itself by force.

Westminster rose gradually, announced first by sound—wagon wheels, voices, the indistinct murmur of trade—and then by sight. Atlas lifted his head slightly as they entered the busier road, ears forward, alert but untroubled. Josephus gathered the reins just enough to signal attention, nothing more.

The Anchor Hotel stood where Christian had said it would, the 'west end' as people called it, near the forks where West Main Street and Pennsylvania Avenue divided. It was a practical place, neither grand nor mean, its sign swinging gently in the afternoon breeze.

He dismounted and looped the reins. Atlas stood as if rooted, patient as ever.

Inside, the air smelled of wood smoke and ink. Men talked in low voices over cups and papers. Someone laughed. Someone argued. Not sharply. Not yet.

Josephus felt no urge to hurry.

He adjusted his coat, straightened once, and stepped forward to ask for Elias Koontz, his purpose clear. Whatever else the world was busy deciding about itself, this much he knew: he was here to build.

VI

The common room of the Anchor Hotel was half-full, the hour balanced between supper and the work still left in the day.

Papers lay open on tables beside mugs gone cold. Two men argued quietly over figures near the window. Someone laughed, then thought better of it.

Elias Koontz sat alone near the wall, coat off, sleeves rolled, a folded sheet of paper spread before him, weighted at the corners with a knife and a stub of pencil. He was neither young nor old. Early thirties, perhaps a little past, with the look of a man who had learned early that carelessness was expensive. His hair was dark and neatly kept. His posture was attentive without being stiff, as though he expected interruption and would not resent it.

Josephus crossed the room. "Mr. Koontz?"

Koontz looked up at once. His eyes were quick, assessing, but not guarded. "Ja? How may I help you?"

"My name is Josephus Marlowe. My father sent me."

Koontz nodded, already standing. "Christian Marlowe."

"Aye, sir."

Koontz offered his hand. His grip was firm, unshowy. "Come. Sit. Tell me what you're thinking of building."

Not *what you can afford.* Not *how much land.*

Josephus sat and spoke plainly—of the rise above the creek, the water, the wind, the light. He spoke of a mill that would work without drowning the house in noise, of outbuildings placed with intention rather than convenience. Josephus didn't speak quickly, but neither did he hedge.

Koontz listened without interrupting, eyes dropping now and then to the paper, something already half-formed in his mind.

When Josephus finished, Koontz nodded once. "You've walked it."

"Aye."

"That helps." Koontz tapped the page with his pencil. "You don't build against land like that. You build with it. Otherwise, you spend the rest of your life correcting the mistake."

Josephus smiled, surprised and relieved. "My father says the same."

Koontz's mouth curved slightly. "Your father's reputation reaches farther than you think."

He turned the paper around. On it was the beginning of a plan—not precise, not yet, but thoughtful. The proportions were sound. The orientation was right.

"I would not rush the stone," Koontz said. "Timber, we can manage. Six months if the weather holds. I have men who know how to work steady instead of fast."

"That's what I want," Josephus said. "Steady."

Koontz glanced up. "You intend to be on site?"

"As much as I can."

"Good." Koontz folded the paper carefully. "A house raises better when the man who means to live in it knows where the nails are driven."

There was a pause. Not awkward, but deliberate.

"You should know," Koontz said, "I am particular about my crew. No slave labor."

Josephus didn't hesitate. "A condition I insist upon."

Koontz studied him a moment longer, then nodded. "Then we shall do well enough."

They spoke a while longer—of costs, of timing, of the millrace and how water might be coaxed without forcing it. Koontz mentioned his wife, Emma, and their children in passing. Four now, his eldest, Samuel, in his early teens. He spoke of them the way he talked of his work: with pride, but no embellishment.

When they stood at last, the light outside had begun casting long shadows.

"I shall come out and see the land myself," Koontz said. "Before we settle anything."

"I would expect nothing less," Josephus replied.

Koontz smiled at that. A genuine thing, quick and gone. They shook, firm and solid. "Then we understand each other."

Josephus stepped back into the afternoon with his purpose firm. Behind him, the Anchor Hotel's door swung shut, the sound final and sure.

Fairlight was no longer just an idea.

It had hands now.

CHAPTER VI

Friday, May 24, 1997

I

Josephus Marlowe—Journal
Undated, the night after Josephus named Fairlight

This morning, we rode before the light had properly made up its mind. Father said little, but he did not need to. The land spoke plainly enough, and I felt, standing there, that it would remember us if we behaved ourselves upon it.

I have named the land Fairlight. Father approved the name. That alone would have been enough for the day.

Jacob was restless. He has been so more often of late. I cannot say when it began, only that it seems to come upon him suddenly, like weather, sharp and ill-timed. I do not think he means me harm, though at moments his words strike as if they do. He speaks as though my wanting to do a thing carefully is an accusation against him. I cannot say why.

When he spoke today of men being owned, I felt something rise in me before I could consider it. I answered too quickly, perhaps, but I do not regret the answer. I would rather not build at all than build wrongly.

I love my brother. I believe he loves me, though he shows it less easily now. I hope this is only a season and that whatever presses upon him will loosen its grip in time. We have always stood together. I cannot imagine it otherwise.

I rode to Westminster this afternoon and spoke with Elias Koontz. He is a steady man. I think we shall work well together. It comforts me to know there are still men who understand that good work is not hurried, and that some choices, once made, must be lived out.

The land felt right again this evening. I take that as a kindness.

II

Christian Marlowe—Journal
Undated, the night after Josephus named Fairlight

I walked the ground with my sons today and saw, more clearly than I would have wished, how differently they now look upon the same earth.

Josephus listens. He always has. He receives a place as one receives instruction, with care, and without needing to master it at once. Fairlight will suit him. It will test him, but it will not corrupt him. Of that I am as certain as a man may be of anything not yet built.

Jacob does not listen. He measures. He weighs. He presses. I have watched this habit grow in him, and I can no longer tell myself that it is merely youth or restlessness. There is a narrowing in his thinking that troubles me. He speaks of order, but what he means is control. He speaks of realism, but what he seeks is permission.

Today, he nearly spoke a word I will not write. That he stopped when commanded does not comfort me as much as it ought. Obedience is not the same thing as conviction.

I have tried to teach him that restraint is not weakness, that authority need not announce itself loudly to be real. He does not believe me. Worse, I fear he believes he has evidence to the contrary.

I sent him home. It was necessary. It will not be sufficient.

Mary would ask what weighs upon me, and I would give her some careful fraction of the truth. She would hear it kindly, and that kindness would not alter the facts. Some reckonings are not eased by sharing them.

The land itself remains sound. That, at least, has not failed us.

I pray that time will do what instruction has not. But I have learned these past years that time is an unreliable ally.

III

The fire had subsided to glowing embers as Ernest paused, watching his audience's faces for a flicker of understanding.

From his perch on the log, Todd hunched forward, scooped up a substantial pile of sticks and branches, and tenderly arranged them within the fire pit. Just as he was about to add dry kindling, the smallest sticks burst into flames, sending up a tiny plume of smoke. Seconds later, the fire flared, bathing them in its warm, bright glow against the darkness.

Ryan nodded toward Ernest's open pack, where the leather-bound journal lay wrapped in cloth, its spine catching the firelight. "Josephus kept one, too," he said. "Did Jacob?"

Ernest didn't answer straight away. He closed Josephus's journal carefully, smoothing the cloth back over it before returning it to the pack. His gaze, outwardly blank, held on Ryan a moment longer, hinting at unspoken thoughts. "No."

He offered no further explanation, and the silence that followed was devoid of any expectation of one. Carrie noticed the way Ernest's gaze moved briefly away, toward the dark beyond the firelight, as though the answer weren't straightforward—only chosen.

After a moment, Ryan tried again. "You've mentioned Big Pipe Creek frequently. I'm assuming there's importance there."

Ernest nodded. "The creek was more than the houses, more than the roads. Water was the work." He picked up a stick and drew a loose line in the dirt, branching it once, then again. "A gristmill needs a steady flow. Not force, mind you, but steadiness. Big Pipe runs year-round. It doesn't dry out or flood. Well, flood easily, anyway. That made it an engine before engines existed."

"So Fairlight wasn't unusual," Carrie said, stating more than questioning. "It was another gristmill along the creek."

"It was intentional," Ernest replied. "There were other mills. Trevanion, obviously. But also Myrtle Hill. It was older and closer to the Monocacy River."

Carrie looked up. "That's the first place Todd took us to see…in Bruceville."

"Yup," Ernest said. "Out of the way." Todd received a small, easily expected grin from him. "On purpose."

Carrie smiled faintly, reaching across Deborah to give Todd a gentle push. "Figures. That's totally Todd!"

"And Trevanion?" Ryan asked. "You mentioned competition."

Ernest's mouth tightened just slightly. "There was always competition. Mills didn't just grind grain, wheat, or corn. They controlled time. Whose wheat got milled first, who waited, who paid less. And who owed favors. Don't worry, dude. We'll get to Trevanion soon enough."

The fire crackled and popped.

Carrie hesitated, her eyes darting over to Todd, "You mentioned a woman earlier. Hannah. When I said the sound of the water could put me to sleep."

Todd nodded, but Ernest replied. He looked at her then, genuinely looked—not surprised, but attentive. "Myrtle Hill belonged to the Mehrings," he said. "George Mehring ran the place until his wife died. Later, by the mid-1850s, he was the postmaster in Bruceville. His oldest son, Frederick, kept the mill running and established a phosphate factory on the creek."

"What happened to his wife?" Deborah asked, her intuition already sketching out the inevitable reply.

"There was an outbreak of cholera in the early 1850s," Ernest said, his expression tightening. "They lost three children in 1852. Julia, who was eleven. Mary, who was seven. And Julianna, who was only a baby." He paused, sighed, then added, "A year later, Elizabeth Mehring hanged herself in the barn."

No one spoke.

"The remaining children lived," Ernest continued. "Frederick took over the mill, and Maggie was still a young girl then, attending common school in Bruceville."

"And Hannah?" Carrie asked.

Ernest's voice softened. "George sent her to school in New Windsor. Joanna Kleefisch's Academy for Girls. Reading, writing, deportment. All skills considered necessary in that era."

"And Myrtle Hill?" Ryan asked.

"Wasn't Fairlight," Ernest said. "Myrtle Hill was work first and family second. Fairlight tried to be both." He leaned back, looking into the fire. "Hannah grew up hearing water the way some people hear lullabies. She knew what mills took from a place, and what they gave back."

The silence that followed felt different. It was expectant rather than heavy.

"Hannah came home to Myrtle Hill in May 1857, a full month after construction of Fairlight had started," Ernest said. "That's where we go next."

The fire crackled softly, as if in agreement.

CHAPTER VII

Friday, May 29, 1857

I

The carriage wheels kept a steady rhythm on the road, neither hurried nor slow.

George Mehring sat opposite his daughter, Hannah, his hat resting on his knee, his gaze fixed ahead.

Hannah folded her gloves once, then again, and set them beside her, watching the country pass without comment. They spoke only when necessity demanded it. By the time Myrtle Hill came into view, the silence had settled into something familiar.

From the road, Myrtle Hill appeared almost austere in its whiteness. Hannah had never thought it beautiful in the way other houses were called so. It didn't bloom, nor did it sprawl. It stood.

The shutters were always closed evenly at night. The porch chairs were aligned before anyone thought to look. Even the hedge along the road seemed trimmed not for appearance, but for principle.

She'd grown up beneath its straight lines and shadowed arches, beneath the steady shade of the two trees that flanked the porch. The house didn't surprise. It remained in place. It endured.

And in that endurance, she was shaped.

The mill was already running when Hannah arrived.

The sound reached her first, steady and unbroken, carrying across the yard with the same persistence it always had. Water on stone.

Wheel on shaft.

Myrtle Hill didn't pause for her arrival, and she didn't expect it to. Hannah stepped down from the carriage, smoothing the creases from her dark traveling dress, and waited a moment. Her hand rested on the carriage rail, listening until the rhythm settled into something she could measure.

It was the same sound she remembered…and not the same. The flow held, but it pulled harder now, as though the creek had learned to give nothing freely. Where it once lulled, it now labored. Hannah didn't frown at this. She noted it, the way one notes a change in the weather that has already come.

George had come for Hannah himself, bringing her home from New Windsor without remark or ceremony.

He dismounted without hurry, not looking back at her right away. He had the habit of finishing what he was doing before turning his attention elsewhere. Hannah waited while he secured the horse and checked the gate. Only when the latch sat correctly did he turn.

"You'll want to wash up," he said. "We'll have supper before dark."

His voice was not unkind. Nor was it tender. He ordered his days by what must be done.

Inside Myrtle Hill, little had changed. The floors bore the same wear. The table stood where it always had. What was absent wasn't named. Hannah moved through the space with practiced ease, setting her gloves aside, rolling her sleeves, and drawing water. She noticed where the boards near the door had been repaired—well enough, but not by her hand.

George spoke while she worked. Of accounts. Of grain. Of how Frederick was managing more of the mill now, besides the phosphate factory. Then, without shifting his tone, he said, "You turn eighteen this spring. It's time we thought ahead."

Hannah nodded once without stopping what she was doing.

"There are families worth knowing," he continued. "Men who keep their affairs in order. I have business with the Marlowes again next week. You'll come with me."

George didn't present his request as a question. It didn't need to be. Hannah rinsed her hands and dried them carefully, taking a moment to feel the cloth's grain. Through the open door, she could hear the mill wheel turn, steady as breath.

"All right," she said.

Later, when she stepped outside alone, she didn't walk toward the house or the road. She followed the sound of water instead, stopping where the ground dipped, and the creek showed itself behind the Virginia pine trees. She watched the current for a while without thinking of what it carried or where it led.

It would hold, she decided. But it would take its due.

When she turned back toward the house, the mill was still running. George was already inside. Nothing had shifted yet, but something had begun.

II

Monday, June 1, 1857
Three days later

The Marlowe farm presented itself gradually, fields opening into orchard, the fence lines newly set and not yet settled into the ground. Hannah stepped down from the carriage beside her father and stood where she was, letting the farm finish declaring itself before she moved. The summer sun caught in her dark hair, drawn back and braided in the plain style she favored, warming her face without pressing too hard. Maryland summers could be cruel when they wished, but this one was not. She lifted her gaze to take in the land, her gray-green eyes narrowing slightly against the light, attentive rather than appraising.

It was not quiet in the way Myrtle Hill was quiet. The sounds here were sharper—hammer on post, wire drawn taut, the measured labor of something being built rather than kept. Hannah didn't search for comfort in it. She listened, as she always did, for steadiness.

Near the apple trees, a young man worked along the fence line, his back to them, sleeves rolled, his movements unhurried and exact. He didn't look up at once. When he did, it was without surprise, as though the land itself had told him someone had arrived.

Josephus Marlowe rested his hands on the rail and straightened. For a moment, he only looked. The girl he remembered from fairs and meetings—quiet, often standing just behind her father—had grown into herself. There was no sense of sudden change, only the unmistakable knowledge that time had done its work.

Christian Marlowe came forward then, greeting George with the ease of a man accustomed to standing his ground. The two spoke briefly, voices low, already turning toward the house.

"Hannah," George said, pausing. "You'll remember Josephus."

She did. Not as he was now, but as he had been: careful, even-tempered, never one to draw attention to himself. Seeing him here, set into the work of the farm, she felt the faintest click of recognition, as though something unfinished had settled.

"It's good to see you again," she said.

"And you," Josephus replied.

They stood for a moment longer. Then Christian held the door, and George followed him inside without looking back.

Hannah glanced once toward the orchard. "Your apples are coming along."

Josephus's mouth betrayed a faint, fleeting curve. "They'll take their time. It's best not to rush what won't be rushed."

"That seems wise."

He smiled and nodded.

When the door closed behind George and his father, Josephus returned to his work without looking back. Hannah remained where she was a moment longer, watching the line of the fence as though committing its shape to memory. Then she turned and followed her father inside, the sounds of the farm settling around her.

III

Monday, June 8, 1857
A week later

Hannah had been to the Marlowe farm enough throughout the week that the place had lost its novelty. She knew where to stand without being told. She knew which rooms were meant for business and which weren't.

Her father was inside with Christian.

Josephus was outside, repairing a fence post that didn't much require repair. Christian had mentioned, in passing, that George intended to return the following Monday, and Josephus had taken that for what it was.

He worked carefully, setting the post straight, though it hadn't leaned far to begin with.

Hannah paused near the yard, unsure whether to wait or wander. Josephus looked up. Not startled, not expectant.

"You can sit there if you like," he said, nodding toward the low stone wall by the apple trees. "The ants won't bother you. They've moved on."

She smiled, surprised that he'd noticed that at all. "I'll remember that."

He went back to his work without hovering or watching.

After a while, she spoke again, more to the air than to him. "It's quiet here."

Josephus stopped, considering Hannah's comment. "Only if you listen for the right things."

That made her laugh. Not loudly. Just enough.

"Does your family still worship at Meadow Branch?" Josephus asked.

"Yes," she replied. "We've been there as long as I can remember."

He nodded. "The Methodist circuit comes through here twice a month. Father doesn't miss it."

With a gentle smile and a nod, Hannah showed she understood.

They didn't speak again.

When her father finally came to fetch her, Christian followed him out, lingering at the door a moment, watching his son and Hannah. He spoke quietly to George before stepping aside.

Hannah turned back once and found Josephus already watching. Not her, exactly, but the place where she had been.

He nodded and smiled.

She nodded in return, then followed her father toward the carriage while Josephus returned to his work.

George did not look displeased.

Beyond the orchard, half-shadowed by the rise of the field, Jacob Marlowe stood with his hands braced on his hips, watching. He didn't move when Hannah turned away. His jaw tightened, the muscles there working once before he set his face and looked out across the land, as though measuring what ground remained to him.

Nothing had happened.

Yet everything had.

The farm settled again, though not as before.

IV

Saturday, June 13, 1857
Five days later

The light was thinning as the sun dropped behind the trees, laying long bands of gold across the clearing, when Josephus set the last board in place.

Now squared and nearly weather-tight, the tenant house at Fairlight stood firm, its door hung plumb and its hearth drawn clean. He stepped back and looked at it, not with pride, but with the simple relief of knowing it would hold. Tomorrow, he would finish weatherproofing the structure and could sleep there.

Beyond it, the mill had taken its final shape. The wheel was mounted, the race cut true, the stones dressed and waiting. Up the slope, the ground for the main house lay open, trenches marked and half-laid with stone, the beginnings of the bank barn rising farther off like a thought not yet finished. Beside it, at a respectable distance, were the stables where Atlas and the other eventual animals would shelter. Fairlight no longer felt imagined; it felt claimed by work.

Josephus was fitting the latch when he heard the horse.

Jacob rode up without calling out, as he typically did, drawing rein near the edge of the cleared ground. With Brimstone halted beside Atlas, he drew a long breath.

He took Fairlight in at once—the mill, the house, the ordered lines of effort—and let out a low whistle. "You've been busy."

Josephus wiped his hands on his trousers. "Aye. It needed doing."

Jacob dismounted and walked the length of the tenant house, running his hand once along the siding. "You'll be staying out here, then."

"Tis the plan," Josephus said. "Once the fair is done, at least."

Jacob's eyes flickered toward him for a moment. "You're not going?"

Josephus shook his head. "Not this year. I would rather finish what I've started."

"Father won't like a Marlowe missing at the fair," Jacob said, smiling at that, easy and quick. "I can go in your place…if he approves."

He considered the offer, then nodded. "That would save him the trouble."

Josephus swiped the sweat from his brow, the heat of the day still clinging to him as they walked toward their waiting horses. As daylight faded, they mounted their horses side-by-side, heading back toward the farm with the creek murmuring alongside them. Josephus looked once over his shoulder at the tenant house, already imagining the quiet of the night there.

Jacob did not look back.

V

Sunday, June 14, 1857
The next day

The Sauble family often hosted agricultural fairs on their property at the edge of Westminster, where the grass had been worn thin by years of wagons and feet.

Past the tents and tables, nearer the bend of Little Pipe Creek, the main County Almshouse sat apart from the noise of the adjacent property, its long red brick front plain and unadorned, built to take in those who had no family left to do so. A white-covered walkway extended from the south side, connecting to the second level of the men's dormitory. The property operated its own smaller 307-acre farm where residents were expected to work. People passed it without comment, turning their faces instead toward the color and commotion of the day.

Christian Marlowe noticed Jacob's absence before he noticed anything else.

He'd set Jacob to mind the family's display, a task he'd accepted with little comment and less interest. When Christian looked back from a conversation and saw the space standing empty, he frowned once and excused himself.

Jacob was nowhere near the pens or tables. He'd crossed the grounds with purpose, scanning the crowd for familiar faces, finding the Mehrings first—George's height unmistakable, Frederick close beside him—and changed course without hesitation.

Jacob slowed near the tables beneath the sycamores, where the quieter work of the day was managed by women who knew who belonged where. Hannah stood beside Mrs. Bixler, the foreman's wife from Trevanion, folding linen napkins that had already been folded once before, her hands moving out of habit more than need.

Jacob lingered within sight, removing his hat, turning it once at the brim. He didn't interrupt.

"Hannah," Mrs. Bixler said at last, not looking up, "you'll remember Jacob Marlowe."

Hannah lifted her eyes. "Yes," she said after a moment. "Only slightly."

Jacob nodded. "It's good to see you home again. Your father must be proud."

"That's kind of you," Hannah answered. She inclined her head. Not a bow, but something close enough to one that it ended the moment properly.

Mrs. Bixler gathered the folded napkins and moved away, satisfied.

For a beat, they stood in the space she'd left behind.

"You were away some time," Jacob said. "School, wasn't it?"

"Yes."

"I hear they teach young ladies all manner of things now."

"They teach us to read," Hannah said. "And to think."

Jacob smiled at that. Not unkindly, but as if indulging a phrase he'd heard before.

"Well. Those are useful, I suppose."

A pause followed. It wasn't uncomfortable. Not yet. Just long enough for the sounds of the gathering to press in again: laughter, cutlery, a child calling for water.

"You'll be staying?" Jacob asked.

"For the season."

"That's good," he said. "It's quiet when people leave. Things feel… unfinished."

Hannah met his eyes then, measuring something she couldn't yet name. "Yes. They can."

From across the lawn, her father glanced their way. Not sharply, not with concern. Simply noting. The way men did when something had begun.

Jacob noticed the look and mistook it for permission.

VI

Sunday, June 21, 1857
A week later

Jacob arrived at Myrtle Hill in the late morning, not long after the Mehrings' return from the Meadow Branch Meeting House, where the German Brethren held their services. The house was still quiet with the weight of the morning.

Brimstone lathered lightly at the neck. Jacob dismounted without waiting to be seen and tied the reins to the rail, smoothing Brimstone's coat before stepping toward the house. The mill was running. He paused only long enough to note that before knocking.

George Mehring answered himself. "Ja? How may I help you?" he said, already measuring the hour.

"My name is Jacob Marlowe, sir," he said, removing his hat. "I hope I'm not intruding."

George looked him over for a moment. He knew the name. He knew the family. After a measured pause, George stepped aside. "Come in."

They sat at the table where accounts were usually kept. Jacob didn't wait to be offered a seat. He spoke plainly.

"I won't take much of your time, sir. I wanted to speak to you directly, as is proper." George nodded once. "I've had occasion to speak with your daughter recently. At the fair. I would like your permission to pay her proper attention."

He said it carefully. He didn't ask whether Hannah wished it.

George folded his hands on the table. "You're young," he said. "And my daughter has only just come home."

"Aye, sir," Jacob replied quickly. "But she's of age. And our families are well known to each other." George did not dispute that. "I won't pretend my intentions are idle. I'm a Marlowe. I work hard. I intend to make something of myself."

"That may be," George said. "But intention isn't possession."

Jacob smiled faintly, as though accepting a mild correction. "Aye. Of course, sir."

For a moment, only the sound of the mill filled the room.

"I shall speak with my daughter," George said at last. "And give you an answer when I have done so."

Jacob bowed his head. "I'd appreciate that."

George stood, replacing his hat.

"I'll await your word," Jacob said.

George watched him go. He didn't return the smile.

VII

Myrtle Hill had not fully woken again after church.

The windows stood open, but the air moved sluggishly, as though the morning had taken its stillness with it when it left. Hannah changed out of her meeting dress and was smoothing it carefully before hanging it away when her father called her name.

"Hannah, in here," George said. He sat at the table with the ledger closed before him. Not working. Waiting.

She crossed the room and stood where she'd stood all her life when summoned—near enough to be addressed, not so close as to presume familiarity. She folded her hands; the habit settling in before thought.

"Jacob Marlowe called today," George said.

Hannah didn't react at once. She'd known this moment was coming since the fair, had felt it gathering like storm clouds. Still, the words landed with a soft, unmistakable finality.

"Yes," she said.

"He asked my permission to pay you proper attention." George watched her then. For composure. "I told him I would speak with you first. Which I have done."

Hannah nodded, keeping her eyes level and her expression unchanged.

"He's a known family," George said. "His father is well-regarded. He has work and prospects. He spoke respectfully." Hannah waited, meeting her father's eyes. "I shall give my leave on condition. Visits will be in the evening, and they will not be long. I shall expect him here this Thursday."

There it was—the shape of the thing, named and set in place.

Hannah drew a slow breath. "And what would you have me do, Papa?"

George's brow creased, just slightly. "I would have you receive him."

She considered that phrasing: *'receive,'* not *'welcome,'* not *'desire.'*

"I will," she said.

George relaxed then with the smallest measure. "Good."

Hannah hesitated, only for a moment. "May I ask why him?"

George didn't bristle. He'd expected the question. "He asked. And you are of age. It's time to see what sort of man he is."

Hannah dipped her head. The motion was practiced. Correct. "Yes, Papa."

He rose then, signaling the end of it. "I'll ride out before evening and speak to Christian. These things should be done plainly."

Hannah stepped aside to let him pass. As he reached the door, she spoke again, her voice steady. "And if I find him not to my liking?"

George paused. He didn't turn.

"Then we shall know that too," he said, closing the door behind him.

Hannah remained where she was for a long moment after, listening to the mill beyond the house, the wheel turning as it always had. She didn't weep. She didn't argue. She took up the dress again and smoothed it once more, though it no longer needed it.

Thursday had been decided.

VIII

George Mehring rode out before supper, the sun already angling low enough to lengthen the shadows along the road.

He kept a steady pace, neither hurried nor slow, his thoughts settled by the rhythm of the horse beneath him. This was not a visit. It was a duty, and he intended to discharge it plainly.

The Marlowe farm came into view with the same order it always presented: fields kept, fences sound, the work of the day not yet fully put away. Christian Marlowe was near the yard when George approached, sleeves still rolled.

George drew rein and stopped. He didn't dismount. "Marlowe."

Christian straightened at once, wiping his hands on a cloth as he came closer. "Mehring."

"I won't keep you," George said. "Your son, Jacob, came to see me this morning."

Christian's expression shifted. Not surprise, exactly, but recognition. "Aye. I see."

"He asked my permission to pay Hannah proper attention," George continued. "I've agreed, under condition."

Christian nodded once. He didn't ask what those conditions were. He already knew there would be some.

"Visits will be at my house," George said. "In the evening. An hour at most. The first will be this Thursday."

"Understood," Christian said.

George inclined his head. The matter was nearly settled.

Jacob had come into the yard by then, drawn by the horse. He stopped a few paces back, his posture already expectant.

George turned slightly in the saddle. "Jacob."

He stepped forward. "Sir."

"You may call at Myrtle Hill this Thursday evening. Come to the door. You shall be received."

Received. The word was deliberate.

"Aye, sir," Jacob said, quick and certain.

George studied him a moment longer than courtesy required. "That will be all."

Jacob nodded, satisfaction already set in his face.

With a gentle nudge of his heels and a double click of his tongue, George guided the horse back to the road. He didn't look back.

Christian watched him go, his mouth set, gaze at last shifting to Jacob.

"Inside," he said shortly. "Now."

The light was fading. Supper would not wait.

IX

Supper was nearly ready when they gathered.

Mary Marlowe and Molly set the table without ceremony. The

food was sufficient and straightforward; the day's labor was still present in the set of shoulders and the lines around the eyes. Christian took his place at the head, Mary across from him, the boys settling where they always did.

Jacob waited until the plates had been passed. "I rode out to Myrtle Hill today," he said, as though reporting the weather. "I spoke with George Mehring."

Josephus looked up, just briefly, then back to his food.

Christian didn't respond at once. He took a bite, chewed, and swallowed. "And?"

Jacob smiled. "He's given his permission. I'm to call on Hannah this Thursday."

The words sat there, claimed space.

Mary's hands stilled. She glanced at Christian, then at Josephus.

Christian laid his fork to rest on the table. "You rode out without saying so."

Jacob shrugged. "I knew where I was going."

"That was *not* the question."

"I handled it," Jacob replied, his smile thinning.

Josephus lifted his eyes then, not to Jacob, but to his father.

Christian's gaze stayed on Jacob. "You didn't think it worth mentioning beforehand?"

"I didn't see the harm," Jacob said. "It's done properly now."

He leaned back slightly, the sound of his chair creaking a soft punctuation in the quiet room. "Properly," he repeated.

"Aye," Jacob said. "George agreed."

Josephus cleared his throat. "That's good," he whispered. "Hannah Mehring is a fine girl."

Jacob glanced at him, surprised, then pleased. "I thought you'd see it that way."

Christian turned his head then, looking at Josephus as though seeing him anew. "And you?"

Without a flicker of doubt, Josephus looked directly into his father's eyes. "What's meant will come clear," he said. "I have work to finish."

There it was. The letting go.

Christian held that moment longer than was comfortable for the table, then looked back at Jacob. "You speak of this as though it were settled."

Jacob frowned. “It is settled. He said yes.”

“He said you may call,” Christian replied. “That is *not* the same thing.”

Jacob's frown deepened, his jaw tightening. “I don’t see the difference.”

“That concerns me.”

Silence fell across the room, heavier now.

Mary gestured toward the bowl sitting on the table. “Eat while it’s warm, Jacob.”

Jacob pushed his food once, irritation flickering through the set of his shoulders. “I don’t know why this is being made into more than it is.”

Christian’s voice stayed even. “Because you talk about a woman as though she were a field you’ve marked.”

Jacob looked up sharply. “That’s not fair.”

“No,” Christian said. “It’s precise.”

Josephus lowered his eyes again, his hands steady. He didn’t defend. He didn’t retreat. He simply accepted the order of things as they stood.

Christian rose, signaling the end of it. “You’ll mind your work tomorrow, Jacob. All of it.”

Jacob gave a single, rigid nod. “Aye, sir.”

The meal resumed, but the ease didn’t return.

Later, when Molly had cleared the dishes and the light had gone from the windows, Josephus stepped outside alone. He stood in the yard a while, listening to the quiet, already thinking of Fairlight.

Behind him, inside the house, Jacob sat rigid with certainty.

Nothing had been resolved.

Yet everything had been revealed.

CHAPTER VIII
Friday, May 24, 1997

I

Christian Marlowe—Journal
Undated, written following the fair

I have learned in these weeks that the manner of a thing often tells more truth than the thing itself.

Jacob has asked leave to court Hannah Mehring, and the leave was properly given, according to form. George Mehring did not act rashly. He set terms. He placed limits. In this, I find no fault.

My concern is not that my son asked, but that he spoke as though the asking were already an answer.

There is a difference between permission and possession. One is granted. The other is assumed. Jacob does not appear to know where that line lies, and if he does, he has no patience for it. He hastens, as though speed itself were a virtue. I have seen men mistake urgency for purpose before, and it rarely ends well.

Josephus has said little. He has taken himself more fully to the work at Fairlight, and I do not discourage it. The mill is nearly fit now. The tenant house stands sound. The land is changing under steady hands. There is a rightness to that labor which I cannot easily put into words, save this: it does not hurry what must be borne.

I watch my sons and see two different answers to the same

question. One reaches outward, eager to claim. The other bends inward, willing to build.

I pray that time will instruct where I have not.

A man may be known by what he desires. He is known as surely by how he goes about taking it.

II

Mary Marlowe—Journal
Undated, written following the fair

There are times when a house holds more than it says.

These past weeks have been like that. The days pass in their usual order. Meals taken, work done, prayers said, and yet something has shifted in the spaces between. It is not spoken of directly, but it is present all the same.

Hannah Mehring has been here often. She is a quiet girl, though not in the way that invites dismissal. She listens. When she sits, she does so as though she means to remain where she is placed, not to draw attention to herself. I have watched her hands while she speaks. How they fold. How they rest. She is not careless with her choices, even when they are not fully her own.

Jacob speaks of her readily. More readily than he should. He names her as one names a plan already set in motion. I do not think he means harm by it. I think he does not notice the weight of what he says.

Josephus has not spoken of her at all.

He is seldom here now. Fairlight takes most of his hours, and when he does return, he carries the look of a man who has already set his mind elsewhere. I do not fault him for this. There is a kind of peace in honest labor that spares a person from measuring himself against others.

I have seen George Mehring watch his daughter when he believes no one is looking. There is care there, and worry, and something like resignation. I do not judge him. We all do what we believe will see our children safely settled in the world.

Still, I find myself uneasy.

A woman may endure many things without complaint and be

praised for it. That does not mean she is unharmed. I wonder sometimes whether we mistake composure for consent and silence for agreement.

I pray for wisdom. Not the kind that rushes to correct, but the kind that knows when to stand close enough to matter.

III

Josephus Marlowe—Journal
Undated, written following the fair

The tenant house at Fairlight is fit now. I slept there for the first time two nights ago. The hearth draws well, and the door holds against the wind. I will need to adjust the latch before winter, but it will serve.

The mill wheel was set this week. The race runs true, and the water keeps its course even after the last rain. I am glad. There is comfort in knowing a thing will do what it was made to do.

I have spent most of my hours here. There is more ground to break for the main house, and the stonework for the barn has begun. The men work better when there is no confusion about the day's purpose. I try to keep it so.

Father says the fair went well enough. I am sorry I was not there to help him, but I do not regret staying. Some work is easier done when one does not leave it half-finished.

Labor asks no explanations. If a beam is square, it stands. If it is not, it must be set again. The land does not concern itself over what might have been done differently.

In the evenings, when the light fades, the sound of the water settles me. I am grateful for that. Some things are best met with steady hands and a willingness to begin again the next morning.

I will continue as I have.

More remains to finish.

IV

Todd glanced at his watch. "It's almost midnight."

The coals of the fire barely flickered when the sound broke the stillness of the night.

A crashing rush through the woods—sudden, violent enough to break the quiet—tore through the trees beyond the clearing.

Deborah gasped and caught Todd's arm.

Ryan was already on his feet.

Another crack followed, farther off this time, branches snapping in sequence as though something significant had lost its balance and taken others with it.

"A tree came down," Ryan said.

"You don't know that," Todd replied. Ryan didn't answer.

Ernest stared into the darkness, his face unreadable, as though he were listening for something that had already passed.

Carrie tilted her head, not tracking the sound itself, but the way it moved, how it traveled, and how it ended.

Then it was gone.

The woods resumed their ordinary noise. Crickets. An occasional frog. The faint stir of leaves. The distant, steady voice of the creek.

Todd laughed—a little too loudly.

"It was probably just the wind," Deborah said.

Ryan sat back down. "There wasn't any wind."

No one replied.

The fire popped once, a coal collapsing inward, and a brief scatter of sparks lifted into the trees before the dark closed over them again.

Deborah coaxed the dying embers back to life. The pile of sticks and branches they'd gathered was now visibly diminished.

Ernest closed Josephus's journal carefully and returned it to the backpack. He looked around the circle, gauging them. "This is the world that holds."

"Well, it totally sucks!" Carrie said, wiping at her eyes. "I feel so bad for Josephus. I mean, no disrespect to your family, but Jacob isn't the nicest guy. He doesn't deserve Hannah."

"I don't disagree with you," Ernest said. "As Christian implied, you have to let it play out. Josephus saw that. He didn't even need his father to tell him so."

"*Que sera, sera*," Ryan said.

Ernest nodded.

Leaning across Deborah, Carrie turned to Todd, her eyes tracing the fiery dance of shadows that played upon his face. "You didn't tell me the wrong guy was gonna get the girl! I hate stories like that. There's always supposed to be a happy ending!"

With a concerned frown, Ryan slipped his arm around her shoulders. "Scout, I'm getting the idea, since we're sitting on the ruins of a mill when the Marlowe farm, Myrtle Hill, and Trevanion are still standing, that this isn't going to have a happy ending."

With a pout, Carrie nestled closer to him. "I hate all of you."

Deborah chuckled, rubbing her back. "You need to wait for it, hon."

"The story will end as it's supposed to," Ernest said. "Happy or sad, it won't matter nearly as much as whether anyone stood the way they were meant to."

He lit another Marlboro; the flare was brief and bright before the dark closed in again.

"Courtships worked differently back then. It wasn't like dating as we know it today," he said. "There wasn't much room for… anything physical. Not unless you were engaged. Even then, families watched closely. Reputation mattered."

Carrie leaned in, captivated by Ernest's story. "I assume the community saw your family and the Mehrings as reputable?"

Ernest nodded. "They were. Taneytown and Westminster were literally small towns in the eighteen hundreds. Grandpa Christian was well-known and well-regarded. The Mehrings were also because of their positions in Bruceville and Westminster. But there were other families whose names carried a lot of weight." Ernest counted on his fingers as he listed some of them off. "The Shivers in Union Mills. In Westminster, we had the Gists, the Roops, the Royers, the Englars, and so on."

Ryan said, "I have friends with all those surnames."

Ernest nodded once toward Ryan. "The Thomas family was, too."

Carrie whirled around, her eyes wide as she fixed her gaze on Ryan. "Really? I never knew that."

Ryan offered a small, knowing smile as he idly traced patterns on the dirt with his shoe. "Somewhere in the family line, there was a man named W.B. Thomas, William, who built a rather imposing Victorian-style house at the corner of East Main and Longwell Ave."

"Isn't that where the post office is?" Deborah asked.

Ryan gave a swift nod, a quick flicker of agreement. “Eventually, they sold it to the B.F. Shriver Canning Company, which used it as offices. Then, in 1932, the city tore it down to build the post office.”

Carrie nuzzled into Ryan, her head resting on his shoulder. “I didn’t know I was engaged to local royalty.”

Ryan let out a soft chuckle, his gaze still fixed on the ground where his foot had finally stopped. “I wouldn’t go that far, Scout.”

She looked up at him, blinking her big silver-blue eyes. “Would you have courted me with the kind of restraint and patience they showed in the nineteenth century, MacGyver?”

Ryan's eyes softened with affection as he smiled at her. “Every time.”

Carrie turned back to Ernest. “Tell us more about how men courted women. To pay them ‘proper attention’.”

“I only have a basic idea of how it all worked,” Ernest said. “The couple would sit together at a respectable distance, either on the porch or in a sitting room. Family would supervise, either in the same room or sitting nearby, always listening, observing…and judging.” Ernest smiled slightly. “A suitor's prospects and potential to provide were important. His treatment of the woman he courted was also a huge factor. There was never any talk about the relationship, things like ‘how are we doing’ or ‘where is this relationship going’. Courtship was basically an audition for marriage. Life expectancy was lower back then, so it was important to get married early and have a family to continue the lineage.”

“Wow,” Deborah whispered. “Time was clearly not a luxury.”

“No, it wasn’t,” Ernest said. “The words ‘I love you’ also weren’t spoken often. Instead, kind gestures and thoughtful actions showed love.”

Carrie tilted her head back and laughed. “Oh, boy. I’m guessing Jacob totally struggled with it. Didn’t he?”

“Well, let’s just say that Jacob kept his Thursday appointment.” Ernest offered Carrie a gentle smile. “And it didn’t go as he expected.”

CHAPTER IX

Thursday, June 25, 1857

I

The lantern had been lit at Myrtle Hill before Jacob arrived. Its glow caught along the porch rail and the edge of the doorframe.

Hannah Mehring wore lavender that evening—a fine silk with a faint woven pattern that only showed itself when the light shifted. The bodice fit closely at the waist, and the shoulders gently sloped in the current style. Her sleeves widened at the wrist, trimmed in a soft fringe that stirred when she moved.

The skirt held its full bell shape over a steel frame beneath, giving her more breadth than her slight figure suggested. A small pelerine fastened neatly at her throat, and her velvet bonnet, trimmed with pale roses, rested beside her chair.

She sat in the seat her father directed, her hands folded, her posture straight without appearing rigid, composed as she had been taught.

George Mehring settled himself inside, close enough to hear, far enough not to intrude.

Jacob didn't sit down at once after he arrived. He reined Brimstone to the rail in front of the house and climbed the stairs onto the porch, removing his hat as he did. His dark wool coat was brushed clean but worn faintly at the seams, a plain waistcoat drawn snug across his chest. The collar of his white shirt rose high against his jaw; his cravat was tied carefully, if without flourish.

Jacob paced the length of the porch once, boots sounding firm against the well-used boards, though freshly polished for the call. He held his hat in both hands as he turned, fingers roughened from work, knuckles faintly scarred.

Then he smiled.

"It's good to see you again," he said. "Without all the noise this time."

"Yes," Hannah said, smiling politely. "It is."

He took the chair opposite her and leaned forward, elbows on his knees. "I've been meaning to ask…how did you find New Windsor? Was it what you expected?"

"It was useful," Hannah replied.

"Useful," he repeated, nodding. "That makes sense. I imagine it's a comfort, knowing you've had such preparation."

She tilted her head a little. "Preparation for what?"

Jacob blinked, then laughed softly. "Well, for life, I suppose. For managing a household. For being of use."

Hannah smiled, faint and careful. "I expect that depends on the household."

Jacob waved that aside and moved on. "Still, it's good you've had it. Not every young woman does."

They fell silent for a moment. The cicadas had begun their steady chorus in the trees beyond the yard.

Jacob cleared his throat. "The fair was well attended this year. Father was pleased. He said it reflected well on the county."

"I'm glad of it," Hannah said.

"You didn't stay long," he added.

"No."

Another pause. Not uncomfortable.

"I expect things will be busy for you now," Jacob said. "Being home again. People will be calling. They'll be curious."

Hannah looked out toward the yard. "Some have already."

Jacob smiled at that, satisfied. "Well. That's to be expected."

The lantern flickered as a breeze moved through the porch, cooling the evening.

"I've been thinking," Jacob said, leaning forward again, lowering his voice as though sharing something private. "Once the season settles, it would be good to know where things stand. So no one is misled."

Hannah turned back to him then. "Misled?"

He hesitated, then pressed on. "About intentions. It's better when these things are clear."

"Yes," she said. Her tone was polite. Neutral. Not encouraging. "It is."

From inside, George shifted in his chair. The sound carried.

Jacob straightened and glanced toward the door. "I won't keep you," he said quickly. "I know your father is particular about time."

She offered a small, respectful nod. "He is."

Jacob rose, smoothing his coat. "I'll call again."

He didn't ask if he should. Hannah noticed. So did George.

Hannah rose to her feet, giving a slight, graceful dip of her head. "Good evening, Mr. Marlowe."

"Good evening," he said, offering a small, courteous bow.

Inside, George cleared his throat.

The hour wasn't yet finished.

Jacob left anyway.

II

Hannah entered the house quietly and closed the door behind her. The lantern light faded at once, replaced by the softer glow of the lamp in the sitting room.

George looked up from his chair. "You're early."

"Yes."

He nodded once without asking why.

Hannah moved to set the chairs back in order, straightening what didn't need straightening. Her gloves rested, folded in her hand.

After a moment, George said, "Did he conduct himself properly?"

"Yes."

Another nod. "And you?"

Hannah paused, then answered carefully. "I conducted myself as expected."

That concluded everything.

George rose and took the lamp to extinguish it. "Very well.

You'll receive him again next week."

Hannah lowered her eyes. "Yes, Papa."

The matter, for now, was settled.

III

Jacob found his father in the yard after dark, the air still holding the heat of the day.

"How did it go?" Christian asked.

"Well enough," Jacob said. "She's quiet. Thoughtful. Not quick to give herself away."

Christian watched him for a moment. "And?"

"And I think she understands what is being asked of her," Jacob continued. "It will take time. That's all."

Christian said nothing.

Jacob smiled. "She didn't object."

"That's not the same thing."

Jacob shrugged. "It's how these things are done."

Christian turned back to his work. "See that you remember the difference."

Jacob didn't answer. He believed he already had.

IV

Thursday, July 2, 1857
A week later

The lantern was lit the following Thursday, its glow steady against the gathering dusk.

Hannah took her place on the porch as before, the chair set at the proper distance, the hour already measured in her mind.

Jacob arrived promptly. Too promptly.

"Good evening, Hannah," he said, stepping up onto the porch with an amiable smile.

She didn't return it. Instead, she fixed Jacob with a steady, unblinking stare. "Good evening, *Mr. Marlowe.*"

The correction was gentle but unmistakable.

He paused, then laughed softly. “Aye. Of course. Miss Mehring.”

She dipped her head and sat. Only then did Jacob take his chair.

“It’s a fine evening,” Jacob said. “The sort that makes a place feel settled.”

“Yes.”

He leaned back, stretching his legs. “I’ve always thought a household runs best when things are settled. When everyone knows what’s expected of them.”

She folded her hands. “Expectations can change.”

Jacob smiled, indulgent. “They can. But not everything should.”

The sounds of the yard carried up to them: a gate closing, the indistinct murmur of voices inside. The house was listening, as it always did.

“I’ve been busy lately,” Jacob continued. “The farm keeps a man moving, especially now that Jos is living at Fairlight. In the tenant house. There’s a great deal to manage when people depend on you.”

“I imagine there is,” Hannah said. “Is Fairlight the name of your brother’s farm?”

“Mill,” Jacob corrected. “Still, some men aren’t suited to that kind of responsibility. They prefer to be told what to do. There’s no shame in it, really. Everyone has their place.”

Hannah lifted her eyes then, meeting his for the first time that evening. “Do you believe that?”

Jacob hesitated, surprised by the question, then answered easily. “I believe order matters.”

A pause followed. Not silence—weight.

“I was taught,” Hannah said carefully, “that order is something we make, not something we inherit.”

Jacob laughed softly. “School will do that. Fill a head with ideas.”

Hannah didn’t smile.

He shifted forward again, lowering his voice. “It’s not a criticism, Hann…Miss Mehring. It’s only that the world works better when it isn’t questioned too much.”

From inside the house, George cleared his throat. The sound wasn’t sharp, but it carried.

Jacob straightened. “I won’t keep you,” he said, peering toward the door. “I know your father values punctuality.”

“Yes. He does.”

Jacob rose, satisfied enough to be confident, not perceptive enough to be cautious. “Until next week.”

He didn’t wait for her reply.

When he’d gone, Hannah remained seated for a moment longer than she thought appropriate, listening to the night settle back into place, the creek’s running water rushing further off. When she finally stood and went inside, George looked up at once.

“He speaks freely,” he said.

“Yes.”

George studied her. “And you?”

She paused. “I listen.”

George nodded, but his expression didn’t ease.

V

Thursday, July 9, 1857
A week later

The lantern glowed, casting a warm pool of light despite the lingering twilight.

The sky held its color longer now; the days stretching toward their end with a stubbornness Hannah felt in herself.

Jacob arrived on time. Not early. He greeted her properly this time. “Good evening, Miss Mehring.”

She inclined her head. The chair scraped slightly as he sat closer than before.

“You look well,” he said. “Home suits you.”

“Does it?”

He smiled, pleased. “It does. Some people are meant to belong to a place.” The porch creaked as he shifted forward. “I’ve been thinking about what you said last week. About order being something we make.”

She waited.

“There’s truth in it,” he continued. “But only to a point. A man can make improvements, aye. But the shape of things, that’s already given.”

“By whom?”

Jacob blinked, a slow, deliberate movement, before chuckling.

"By how the world works." The answer was meant to be sufficient. "The trouble with too much questioning is that it unsettles people who rely on steadiness. Folks who need to know the ground won't move under them."

"And those who don't?" Hannah asked.

"They ought to be mindful," Jacob said. "Change carries consequences. I've seen what happens when people start pulling at threads they don't understand. It creates unrest. Confusion. Such things spread."

Hannah folded her hands tighter. "You speak as though unrest is always a failing."

"It usually is," Jacob said without flinching. "Most people are better off when someone else keeps order."

She looked at him then, thoroughly. "And you see yourself as that someone?"

Jacob hesitated, just long enough, then nodded. "Someone has to."

From inside the house, a chair shifted. George's presence pressed closer to the edge of hearing.

"I don't think we mean the same thing by order," Hannah whispered.

Jacob smiled, certain now. "I think you do. You've just been taught to doubt it."

The certainty in his voice was new. Settled. Dangerous.

The silence that followed didn't invite him to continue. It pressed.

George cleared his throat.

Jacob straightened, irritation flashing across his face before he smoothed it away. "I won't keep you," he said, already rising. "I know how your father is."

"Yes," Hannah said plainly. "You do."

He paused. "Next week, then."

She didn't answer.

Jacob left with the hour unfinished.

VI

Hannah entered the house and closed the door more firmly than before.

She didn't go to her room. She remained where she was.

George stood by the table, not pretending to be occupied. "You needn't sit again."

They stood in the space between the lamp and the door. Neither spoke at first.

At last, George faced her and asked, "At what point did it turn?"

Hannah considered the question. "I don't think it did. I think he's always been like this." George nodded slowly. "He speaks as though agreement is inevitable. As though my silence were consent."

"That's a mistake," George said.

"Yes," Hannah said. "But one he's determined to make."

George looked at her fully now. "And you?"

"I am tired," she said plainly, not weakly. That, more than anything, settled it.

"You'll receive him once more," George said after a moment. "If you choose."

She met his eyes. "I would like to end it."

George didn't answer at once. "Then we shall do so properly."

Relief crossed her face—not joy, not triumph. Release.

"Thank you," she said.

George tilted his head slightly in acknowledgment. "Rest tonight."

Outside, the lantern burned until it was no longer needed.

VII

Thursday, July 16, 1857
A week later

The lantern was lit, although Hannah hadn't asked for it.

The night had come down heavy and warm, the air unmoving, the sound of the creek farther off than usual. Hannah took her seat on the porch and didn't arrange it this time. She sat as she was.

Jacob arrived a few minutes late. He apologized for nothing.

"Good evening, Miss Mehring," he said, careful now. Almost formal.

"Good evening, Mr. Marlowe."

He sat, glancing once toward the house, then back to her. “Your father told me you wished to see me again.”

“Yes.”

Jacob smiled, relieved. “Good. I thought it best we speak plainly.”

Hannah waited.

“I’ve been thinking about what we discussed last week. About order. About steadiness. It’s been on my mind.”

“I imagine it has,” she said.

He leaned forward, confident again, the ease returning. “There’s a great deal of talk these days. People questioning things that have worked for generations. It’s dangerous letting that sort of thinking run loose.”

Hannah felt it coming and didn’t stop him.

“At Trevanion, they’ve had trouble lately. Men stirred up by ideas that don’t belong to them. It unsettles everyone. It makes people forget their place.”

Hannah folded her hands together, firm.

“You understand the danger in that, don’t you?” he asked. Not accusatory, but expectant.

She met his eyes. “I understand danger.”

Jacob nodded. “Then you see why it’s important to stand firm. To keep things as they are. Some people aren’t meant for freedom the way others are.”

Between them, the words lay bare.

“Some people,” Hannah said slowly, “have never been given the chance to decide what they are meant for.”

Jacob frowned. “That’s not how the world works.”

“No,” she said. “It’s how you work.”

He tensed. A sudden rigidity took hold of him. “I’m speaking of practicality. Of keeping order.”

“You’re speaking of owning other human beings,” Hannah said, sharper than she intended.

A spark of irritation ignited within Jacob. “I’m speaking of responsibility. Someone has to govern. You can’t just upend everything because it makes you uncomfortable.”

Hannah stood then. Not abruptly, but deliberately.

“I am uncomfortable,” she said. “But that is not why I cannot continue this.”

Jacob rose as well, startled. "Hannah—"

She lifted a hand. "Miss Mehring."

The correction landed hard.

"You asked for my father's permission," she said directly. "You did not ask for mine. You assumed it. You have assumed much from the beginning."

"That's not fair," he protested, his voice tight with rising anger. "I've been patient. Proper."

"You have been persistent," Hannah said. "There's a difference."

From inside the house, George's chair shifted.

"I will not marry a man who believes the world must remain cruel in order to function," she said. "Nor one who believes silence is agreement."

Jacob's jaw tightened. "You're letting ideas get in the way of sense."

"No," she whispered. "I am finally listening to myself." The porch held them in a silence that wouldn't soften. "This is finished, Mr. Marlowe. I wish you well. But I shall not receive you again."

Jacob stared at her as though the ground had shifted beneath him. "You don't mean that."

"I do."

He laughed once, sharp and disbelieving. "You'll regret this."

Hannah didn't answer.

George stepped into the doorway then. "That will be enough."

Jacob turned, his face flushed. "Sir—"

"You have been heard," George said. "Now you shall leave."

Jacob looked back at Hannah one last time, searching for something—doubt, softness, anything.

There was nothing.

He left without the hour ending properly.

The lantern burned on.

VIII

Hannah remained standing until she heard Brimstone's harsh stamps fade.

Only then did she sit, her hands trembling now that they no longer needed to be steady.

George didn't speak at once.

"You did right," he said finally.

She nodded, exhaustion settling in. "I know. But it still hurts."

George rested his hand on the doorframe. "Most necessary things do."

The lantern guttered.

Hannah reached out and extinguished it herself.

IX

The Marlowe house was dark when Jacob arrived; the lamps already lowered, the day put away.

Christian was in the yard, setting a tool back where it belonged, while Jacob stabled Brimstone for the evening.

"You're late," Christian said without looking up.

Jacob stopped short. "I rode to Myrtle Hill."

"Aye. I know."

Jacob paused. "George told you?"

"He did."

Jacob's breath hitched, a sharp sound in the quiet. "Then you know she's ended it."

With a deliberate, unhurried movement, Christian rose to his full height and met Jacob's gaze. "I know she refused you."

Jacob's lips curled into a sneer. "For no good reason!"

Christian studied him for a long moment. "I doubt you believe that."

"I did everything properly," Jacob said, bristling. "I asked. I waited. I conducted myself as expected."

"You conducted yourself as though the answer were owed."

Jacob scoffed. "That's not fair."

"No," Christian said. "It's accurate."

Jacob stepped closer, peering at his father. "She let ideas turn her against me. Things she doesn't understand."

Christian didn't move. "She understood you."

Jacob shook his head, agitation rising. "You don't throw away stability for sentiment. You don't hand the world over to people who don't know how to keep it running."

Christian's voice remained even. "You speak of people."

"I'm speaking of order."

"You speak of control."

A muscle in Jacob's jaw twitched, betraying the tension he held within. "Someone has to."

Christian's gaze hardened then, not with anger, but with certainty. "No, Jacob. Someone has to choose rightly. That is *not* the same thing."

Jacob's laugh was a short, sharp sound, laced with deep bitterness. "So you take her side."

"I take truth where I find it," Christian said. "Tonight, it's not with you."

Silence pressed in, thick and final.

"You think Josephus would have done better," Jacob said at last.

Christian didn't answer immediately. When he did, his words were measured. "Josephus would not have mistaken her silence for consent."

Jacob turned away, hands clenched at his sides tight enough to whiten his knuckles. "So that's it, then!"

"Aye," Christian said. "You were given a chance. You showed who you are with it."

Jacob looked back, eyes bright with something sharp and dangerous. "You always did prefer him."

"No," Christian said, his expression unchanging. "I always expected more of you."

The words landed and stayed.

Jacob left without another word.

Christian stood alone in the yard for a long time afterward, listening to the night settle, knowing that something had passed from disappointment into grievance—and that it would not rest there.

CHAPTER X

Saturday, May 25, 1997

I

Christian Marlowe—Journal
Undated, written after Hannah Mehring ended the courtship

There are moments when a thing ends cleanly, and moments when it ends rightly. The two are not always the same.

Hannah Mehring has refused Jacob. She did so without spectacle and without malice, and I find no fault in her manner or her judgment. If there was disappointment in it, it was not hers. She bore herself with more steadiness than many grown men I have known.

Jacob does not see it so.

He came home bearing grievance as though it had been placed upon him unfairly. He speaks of order, of stability, of the danger of yielding ground. He does not speak of her, except as something withheld. This troubles me more than the refusal.

I have tried to teach my sons that restraint is not weakness, and that patience is not passivity. Josephus understands this without needing it explained. Jacob hears the words and mistakes them for obstacles.

I see now that I have mistaken firmness for guidance. There are lessons a man must choose to learn, and I fear Jacob has chosen otherwise.

Josephus remains at Fairlight most nights now. The mill is nearly fit to run. The tenant house stands sound, and the work has a steadiness to it. There is something honest in building a thing that does not answer back.

I am grateful he has that refuge.

As for Jacob, I am watchful.

A man who believes himself wronged is capable of justifying many things. When order becomes possession, and restraint becomes resentment, the ground grows uncertain underfoot.

I pray that time will temper him. But prayer is not the same as vigilance, and I will not mistake it again.

Some choices reveal themselves only after they are made.

Others reveal the man who made them.

II

Mary Marlowe—Journal

Undated, written after Hannah Mehring ended the courtship

The porch has been dark these evenings.

I noticed it first because I went to light the lantern and found no need to. The hour passed without it, and the night took its place without disturbance. There are changes that announce themselves, and others that are known only by what no longer must be done.

Hannah Mehring came by yesterday with her father. She looked tired, but not unwell. There was a steadiness about her that had been missing these past weeks, as though she had set something down and no longer feared it would follow.

She spoke little. I did not ask her to speak more.

Jacob has been restless. He moves through the house as though it had narrowed around him, as though the walls had shifted without warning. I have seen this before in men who believe themselves denied rather than answered.

Josephus has not returned often. Fairlight keeps him, and that is for the best. There are seasons when a man must put his hands to something solid in order to keep his thoughts from hardening.

I am grateful that Hannah trusted herself when the moment came.

That is no small thing for a young woman to do, even when she is supported. Perhaps especially then.

There is relief in this house, though it is a quiet kind. It does not announce itself, and it does not erase what has passed. It simply allows us to breathe again.

I pray that what has been spared will not be forgotten, and that what has been revealed will not be dismissed.

Some endings leave a mark not because of what they break, but because of what they refuse to become.

III

The fire had burned down again, the embers low and breathing.

Midnight passed without ceremony.

Carrie sat cross-legged on the blanket, her chin propped in her hand now that the log had grown too uncomfortable. She hadn't spoken for a while.

"You know what gets me?" she finally said.

Ryan looked over. "What?"

With a vague wave of her hand, she indicated the darkness, a space filled with a history yet to be revealed. "For a man who wants control…Jacob has very little of it when he's irritated."

There was a pause.

"That's not wrong," Ernest said quietly.

Todd let out a low whistle. "Damn."

Carrie frowned. "It's like every time someone doesn't do or say what he expects of them, he gets flustered instead of listening."

Ryan nodded slowly. "Then it's not about order."

Ernest tapped ash from his cigarette. "No. It's about possession."

Carrie drew her knees in close. "That never ends well."

"No," Ernest agreed. "It doesn't."

She wiped at her eyes and gave a small, embarrassed laugh. "Still. I'm glad Hannah ended it. I was totally worried there for a minute."

"So was I," Ryan said.

Todd stretched his legs toward the warmth. "She and Jacob would never have worked out."

Ernest closed Mary's journal and slid it into the pack. "They wouldn't have."

Carrie leaned forward. "So that's it, right? She's free. He's gone. We get to move on."

Ernest looked at her then with a hint of a smile. "Yes."

"That didn't sound reassuring," Carrie said, frowning.

Deborah smiled faintly and glanced at her. "It never does."

Ernest nudged the embers with his boot. The fire flared briefly, then settled again. He glanced toward the dark where the millstones lay scattered in shadow. "This next part? This is the world that burns."

The fire crackled softly, as if it already knew.

ACT II

THE WORLD THAT BURNS

CHAPTER I

Tuesday, September 22, 1857

I

The main house at Fairlight was never meant to impress from a distance.

It revealed itself slowly, the way good places do, by sound first, then light, then presence.

Set above Big Pipe Creek, the house stood of pale local stone, its walls thick enough to hold coolness in summer and memory in winter. The creek didn't rush here; it spoke. A constant, low voice that carried through open windows and settled into the bones of the house. On still nights, the millwheel downstream added its own rhythm, a patient turning that became part of the household's breathing.

The house faced the fields at a slight angle, not squarely—an unconscious humility, as if it understood it belonged to the land rather than commanded it. Shutters framed the windows, practical and unadorned, painted once and touched up often. The front porch that wrapped around the ell side was narrow but solid, built for waiting, for quiet conversation, for the kind of evenings that end without anyone noticing when the light had faded.

Inside, the rooms were spare and purposeful. Floors bore the soft unevenness of hand-laid boards. The hearth was central, not decorative, but functional. This was a house that earned its warmth. Upstairs, the bedrooms sat close beneath the roofline, the windows lower there, the ceilings angled just enough to make one aware of shelter.

Behind the house, slightly downhill, the springhouse waited in shade. Stone again, cool even in August, water threading through its shallow channel. It was here that time slowed most noticeably. Milk rested. Apples waited. And sometimes, someone sat—not to work, not to think, but simply to listen.

Fairlight wasn't grand. It didn't announce prosperity. What it offered instead was steadiness. A sense that effort here meant something. That labor was answered. That the land, the water, and the house were in quiet agreement.

It was a place where people learned how to stand.

By its third week, Fairlight no longer needed announcing.

The roads that led to it bore the proof: wagon ruts pressed deeper into the packed earth, the grass at the edges worn thin by waiting teams, the sound of water and stone carrying farther than it had any right to. Men came early now, some before sunrise, grain sacks stacked higher than necessity alone would justify.

They came because the work was steady.

Fairlight didn't hurry, and it didn't stall. The water from Big Pipe Creek ran as it always had, guided cleanly into the race, the wheel turning with a rhythm that required nothing of the men but patience. Grain was weighed plainly, ground in order, and returned without fuss. No one was asked who they knew, or how long they had been coming, or whether another mill had kept them waiting the week before. Fairlight took what was brought and did the work set before it.

That alone would have been enough.

The mill stood finished now, its stone settled and dressed, the timbers already darkening with use. The tenant house beside it bore the marks of habitation—smoke rising from the chimney at midday, boots left by the door.

Across from the bank barn, but not yet so far as the slope that led down toward the springhouse, a small smokehouse had been raised—squat, square, and deliberate. Its chinked logs held the scent of curing hams and slow fire. A narrow vent near the peak exhaled a thin, patient thread of smoke that drifted low before dissolving into the afternoon. It stood apart by design, close enough for convenience, far enough that an errant spark would find little to claim.

Farther up the rise, the main house stood complete at last, its windows still bare of curtains, its rooms clean but not yet softened by habit. The bank barn and stables loomed solid behind it, doors wide, ready for a season that would test them soon enough.

Nothing at Fairlight was decorative. Everything answered a need.

By midmorning, the mill yard filled and emptied in a steady pulse. Wagons arrived, were unloaded, and moved on. Men lingered less than they once had at Trevanion, where waiting could stretch a morning into a grievance. At Fairlight, waiting felt like part of the work, not a test of endurance.

At noon, the yard quieted just enough for eating. Bread was broken, cheese cut, and apples passed hand to hand when there were apples to spare. They ate where they could, by the tenant house, along the low wall, standing when there was nowhere to sit. Josephus Marlowe ate with them when he could, whatever was at hand, rising again when the wheel called him back.

By afternoon, the wheel turned on, unremarked now.

Fairlight had found its place.

II

What Fairlight required of men, it required plainly.

Elias Koontz kept the day's order. He didn't shout, and he didn't hurry work that was already moving as it ought. Grain was taken as it arrived. Stones were dressed when needed. If something slipped or bound, it was set right without commentary. Elias stood where he could see the yard at once, and when he spoke, it was because the work itself demanded it.

Josephus worked among them, not above them. He took the lever when it was needed, hauled sacks when there were too many hands at the stones, and reset boards along the race when water worried them loose. He asked questions when he did not know a thing and listened when an answer was given. Men learned quickly that he didn't mind correction, provided it was honest.

The hands came and went with the light. Two younger boys from neighboring farms worked longer days and went home in the evening, their wages counted plainly at week's end. John Dorsey, a freed black man from Taneytown, arrived most mornings on foot, his sack over one shoulder, sleeves already rolled up. He took his place where Elias set him and worked without instruction. At dusk, he washed at the springhouse and took the road back the way he'd come.

No one remarked on it. The work made room.

Men who had known Christian Marlowe watched Josephus without comment. Some nodded once when he passed, as though something had been confirmed. Others brought their grain back a second time. Word traveled faster than wagons, and Fairlight didn't suffer for it.

No favors were kept there, no debts tallied beyond the measure of grain and the turning of the stones.

That, more than the newness of the place, held them.

III

Wednesday, September 30, 1857
A week and one day later

George Mehring came to Fairlight on a clear morning, the kind that made distance feel shorter than it was.

He brought Hannah with him.

She'd dressed with care. Not finery, nothing that would have drawn comment, but intention showed in the details. Her dress was a deeper blue than she wore at home, plain in its cut, the bodice appropriately fitted, the sleeves fastened with small, neat buttons. She braided her brunette hair and pinned it back cleanly, no loose strands left to chance. She wore her good boots, recently brushed, and carried her gloves in her hand rather than tucking them away, as though prepared to use them, or not.

Josephus noticed it all and said nothing.

The mill was already running when they arrived. The wheel turned with its usual steadiness, the sound of stone on grain carrying across the yard without strain. Wagons stood in a loose line, some already unloaded, others waiting their turn. Elias Koontz was near the scale, speaking with a farmer George recognized from the Bruceville side of the creek.

George stopped for a moment to take it in. "So this is it."

Josephus nodded, letting a small grin slip. "It is."

Elias came over then, wiping his hands on a cloth. Josephus made the introduction and stepped aside as the two men spoke. George asked his questions directly—about rates, about timing, about how grain was handled once it was taken in. His own mill would not have room for it until the end of the week. It made sense, this time, to let another man's water do the work. Elias answered without embellishment, pointing when needed, calling over a hand to demonstrate how the sack was hoisted, how the grain was poured, how the stones were set just close enough to do the work without burning the meal.

Hannah watched quietly. She noticed how often men glanced toward Josephus before returning to their work, not for permission, but for confirmation. She saw, too, that when a question was asked, it was answered once and not repeated.

"I'll bring my grain here next time," George said finally. "It's closer, and I don't see the sense in riding past good work."

Elias inclined his head. "We'll be here."

George nodded and turned back toward Josephus. "I'd like to see the springhouse."

Josephus gestured up the rise. "This way."

They walked together, the sound of the mill dulling behind them. Halfway there, George paused. "Instead, I shall speak with Elias a moment longer." He addressed Hannah. "You needn't wait."

Josephus hesitated only long enough to be polite. Hannah had already stopped, her eyes on the springhouse, its stone walls cool and pale in the sun.

"I'll show you," Josephus said. "Come."

They walked the rest of the way in silence.

The springhouse was as Hannah imagined it would be: cool even on a warming day; the water running clear beneath its low roof, shelves already set with crocks and wrapped butter. Josephus explained how it drew from the creek, how the flow stayed steady even in dry weeks, how it kept without fuss.

"It's peaceful," Hannah said.

"Aye. It is," he agreed. "I come here when the stones are loud."

She smiled at that, then grew more serious. "I'm glad this place exists, Mr. Marlowe."

He looked at her then with a faint smile. "So am I."

She hesitated, then spoke as though answering something unasked. "What happened before...with Jacob...it wasn't your doing. I wanted you to know that."

Josephus bowed his head, a deep, respectful inclination. "I never thought it was, Miss Mehring."

George returned shortly after, his business concluded. They walked back toward the yard together, the mill taking up its sound again around them. Before they parted, George looked once more at the land—the water, the work, the men moving with purpose—and nodded to himself. "This was done properly."

Josephus met his eyes. "Aye. That was the hope, sir."

As George and Hannah took the road home, she looked back once, not at the mill, but at the springhouse.

Fairlight received them, asking nothing in return.

IV

Friday, October 2, 1857
Two days later

George Mehring returned to Fairlight two days later, his wagon lighter this time, the grain already accounted for.

Hannah rode beside him, the morning cool enough to justify the shawl she'd brought, though she didn't keep it on long.

Fairlight met them as it had before, not with ceremony, but with motion. The wheel turned. The yard shifted. Men worked and moved on. George nodded once, satisfied, and set off toward the mill with Elias, business already resumed as though it had merely been paused.

Josephus waited only long enough to be sure he wasn't needed.

"Would you care to walk?" he asked Hannah.

"Yes," she said at once, as though she had expected it.

They took the path without naming it. The springhouse came into view between the trees, its low roof catching the light, the water's sound growing clearer with each step.

"You come here often," she said.

"Aye. I do," Josephus answered, glancing at her with a warm smile. "It keeps its own counsel."

Hannah smiled at that. "I understand the appeal."

The air cooled as they stepped inside, the stone holding the day at bay. Water ran beneath the floor, clear and constant; the crocks set where they had been before. Nothing had been disturbed.

"It's the same," she said.

"It ought to be," he replied. "If it needs managing, I've done something wrong."

She rested her hand against the stone wall, feeling the chill through her glove. "Myrtle Hill has a place like this. Not the same, but close enough to be familiar."

Josephus nodded. "Some places teach you what you need without insisting."

They stood there a moment, neither of them hurried.

"I'm glad my father chose to come here, Mr. Marlowe," Hannah said. "It's easier—being somewhere that doesn't feel like it's measuring you."

Josephus considered that. "I've found most things work better when you don't press them."

She studied him then. "You're very unlike your brother."

The words were offered plainly. He accepted it. "I know."

She waited, but he didn't explain further. "I'm sorry. That wasn't meant unkindly."

"It wasn't taken so, Miss Mehring," he replied. "Truth rarely is."

Footsteps sounded on the path outside. George's voice carried faintly, his business concluding.

They stepped back into the light together.

As they returned to the yard, Hannah noticed how easily Josephus rejoined the work—not leaving her behind, but not rearranging himself around her either. She found that this steadiness felt like an invitation rather than a distance.

When George came to fetch her, he paused once more to look over the place, his eye lingering on the springhouse this time.

"It holds," he said, not to anyone in particular.

"Yes," Hannah whispered, softly smiling. "It does."

They took the road home soon after, the sound of the wheel fading behind them.

Hannah didn't look back at the mill.

She looked back at the springhouse.

V

Monday, October 5, 1857
Three days later

The third visit felt less like an occasion and more like the forming of a habit.

George brought Hannah to Fairlight again, this time with grain to be left and collected later. He spoke with Elias briefly, then moved on toward the barn, already thinking ahead to winter and what would need mending before it arrived.

Josephus waited near the yard, his hands clean but not idle. "The springhouse, Miss Mehring?"

Hannah smiled, her gray-tinted green eyes catching the light that broke through the trees. "I was hoping you'd say that."

The path was familiar now. Leaves had begun to turn along the edges to shades of scarlet, orange, and gold, the air carrying the first real promise of cold. The sound of water met them before the stone came into view, steady as ever.

Inside, the cool held. The crocks had shifted since Hannah's last visit, butter wrapped fresh, milk set earlier that morning. The place was used, not kept.

"You don't change it much," she observed.

"There's no need," Josephus said. "It does what it's meant to."

She rested her hands on the stone ledge, ungloved now, feeling the chill without flinching. "I think that's why I'm drawn here. It doesn't ask me to be anything other than what I am."

He considered that, then nodded. “That’s a fair thing to want.”

They stood in silence. It held easily.

“My father trusts this place, Mr. Marlowe,” Hannah said at last. “I can tell. He doesn’t speak of it, but he watches less.”

Josephus smiled faintly. “That’s how you know.”

Then, she turned to him, a quiet strength now clear in her eyes. “If you were to ask him something,” she said carefully, “he would listen.”

Josephus didn’t answer at once. When he did, his voice was steady. “I would not ask unless I believed it would be welcome.”

“I think it would,” she said, allowing herself a small smile.

Footsteps approached outside—George returning, his presence no longer a disruption. The moment had reached its natural end.

They stepped back into the light together.

As they walked toward the yard, Hannah didn’t linger. She didn’t look back this time.

The springhouse didn’t need watching. It would be there.

VI

Thursday, October 8, 1857
Three days later

Jacob Marlowe arrived at Fairlight near the end of the day, riding hard enough that Brimstone tossed his head when he drew rein.

He didn’t call out as he approached, only dismounted and came forward with the confidence of someone who expected recognition.

Josephus looked up from where he stood near the tenant house, pausing. He greeted his brother politely, but without the warmth Jacob remembered from earlier years.

“You’ve finished then,” Jacob said, glancing past him toward the mill, the house, the yard. “I thought I’d come see how you were settling.”

“We are,” Josephus replied. “You’re welcome to stay for supper.”

Jacob seemed satisfied.

They ate at the tenant house, where Emma Koontz had set the

table, the food plain and well-prepared. Elias took his place at the head, Josephus beside him. The others sat where there was room. John Dorsey came in last, washed and quiet, nodding once before taking his seat.

Josephus made the introductions as they sat. Jacob barely dipped his head.

Conversation moved cautiously at first; talk of grain, of the weather turning, of how long the stones might hold before needing to be dressed again. Dorsey spoke little, answering when spoken to, his voice even, his words chosen with care.

At one point, he commented the creek was running lower than usual in a dry year.

Jacob looked at him then, openly. “No one asked you, boy!”

The table went still.

Elias raised his head, but not his voice. “That will *not* do,” he said firmly. “Every man at this table is here by his own labor. There is no one above another at Fairlight, not in this house, and not in the eyes of God.”

Jacob stared at him, color rising in his face. He looked around, expecting support, and found none.

“Fine,” he said at last, pushing his chair back. “Have it your way, then!”

He dropped his napkin onto the table and left without another word. Outside, Brimstone stamped and snorted, the sound sharp against the quiet yard as Jacob swung into the saddle and rode off.

No one spoke for a moment.

“I apologize,” Elias said finally, turning to Josephus. “I spoke plainly, but I will not have that sort of thing here.”

Josephus shook his head. “You did right. This place is yours to keep as you see fit.”

Elias nodded once, the matter settled.

Dorsey hesitated, then spoke quietly to Elias. “Thank you, sir.”

Supper resumed. The conversation didn’t return to where it had been, but it found another course soon enough.

Later, when the table was cleared, and the evening settled back into its work, Josephus stood alone for a moment and listened to the mill wheel turning on in the dark.

Jacob guided Brimstone along the dusty road leading to

Trevanion, eventually leading him across his father's land toward the Marlowe farm. He didn't once look back toward Fairlight. When Trevanion passed on his left, he glanced at it.

Wondering. Considering.

VII

Saturday, October 10, 1857
Two days later

Josephus left Fairlight in the late afternoon, once the day's work had settled into its own keeping.

Elias would see to what remained. The wheel would turn until dusk. There was nothing that required his hand now.

He rode hard enough to make the distance count, but not so hard as to invite questions when he arrived.

Christian was in the southernmost field, as expected, setting a post back into line where the fence had begun to give. He straightened when Josephus dismounted Atlas, wiped his hands on his trousers, and took Atlas's reins.

"Is Jacob nearby?" Josephus asked quietly.

"East field," Christian replied. "He'll be there a while."

That was enough.

They walked the length of the fence together before Josephus spoke again, the evening light thinning around them, the work familiar enough to steady his voice.

"He came to Fairlight," Josephus said. "Thursday."

Christian didn't look up. "So I gathered."

"He didn't take to it well," Josephus continued. "Nor to the men. Elias spoke to him when he crossed a line."

Christian set the post and tamped the surrounding earth with his boot. "And Elias was right to do so."

"Aye," Josephus said. "I told him as much. But Jacob has been coming unannounced. Staying for supper. Speaking as though the place were his to move through as he pleases. That isn't what Fairlight is meant to be."

Christian leaned on the fence rail and considered the field ahead of them. “No. It isn’t.”

Josephus hesitated. “I don’t know what to do with him. I won’t have him made small in his own home, but I can’t allow him to make others smaller in mine.”

Christian nodded once. “Leave that with me. You’ve done nothing wrong, and I shan’t ask you to carry it.”

With a sigh, Josephus released the breath he'd been unconsciously holding.

They walked a few more steps in silence, the fence line finished for the day.

“There’s another matter,” Josephus said at last. “George Mehring has been coming to Fairlight. With Hannah.”

Christian turned then, his attention sharpening.

“I didn’t set it in motion,” Josephus continued. “But we’ve spoken while business was being done. Nothing improper. Only…enough to matter.”

Christian’s expression softened, though his voice remained measured. “Enough tells me what I need to know.”

Josephus stopped. “I would not ask lightly.”

“I know,” Christian said. “And I would not offer lightly either.” He rested his hand on the fence rail. “You’re better suited to her than your brother. That isn’t a failing in Jacob, but a truth in you.”

Josephus said nothing. He didn’t need to.

“If you wish to ask George’s leave to call on his daughter,” Christian continued, “I will ride with you. That is the proper way.”

Relief crossed Josephus’s face, unguarded and brief.

“Tomorrow,” Christian added. “After services. The Mehrings worship at Meadow Branch. We’ll ride in the early afternoon.”

Josephus inclined his head. “Thank you, Father.”

“You should return home before the light goes entirely. You’ll want a clear head tomorrow.”

Josephus mounted Atlas and turned toward the road. As he rode off, the field behind him lay quiet, the fence set straight again, holding what it was meant to keep.

VIII

Sunday, October 11, 1857
One day later

Josephus and Christian rode out after the noon meal, once the roads had emptied again.

Christian set Elder's pace, steady and unhurried on the Monocacy Road, as he did when there was no reason to arrive early and no need to be late. Josephus rode beside him, saying little, his attention turned inward.

Myrtle Hill gradually came into view as they reached Bruceville, the mill sound reaching them before the house did. Water on stone. Wheel on shaft. The familiar labor of it settled Josephus more than he'd expected.

George Mehring met them at the rail.

He took in the sight of them together—father and son, horses well kept, posture unassuming—before offering his hand. Christian dismounted first, Josephus following a moment later.

"Mehring," Christian said. "Thank you for receiving us."

"Marlowe. You're welcome," George replied. His eyes moved briefly to Josephus, then back. "Come inside."

They sat in the front room, the door open to the afternoon, the mill's sound never quite leaving.

Christian spoke plainly. He didn't speak long. "My son wishes permission to court your daughter. He has asked me to ride with him, as is proper."

George listened without interruption. When Christian finished, he turned to Josephus.

"Have you spoken with her already?" George asked.

"Aye, sir," Josephus answered. "Only while business was being done. I would not presume further without your leave."

George nodded. He didn't smile, but something in his expression gave way. "You've built something solid at Fairlight."

"I've tried to," Josephus said.

"That matters." George stood then and nodded once. "I have heard what you've said. And I appreciate that you came as you did."

Josephus dipped his head. "Thank you for receiving us, sir."

"I will speak with Hannah," George said.

That was all.

Christian rose at once. Josephus followed without hesitation. There was no disappointment in it, only recognition of form.

At the door, George paused. "I shall give you my answer soon."

"Aye, sir," Josephus said.

"We shall wait at my farm," Christian said.

They rode away without knowing more than they'd brought with them.

IX

George waited until the sound of hooves had thinned into the distance before closing the door.

Hannah stood near the window, hands folded, her posture correct in a way that didn't quite mask the energy beneath it. She hadn't sat down.

"Well," George said, turning to face her. "You heard why they came."

"Yes," Hannah replied. Her voice was steady. Too steady.

He studied her for a moment. "And?"

She hesitated. Not long, but long enough to gather herself. "Josephus has been respectful. He's not hurried me. He's not spoken as though I owed him anything."

George nodded. "That matters."

"It does," she said. "He listens. And when he speaks, it's because he's thought first."

A faint color had risen in her cheeks. She didn't try to hide it.

"You like him," George said, not unkindly.

Hannah lowered her eyes. "Yes."

That was all. No embellishment. No apology.

George walked to the table and rested his hand on it, feeling the grain beneath it. "This would be a courtship, Hannah," he said. "Not a promise."

"I understand."

"Visits as agreed. Time kept. Nothing taken for granted."

"Yes, Papa."

He looked at her then, truly looked, at the way she stood, at the way she held herself, at the composure she'd learned young and worn well. "You are certain?"

She met his eyes. "As certain as I know how to be."

The smile came then, unbidden and bright, before she could catch it. She pressed her lips together at once, embarrassed by it.

George's expression softened. "That answers me."

Hannah's shoulders dropped as she exhaled, the tension easing with it. "Thank you, Papa."

"I'll ride to Marlowe this evening," George said. "I shan't keep them waiting long."

Her fingers tightened once, then stilled. "I shall be ready."

George nodded. "I know you will."

As he turned to go, Hannah returned to the window. Myrtle Hill carried on as it always had—the wheel turning, the water running—unchanged by the decision just made inside its walls.

She stood there a moment, smiling to herself, careful not to let it show to anyone else.

Joy, like most things worth keeping, was best held that way.

X

George rode out before supper, the light still clear enough that the road showed itself honestly.

He didn't hurry, but neither did he linger. Myrtle Hill fell away behind him, the sound of the wheel thinning until it was only a memory.

The Marlowe farm was settled when he arrived. Christian was in the yard, finishing a task he had no need to rush. Josephus stood nearby, sleeves rolled, hands idle in a way that told George everything he needed to know.

George dismounted and tied his horse without remark.

"Marlowe," he said.

"Mehring," Christian replied. He glanced once at Josephus, then back. "You've come with an answer."

"I have."

Josephus didn't step forward. He waited where he was.

George turned to him. "I have spoken with Hannah."

"Aye, sir," Josephus said, finally approaching.

"She is willing to be courted."

The words landed cleanly, without warning. Josephus bowed his head respectfully, his composure holding even as something bright broke through it.

"I will expect the same conduct I outlined with Jacob," George continued. "Visits as agreed. Time kept. No assumptions made."

"You have my word," Josephus said. "On all of it."

George studied him a moment longer—not searching, only confirming—then nodded. "That will do."

Christian exhaled quietly, a sound so slight it might have gone unnoticed by anyone else.

George turned to him. "You raised him to listen. That counts for something."

Christian accepted the words without false modesty. "He has chosen his own way. We only gave him the tools."

George mounted again, settling himself in the saddle. "Then we are agreed."

As he turned his horse back toward the road, Josephus spoke once more. "Thank you, sir."

George paused just long enough to look back at him. "Do right by her."

"Aye, sir. I intend to," Josephus said.

George nodded and rode on.

Christian turned back toward the yard. Josephus had already stepped away, leaving the yard to its evening.

Permission had been given. And this time, it fit.

Beyond the far fence line, where the ground dipped toward the trees, Jacob stood half-hidden in the long grass, a bridle hanging loose in one hand. He'd not heard every word—only enough. His brother's name. George's voice. The shape of an ending he hadn't been invited into.

When the Marlowe yard settled again, Jacob slipped away without sound, the resentment he carried deepened not by what was said, but by what was no longer possible.

CHAPTER II

Saturday, May 25, 1997

I

Christian Marlowe—Journal
Undated, written mid-October 1857

Fairlight is in operation now, and it shows itself rightly ordered. The wheel turns as it should. Men come, are served, and go again without grievance. This is no small thing.

Josephus has taken to the work as though it were his own. He does not command. He attends. Elias Koontz keeps the day's order well, and I am satisfied with the arrangement. Authority that does not need to raise its voice is authority properly held.

Jacob has been there more often than invited.

I will not set down more than this: Fairlight is not the place for a man who mistakes possession for stewardship. I must consider how best to correct him without hardening him further. Silence is sometimes mistaken for permission. I will not allow that error to stand.

George Mehring came to Fairlight with his daughter. Then Josephus came to see me. I knew before he spoke what would follow. He asked properly. I agreed to ride with him, as the request was not made lightly.

George granted permission this evening.

I have taught my sons that restraint is not weakness, but strength. One of them has learned it. The other resists it still.

I pray the difference does not become a division I cannot mend.

II

Mary Marlowe—Journal
Undated, written the same week

The house is quieter than it has been in years, and not for lack of people. Fairlight has taken Josephus from us most days, and I think that is as it should be. A man must be where his work can find him.

I went out there this week. The mill is handsome in its way. Not pretty, but sure of itself. I like the springhouse best. Water remembers what hands forget.

George Mehring brought Hannah with him. She has come into her own. I saw it at once. There is a gentleness in her that is not uncertainty, and a steadiness that does not ask permission to exist.

Josephus was careful with her. Care is a form of love long before love names itself.

Jacob was there one evening. He did not stay long.

I worry for him more than I say aloud. Anger is easier to bear than grievance, and he has taken too easily to the latter. Christian believes time will correct what force cannot. I hope he is right.

Tonight, George rode out and returned satisfied. That is not a thing he does without reason.

I will set an extra place at the table when Josephus brings her here for the first time.

III

Josephus Marlowe—Journal
Undated, written after George's visit

The mill runs clean.

Elias keeps the men steady. John Dorsey works as though the work were reason enough. I have learned more by listening than I ever did by deciding alone.

Hannah has come with her father several times now. We spoke while business was being done. I expected no more than that, and yet more came of it. I was careful. She noticed.

I asked Father if he would ride with me to Myrtle Hill. He agreed without surprise. I took that as enough.

George heard us and sent us away without answer, as was his right. When he returned with his answer, it felt less like a door opening than a path already cleared.

I will not hurry this. What is sound does not need pressing.

Fairlight is holding. I intend to do the same.

IV

The fire had sunk to a bed of coals, the flames no longer leaping, just holding.

Ryan gathered some larger branches, the glowing embers eagerly awaiting new wood. He gathered some larger branches from nearby and stacked them upright in the fire.

Todd glanced at his watch and raised his eyebrows. "It's a little past one."

Carrie smiled, tired but unmistakably pleased. "So she said yes. Josephus did it properly and with permission." She pushed herself upright, smiling. "The good guy gets the girl. As it should be. I totally needed that!"

Ryan nudged her shoulder, grinning broadly. "You earned it, Scout."

Ernest closed the journal and slid it back into his backpack. He didn't speak right away, only watched the embers settle. "Josephus understood something early. That wanting isn't the same as taking."

Deborah nodded. "And Hannah?"

"She knew the difference," Ernest replied.

Carrie leaned back on her hands, looking up at the stars through the thinning smoke. "And now it all works out like it's supposed to."

A faint smile crossed his face. "For a time."

No one rushed to fill the silence.

The fire breathed on, steady and contained.

CHAPTER III

Sunday, October 18, 1857

I

The lantern was already lit when Josephus Marlowe came up the steps, its glow catching on the porch rail and the edge of the doorframe.

He paused long enough to wipe his hands on his trousers, more from habit than need, before knocking once.

George Mehring answered and stepped aside. "You have the hour."

"Aye, sir."

Hannah wore a pale blue muslin that afternoon. The bodice fitted neatly at the waist, and the sleeves fell in modest folds to her wrists. The skirt spread in a careful bell shape over its frame, neither ostentatious nor plain. A narrow ribbon marked her collar, precise and unobtrusive.

Josephus removed his hat before he reached the steps; the motion settled long before the moment required it. His coat was clean and properly kept, his collar set without fuss, his boots polished but unremarkable. When he offered his hand, it was steady and calloused—a man who worked, but not carelessly.

He moved without haste, bowing his head slightly before taking his seat.

Hannah was seated where she had been directed, hands folded in her lap, posture correct but not stiff. She rose when Josephus entered, then sat again as he did. The space between their chairs was measured and intentional.

For a moment, neither spoke.

The night carried itself well. Cool without being cold; the air holding the faint sweetness of fallen leaves and distant water. From somewhere beyond the house, Big Pipe Creek kept its steady counsel.

"I'm glad you came," Hannah said at last.

"So am I," Josephus replied. He didn't embellish it.

The quiet settled easily between them.

Josephus spoke first of the mill. Not of its success, but of its steadiness. How the wheel had taken to its work. How the stones had dressed cleanly. How his foreman, Elias Koontz, had remarked that the creek seemed content with its course.

Hannah listened, her attention unforced. "I like that you speak of it as though it were alive."

"I suppose it is," he answered. "Or as close as a thing made by hands can be."

She smiled at that, a small, genuine thing. "Myrtle Hill sounds that way to me. When I'm home long enough, I stop hearing the wheel—until I miss it."

Josephus nodded. "I know that feeling."

The hour moved without being pushed. They spoke of work, of books she'd read, of how New Windsor had changed her, and how home had not. When silence came, it didn't hurry them to fill it.

At one point, Hannah glanced toward the door, then back at him. "My father says time kept is a kindness."

A faint smile touched Josephus's face, a mere hint of amusement. "Aye. He's right."

When George cleared his throat inside the house, the sound was neither sharp nor abrupt; only a marker, gently placed.

Josephus stood at once. Hannah followed, regret flickering across her face before she could hide it.

"Thank you, Mr. Marlowe," she said.

"For the hour," he replied. "It was well spent, Miss Mehring."

She inclined her head, and he did the same.

Josephus stepped off the porch and into the night.

Nothing had changed. And yet, something had settled into place that hadn't been there before.

Atlas dipped his head as he approached, the leather creaking softly as Josephus took the reins. He paused a moment longer than he needed to, then turned toward the road.

The lantern burned on, steady and contained, as it was meant to.

II

George waited until the sound of Atlas's hoofs had faded from the yard before speaking. "Well?"

Hannah remained standing, her hand still resting on the chair back. "He kept the hour."

George nodded. "That was expected."

"He listened," she added. "And when he spoke, it was to answer something I'd already said. Not to turn it aside."

"That matters," George said.

She smiled then—quickly, as though she hadn't meant to—and caught herself at once. "Yes."

George watched her with the quiet satisfaction of a man proven right. "You were at ease."

"I was," Hannah said without hesitation.

George folded his hands behind his back. "That is what courtship is meant to reveal. Not persuasion. Not pressure."

"I know," she replied. "And I'm grateful."

He nodded once, the matter settled. "We shall keep to the schedule."

"Yes, Papa."

Hannah moved toward the stairs, then paused. "Thank you," she said. Not for permission, but for care.

George lowered his head. "Get some rest."

When she was gone, he stood a moment longer in the quiet, listening to the night take its place around the house. For the first time in many weeks, there was nothing to weigh.

That, he thought, was its own answer.

III

Josephus stopped at the Marlowe farm on his way back to Fairlight, the light already thinning enough that the windows glowed warm against the dusk.

Mary was in the kitchen when he came in, her sleeves rolled up, the table not yet cleared.

"You're late," she said, and smiled. "Did it go well?"

"Aye, ma'am. It did."

"That's good." She looked him over once, then toward the hearth. "Have you eaten?"

"No."

"Sit," she said, already moving. "I shall make you a plate."

He hesitated. "I shouldn't linger. Elias will—"

"Elias will manage," Mary said gently. "You will eat."

Josephus sat.

She set a plate before him—simple food, still warm—and he began at once, mindful of the time but grateful all the same. Christian was coming in from the yard when Jacob entered from the other room, his boots loud against the floor.

He stopped short when he saw Josephus at the table. "Well? How was she?"

Josephus didn't answer. He kept chewing, his eyes on his plate.

Christian didn't look at him. "That is *not* a proper question, Jacob."

Jacob scoffed. "I only meant—"

"You meant to pry," Christian said evenly. "And it's none of your business unless your brother chooses to make it so."

Jacob turned to Josephus. "Well?"

Josephus met his gaze at last. He swallowed, nodded once, and said nothing.

Christian folded his arms. "There is another matter, Jacob."

Jacob's lips pressed into a thin line, his jaw clenching with tension.

"Fairlight is your brother's house," Christian continued. "If you visit there, it will be after the day's work is done, or on a Sunday after services. You will conduct yourself as you would here. You will show respect to every person under that roof, or you will not go at all."

Jacob looked again at Josephus.

Josephus said nothing.

"Fine," Jacob snapped. "I see how it is." He turned toward the door, muttering as he went. "Jos does no wrong. The favorite son. It's always been that way."

The door closed hard.

Josephus exhaled and shook his head.

Mary set a hand briefly on his shoulder. "Don't fret over it," she whispered. "You're doing right."

He nodded, though the ease of it had gone.

Christian watched the door a moment, then turned back to the room, the evening settling around them again.

For now.

IV

Sunday, October 25, 1857
A week later

The lantern was lit again, though earlier this time, the dusk coming on more quickly now that October had found its footing.

The porch smelled faintly of oil and cooling wood. Hannah took her seat where she had the week before, the chair angled just enough that she could see the yard and the road beyond it.

Josephus arrived a few minutes after the hour, breathless only from haste, not nerves. Atlas bowed his head as Josephus guided him toward the adjacent rail, reining him there. "I hope I'm not late."

"You're not," Hannah replied. "I was watching the light change."

He followed her gaze for a moment. "It does that faster now."

"Yes," she said. "As though it's decided not to linger."

They smiled at that, both of them, and the quiet eased.

They spoke first of small things. The way the apples had come in early this year. How the creek sounded different once leaves collected along its edges. Josephus mentioned Elias's wife, Emma, had begun drying herbs near the tenant house, and Hannah said she had always liked the smell of sage, though she couldn't say why.

At one point, a gust of wind rattled the porch rail and startled her just enough that she laughed softly.

Josephus looked at her then, smiling. "I thought it was only the lantern."

"So did I," she said, still smiling. "It seems I was wrong."

"Wrong is allowed," he replied. "So long as nothing breaks."

That made her laugh again, a little more freely this time.

The sound settled something in him. He leaned back, careful not to crowd the space between them, and let the hour pass.

She asked him about Fairlight. Not the mill this time, but the house. Whether it felt like his yet.

"Not fully," he admitted. "But it's beginning to. I think places come to it in their own time."

"I suppose people do as well," she said.

He considered that. "I think that's true."

When the sound from inside came, the faint, familiar clearing of George's throat, they both knew the hour had reached its end.

"That went quickly," Hannah said, not meaning to say it aloud.

Josephus stood. "It did." He hesitated, then added, "I'm glad you laughed."

She met his eyes. "So am I."

They inclined their heads—no lingering, no hurry—and parted as they were meant to.

From the doorway, George's gaze lingered on them, a moment too long to be casual. Nothing was said. It didn't need to be.

The lantern burned on, steady and warm, as the night gathered itself around the house.

V

Sunday, November 15, 1857
Twenty-one days later

The weeks turned without announcement.

The trees, now bare, had shed their leaves, which collected in drifts along fence lines and in the slow-moving, eddying bends of the creek. Josephus came when the schedule allowed and didn't when it did not. Hannah came to know the pattern without remark.

Some visits passed with little to mark them besides familiarity: the lanterns lit earlier, the chairs drawn closer against the cold, and conversation warming as the air cooled. They spoke of ordinary things and let them be enough.

George observed and did not intrude.

Fairlight held.

Myrtle Hill kept its sound.

By November, the ease between them no longer needed proving.

The porch hour began with the light still holding, the sky a pale, disciplined blue. When George stepped inside to attend to a matter of his own, Hannah hesitated only a moment before speaking.

"If you like," she said, "we could walk."

Josephus nodded. "If that pleases you."

They kept to the path that led toward the springhouse, their steps measured, the space between them unchanged. The ground was firm with cold now; the leaves crisp beneath their feet.

The springhouse stood as it always did; stone cool to the touch, water clear and steady beneath its roof. Hannah paused there, resting her hand against the wall as though greeting something familiar. "I like places that remember what they're for."

Josephus smiled faintly. "So do I."

They paused there, listening.

"My father believes," Hannah said carefully, "that order is something you tend, not something you enforce."

Josephus considered that. "I believe that, too. Order that has to be defended too loudly is usually already failing."

She glanced at him, a question in her eyes. "That hasn't always been your experience?"

"No," he said. "But it has been my instruction."

She looked back toward the water. "I was afraid, once, that I would be asked to become smaller in order to be agreeable."

Josephus didn't answer at once. When he did, his voice was steady. "I wouldn't know how to live that way."

She turned to him fully then. "I hoped you'd say that."

They didn't linger long. When George returned, they were

already making their way back; conversation settled into its quiet course again.

The hour ended as it always did: without hurry, without regret. As Josephus stepped away into the cooling dusk to prepare Atlas to ride, Hannah remained a moment longer, watching the springhouse, listening to the sound of the water.

Something solid had taken shape there, though neither spoke of it.

VI

Josephus stopped at the Marlowe farm before riding on, dusk settling into the rooms they kept warm this time of year.

Mary had drawn the chairs closer to the hearth, and Christian sat with a book open on his knee, though he wasn't reading.

Josephus retrieved a book he'd left behind after moving to Fairlight, turning it once in his hands. "I thought to give this to Hannah," he said. "If you think it suitable."

Mary smiled. "That would be very suitable."

Jacob, who had been leaning against the mantle, glanced over. "A book?" he asked lightly. "If you want something with spirit, you should give her *The Count of Monte Cristo*."

Josephus looked at him without expression. "I didn't know you cared for it, brother."

Jacob shrugged. "A man wronged by the world sets it right. There's order in that."

Josephus considered him for a moment. "Dumas had an interesting sense of order."

"What's that supposed to mean?" Jacob asked, his frown deepening with each word.

"He was of mixed descent," Josephus said. "His father, certainly."

Christian shifted slightly but said nothing.

Jacob scoffed. "That's nonsense!"

"It's not," Josephus replied. "You can look it up."

The room cooled while Jacob's mouth slowly twisted. "Figures. A man like that writing about revenge."

Mary set her knitting down. "Jacob," she said, not sharply. "That's enough."

He looked at her, startled more than offended. "I was only saying—"

"You were prying into what doesn't concern you," she said. "And speaking where no invitation was given."

Jacob stared at Josephus.

With a quiet snort of breath, Jacob pushed himself away from the glowing embers of the hearth. "Give her whatever you like," he muttered. "It won't matter in the end."

He left the room, climbed the stairs with more vigor than necessary, and slammed his bedroom door shut.

Mary picked up her knitting again, nodding toward the book in Josephus's hands. "*The Pilgrim's Progress*," she said. "She'll understand why you chose it."

Josephus nodded. "Aye. Thank you, Mother."

Christian closed his book. "Ride safely, son."

Josephus did, carrying the book with him and leaving behind something he no longer meant to carry.

VII

Sunday, November 23, 1857
A week later

The lantern was lit before Josephus arrived, its light drawn close against the cold.

Snow lay along the edges of the yard and gathered at the base of the porch steps, packed hard where it had been walked over and softened where it had not. Hannah waited with her shawl drawn tight, her breath faintly visible when she spoke.

"You made good time," she said.

"The road was clear," Josephus replied. "Cold keeps things honest."

She smiled at that.

They sat as they usually did, chairs set with care, the space between them unchanged. The winter had pressed the world inward, and the hour felt smaller for it. Not constrained, only contained. From inside the house came the muffled sound of movement, quiet and regular. George was nearby, not listening, but present.

Josephus spoke of Fairlight first because it was easiest. How the wheel had slowed with the ice, how Elias had set the hands to clearing the race each morning before anything else was done. How the tenant house held its heat better now that the seams had settled.

"It sounds like Fairlight is learning the season," Hannah said.

"Aye. We are."

She nodded, tucking her hands deeper into her sleeves. "Myrtle Hill does that, too. Winter shows you what you've neglected."

They fell quiet for a time, listening to the wind move along the eaves. The cold didn't hurry them. It had no interest in spectacle.

"I was afraid once, when I was younger," Hannah said softly, "that winter would make everything harder."

Josephus considered that. "It makes some things clearer."

She glanced at him. "You don't mind it?"

"No," he said. "It tells the truth."

That seemed to satisfy her. She leaned back, her posture easing in a way it hadn't months earlier, as though the chair itself had become familiar.

Josephus reached into the pocket of his coat and drew out a small, plainly bound book, its corners softened by handling.

"I brought you something," he said, holding it out to her. "If you would like it."

She took it, surprised by its weight more than its presence. "You didn't have to."

"I wanted to," he replied. "It's one I return to when I need reminding."

She turned it once in her hands, reading the title. "*The Pilgrim's Progress.* I've heard of it, but I've never read it."

Josephus nodded. "It's not a story about arriving," he said. "It's about continuing. A man spends most of it walking, not knowing whether the ground beneath him will hold. He's given help when he asks for it, and trouble when he assumes too much."

Hannah glanced up at him. "Does he ever stop?"

"No," Josephus said. "But he learns how to tell the difference between a burden meant to be carried and one meant to be set down."

She considered that, then smiled. Not brightly, but with recognition. "That seems…useful."

"It has been."

When the sound came from inside—the faint clearing of George's throat—it was earlier than usual. The cold shortened the hour without apology.

Josephus rose at once. "Thank you, Miss Mehring," he said, his nod acknowledging the cold. "For braving it."

Hannah stood as well and smiled, meeting his eyes, the book held close against her side. "You may call me Hannah, if you like."

Josephus smiled. "Thank you…Hannah."

"I don't mind the cold. Not when I know when it will end."

He bowed his head, understanding the gift of the words without pressing them.

As he stepped down from the porch, his breath clouded the air between them and vanished. Hannah remained a moment longer, the book still warm in her hands, watching the lantern's steady glow hold against the dark.

Winter had not changed him.

That, she thought, was its own assurance.

VIII

Sunday, March 28, 1858
Four months later

The cold began to loosen its grip without asking permission.

Snow retreated from the fence lines and gathered only where shadow held it fast.

At Fairlight, the race ran freer; the wheel finding its full voice again after months of restraint. Elias spoke of planting before the frost was fully gone, and Josephus found himself thinking ahead more often than back.

At Myrtle Hill, Hannah marked the days by light rather than calendar. The evenings lengthened. The porch no longer required a shawl drawn tight. When her eighteenth birthday passed, it did so quietly, without announcement. It was another threshold crossed and kept.

By the time Josephus rode out again, the season had already decided it would wait no longer.

The porch no longer held the cold the way it once had. The lantern was still lit, but more out of habit than necessity; its glow soft against the lengthening evening. Beyond the yard, the first honest signs of spring were visible: damp earth and the hint of green where winter had finally loosened its grip.

Hannah came out without her shawl.

Josephus noticed, but didn't remark on it.

They sat as they usually did; the chairs placed with care, the space between them familiar now rather than measured. The hour opened quietly, as though it already knew its purpose.

They spoke then of ordinary things: Fairlight's race running freer, Elias planning for grain planting, the way the creek had changed its voice again. Hannah mentioned that Myrtle Hill's wheel had needed tending twice that week. Josephus listened as though it mattered, because it did.

When the conversation paused, it didn't settle into silence at once.

"Hannah," Josephus said. He used her name carefully, as though it were something newly entrusted. She looked at him, attentive, unguarded. "I would not ask your father a question I'd not already asked you. And I would not continue as we are if you didn't wish it to tend somewhere."

She didn't answer immediately. She took a moment.

"I have been content," she said at last. "Not because it was easy, but because it was right." His posture eased slightly, though he didn't move closer. "I don't need promises, Josephus. Only honesty."

"You have that."

She smiled then, openly now, the restraint that had shaped her no longer a barrier, only a habit. "Yes. I believe I do."

They sat with that for a moment; the decision settling into place without ceremony. From inside the house came the quiet sounds of evening—a chair shifted, a door eased shut—but no signal yet that the hour had ended.

Josephus rose first when it came. "Thank you. For your candor."

Hannah stood as well. "Thank you. For waiting."

They inclined their heads, not as strangers now, but not yet as something named. As Josephus stepped off the porch, he carried with him no urgency, only certainty.

Inside, Hannah remained by the door a moment longer, her hand resting against the frame, the world newly arranged, though nothing appeared changed.

The next step would be taken properly.

And soon.

IX

Josephus stopped at the Marlowe farm on his way to Fairlight, well after dark, the house already drawn in against the night.

Mary was at the table with a lamp turned low. Christian looked up as Josephus entered the house, reading his face before he spoke.

"Father, I would ask your leave," Josephus said. "To ride with you to Myrtle Hill. Soon."

Christian did not ask why. "Tomorrow?"

"No," Josephus replied. "Next week. I want to do it properly."

Christian nodded once. "Your mother should come."

Mary's hand stilled on the table. She smiled, small and knowing. "I would like that."

Josephus bowed his head, gratitude evident but contained. "Thank you."

He didn't linger. The light was fading, work awaited, and he meant to return to it with a clear mind. When the door closed behind him, the house settled again into its quiet.

Christian rose a moment later and moved down the hall.

Jacob stood just inside his room at the top of the stairs, one hand resting against the doorframe, the other resting on the latch, as though he'd only just drawn it back. He'd not meant to be seen.

For a moment, they looked at each other.

Christian didn't speak. He didn't step closer. He didn't ask how much Jacob had heard.

Something in Jacob set, not outward, but inward. He eased the door shut with care; the latch settling without sound.

Christian stood where he was until the stairwell returned to stillness, then turned back toward the front of the house.

Something had closed. It would not open again.

X

Sunday, April 4, 1858
A week later

George Mehring received Josephus and his parents in Myrtle Hill's front room, the windows open just enough to admit the afternoon air.

The creek could be heard beyond the rise, steady as ever. Christian removed his hat at once. Josephus followed suit, standing straight but not stiff, his hands at ease at his sides.

George didn't invite them to sit. That, too, was a choice.

"You wished to speak with me," George said, his gaze moving from Christian to Josephus and resting there.

Josephus nodded. "Aye, sir."

Christian said nothing. This was not his question to ask.

"I have been in Hannah's company these past months," Josephus continued. "Always by your leave, and always under your roof or on the grounds of Fairlight. I would not have continued if I had not found her regard steady and her judgment sound."

George's expression didn't change, but he shifted his weight slightly. A slight movement, one that did not escape Christian's notice.

"I am asking permission," Josephus said, "to ask for your daughter's hand in marriage."

He spoke the words plainly. No flourish. No claim.

George studied him for a long moment. His eyes took in the set of Josephus's shoulders, the way he didn't fill the silence, the fact that he had come with his mother and father rather than alone.

At last, George nodded once. "I have seen how you conduct yourself," he said. "At Fairlight. Here. With my daughter."

That was not assent, nor was it a refusal.

"I will speak with Hannah," George continued. "As is proper."

Josephus dipped his head. "Aye. Of course, sir."

Christian replaced his hat, signaling the end of the visit without pressing for more. They took their leave with no urgency, the matter left where it belonged.

XI

George found Hannah in the kitchen, her sleeves rolled up, her hands busy with a task she'd already finished.

She looked up at once. "They came?"

"Ja," George replied. He set his hat on the table and leaned against the doorframe.

"Josephus asked my permission to ask for your hand in marriage."

She didn't feign surprise. Still, the color rose in her cheeks, and she turned slightly away, composing herself before answering. "And what do you think?"

George watched her carefully now—the restraint, the way she waited rather than rushing to fill the space. "I think he asked as he should have. I think he waited when waiting was required. And I think he listened when listening mattered more than speaking."

Hannah nodded, her hands stilled.

"And you?" he asked.

She met his eyes then, openly. "I would like him to."

That was all she said.

George let out a breath he hadn't realized he'd been holding. He reached for his hat. "I shall ride out this evening. They should not be kept waiting."

XII

The light was thinning by the time George Mehring rode up to the Marlowe farm.

Christian met him at the fence, already aware of the purpose without it needing to be stated.

Josephus came at once when called.

George did not dismount.

"I have spoken with my daughter," he said. "She is of age. She is of sound mind. And she is willing for you to ask for her hand in marriage."

Josephus didn't speak at once. His posture changed. Relief, gratitude, and resolve settling together.

"You have my permission," George continued. "You will conduct yourself as you have thus far. With patience. With respect. And with her regard held above your own convenience."

"Aye," Josephus said. "I shall, sir." He hesitated only a moment before continuing. "If I may, I would ask your leave for the manner of it as well."

George regarded him.

"There is a place at Fairlight," Josephus said, "the springhouse. It's quiet, and she's fond of it. If it meets with your approval, I would ask her there. Privately, but properly."

George considered this, his expression thoughtful rather than guarded.

"I shall bring her by in the morning," he said at last. "I will have business to attend to. You may take the time that is due."

Josephus inclined his head. "Thank you, sir."

George tipped his hat to Christian. He turned his horse and rode back the way he had come, leaving the yard lighter than he'd found it.

XIII

George's horse had barely cleared the rise before Christian turned back toward the house.

Josephus remained still near the fence, where George had left him, the weight of the permission settling more slowly than the words themselves.

Mary stepped out onto the porch, her hands folded loosely, her face already softened by what she could read without being told.

"It went as it should," Christian said.

Josephus nodded. "Aye. It did."

Christian motioned him inside. "You'll eat."

"I should return to Fairlight," Josephus replied. "There's still light."

"There will be supper again," Mary said gently. It wasn't a question.

Josephus hesitated, then bowed his head. "Briefly."

They didn't see Jacob at first. He stood just inside the doorway, half in shadow, one shoulder against the frame, as though he had only just arrived. Or had never left. His hat was still on. One hand rested on the back of a chair he'd not pulled out.

Christian noticed him when Jacob shifted his weight.

No one spoke.

Josephus didn't look his way. He'd learned by now which silences were meant to be kept.

George's words—*her hand in marriage*—still hung in the air.

Jacob held himself still, too still to be at ease. He watched his brother move through the room with a steadiness that didn't glance sideways for approval or fear correction.

Mary set a plate on the table. "Sit, Josephus."

Jacob's fingers curled once against the chair back as his brother took the chair. He didn't sit.

Christian met Jacob's eyes then, not sharply, not with warning, only with recognition.

Jacob held the look a moment longer than courtesy required. Then he turned away, climbed the stairs, the door easing shut behind him without sound.

Outside, the yard remained unchanged. The fence stood. The fields waited. Somewhere beyond them, Fairlight's wheel turned on.

Inside, the house settled again.

Some permissions were granted aloud.

Others were withdrawn without a word.

XIV

Monday, April 5, 1858
A day later

The morning was already warm enough that the mist had lifted from the creek before Hannah Mehring arrived at Fairlight.

George left her at the foot of the path without ceremony, tipping his hat and turning back toward the mill as though this were only another matter of business.

The springhouse sat just off the rise, stone cool and pale against the greening grass. Water ran beneath it in a steady, quiet channel, the sound neither hurried nor still; only present.

Josephus was waiting.

He stood with his hat in his hands, not pacing, not rehearsing. He'd come early enough to be finished with waiting by the time Hannah arrived.

"Hannah," he said.

She smiled at the sound of her name and stepped inside, the stone drawing the warmth from the air as it always had. Sunlight filtered through the narrow window, catching on the water as it passed.

"For a place built to hold cold," she said, "it always feels kind."

"It tells the truth," Josephus replied. "And then let's you decide what to do with it."

She turned to him then, attentive and calm. He didn't reach for her hand.

"I asked your father for permission," he said. "And he has given it."

Her breath caught, just slightly, and she nodded, as though she'd been expecting the words and was still unprepared to hear them spoken.

"I would not have done so," Josephus continued, "if I did not believe I already knew your answer. But belief is not the same as hearing it." He paused, letting the space remain unfilled. "I would like to spend my life with you. In work and in quiet. In seasons that go easily, and those that do not. I would like to build a household that does not ask you to become smaller in order to fit inside it."

Only then did he reach for her hand; not taking it, just offering his own.

"If you are willing," he said, "I would ask you to marry me."

Hannah didn't answer at once.

She looked at him, truly looked, as though confirming something she'd known for some time but had never allowed herself to say aloud. The water ran on beneath them. Somewhere beyond the trees, the mill wheel turned.

"Yes," she said.

The word was quiet, but it changed everything.

She placed her hand in his, her fingers warm against his palm. He didn't lift it. He didn't kneel. He simply held it, as though that were the most natural thing in the world.

"I am willing," she added. "I have been."

Josephus let out a breath, the tension easing. His thumb brushed once against the back of her hand. Not a caress. Not yet.

"It's you," he whispered. "It's me. It's us."

They stood that way for longer than a moment, looking at each other, unguarded.

When they stepped back into the light, the world looked no different than it had an hour before.

Fairlight stood. The creek ran. The wheel turned.

But the place had been claimed. Not by deed or labor, but by promise.

And that, Hannah thought, was how the truest things were done.

CHAPTER IV

Saturday, May 25, 1997

I

Josephus Marlowe—Journal
Undated, the day Josephus proposed to Hannah

I asked her today.

I have built houses and set stone and stood beside men when fire or water tested them, and none of it prepared me for how quietly the world can change.

She did not answer quickly. I am grateful for that. When she did, it felt as though something already true had simply been named.

I do not yet know what kind of husband I will be. I know only that I intend to be worthy of her regard.

Fairlight ran today as it always does. The wheel turned. The water held.

It seems right that something so steady should witness this beginning.

II

The fire had burned down again, the embers low and breathing.

Todd checked his watch and said nothing. The night's quiet deepened as another hour passed, bringing the time to 2:30 a.m.

Ernest closed Josephus's journal carefully and returned it to the backpack, smoothing the cloth over it as though the book might feel the gesture. He scanned the quiet circle, assessing the stillness as one might gauge an approaching storm.

Carrie didn't wait. She raised her arms in the air. "Jos totally got the girl!" She turned to Todd and peered at him, pursing her face in faux anger. "You knew, didn't you? You should have spoiled it for me instead of making me wait! I was *so worried* this was going to be some epic Victorian tragedy!" She straightened her posture and stood with her hand on her heart. "For never was a story of more woe than this of Hannah and her Josephus." With a victorious smile, she turned to face Ryan. "Not!"

Ryan smiled despite himself. "Scout—"

"No!" she said, pointing at him. "Don't even, MacGyver! Let me have this!"

Deborah laughed softly and tugged her back down onto the blanket. "It doesn't mean the story's finished."

"I know," Carrie said, leaning back into Ryan's arms. "As George Mehring liked to say, 'It matters.' Josephus and Hannah. Fairlight. The whole story."

Ernest nodded. "That's exactly it."

He reached back into the pack and withdrew another journal.

III

Christian Marlowe—Journal
April 4, 1858

I rode with my son to Myrtle Hill today and watched him ask a question I once feared he would never need to ask.

George Mehring is a careful man. I respect that. He weighs character before outcome and listens for steadiness rather than charm. He heard what mattered.

Josephus did not speak of desire. He spoke of life. Of order that does not require force. Of patience that is not idleness.

This is what I hoped for him. Not ease, but alignment.

Mary wept when we returned home. I did not stop her.

Some doors close without being forced. Others open because they are ready.

IV

Mary Marlowe—Journal
April 1858

I have been holding my breath longer than I realized.

Josephus came home changed today, though nothing in him was altered. That is how I know it is right.

He did not boast. He did not hurry to speak. He simply stood in the doorway as though the world had shifted and he was waiting for it to settle.

Hannah Mehring will be a good wife. Not because she is gentle, but because she is exacting in the right ways. She does not bend where bending would cost her something essential.

I am glad Josephus chose her. I am glad she chose him.

I shall allow myself this joy tonight. Tomorrow, there will be work again.

V

Ernest closed the last journal, slid it inside his backpack, and leaned back against the log.

"This," he said, gesturing vaguely at the dark and the ruins beyond, "is the world when it's in balance."

Carrie wiped at her eyes, unashamed. "I love them."

Ryan wrapped an arm around her. "I think that's the point, Scout."

Carrie watched the embers, her gaze fixed. "So how long does it last? Will Jacob find a way to ruin it all? He seems totally hell-bent on doing so."

Ernest took out another Marlboro and lit it; the flame briefly brightened against the night. “Long enough. Which is to say, not long at all.”

The fire crackled softly. Ernest brought the cigarette to his lips and drew in a long, slow drag, the tip glowing red. “Carrie, you quoted Shakespeare a minute ago.”

“Butchered it, actually,” Ryan whispered, pulling Carrie into a tight hug, his voice laced with playful teasing. “Billy Shakes is spinning in his grave.”

Carrie playfully slapped Ryan’s arm. “Bite me, MacGyver!”

“I’ll answer your question about Jacob with a different quote,” Ernest said. “‘Cowards die many times before their deaths.’”

Everyone sitting opposite Ernest replied at once, in a staggered cadence. “Julius Caesar!”

“Jinx!” Carrie called out, raising her hand. “You all owe me a Coke!”

Laughter broke out, light and easy, which faded into the quiet as Ernest cleared his throat. His voice cut through the air as he surveyed them by the renewed firelight, the flickering flames casting shadows. "This next part is about the world that believes it's complete." He exhaled smoke into the darkness. “It never is.”

CHAPTER V

Monday, April 5, 1858

I

Hannah Mehring returned to Myrtle Hill, riding beside her father with her hands folded in her lap, her posture unchanged.

The creek ran alongside the road for a time, steady and unconcerned. The afternoon light slanted low through the trees, touching the tops of the fields but leaving the hollows cool.

They didn't speak at once.

When the house came into view, George slowed the horse. Hannah stepped down carefully, smoothing her skirt before moving away from the carriage. It was the same dress she'd worn before—sensible, plain—but she took more care with it now, as though the act mattered differently than it had that morning.

Inside, the house held its usual order. A kettle simmered. The clock marked the hour. Nothing had been rearranged to meet her.

From the kitchen came the faint sound of a drawer closing and Maggie's steps passing, then pausing, as though she'd understood without being told.

George removed his hat and set it upon the hatrack by the door. He watched Hannah a moment, not searching her face, but only confirming what he already knew.

"There will be letters to write," she said.

"Ja," he replied. "Not many."

She nodded. That was enough.

She untied her bonnet ribbon and laid it on the sideboard, her movements deliberate, as though teaching her hands how to behave in this new arrangement of things. When she turned back toward her father, her expression remained composed, though the color in her cheeks had not yet faded.

"I told him as much," George said. "That I would not keep him waiting longer than was proper."

"I'm glad," she answered. After a pause, she added, "Thank you."

George dipped his head—not solemnly, not with ceremony—simply acknowledging that the thanks belonged where Hannah placed it. "That shall be all for today. You may finish what you were doing."

Hannah hesitated only a moment, then went toward the kitchen. She paused at the threshold, resting her hand against the frame, listening to the quiet settle back into its accustomed places.

The house remained precisely as it had always been.

Despite that, it all seemed to have changed.

II

Josephus rode to the Marlowe farm after the work at Fairlight was done. Daylight faded, the fields softening into dusk.

Atlas knew the way and didn't hurry. The road was familiar; he didn't need to watch it. His attention moved instead between what had been said and what hadn't.

The house stood, solid and unremarked upon, smoke lifting straight from the chimney. Mary was visible through the front window, moving at the table. Christian was not in sight, though Josephus didn't doubt he was close.

He dismounted without calling out and led Atlas to the rail. Before he'd secured the reins, the door opened.

Mary stepped out first, wiping her hands on her apron. She looked at him once, only once, and smiled. "You needn't rush off again. There's food enough."

"Aye, ma'am," Josephus replied. He meant to say more, but didn't.

Christian appeared behind her, hat still on, his coat unbuttoned as though he'd come from the yard. He stopped at the threshold and studied his son with the same careful attention he gave weather and stock; not searching for answers, only confirming what he already suspected. "It went as it should?"

Josephus nodded. "Aye."

Nothing more needed to be said.

Christian reached up and removed his hat, a slight gesture, but not an idle one. "Then come inside."

They ate simply—bread, stew, the kind of meal that filled a man without comment. Josephus ate steadily, aware of the quiet but not troubled by it. This was not a silence that pressed. It held.

"Where is Jacob this evening?" Josephus asked.

"He left earlier this afternoon without saying," Christian replied. "I suspect he rode to Westminster to attend another of Shaw's palavers."

Josephus frowned and let the subject rest. The tone in his father's voice needed no interpretation.

Mary poured him another cup of cider without asking. "You did right...waiting."

"Aye, ma'am."

Christian said nothing further until the meal was nearly done. Then, as Josephus set his spoon aside, he spoke. "You understand what follows?"

"Aye, sir."

"And you're prepared for it?"

Josephus met his father's eyes. "I am."

Christian inclined his head once, the way he did when a matter was settled. "Then that's enough for tonight."

Josephus rose and thanked Mary, then stepped back out into the yard. The air had cooled, the last of the light slipping behind the trees. He stood a moment longer than usual, listening to the sounds of the house settle: the scrape of a chair, the murmur of voices.

He sensed that all remained precisely as it was.

And yet, everything had changed.

He mounted Atlas and turned him toward Fairlight, the road ahead clear and known, carrying not urgency but purpose.

III

Tuesday, April 6, 1858
A day later

The news did not announce itself at Myrtle Hill so much as it settled in.

Frederick heard it first, not from Hannah, but from George, as they stood together in the mill yard before supper. George said it plainly, as he did most things, and Frederick listened without interruption. When his father finished, Frederick nodded once and went back to the work at hand, tightening a strap that didn't strictly need it.

"That's good," he said after a pause.

"Ja," George replied. "It is."

Maggie found out later, in the kitchen, where Hannah stood at the table, folding linen she'd already folded once. Maggie watched her sister for a moment before speaking.

"So," she said, careful not to sound like she was prying.

Hannah looked up with a hint of a smile. "So."

Maggie smiled, quick and unguarded. She crossed the room and hugged her once, brief, fierce, and gone again. "I always liked him," she said, as if that settled something.

By Sunday, the matter had reached the congregation at Meadow Branch.

It passed between women first, not in whispers, but in the quiet confirmations of glances and nods. Hannah felt it before she heard it: the slight shift in how she was regarded as she took her place, the way eyes lingered a fraction longer before moving on. No one addressed it aloud. That, too, was a courtesy.

After the service, George lingered near the gate as he habitually did, speaking with men who'd known him long enough not to circle their meaning. A few offered congratulations. Others offered none at all, but their expressions softened when they spoke of Fairlight, of Josephus, of how the mill had changed the shape of things along the creek.

By midweek, the news had reached the post office in Bruceville.

George made no mention of it. He had learned long ago that news traveled best when left to its own devices. Still, as he sorted letters and handed them across the counter, more than one hand lingered. More than one smile held just a moment longer than business required.

"Your daughter," someone said, as though it weren't already known.

"Ja," George replied. "She is well."

That was sufficient.

By the time Hannah walked down to the springhouse again, the world had not changed its course. The creek ran as it always had, the wheel turned, and the day moved forward, but something had been set in place.

Not announced. Not celebrated. Acknowledged.

IV

Sunday, April 18, 1858
Twelve days later

By mid-April, Josephus noticed the difference not in his thoughts, but in his hands.

Work still filled the day. Grain to be weighed, stones to be watched, boards to be reset where the water had worried them loose, but the work no longer ended when the task was finished. He found himself standing longer than he usually did, looking not at what needed doing, but what would need doing *again*.

Fairlight no longer felt provisional.

The mill had settled into its rhythm; the wheel turning with a confidence that didn't ask to be admired. Elias moved through the yard as he always did, unhurried, keeping the work aligned without announcing himself. The hands came and went. Grain arrived, was ground, and left again. Nothing in that had changed.

What had changed was Josephus's attention.

He noticed the way the tenant house held the evening chill longer than it should and made a note to seal the sill before the next frost. He paused at the springhouse longer than he used to, aware now how the stone kept the milk cool, how the shelf might be better set higher, out of the damp. When he crossed the yard at dusk, he imagined a light left burning; not because it was needed for work, but because someone might be expected to come looking for it.

He hadn't yet said her name aloud in those moments.

Instead, he measured.

Elias remarked on it once, not directly. "You're thinking past tomorrow," he said, as they stood watching the wheel run clean.

Josephus nodded. "I should have been sooner."

Elias shook his head. "No. Just sooner than before."

That evening, Josephus ate alone at the tenant house, a simple meal taken standing at the table, boots still on. The room felt unfinished in a way it hadn't before. Not lacking walls or furniture, but intention. He looked at the bench by the door and realized it wouldn't do as it was. Not if someone else were to sit there. Not if it were to be used for anything but rest between hours.

He carried his plate to the door afterward and stepped out into the yard.

The light was dimming, a spring evening that stretched longer than it should. The mill wheel turned on, steady and unremarked. Beyond it, the house stood clean and bare, waiting not for occupation, but for use.

Josephus understood then that Fairlight was no longer a place he was merely *building*. It was a place that would have to be *kept*...but not alone.

The thought didn't hurry him. It didn't unsettle him. It steadied him.

He turned back toward the tenant house, already planning which boards to set first in the morning, and which matters could wait. There was time enough for both work and care now. Not because the labor had lessened, but because its purpose had sharpened.

Fairlight was still his responsibility.

But it was no longer *only* his.

V

Thursday, April 22, 1858
Four days later

Hannah didn't go to the Fairlight springhouse because she wished to be alone.

She went because there were things that needed seeing.

The day was mild enough that she didn't bring a shawl, though she carried one over her arm out of habit. The path down the rise, with its occasional stone steps, was familiar now; the grass pressed thin where she had walked. The creek spoke ahead of her, steady and unchanged, and she felt the comfort of that before she reached the stone door.

Inside, the air cooled at once.

She stood a moment without moving, letting the quiet reassert itself—the drip of water, its faint echo against stone. The shelves were as Josephus had left them: clean, practical, set for use rather than display. Milk crocks rested where they always had. Butter lay wrapped and waiting.

It occurred to her then that *waiting* had begun to feel different.

Hannah set the shawl aside and reached into the basket she'd brought with her. Inside were minor things: folded cloth she'd cut herself, a length of muslin she thought might serve better than the linen currently used, a narrow ribbon she had no use for yet, but didn't wish to misplace. She laid them out carefully on the stone ledge, not arranging them so much as acquainting herself with where they might belong.

She ran her fingers along the edge of the shelf and frowned slightly. It would be better raised. Not much—an inch or two, but enough to keep damp from creeping in during the heavier months. She made a note of it in her mind, knowing she wouldn't need to explain it when she mentioned it to Josephus later.

The thought didn't feel presumptuous. It felt responsible.

Hannah moved slowly through the space, seeing not what it was, but what it *held*, what it protected. The springhouse had always been a place of keeping—coolness, sustenance, continuity. She understood now why she'd been drawn to it before she had words for the reason. Some things endured because someone tended them.

She sat on the low stone step and let the water speak while she listened. Not for answers. She'd never believed the world worked that way, but for steadiness. For assurance, not everything required deciding at once.

When she rose, she gathered the cloth again, returning it to the basket. Everything was precisely as it was, no alterations made. Yet, a measurement had been taken.

Hannah paused at the threshold before leaving, her hand resting briefly against the stone. The future didn't rush her. It didn't demand names.

It waited.

And she knew now that when it came, she would meet it prepared—not with grand plans, but with small, careful acts that made room for what was meant to last.

She closed the door behind her and took the path back up toward the house, already deciding what she might bring next time.

VI

Tuesday, April 27, 1858
Five days later

Josephus noticed the difference before he could have said what it was.

The springhouse door was shut when he passed it that morning; not latched, only set to, and for a moment, he thought nothing of it. He'd learned which things at Fairlight required attention and which did not, and the springhouse had always been content to mind itself.

Still, he paused when he came back through the yard later.

Inside, the air held its usual coolness, but the space felt altered. Not disturbed, only *considered.* The crocks had been shifted slightly, raised just enough that damp no longer kissed their bases. A length of cloth lay folded on the stone ledge, clean and unused, its purpose not yet set. Nothing had been added that didn't belong. Nothing removed that did.

Josephus lingered a moment longer than the errand required.

He didn't smile. He didn't reach out.

He understood.

Josephus went on with his work after that, carrying the knowledge with him like a tool newly added to his belt. Not to be admired, but to be used carefully.

When Elias passed him later and remarked, without looking at him, "Someone's been thinking ahead."

Josephus only nodded. "Aye. I believe she has."

VII

It was late afternoon when Jacob arrived.

He rode in without warning, as he often did, Brimstone restless beneath him, the horse's ears flicking back, already irritated by the place. Jacob took in the yard with a practiced eye—the mill running clean, the hands moving without confusion—and felt, again, that tightening behind his ribs that came when order existed without him.

He dismounted and walked the yard as though invited.

At the springhouse, he stopped. The door was shut.

That alone would have been nothing, once. But Jacob opened it anyway, pushing into the cool air with the impatience of someone used to being answered. His gaze swept the interior quickly, searching not for use, but for claim.

He saw the cloth.

It took him a moment to understand.

This wasn't work. Not entirely. Not the kind of improvement meant to prove anything. The changes were slight, domestic in a way Fairlight hadn't been before. They weren't soft, but *intentional.* Someone had stood here and thought about what would last through seasons rather than days.

Jacob's expression hardened.

He shut the door harder than needed and pivoted back to face the yard. Josephus was there, speaking with one of the hands, his attention on the work, not the visitor. When he looked up and saw Jacob, he nodded once—polite, contained, and done.

"You're here," Josephus said.

"For now," Jacob replied.

His eyes went back to the springhouse door, then away again, as though it had no right to be closed to him.

Josephus followed the look and said nothing.

That was what unsettled Jacob most.

Fairlight no longer bore the marks of something being built. It bore the marks of something being kept. And whatever had changed here hadn't been done loudly, or with permission asked of him.

It had been done without him in mind at all.

Jacob mounted Brimstone again before dusk, riding out with the same restlessness he'd brought in. He didn't look back at the mill. He didn't look at the springhouse.

But the image followed him all the same; not as loss, exactly, but as exclusion.

Josephus watched him go and returned to his work.

Some changes announced themselves.

Others simply took hold.

Fairlight now chose what it would allow.

VIII

Tuesday, May 4, 1858
A week later

They didn't mean to make plans.

It happened while Elias was occupied with a wagon at the mill, and the yard had gone briefly quiet. Josephus walked the length of the race with Hannah beside him, neither of them in a hurry, both aware of the water's sound as it met the stone.

"The damp gathers there," Hannah said, nodding toward the corner where the race met the wall. She didn't point. She didn't explain.

Josephus followed her gaze. "In winter, aye. I've thought of setting the board higher."

She considered that. "It would help."

They walked on.

Near the tenant house, Hannah paused again—not stopping, only slowing. "The bench by the door. It's useful, but it catches the cold."

Josephus nodded. “It does.” After a moment, he added, “It could be turned. Set against the inner wall instead.”

“That would keep it drier.”

Neither of them wrote it down.

When they reached the springhouse, Josephus waited at the threshold while Hannah stepped inside. She didn’t invite him in; she didn’t need to. He remained where he was, listening as she moved about, the soft sound of cloth brushing stone.

“The shelf holds well,” she said from within. “Another would make sense. For winter.”

Josephus smiled, though she couldn’t see it. “I’ll set one.”

She came back out and stood beside him again, their shoulders not quite touching.

“I don’t wish to change things that work,” she said.

“I wouldn’t see it done,” he replied, not sharply, only certain.

That made her laugh; not aloud, just enough to catch and disappear.

They turned back toward the yard together, the wheel running steady behind them. No decision had been made that required naming. No future had been promised that hadn’t already begun.

The plans remained small.

Which was how Josephus knew they were sound.

IX

Sunday, May 9, 1858
Five days later

Josephus didn’t come by carriage that afternoon after the Mehrings’ services at Meadow Branch Meeting House.

Hannah heard Atlas before she saw him—the measured cadence of hooves along the road, unhurried, deliberate. She stepped to the front window and watched as Josephus reined the bay in beside the gate, dismounting with the same quiet care he gave everything.

George noticed her movement, but said nothing.

By the time Josephus reached the walk, George was already at the door. Introductions were no longer needed. Manners were.

Josephus removed his hat and waited for instructions he didn't need.

"Come in," George said. Not invitation. Permission.

They spoke first of Fairlight, of the creek after thaw, of how the mill had settled. Josephus answered plainly, never overstating, never shifting credit. Hannah listened, hands folded, aware of how naturally the conversation held itself.

When Mary's name came up in passing as part of Christian's household, George's gaze flickered briefly toward the kitchen before returning.

"You've ridden some distance," he said at last. "You'll stay for a bite."

The offer was made evenly.

Josephus hesitated just long enough to be proper. "I thank you, sir. But I ought not."

George studied him, weighing not the refusal but the man making it.

Another day, the offer might have been pressed. Today, it was allowed.

"As you wish," George said. "Another time."

Hannah rose when Josephus did and walked him to the door. The movement went unremarked, as though it had always been so.

Outside, near the fence, a chestnut mare stood tied in the shade—narrower through the shoulder than a plow horse, built for riding, not pulling. She lifted her head as Josephus stepped out, ears forward but untroubled.

Josephus glanced toward her. "Yours?"

Hannah nodded. "Lark."

"She's young."

"Two this spring."

"She suits you," he said.

Hannah didn't look at him when she answered. "She's steady."

Josephus mounted Atlas and settled the reins. "Thank you for the afternoon."

"For the afternoon," Hannah replied.

He smiled at that, small and genuine, and turned Atlas back toward the road. Hannah watched until horse and rider had passed beyond the rise, then remained a moment longer.

Inside, George had already returned to his seat.

Some thresholds were not meant to be crossed all at once.

X

Sunday, May 16, 1858
A week later

Jacob rode the length of Bruceville Road to Myrtle Hill without slowing.

Josephus heard him before he saw him. The gait was wrong for Atlas. It was too quick and uneven. Hannah, standing near the fence, turned at the sound.

Jacob reined Brimstone in hard enough that the horse tossed his head, and the iron rang once against the bit. "Elias sent me," he said before either of them spoke. "Said you were here with George Mehring. There's trouble at the forebay."

Josephus did not move. "What kind?"

Jacob's eyes flicked briefly toward the house, then back again. "It's holding uneven. Stones pulling heavier to one side. He thought you'd want to see it."

"I already have," Josephus said.

Jacob blinked. His gaze slid past Josephus to the doorway where Hannah stood. He shifted his grip on the reins. "Oh. I didn't know you were here today."

"I am," Hannah answered. The words were simple. They landed anyway.

Jacob nodded once, shifted his gaze back to Josephus, then again. "Father always said things should be done in order."

"They are," Josephus replied.

For a moment, Jacob stood as though waiting—for permission, perhaps, or correction. When it didn't come, he shifted his weight. "They let Dorsey run the stones," he said. The words came careful. "I thought you'd—"

He stopped.

Josephus waited.

"I thought you'd made it plain he'd keep to hauling," Jacob finished instead.

"He was capable," Josephus said. "The work needed doing."

Jacob's mouth thinned. "Capable," he repeated, the word edged but quiet.

The front door opened behind them.

George Mehring approached the doorway and stood beside Hannah, hands resting lightly at his sides. He'd heard enough to understand the shape of it, the intention. He didn't speak.

Jacob saw him plainly. Whatever had risen next in his throat—sharper, less guarded—stilled. After a moment, with breath tight, he said, "Well, that's all, then."

He turned Brimstone without another word and rode back down the lane.

Josephus listened until the sound of hooves thinned into the distance.

Hannah didn't move.

Neither did the house.

CHAPTER VI

Saturday, May 25, 1997

I

Josephus Marlowe—Journal
Undated, written after Jacob's visit to Myrtle Hill

There are moments when order is mistaken for silence.

Jacob came today under the guise of necessity. I recognized it at once: a reason that would excuse him if accepted, and injure him if not. I did not accept it.

He spoke of the mill as though it were still unsettled. He spoke of Father as though instruction and permission were the same. He talked of Dorsey as though fairness were a temporary arrangement.

Hannah said very little. She did not need to say more.

I have learned that some men mistake proximity for standing. When space no longer opens for them, they believe it has been closed *against* them. That is not always true. Sometimes the world has simply moved into proper alignment.

The creek runs steady. The work holds.

What troubles me is not the resentment but the ignorance beneath it all.

II

The fire had died down to a bed of glowing orange embers.

Ernest closed the journal and rested it on his knee. He didn't speak. The night filled the space easily. The crickets were loud enough that no one felt obliged to break the silence.

Carrie had leaned forward without realizing it. Her eyes fixed on the shadows beyond the fire, as though she were seeing something else entirely; her hands clasped so tightly that her knuckles turned white.

After a moment, she said, "That wasn't about the Fairlight mill."

Ryan glanced at her. "What was it about, then?"

Carrie shook her head once. "I don't know." She hesitated, then tried again. "He went there expecting things would still be there for him. Like everything hadn't changed." She swallowed. "And it totally wasn't."

Deborah shifted on the log. "People get shut out all the time."

"True," Carrie said. "But usually they know when it's happening." She pressed her thumb into her knuckle, as though trying to feel something. "He didn't. Not yet anyway."

Ernest continued to watch the fire.

Ryan asked, more carefully now, "So this is where it starts for him? Jacob realizing the world is moving on without him?"

Carrie considered the question. The woods beyond the clearing held their shape, unresponsive. "No, it's already started. It already happened." She offered Ryan a small, uncertain smile. "He's only just figuring it out." She let out a breath, glancing back at the embers of the fire, and reached for more kindling. "And that's worse."

The fire cracked once, sharp and brief as it flared up.

Ernest picked up the journal again, turning to the next marked page, and listened to the crickets and frogs settle before breaking the silence.

CHAPTER VII

Saturday, October 9, 1858

I

The carriage left Myrtle Hill just after sunrise.

Hannah Mehring sat facing forward, gloved hands folded in her lap, her cloak tucked clear of the wheel. The air had cooled enough that breath showed when the horse was first set moving, though the frost had not yet come. The road still held its summer shape—ruts shallow, dust packed—soon to be undone by rain and weight and winter traffic.

She watched the fields pass without comment.

October had settled the land into usefulness. Corn stood shocked and bound. Fence rails had been reset where cattle had tested them. Smoke lifted in thin columns from chimneys that had not been used in months. Nothing hurried. Nothing lingered.

At Fairlight, the wheel was already turning.

Hannah stepped down when the carriage halted, waiting for the driver to secure the horse before moving toward the mill. The sound met her first; water held to purpose, stone answering stone. She'd learned to listen for what varied within it. Today, the rhythm held even.

Josephus wasn't yet in sight. Elias Koontz stood near the forebay with two of the hands, sleeves rolled, heads inclined as he spoke. John Dorsey worked the stones, his movements economical, his posture steady. No voices were raised.

Emma Koontz looked up from the doorway of the tenant house and nodded once in greeting. Hannah returned it and went inside.

The morning's work waited where it had been left the day before. Accounts to be checked. Supplies noted for winter. Cloth folded and set aside. Hannah moved through the space without needing to ask where things belonged. This wasn't her house. It was not *not* hers, either. The distinction mattered.

When Josephus came in, he didn't interrupt her. After a moment, he said, "You're earlier than yesterday."

"The road was clear," she replied. "And the creek is holding."

He nodded. "It should."

They spoke of small things. A delivery due next week. The need for extra sacks before the weather turned. Emma joined them briefly, asked one question, received an answer, and returned to her work.

Later, Hannah stepped back outside and stood where the path narrowed toward the trees. The mill held behind her. The land opened ahead. She didn't choose between them.

The carriage waited for her again by mid-morning with her father at the reins.

This time, the road led toward Westminster.

Church notices had gone up the evening before. Hannah had seen them after supper: committee names, winter arrangements, reminders about provisions. Her father had read them carefully and said nothing, which meant they were not nothing.

At the edge of town, the pace changed. Horses were tied where they had no business lingering. Voices carried farther than they needed to. The season had turned people outward, toward rules and arrangements and decisions meant to last until spring.

Hannah remained seated while George spoke to a man she didn't know. She noted how long the conversation lasted. How often the word *order* appeared, and how rarely it was defined.

Their path to the Trumbull Farm led them past the Carroll County Almshouse.

It stood as it had since 1853—clean enough, quiet enough, windows set high. Hannah had seen it before, usually at the agricultural fairs hosted by the Sauble family and held on their property next door. Everyone knew it. It wasn't a place one entered without cause.

They kept riding without interruption. She didn't look back at it.

The carriage rolled on. The horse kept its pace.

Behind them, at Fairlight, Myrtle Hill, and even Trevanion, water continued to move, steady and unremarkable, as though nothing yet had demanded otherwise.

II

By mid-October, the government of Westminster could no longer keep the matter of the county Almshouse out of committee rooms.

It existed, as such places did, at the edge of attention—acknowledged, funded, and rarely entered by those who governed it. Its purpose was understood in principle and avoided in practice. One didn't speak of it unless necessary. One didn't look at it unless required.

That changed as the season turned.

The first reports were imprecise. Newspapers described the conditions as poor, though what that meant varied from editor to editor. Almshouse inmates were said to be inadequately clothed for the weather. Food was described as sufficient by measure, wanting in effect. Heating was irregular. Some rooms were warm enough. Others were not. The sick were attended to when the attendant was present. When he wasn't, they waited. Those suffering from mental infirmity were housed with the general population, not by design but by default; a distinction often noted and rarely acted upon.

None of this was new. What was new was that it had been said aloud.

Questions of money followed. The county Democrats in power appropriated funds for supplies that didn't appear to be in use. Ledgers were produced. Receipts were shown. Contracts were traced through familiar names, some of them long established, others recently favored. When pressed, responsibility diffused. Clerks deferred to overseers. Overseers cited precedent. No one denied that money had been spent. No one could say with certainty where its effects had gone.

Proximity was more concerning to many than the gnawing hunger or the chill in the air.

Women and children were housed nearer than custom allowed. Children often shared space with adults who weren't kin. The men's dormitory, sitting at a right angle to the main house, was said to be unlivable. Reports spoke cautiously of moral impropriety, a phrase that carried more weight than detail. No one described what had occurred. It was enough that something might have. In a society governed as much by implication as by statute, this was sufficient to provoke alarm.

The newspapers quickly seized upon the matter.

One framed the Almshouse as a symbol of long-standing misrule, the inevitable result of lax oversight and political favoritism. The poor, it argued, had been neglected not through accident but through indifference. The language was vivid. Children were invoked often. Reform was demanded broadly and defined narrowly.

The other dismissed these accounts as fabrication and theater. It accused its rival of exploiting the unfortunate for political gain and of stirring sentiment without regard for the consequences. Discipline, it insisted, was not cruelty. Order wasn't neglect. The poor, it argued, suffered more from instability than from regulation.

Each accused the other of lying. Each accused the other of recklessness. Neither lingered on the daily lives of those housed within the institution itself.

Meetings were called. Committees convened. Men spoke at length about precedent, economy, and deterrence. The Almshouse became a matter of public morality rather than private care. It was discussed in the same breath as elections and budgets, its inhabitants rendered abstract by the language used to defend or condemn them.

Amid this, a particular incident emerged, first as a rumor, then as an example.

A pauper family—father, mother, and children—had violated a technical rule of residence. Accounts differed as to the nature of the breach. Some said the father had left the grounds without leave. Others said he refused assigned labor. What remained consistent was the response. Relief was denied. The family was ejected. The decision was reached in accordance with the regulation, properly recorded, and enacted without delay.

The weather had turned by then.

Those who defended the action called it unfortunate but necessary. Rules, they argued, existed for a reason. Without enforcement, the institution couldn't function. Mercy, extended too freely, invited disorder.

Those who condemned it described the same facts differently. They spoke of punishment disguised as procedure. Of children turned out as a lesson to others, of rules applied without regard for circumstance.

The family itself was rarely mentioned again.

By the time the matter reached its loudest pitch, positions had already hardened. The Almshouse was no longer a place, but a symbol. What it symbolized depended upon who was speaking.

For some, it represented the dangers of indulgence and inefficiency. For others, the costs of indifference dressed as order. For most, it remained something to be argued over rather than entered.

Winter approached. The debates continued.

And beneath them, unchanged, the institution endured—its routines intact, its rooms filled, its purpose contested, but its doors still closed to those who belonged there only by necessity.

III

From the Carroll County Democrat
October 15, 1858

THE LATEST ALMSHOUSE CLAMOR: A FABRICATION OF NECESSITY

Joseph Shaw, Editor

It has become fashionable, in recent weeks, to decry the administration of the County Almshouse as though it were a scene of barbarity rather than a public institution governed by law, necessity, and long-standing precedent. The loudest voices in this outcry are, notably, those who have shown little prior concern for the poor except when political advantage may be extracted from their condition.

Let us speak plainly.

The Almshouse exists to provide relief to those unable to provide for themselves, not to reward indiscipline nor to serve as a refuge from consequence. Rules are not cruelty. Discipline is not neglect. An institution without enforcement is no institution at all, but an invitation to disorder and abuse.

Recent accounts in rival publications have relied upon implication rather than fact, employing suggestive language designed to inflame sentiment rather than improve conditions. Claims of neglect, impropriety, and corruption have been repeated with theatrical insistence, yet rarely substantiated beyond hearsay and conjecture. Where evidence has been demanded, it has been replaced with outrage.

Much has been made of a recent incident involving a pauper family removed from the institution for violation of established regulations. The facts of this matter are straightforward. Rules governing residence and conduct were knowingly breached. Proper authority was exercised. Relief was withdrawn accordingly. This was not punishment, but procedure.

Those who object appear to believe that mercy consists in abandoning all distinction between deserving and undeserving, obedient and insubordinate. Such thinking, however well-intentioned, would render the Almshouse ungovernable and ultimately useless to those who truly depend upon it.

As to allegations of financial impropriety, county accounts remain open to inspection, as they always have. Contracts have been awarded through lawful channels. Supplies have been procured as appropriated. That rival editors choose to hint darkly at corruption without naming it speaks more to their methods than to any proven mismanagement.

It is regrettable that the poor should be dragged into partisan conflict, their circumstances exaggerated to score points against those charged with maintaining order. The true harm lies not in firm administration, but in the reckless erosion of public trust through sensational accusation.

Let the Almshouse be improved where improvement is

warranted. Let oversight continue where oversight is proper. But let us not mistake discipline for cruelty, nor confuse agitation with reform.

IV

From The American Sentinel
October 20, 1858

ORDER WITHOUT MERCY IS NOT ORDER AT ALL

William H. Grammer, Editor

The defenders of the present Almshouse administration would have us believe that hunger is a necessary instructor, that cold is a moral corrective, and that children turned from shelter serve the greater good by their example. We reject this doctrine outright.

What is now dismissed as "clamor" consists of facts long ignored and finally spoken. The conditions of the County Almshouse have been poor for years. That they are now acknowledged only under pressure is no argument in their defense. Inadequate clothing, irregular heating, and insufficient medical attention are not inventions of the press. They are realities endured by those with no voice to protest them.

We are told that rules were enforced. This is not disputed. What is disputed is whether rules, once written, absolve those who apply them of judgment.

A pauper family was removed from the Almshouse for a technical breach. Relief was denied. Children were ejected alongside their parents as an example to others. All was done correctly, according to regulation. And yet something essential was lost in the correctness of it.

Those who govern public institutions do not escape moral responsibility by invoking procedure. Economy is not virtue when it starves the helpless. Discipline is not order when it punishes without regard for consequence.

Financial questions remain unanswered. Funds allocated for food, clothing, and maintenance have not produced their expected effect. Contracts circulate among familiar hands. Oversight diffuses when pressed. These matters warrant scrutiny, not dismissal.

We are accused of sensationalism. We answer that silence has been the greater cruelty.

The poor of Carroll County are not abstractions. They are men, women, and children placed under public care because no other care remains to them. To invoke their suffering only to deny it, to name "order" while refusing to enter the rooms it governs, is not administration. It is abdication.

If the present system cannot sustain both order and mercy, then the system—not the poor—must change.

V

Sunday, October 24, 1858
Fifteen days later

The papers didn't settle the matter. They sharpened it.

Positions hardened quickly, not around what had occurred, but around what it was permitted to mean. Men repeated phrases they'd read. Others answered them with different phrases, equally certain. Meetings were called. Names were recorded. The Almshouse was spoken of more often than it was entered, although most called it 'poorhouse' instead of its proper name.

It was in this climate, rather than because of it, that George Mehring was required in town.

The business was ordinary enough: committee obligations, signatures, the minor civic duties that accrued to men whose names were trusted to steady them. Hannah accompanied him, as she'd begun to do more often, not as a courtesy but as preparation. Josephus joined them later, called by the same web of concerns that now bound Fairlight to county matters, whether he wished it or not.

Jacob arrived separately of his own accord.

No one remarked upon this. There was no need. He'd already attached himself to the question in ways that required neither invitation nor approval.

The Almshouse wasn't the destination. It emerged from the

proceedings as a consequence: an inspection noted, a verification requested, a matter best settled by sight rather than argument. The decision was made without drama, and the party moved as though this had always been the next step.

Hannah had not expected to enter.

George conducted a brief exchange at the gate with a man whose name she didn't catch. The door was unlocked, then opened, as though it were not accustomed to the motion. Hannah followed because no one told her not to.

The air changed at once.

It wasn't foul, as the newspapers led her to expect, but close. The smell was of damp wool and boiled grain, of bodies kept indoors too long. The hallway was narrow, its windows set high, admitting light without view. The floor had been scrubbed recently. That, too, was clear.

They were received by the overseer, a man careful in his manner and precise in his speech. He spoke of capacity and compliance, of rules observed and infractions noted. He used the word *unfortunate* more than once. Hannah listened and didn't interrupt.

A woman sat on a bench near the wall, hands folded around a child's wrist. The child's shoes were too thin for the season. Hannah noticed this and then noticed herself noticing it. She didn't look again.

They were shown the common room. Men and women sat at intervals, some idle, some mending. A few looked up as the party passed. Most didn't. One man laughed suddenly, then fell silent when the overseer glanced his way.

"The winter arrangements are already in place," the overseer said. "We anticipate no difficulty."

In the infirmary, two beds were occupied. A third stood ready. The attendant was absent. The overseer explained this as a matter of rotation. Hannah noted the explanation and the absence separately.

They did not linger.

Outside, a small group had gathered near the yard fence. A man stood apart from them, his hat in his hands. Two children clung to his coat. A woman stood slightly behind, her gaze fixed on the ground.

"That's the family," the overseer said. "The matter we

discussed."

Hannah understood which matter this was.

The man spoke as they approached, his voice low and careful. He didn't raise it. He didn't plead. He explained, as though explanation might still be useful. The overseer answered him in the same tone, citing regulation and precedent. The words passed between them without friction.

Josephus stood apart, his hands at his sides. Jacob stood closer to the overseer, his posture attentive.

"The rule exists to prevent abuse," Jacob said. "If it isn't enforced, there's no point to it."

The overseer nodded, relieved.

Josephus didn't speak at once. When he did, it was only to ask, "And the children?"

Jacob paused, something like a smile forming. "They will learn. So will others."

The woman lifted her head then. Her eyes moved once, quickly, over the group and settled on Hannah.

Hannah met her gaze and didn't look away.

The only sounds breaking the silence were the rhythmic clangs of rail workers laying track for the Western Maryland Railroad to their west.

No one said anything more.

The decision had already been made. It had been made before they arrived, before the words were spoken, before the season turned. What remained was its execution.

When they left, the door was locked behind them with care.

The carriage waited where it had been left. Hannah took her seat and folded her hands in her lap again. The horse stepped forward. The wheels turned.

She didn't speak on the ride home.

But when the road narrowed, and the trees closed in, she found herself thinking not of the family but of Fairlight; of water held and released with intention, of rules that bent toward use rather than punishment.

She said nothing of this.

She didn't need to.

VI

Mary Marlowe and Molly had set the table before the light began to fade.

They laid it as they always did on Sundays, with no more and no less than was proper. Bread cut and covered. Stew kept warm at the back of the hearth. The good cloth brought out. Not for company, precisely, but because the day required it.

Josephus arrived with Hannah just before Mary rang the bell.

Christian met them at the door and took Josephus's hat, then Hannah's cloak, his manner unchanged but his attention exact. Mary kissed Hannah's cheek and stepped back to look at her, as though seeing her anew.

"You are welcome," Mary said, her words carrying an unspoken weight.

Jacob stood near the window, already restless. He nodded once at their arrival and turned back as though he were only marking time.

They gathered at the table. Christian bowed his head. The prayer was brief and unadorned. Gratitude. Sufficiency. Guidance. When he finished, Mary served.

The conversation began, as it invariably did, with the farm. Then the weather and the week ahead. Nothing strained. Nothing hurried. Hannah answered when addressed and listened otherwise, her hands folded loosely in her lap.

It was Jacob who broke the rhythm. "I won't be staying."

Mary stopped while reaching for the bread.

No one spoke.

Christian looked up. "You are expected."

Jacob's lips pressed together in a thin line. "I have other business."

Josephus didn't look at him. Hannah did.

"On a Sunday?" Mary asked.

Jacob shrugged. "It won't keep."

"Then say what it is," Christian said, setting his spoon down.

"There's a meeting at Trevanion," Jacob replied. "Dallas is hosting. Shaw is speaking."

No explanation followed. None was needed.

Christian's gaze remained steady. "Sit."

Jacob didn't comply.

"They're discussing the Almshouse," he went on, as though that were justification enough. "And the election. Douglas has carried the debates, but Lincoln's name is being made useful by men who don't mind stirring panic."

Josephus lifted his eyes then. "You can hear about it tomorrow."

"That won't do," Jacob said. "This matters."

Mary's hand paused over the pot. "So does this."

Jacob emitted a quick, light laugh. "This will still be here."

Hannah spoke then, quietly. "The family we saw today will not."

The words held. Even Jacob seemed unprepared for them.

"There will always be need," he said. "That's the point of order. You can't—"

"I'm not speaking of order," Hannah said, the intensity of her voice raising a single notch. "I'm asking what can be done." No one interrupted her. "They were turned out because it was correct. But correctness does not feed children. Fairlight has grain. Myrtle Hill has stores. There are others who would help if asked." She looked from Mary to Christian. "Is there a way to organize that?"

Jacob stared at her. "You can't just give things away."

Josephus spoke, calm but firm. "She didn't say that."

"It's the same thing," Jacob said, color rising along his cheeks. "Charity without discipline invites abuse. It undermines the system."

Hannah didn't raise her voice. "The system failed them."

Jacob scoffed. "Because it was enforced?"

"Because it was enforced without judgment," she replied, locking his gaze. "There's a difference."

Christian shifted then—not forward, but back, as though bracing. Mary's hand came to rest on the table.

Jacob turned to Josephus. "You're letting her talk like this?"

"She speaks for herself," he replied evenly.

Jacob's mouth parted as if to speak, but then snapped shut.

Hannah met his gaze directly. "You speak as though mercy is weakness. It isn't. It requires more restraint, not less."

No one spoke. The fire settled. Outside, a horse stamped once in the yard.

Christian cleared his throat and turned to Jacob. “If you are going, go now.”

Jacob’s chair scraped sharply as he reached for his coat. “I won’t be lectured in my own father’s house.”

Christian stood. “You will not abandon it either.”

Jacob hesitated, then turned for the door, closing it hard behind him.

From the yard came the sharp, impatient sound of Brimstone’s whinny.

Mary exhaled slowly. She looked at Hannah then, her expression composed but intent. “If you wish to do this, I will help.”

Christian returned to his seat and nodded once. “So will I.”

Hannah respectfully dipped her head. “Myrtle Hill will do what it can.”

Josephus reached for the bread at last. “Fairlight as well.”

They ate then, the meal no longer waiting.

Outside, the farm settled.

Jacob did not return.

VII

The meeting at Trevanion had already broken apart by the time Jacob reached the yard.

Lanterns were doused. Horses shifted at the rail. Voices carried in fragments, enough to know what had been said without hearing how it was framed. Jacob didn’t linger near the door. He’d heard what he came to hear.

Trevanion’s foreman, Silas Bixler, a gruff man in his thirties, with thinning black hair and dark eyes, stood apart, speaking to one of the hands. He finished, sent the man off, and turned as Jacob approached.

“You missed most of it,” Silas said.

“I heard enough.”

Silas studied him for a moment. “You look as if you have something to add.”

Jacob hesitated. Then, as though the decision had been made elsewhere, he said, “Fairlight’s talking about helping the

Almshouse."

Silas's expression didn't change, but something behind it did. "Helping how?"

"Grain. Provisions. All done quietly." Jacob paused. "Myrtle Hill as well."

Silas let out a thin breath through his nose. "That figures."

"It won't last," Jacob said. "It never does."

"No," Silas agreed. He glanced back toward the darkened house. "But it makes noise while it does."

They stood without speaking. Farther down the line, Brimstone stamped impatiently.

"Since that mill opened," Silas said at last, "our numbers haven't been what they were." Jacob nodded as Silas continued. "We've been steady. But steady doesn't mean whole."

Jacob looked toward the road. "The county will need supplies either way."

Silas's mouth curved, not quite a smile. "That's what I was thinking."

Jacob adjusted his coat. "You should move quickly."

"We will."

Without another word, Jacob walked down the line, mounted a clearly impatient Brimstone, and rode off.

Behind him, Trevanion settled back into its routines, the yard quiet once more, as though nothing had been decided.

VIII

Thursday, October 28, 1858
Four days later

Nothing was announced.

Mornings began as mornings did at Fairlight, with water set to purpose and stone answering stone. The wheel took the creek without argument. Grain was weighed. Sacks were filled and tied. The ledger lay open on the bench, its columns half-formed.

Josephus didn't call the men together. He didn't speak of obligation. He altered the count.

Elias Koontz noticed it before anyone said a word. "These are our stores, ja? You want them set aside?" he asked, resting his hand on the nearest sack.

"Aye," Josephus replied. "But not here."

Elias nodded. He didn't ask why. He marked the figure in the margin instead of the column.

By midmorning, Hannah arrived by carriage. She stepped down, thanked the driver, and crossed the yard with her skirts gathered clear of the mud. Mary had come earlier and was already inside the tenant house, sleeves rolled, speaking with Emma over the table.

They did not discuss the Almshouse. They discussed quantities.

"How much can be spared without thinning winter stores?" Mary asked.

"And how often," Hannah added. "So it doesn't look sudden."

Josephus listened, then said, "Weekly. No more than that."

Emma nodded once. "I shall make room."

The work shifted, almost imperceptibly. Fairlight's grain meant for market was weighed twice and redirected. A sack was tied and set out of sight from the road. Another followed. No one spoke of charity. It was treated as allocation.

John Dorsey carried two of the sacks himself, steady and unhurried. When another man reached to help, he shook his head and took a third. "It's all right," he said. "I've got it."

By the end of the day, the space beside the springhouse had been cleared and set. The water there ran cold and even; the stones worn smooth from use. The sacks were stacked carefully, covered against the damp.

Hannah stood back and looked at it, not with satisfaction, but with measure. "This will do."

Josephus nodded. "For now."

They didn't speak of who would receive it. That had already been decided.

The next delivery left before dawn, two days later, taken by a man whose name would not appear on any paper. The wagon returned empty. No notice followed. No thanks were expected.

At Fairlight, the wheel continued to turn.

IX

Thursday, November 4, 1858
A week later

Elias noticed it in the deliveries—but not at first.

The creek had been steady, the stones true. Orders came and went. But by the second week, the rhythm shifted just enough to register.

Fewer wagons from the east. More questions about price.

A miller from Taneytown lingered longer than usual, weighing his words as carefully as his grain. "County's buying up a fair bit of grain," he said at last. "Not from here."

Elias made a note. "From where, then?"

The man shrugged. "Trevanion."

That would have been unremarkable once. Not now.

By midmonth, the pattern held. County wagons passed Fairlight without stopping; their loads already accounted for. Elias saw the marks on the barrels when they came back empty with new stencils and fresh paint—contracts made visible.

He brought it to Josephus that evening, laying the ledger open on the bench between them. "They're moving more grain than before. County scale."

Josephus scanned the figures. "They weren't before?"

"No," Elias replied. "Not since Fairlight's first run of the mill."

Josephus said nothing.

"They've lost trade to us this past year," Elias went on, careful now. "This makes it back. Then some."

Josephus closed the book. "We'll keep doing what we're doing."

Elias nodded. He'd not expected another answer.

As he stepped outside, he saw Hannah near the springhouse, checking the coverings against the coming cold. The sacks were fewer now, the stack diminished by design. What remained was enough…for now.

The wheel turned on. The creek kept its course.

Across the county, ledgers balanced themselves differently.

X

Thursday, November 15, 1858
Eleven days later

Jacob hadn't come home for three nights.

When he did, it was near dusk; his horse lathered and impatient, his movements sharp with fatigue that Jacob didn't acknowledge. He dismounted, led Brimstone to the rail, and went inside without calling out.

Christian was at the table with his accounts. He looked up once, then returned to his work. "You missed the market."

Jacob shrugged out of his coat. "Didn't need it."

Mary glanced up from the stove. "Have you eaten?"

"I'm not staying."

Christian set his pen down. "You are staying."

Jacob hesitated, then took the chair nearest the door. He didn't remove his boots.

Josephus entered a moment later, carrying a sack of feed. He stopped when he saw Jacob, then continued as though nothing had changed.

"The county has contracted Trevanion," Jacob said suddenly. Josephus didn't answer. "It's proper. Order requires predictability. You can't run public institutions on goodwill."

Josephus set the sack down. "No one suggested that."

"That's what it comes to," Jacob replied. "Eventually."

Mary turned from the stove, watching him. "You speak as though you've decided this already."

Jacob offered a tight, almost imperceptible smile. "It's being decided whether you speak or not."

Christian looked at him then. "You're quoting someone."

Jacob's jaw locked. "I'm stating facts."

"No," Christian replied. "You're repeating words you did not arrive at yourself."

Jacob's eyes rolled as he abruptly pushed himself to his feet. "You always think that!"

Christian didn't rise. "I think you used to explain your thinking. Now you borrow it."

Josephus met his gaze. "Who told you that Fairlight was running on goodwill?"

Jacob let out a single, sharp bark of laughter. "Everyone knows!"
Josephus waited. "No one *said* it. It's obvious."

Silence followed. Not strained, just complete.

Jacob pushed his chair back. "I don't have time for this."

Christian nodded. "You rarely do now."

Jacob reached for his coat. "The world's changing, Father. You can't keep pretending it isn't."

Josephus answered quietly, "We're not pretending, brother."

Jacob paused at the door. For a moment, it seemed he might say something else. He did not. The door closed behind him.

Josephus went to the window and watched Brimstone disappear down the lane.

"He didn't argue," Mary said.

Christian folded his papers. "No. He's past that."

Outside, the sound of hooves thinned into the distance.

The house settled back into itself, altered only by what did not return.

XI

Tuesday, November 20, 1858
Five days later

Jacob came down the stairs with unusual care.

He'd washed. His hair was smoothed back, his coat brushed. There was an energy to him that hadn't been present for weeks, a lightness that showed in small things: the way he took the last step two steps at a time, the way he reached for his mug without being told.

Mary glanced up from the stove. "You're early."

"It's my birthday," Jacob said, almost smiling.

Christian was already at the table, the ledger open before him. He looked up once, nodded, and returned to the page.

Jacob sat and waited.

He remembered Josephus's eighteenth birthday. Forty acres along Big Pipe Creek. The note Father had written, brief and precise, promising funds once the plans were drawn. A beginning. A recognition. Jacob carried that memory with him for nearly two years, polished it smooth with repetition like water over stone.

At last, Christian closed the ledger. "Come with me."

They didn't move to the door. They didn't move outside. They walked just far enough down the hall that Mary couldn't hear the words, though she would know what they were about.

Christian stopped where the light from the window fell cleanly across the floor between them. "You are eighteen today."

Jacob straightened. "I am."

Christian folded his hands behind his back. "I shan't pretend this is sudden." Jacob's smile slipped. Christian noticed and continued without raising his voice. "You have been disrespectful. To this household. To the work. To those who have taken up what you leave undone."

"That's not—"

Christian lifted a hand, once. "I have never told you how to think, Jacob. Nor have I ever asked that you agree with me, only that you live within the rules of this farm while you are part of it."

Jacob drew a breath. "I do my share."

"You disappear for days at a time," Christian said. "I don't ask where you go. I can imagine. You miss Sunday mass. You miss Sunday supper. You speak as though obligation were a choice."

Jacob flushed. "Josephus never—"

"This is *not* about Josephus," Christian said. "It *is* about you." The two men stared at each other for a moment. "You turn eighteen today. And you must leave. You shall find your own work. Your own roof. You will learn what I could not teach you here."

Jacob looked at him, disappointment darkening his gaze. "You mean I don't get land?"

Christian didn't hesitate. "You cannot manage chores on this farm. What makes you believe you're prepared to manage your own?"

"That's not fair," Jacob said sharply. "You favor him. You always have. He gets everything!"

Christian's voice didn't change. "It does *not* mean the land isn't there for you, Jacob. It means it will be, when you have learned what it requires to keep it."

Jacob laughed once, brittle. "So that's it. You're throwing me out."

"I'm releasing you," Christian said. "There *is* a difference."

Jacob's hands curled at his sides. His words came faster now, tumbling over one another, the same grievances repeated.

At last, he stopped.

"Well," he said, his voice tight, "Trevanion is taking on new hands. Perhaps they can teach me what you couldn't, Father."

The words were chosen carefully.

Christian didn't answer them.

Jacob turned, took his coat and hat from the peg, and pulled them on with sharp, uneven movements. The door opened hard. A moment later, Brimstone's whinny cut through the morning air, high and impatient.

Christian stood where he was until the sound of hooves thinned as they moved down the lane.

Only then did he turn back toward the kitchen.

Mary didn't ask what had been said.

CHAPTER VIII

Saturday, May 25, 1997

I

Christian Marlowe—Journal
Undated, after Jacob's departure

I have begun to understand that restraint, properly practiced, does not prevent harm. It merely delays its recognition.

Jacob no longer argues. When he was younger, his defiance sought response. Now it seeks only confirmation. He returns with words already shaped, already finished, as though thought were something to be received rather than tested.

I told myself that a man must be allowed to choose his company, his influences, his path. Yet I cannot escape the sense that Jacob has ceased choosing and has aligned himself with whatever voice offers certainty without cost.

Josephus sees this as well, though he names it differently. He speaks of patience, of time, of the creek wearing stone. Still, stone wears slowly. Fire does not.

Hannah asked a question this week that none of us should have needed to be asked. She did not speak of blame or policy. She asked only how help might be given. I am ashamed that the answer required courage.

If there is fault here, it may be that I believed example alone would suffice, and that order, once set rightly, would hold without tending.

Order, left untended, becomes something else.

II

Mary Marlowe—Journal
Undated, after Jacob's departure

Sunday meals are meant to gather what the week scatters.

This one did not.

Jacob left before the table was fully set. He did not look at me. I have learned not to demand a son's attention when he withholds it. There are silences that harden if struck.

Hannah spoke plainly, and I am grateful for it. She did not ask permission to care. She assumed it, as women must, if anything is to be kept whole. I watched Josephus listen to her and thought, *this is how households are made.*

Christian said little. But I saw his hand tighten on the table when Jacob spoke of necessity as virtue. That word has been misused often of late.

I will help Hannah as best I can. Not loudly. Not in ways that invite comment. Bread given quietly feeds the same as bread announced.

I pray Jacob finds his way back to us before the distance teaches him he no longer needs us.

III

Josephus Marlowe—Journal
Undated, written after speaking with Elias

Elias brought me figures today. They were clear.

Trevanion has recovered ground it lost when Fairlight opened.

Not by changing how it works, but by finding where work may be priced without regard for consequence. It is not surprising. It is efficient.

I do not fault efficiency. I fault its misuse.

Jacob spoke this evening as though the matter were already settled, as though the question were no longer what ought to be done, but who has accepted it first. He believes himself ahead of us. I believe he has stepped aside.

Hannah asked how help might be organized. She did not ask whether it would be noticed. I am learning from her more than I expected.

If Fairlight stands for anything, it must stand quiet. The moment it announces itself, it becomes something else.

Water runs because it is allowed. When it is forced, it destroys.

I will keep the stones true.

IV

The fire had burned down to a low, steady bed of coals.

Ernest closed the last journal and rested it on his knee. He didn't look up straight away. The woods beyond the clearing pressed close, the darkness thick enough that the firelight seemed to stop at its edge.

No one spoke. No one knew what to say.

Ryan shifted on the log, then stopped himself, as though uncertain whether movement was permitted. Todd settled himself onto the rustling bed of leaves, leaning his back against the rough bark of the fallen log. Deborah folded her arms. Carrie sat on the blanket beside her, leaning forward, elbows on her knees, hands loosely clasped.

"Wow," Carrie finally whispered. "Christian really did it."

Ernest nodded once.

"He stopped waiting," Todd said. There was no approval in his tone—only acknowledgment.

After a moment, Ryan said, "So…does it ever ease?" Ernest didn't reply. "I mean, the tension between them. Does it—" He faltered, then tried again. "Do they ever work it out?"

Ernest looked at the fire. "Not everything works out."

Carrie nodded slightly, as if confirming something she'd already suspected. "It's in the way he talks."

Ryan glanced down at her while she leaned on his legs. "Jacob?"

She hesitated. "It's not what he says. It's…how settled he sounds. Like he's totally decided what everything means." No one interrupted her. "He doesn't seem angry, or even confused. He's just…already decided." She paused, searching for the right words. "There's no room left in him for anyone else to be right. Does that make sense?"

"That doesn't mean he's right," Deborah said. "It means he's absorbing what's already around him. Lots of people thought that way once. It was normal."

"That's not the same as reachable, Debs," Carrie said. "Jacob wasn't. Not by then. Especially not after his father kicked him out."

Reachable. The word settled into the space between them.

Ryan frowned. "What happens to everyone else?"

Ernest fully closed the journal, his hand coming to rest on the worn leather cover. "They keep doing what they know how to do." He looked out past the edge of the firelight, toward the dark where a house once stood. "As long as they can."

No one asked what came after that.

Ernest slid the journal carefully into his backpack, stood, and stepped closer to the fire to add fresh kindling. The flames caught quickly, flaring once before settling.

He cleared his throat. "I know Todd knows the answer to this, but have the rest of you ever heard of the dorveille?"

Carrie tilted her head, listening intently. "Door-veil? No. Never heard of it."

"In the nineteenth century, farmers would go to sleep shortly after sundown," Ernest explained. "Candles and lamp oil were expensive. They'd light them for an hour or so, then lie down for the first sleep."

"First sleep?" Ryan asked.

"It's biphasic sleep," Ernest said. "Farmers and their families would sleep in two four-hour blocks: the first sleep and the second sleep. The period in between the two sleeps is called the dorveille. It lasted between one and two hours. It faded with gas lamps and electricity."

“That makes sense,” Carrie agreed, a slight nod accompanying her glance toward Ryan.

Ernest continued, “I only mention it because some of this story happened during the dorveilles. It’s important to understand what those are.”

The trees above them swayed and whispered memories of the land on the wind.

From the darkness beyond the fire's reach, the hushed whisper of water finding its path over smooth stones drifted up through the woods.

CHAPTER IX

Tuesday, January 18, 1859

I

Snow had been falling at Fairlight since midmorning; not heavy, but steady enough to soften the yard and quiet the road. Travel had slowed. Grain shipments waited. Elias had set the hands to maintenance instead, checking belts, teeth, and the forebay while the wheel turned at its winter pace.

Josephus sat with him in the main house, ledgers open between them. The stove gave a low, even heat. Ash, the smoky-colored young cur he'd given Hannah for Christmas, lay stretched along the hearthstones, one ear cocked toward the door, the rest of him given over to sleep. Now and again, his tail thumped once against the floor when Elias shifted his chair, then stilled again.

Hannah stood at the far window, adjusting the curtains she'd finished the week before, measuring the light as much as the fabric. Ash lifted his head when she crossed the room, watched her pass, then settled again as she returned to the window. He'd learned the shape of her movements and didn't follow them.

She heard the horse before the men did.

The sound carried differently in snow. Muffled but unmistakable. Hooves near the rail. Leather shifting. A familiar impatience in the stamp.

Hannah's hands stilled. "Jacob has arrived."

Josephus looked up at once. Elias followed, frowning. Neither spoke. They waited.

The knock came a moment later, firm and unhesitating, as though the door had been his.

Ash didn't bark. He stood at the threshold, body angled, ears forward, tail still. His gaze fixed on the door with a concentration that was neither excitement nor fear, but assessment. After a beat, he stepped back once, deliberately, clearing the space as though he knew what was coming through it wasn't meant for him.

Elias rose, already frowning.

Josephus closed the ledger, stood, crossed the room, and lifted the latch.

Cold rushed in with the door, along with a scatter of snow and the unmistakable presence of Jacob Marlowe, though not, at first glance, in any recognizable form.

He stood framed in the doorway dressed as a figure out of season and sense: heavy furs layered awkwardly over his coat, a broad belt cinched too tightly at the waist, a coonskin cap pulled low, and a long brown beard that was clearly false hanging stiffly from his chin. A sack was slung over one shoulder, its contents shifting with a dull weight.

Jacob didn't wait to be invited in. He stepped inside, stamping snow from his boots with exaggerated care, as though arriving at a performance.

Elias stared. Josephus did not.

"Well?" Jacob asked, spreading his arms. "No greeting?"

Ash watched him from the edge of the room, head low, eyes steady. When Jacob's gaze flicked briefly toward him, Ash turned away and moved to the far wall, settling there with his back to the hearth and his face angled toward Hannah instead.

Josephus regarded his brother without expression. "Who are you supposed to be?"

Hannah turned from the window. When she saw him fully, her expression didn't change. "He's pretending to be Belsnickel."

Elias glanced at her. "Who?"

Hannah sighed deeply. "Among the Brethren, Belsnickel brings gifts to children who have behaved themselves. For those who have not, he brings the whip." She looked back at Jacob. "I'm surprised you're not carrying one now, considering our last encounter."

Jacob tugged the beard loose and grinned. "That's past, Hann—. Pardon. Miss Mehring." The correction of her proper name was deliberate. "I thought you might appreciate the effort." He gestured toward himself. "I'd say I got it right."

"I do not," Hannah said. "And you didn't."

For a moment, something like irritation crossed Jacob's face—quick, almost petulant—before he smoothed it away. He tugged the beard loose from his chin and let it dangle from one hand.

"Past disagreements aside," he said, with deliberate emphasis, "I've come in goodwill."

Josephus closed the door behind him. "That was your choice. You aren't expected."

Jacob shrugged, loosening the strap of the sack. "I was *not* passing through."

"I know."

"I'm at Trevanion now," Jacob went on. "They've taken me in as I am."

Elias's lips pressed together in a thin, hard line. "We heard."

Jacob glanced at him, surprised, then pleased. "It suits me. They know how to run a mill properly. Efficiently."

Elias folded his arms. "That mill's name is not what it was last winter."

Jacob laughed. "Those are politics."

"It's business," Elias said. "And ethics."

Jacob waved the distinction aside and turned back to Josephus. "You've made yourself visible, brother," he said intentionally. "That draws attention."

"So does honest work," Josephus countered.

Jacob's eyes flicked toward the window, toward the wheel beyond it. "It depends on who's watching."

For a moment, no one spoke.

"I brought gifts," Jacob said at last, lifting the sack. "Since I didn't see you at Christmas."

Hannah didn't move. Elias didn't speak.

Ash lifted his head once, then laid it back down, unimpressed.

Josephus crossed his arms. "You should have spared it."

Jacob hesitated. "If they are unwelcome, you might as well give them to the nigg—" He stopped, correcting himself with a thin smile. "The colored boy. I imagine Belsnickel arrived at his plantation with the whip more than once. He would be accustomed to it. I'm sure these would be welcomed."

The room went as still as Hannah's hands. Her gaze hardened. Elias's face flushed dark, his jaw set hard. He didn't move.

"Enough, Jacob," Josephus said, stepping forward once. Jacob met his gaze, unrepentant. "You need to leave. You are *not* welcome here like this."

"Like what?" Jacob asked.

"Unannounced. Disrespectful."

For a heartbeat, Jacob looked genuinely surprised, not at the words, but at the lack of reaction behind them. He glanced from Josephus to Hannah, searching for purchase, finding none.

"I thought unannounced was the advantage," Jacob said, his grin thin and satisfied. He let the sack fall to the floor. The sound was dull, unfinished. He pulled the door open and looked back before leaving. "I'll be around. This place matters now."

Cold air swept in. Snow followed.

Ash didn't watch him go as the door closed.

Josephus watched as Jacob crossed the yard, untied Brimstone's reins, and mounted him with quick, practiced movements. The horse whinnied and set off down the lane, hooves striking through the new snow until the sound thinned and was gone.

Only then did Ash rise, cross the room, and settle once more at Hannah's feet—not touching her, not leaning, simply present.

Inside, the stove ticked softly. Josephus reopened the ledger.

Outside, the wheel turned.

Hannah returned to the window and smoothed the curtain where it had slipped. She didn't look toward the road.

II

By afternoon, the road had disappeared.

What had begun as a steady fall thickened into weight. Snow

pressed against fence rails, settling along the stone edge of the forebay, muting even the creek's voice. Elias had gone twice as far as the bend in the drive and returned both times without seeing a wheel mark.

"The Mehrings' driver will not make it back tonight," he said plainly.

Josephus nodded once.

Hannah stood near the window, but didn't speak. The driver had left before the worst of it. If he had turned back, he was already safe somewhere along the road. If he had pressed on, he wouldn't risk the return in the dark.

Elias brushed snow from his sleeves near the hearth. "Emma and I will remain in the house," he said. "Samuel can see to the others."

He didn't offer it as correction. He stated it as order.

Josephus nodded. "Thank you."

Emma arrived not long after, bringing with her the quiet efficiency of a woman who had made such adjustments before. She set about warming the guest chamber in the upstairs ell, banking its small fire higher and laying fresh linens from the cedar chest. Ash followed in Hannah's footsteps as she brought more quilts, folded neatly over her arms.

"The room holds heat well once it's caught," Emma said to Hannah. "You'll be comfortable."

Hannah thanked her and didn't look toward Josephus.

Outside, the last of the hands who'd remained at Fairlight settled either in the kitchen alcove or made their way through the drifts toward the tenant house before the light failed. Dorsey, who'd come on foot that morning, remained without comment when Elias suggested he stay.

By suppertime, the windows showed only white.

Josephus lifted the sack Jacob had left and weighed it once.

Hannah watched him, then glanced toward the hallway where Emma's footsteps moved upstairs. She touched his arm. "Not yet. Later. During the dorveille."

He set it back where it had fallen.

The house continued about its business.

III

Later, during the dorveille between the two sleeps, when the house had settled and the storm pressed steady against the windows, they brought the sack to the hearth table. The lamp was turned down, its light low.

Upstairs, a board creaked once and stilled. Somewhere beyond the ell, Elias coughed.

Josephus untied the cord.

Woolens first. Gloves too thin for real work. A scarf of decent weave but careless stitching.

Hannah touched one of the tools. A small hammer, polished but unused. "He thought this would land," she said quietly. Josephus looked at her. "He wanted to be seen."

Josephus didn't answer. They continued.

A tin whistle wrapped in cloth. A length of cord. A wooden charm painted too brightly to be sincere.

"These can go," Hannah said. Josephus gathered them without comment. "He meant to disturb things."

"They hold," Josephus replied. "As do we."

She met his eyes then and smiled. Not questioning. Confirming. "Yes."

The rest were folded and set apart for distribution with other winter goods already promised. No note was attached; no name was given.

The house did not change.

IV

February 1859

Snow lingered longer that year, pressed into hollows where the sun reached last.

February brought little traffic and fewer visitors. The mill kept its winter pace: steady, reduced, attentive to cold, not demand.

Jacob did not return.

His name surfaced once or twice, but no more. Someone

mentioned he'd taken work at Trevanion, that he'd been seen riding hard through Taneytown. Someone else said he'd missed church. The remarks carried no urgency. They were noted, then set aside.

At Fairlight, the days fell into order.

Elias oversaw repairs that had waited for a lull: belts tightened, boards replaced, a gate rehung that had sagged all winter. Josephus reviewed accounts by lamplight, penciling plans forward rather than back. Hannah moved through the house during her visits as though it had always been hers—quietly, with purpose, leaving nothing unfinished.

March softened the ground. Snow receded, leaving mud that dried unevenly. The roads grew passable again. Orders resumed. The wheel answered without complaint.

Hannah didn't go to the springhouse all winter. The cold held there too long; the stone breathed damp even at midday. She waited without impatience.

When the thaw finally came, it did so without proclamation. The springhouse offered Hannah a place where she could be heard.

She took her shawl one afternoon and walked down the path alone. The door opened easily. The bench was as she'd left it. Water moved beneath the slats, clear and unhurried, carrying winter away inch by inch.

She sat.

Nothing required her attention. Nothing followed her. She simply listened.

Below her, Fairlight went on.

V

Wednesday, March 23, 1859

The creek ran high with the thaw.

Snowmelt from the hills fed it steadily now, not enough to flood the banks, but enough to give the water a new weight. The sound carried farther than it had in winter—less brittle, more insistent. Josephus listened for variation, marking the difference between speed and strain.

The wheel answered cleanly.

Elias had the hands spread along the race that morning, attending to the small work that winter postponed: clearing silt, resetting stones, checking the intake gate for drift that might have lodged unnoticed. It was the kind of work that looked like nothing when done right.

Ash ranged the bank above them, nose low to the wet ground, moving in short passes as though mapping the morning. He paused now and again to watch the men work, then moved on, keeping just out of the way. When the water shifted pitch, he lifted his head and stood still.

John Dorsey stood upstream with a pike pole, testing the edges where water gathered debris before releasing it again. He moved with care, his boots planted wide on the bank, eyes on the surface, not the current.

That's when he saw it.

At first, it looked like shadow; a darker line beneath the water, moving faster than the rest. Dorsey leaned forward, squinting against the glare, then straightened at once.

"Log!" he called. Not loud. Not yet. Just enough to carry.

Josephus turned at the word. Elias was already moving.

Ash froze.

The log broke the surface a moment later, rolling once as the current caught it. It was long, longer than any drift that should've been moving that fast, and stripped clean of branches, its ends blunted as though cut rather than broken. Saw marks. Iron spike scars.

"It's too straight," Elias said, moving his eyes from the log to Josephus. "This is deliberate."

The water had it now.

Dorsey shifted his footing and set the pike into the current, angling the tip just enough to test the log's weight. The force nearly tore it from his hands. "Hard!"

Josephus took in the distance between the log and the forebay in a single glance. He raised his arm once. "On the gate!"

Ash backed away from the race at once, retreating to higher ground without being told. He stood there, body angled toward the water, ears forward, tracking the log's advance.

The nearest hand ran for the lever. The intake narrowed, water backing slightly as the flow changed. A low groan came from the wheel.

The log surged, then hesitated, caught for an instant in an eddy before the race. The current tugged at it, trying to turn it broadside.

"Now," Elias said, pointing at Dorsey.

Dorsey planted the pike again, deeper this time, driving the iron point into the wet wood. Another hand joined him from the bank, then another, their poles crossing like spears as they worked to shift the log's angle.

The current fought them.

Josephus stepped forward and took hold of the gate rope himself, easing it another notch closed. The sound of water changed—higher, sharper—as pressure built.

The log turned. For a moment, it seemed it might still strike the wheel. Instead, it scraped the edge of the race, sending up a spray that darkened coats and faces alike. Dorsey leaned into the pike, jaw clenched, boots sliding an inch before he caught himself.

"Hold," Elias said, his voice even, hand raised.

The log slipped past the intake, carried wide by the narrowed flow, and struck the bank beyond with a dull, hollow sound. It spun once, then lodged against a stand of young trees, water curling around it in tight, angry lines.

Ash released a single breath through his nose and sat, eyes still on the water.

No one spoke in the aftermath.

Josephus eased the gate open again, slowly. The wheel settled back into its rhythm; the strain lifting without complaint.

Only then did Elias exhale. "That was *not* drift."

Dorsey straightened and wiped his hands on his trousers. "No, sir."

Josephus looked upstream, following the course the log must have taken. The creek curved out of sight not far beyond the bend. He turned back to his hands. "Anyone hurt?"

Heads shook.

"Damage?" Elias asked.

Dorsey glanced back at the race, then the wheel. "None."

They stood there a moment longer, waiting for the creek to settle.

Later, when the hands returned to their work and the log had been secured against further trouble, Josephus and Elias stood near the forebay.

"That was close," Elias said.

"Aye. Aren't there laws against this?" Josephus asked quietly.

"Ja," Elias said. "Nuisance law. Using your water in a way that harms another's work."

"But there's no harm."

Elias nodded. "That's the trouble."

Josephus considered the creek again. Ash had resumed his slow circuit of the bank, the danger passed. "How do we keep it from happening twice?"

"Practically?" Elias said. "We add a sluice gate at the intake. And booms across the narrow points upstream. Nothing showy."

"And otherwise?"

Elias was silent for a moment. "We do not answer this with force." Josephus didn't look surprised. "Trevanion is playing at nuisances. That is *not* strength. It's fear. They wouldn't bother if they were not feeling it."

"So we let it be known," Josephus said.

Elias nodded. "Ja. Quietly. The community knows how to read that kind of thing."

The creek moved on.

By afternoon, the log had been cut down where it lay, its pieces stacked neatly along the bank for later use.

The wheel turned as it had all morning.

Orders went out.

From the road, Fairlight looked unchanged.

VI

Jacob heard about it three different ways before noon.

The first came from a man at the hitching rail, speaking as though repeating something already old. A log sent down the creek. Nearly struck Fairlight's wheel. Turned aside at the last moment. No damage done.

The second came from inside the mill, from someone who

wanted to sound informed. Trevanion had been named, not directly, but with the kind of pause that made a name unnecessary to be understood.

The third came from Silas Bixler, the foreman, later, when the day's work had settled.

"They handled it cleanly," he said, almost grudging. "Had the gate closed before it mattered. Dorsey saw it coming."

Jacob looked up from where he was tying off a sack. "Dorsey?"

"The colored hand," Silas said. "Sharp-eyed fellow."

Jacob's jaw became rigid, his teeth grinding slightly. "And the wheel?"

"Turned right on."

Jacob said nothing.

Silas continued. "No proof of anything. One can't take a man to court for what didn't break. Still—" he shrugged. "People are talking."

By the time he stepped outside, the story had already begun to change. It was no longer about a log. It was about how Fairlight had been ready. How they'd anticipated trouble. How the mill had absorbed it without fuss.

Someone laughed and said, "I guess Marlowe's place is sturdier than it looks."

Jacob didn't laugh. He mounted Brimstone and rode out toward the road, the air sharp in his chest. The creek ran alongside him for a stretch, swollen with spring, obedient to its course.

He understood then. They wouldn't stop. That was the problem.

Fairlight would not be shamed into retreat. It would not fail quietly. It would endure the way Josephus always had—by making other men look foolish for trying.

He thought of Silas's tone. Of the way the man had spoken Dorsey's name, with respect. He thought of the way Fairlight had already folded the incident into its own order, denying it the shape of a challenge.

By evening, the story had reached Taneytown proper. It had been smoothed and made respectable. No one said *sabotage*. They said *incident*. They said *near thing*. They said *handled.*

Jacob listened and said little.

That night, he sat on the edge of his bed in Trevanion's tenant house and slowly unbuckled his boots, his movements measured. If Fairlight could turn aside what was meant to damage it, then damage was the wrong instrument.

You didn't warn a thing like that.

You ended it.

Outside, the creek moved on, dark and swollen, carrying what it was given without question.

VII

Sunday, April 17, 1859
Twenty-five days later

The Carroll County Improvement meeting was held that year on the Sauble family's land, under a great canvas pavilion raised just beyond the road to the Almshouse; close enough that no one needed reminding of its presence. The road passed the poorhouse fields on the way in.

The pavilion stood broad and pale against the late light, its center poles rising like stripped trunks, guy ropes staked wide into the trampled grass. The sides had been rolled and tied to let the air move through, though the scent of earth and livestock clung to the canvas all the same. Rough plank benches filled the interior in narrow ranks, and a low platform had been laid at the far end for speakers.

By the time Josephus and Hannah arrived, the benches were already half-filled. Farmers stood in small knots near the open edges, hats in hand. A few tradesmen lingered along the rope line, prepared to slip away if the talk ran long. George Mehring sat near the front, posture attentive but reserved. Christian Marlowe stood a few rows back, hands folded loosely before him, listening more than watching.

The air held a low murmur of expectation. This was not a gathering called for comfort. It was called for correction.

The first speaker expressed concern; the second, outrage. By the third, the language had shifted, as though the matter had already been decided.

Funds for the Almshouse had gone missing.

The phrase passed from mouth to mouth, shifting slightly each time. Misapplied. Unaccounted for. Improperly handled. No one named names. None were needed. The matter, it was said, was no longer one of cruelty or neglect, but of stewardship.

Hannah listened carefully. She noticed clearly that speakers didn't use the term 'Almshouse.' It was always 'poorhouse.'

The poor themselves were mentioned, but mostly in passing, as evidence rather than subject. Their suffering had opened the door, but it was the money that now held the space. What had been allocated. What had been received. What had not, apparently, arrived where it was meant to go.

Someone asked where the funds had been kept.

Someone else asked who had oversight.

A man near the aisle repeated the question that had appeared in print, though he didn't cite the paper by name. Who is responsible? What has become of it?

The words were taken up again, quieter this time, as though repetition might summon an answer.

Josephus felt Hannah shift beside him. Not impatiently. Just enough to mark a change. She didn't look toward the speakers, but toward the tent flaps, where the light fell across the field. Beyond, the road lay dry. Wagons passed. Life continued.

When the talk turned to remedy, the area settled.

There would be safeguards, they were told. New requirements. Clearer accounting. The commissioners would be obliged to publish detailed statements going forward. No more ambiguity. No more discretion without record.

Someone asked whether the conditions at the poorhouse would change.

The answer was careful. Measures were being considered. Committees formed. Assessments made. In the meantime, order must be restored.

Hannah heard the word *order* and thought, not for the first time, how easily it could be made to stand in for justice.

The meeting adjourned without ceremony. Men rose, replaced hats, and shook hands. The crowd thinned in stages, conversation breaking into smaller pieces.

Josephus turned toward Hannah to ask if she was ready when he heard his name spoken behind them.

He turned.

Jacob stood a few paces back, hands loose at his sides, his expression already arranged. He looked neither surprised nor pleased to see them—only certain.

"I didn't know you'd be here," Jacob said. His gaze flicked briefly to Hannah, then back to his brother.

"Aye. We live nearby," Josephus replied.

Jacob smiled faintly. "Of course."

They stood in a small pocket of space left behind as others moved past them. Christian remained within sight, though he didn't approach. George stood near Hannah.

Jacob's attention shifted again, catching a fragment of conversation just behind him.

"Brother Roop has agreed to officiate your ceremony at Myrtle Hill on the fifteenth of May," George said.

Jacob's brows lifted. "May?"

Hannah didn't turn, but Josephus felt the change in her posture all the same. He answered evenly. "Aye."

There was a pause, brief but telling. "When may I expect my invitation?"

The question wasn't framed as one. Josephus didn't answer at once. He glanced at Hannah, then George, then back. "We'll need to discuss it."

Jacob's smile held, though something behind it tightened. "I'm your brother. There's nothing to discuss."

Josephus didn't take the bait. "There is."

Jacob's eyes narrowed, just a fraction. Then he straightened; the moment passing as quickly as it had come. "Very well. You know where to find me."

He stepped back into the flow of people, already turning away.

The tension left Hannah's body as she let out a long, slow breath.

Outside, the road carried attendees past the Almshouse again. The building stood as it had before—doors closed, windows unremarkable. Whatever had been decided under the tent hadn't reached it yet.

Josephus reached for Hannah's hand as they walked. She took it without hesitation.

Behind them, the tent emptied.

VIII

Josephus and Hannah didn't speak of it at once.

They walked from the tent until the noise thinned. The road bent away from town, bordered by early grass showing through winter's flattening. A wagon passed them, then another. No one paid them any mind.

At last, Hannah said, "I would prefer he not be there."

Josephus didn't answer immediately. He nodded once. "I understand."

She kept her gaze fixed forward. "I shan't make this difficult for you, Jos. He's your brother."

Josephus slowed and turned to face her. "This isn't about difficulty."

"It is," she said gently. "Just not in the way he thinks."

They stood there a moment, the space between them settled.

"I would prefer he not attend either," Josephus said. "Not as he is."

Hannah looked at him then. "But you will allow it."

"Aye."

She didn't argue. Instead, she reached for his hand. "If you decide that, I shall stand with you in it."

Josephus exhaled. "There will be conditions. Clear ones."

"Of course."

"He comes as a guest, or not at all."

Hannah nodded. "And if he cannot?"

"Then he will leave."

She didn't smile, but something in her expression softened. "Then I trust you."

They walked on.

IX

Christian was waiting when Josephus and Hannah arrived at the farm for Sunday supper.

He stood near the fence, watching the hands finish with the stock. When he saw Josephus approach, he turned without comment.

Josephus didn't preface it. "Jacob has asked about the wedding."

Christian did not react. "I assumed he would."

"He wishes to attend," Josephus said. "I will allow it. Under certain conditions."

Christian nodded once. "Name them."

Josephus did.

When he finished, Christian remained silent a moment longer, his gaze on the ground beyond the fence. "And if he fails to keep them?"

Josephus met his eyes. "Then he'll be asked to leave. Immediately."

"I shall see to it," Christian said.

Josephus studied him. "I would not ask you to do this if you'd rather not."

Christian shook his head. "It's my place to do so."

This was not authority, but responsibility.

"I won't go to Trevanion," Josephus said. "It isn't fitting."

"No," Christian agreed. "I shall speak to him."

"And if he argues?"

Christian's mouth tightened, just slightly. "Then he'll learn that an invitation is not a right."

Josephus bowed his head. "Thank you, Father."

Christian turned back toward the barn. "Josephus," he said, not looking back. "You are doing right by her."

Josephus stood where he was for a moment after Christian began walking toward the house, the words settling into place.

Beyond the fence, the fields waited. Spring would come whether they were ready or not.

X

Tuesday, April 19, 1859
Two days later

Christian found Jacob at Trevanion.

He waited near the hitching rail, where men came and went with sacks and tools—nothing private could pretend to be otherwise. When Jacob appeared, Christian neither raised his voice nor stepped forward.

"Jacob," Christian said. Jacob stopped, surprised more by the tone. He looked his father over, then smiled faintly. "We need to speak."

"You've come a long way," he said.

Christian didn't answer that. Instead, he said, "Josephus has agreed that you may attend the wedding. Under conditions."

Jacob's smile tightened. "Of course there are."

No politics.
No work.
No commentary meant to provoke or correct.
Conduct yourself as a guest.
Leave when the day is done.

When Christian finished, Jacob laughed softly. "You're afraid I'll embarrass him."

"No," Christian replied. "My concern is that you will dishonor the occasion."

Jacob's eyes flashed. "That's the same thing."

"It's not," Christian said. "And if you cannot abide by it, you will be asked to leave."

"By you?"

"Aye."

Jacob studied his father, then straightened, smoothing his coat as though for inspection. "I accept. You'll see. I'm a man of my word." Christian didn't respond. Jacob leaned closer, lowering his voice. "You're all so careful now. As though order were something fragile."

Christian held his gaze. "Order untended becomes something else, Jacob."

Jacob smiled again, but this time it didn't reach his eyes. "Then I suppose you'll be watching."

Christian turned away. "I always am."

Jacob remained where he was long after his father left, the mill noise closing around him. His hands clenched once, then stilled.

He'd been given permission.

That would have to be enough.

XI

Preparations began without announcement.

There was no moment when the wedding became the center of conversation. It simply entered the days the way the season did: first as expectation, then as work.

At Myrtle Hill, Hannah and her aunts sorted linens that had been kept folded longer than she'd been alive. Some were set aside. Others were returned to their chests, waiting their turn. No one spoke of abundance. They spoke of readiness.

At Fairlight, Josephus adjusted schedules without explanation. Deliveries were arranged to allow for a day's absence. Elias noticed and asked no questions. The mill would run. It always did.

Mary Marlowe sent word that she had something for Hannah and asked only that it be given before the ceremony. Hannah didn't inquire further. She trusted Mary's sense of timing.

George Mehring brought a wagonload of flour to Fairlight and lingered as long as he needed to, speaking only of what could wait.

There were lists, but no one wrote them down.

Hannah walked the path to the Fairlight springhouse again. The cold had lifted enough that the stone no longer breathed damp. She carried nothing at first, only sat and listened to the water moving beneath the boards, steady and unremarkable.

Josephus didn't follow her. He learned the hours she favored and kept his distance. When he passed the springhouse on his way to the mill, he did so without pause, as though it were another structure belonging to the land.

The date moved closer.

No one spoke Jacob's name.

XII

Sunday, May 15, 1859
Twenty-six days later

Hannah Mehring lay awake listening to the house breathe in the dorveille.

Somewhere, a board settled. A clock marked the hour, then stopped.

She thought of the road to Fairlight—the turn where the trees thinned, the rise before the creek.

She didn't think of vows. She didn't think of ceremony.

She thought of morning, when she would become Hannah Marlowe.

When sleep came again, it was brief, and she rose before dawn without regret.

XIII

The room Hannah had slept in since childhood had been cleared of nearly everything that made it familiar.

Her bed was stripped to its frame. The trunk beneath the window stood open and empty. The chair by the wall had been turned to face the light, its cushion newly brushed, its purpose altered. Even the mirror—small, plain, never centered—had been moved closer to the window so the morning could reach it.

Hannah stood before it, hands folded loosely at her waist.

Mary came in without knocking. She closed the door and stood a moment, taking in the room as it was now; not abandoned, but released. Then she crossed to the small table near the wall and set down the box she carried.

It was wooden. Dark-stained. Solid in the way things are when they are meant to be kept.

Hannah turned at the sound.

Mary didn't speak at once. She placed the box carefully, aligning it with the table's edge, then ran her fingers once along the lid, as though checking for a flaw she already knew wasn't there.

"I had this made for you," she said at last.

Hannah stepped closer.

The box wasn't large. It could be carried easily, but not absentmindedly. The lock was simple; the key already tied with a short length of twine and looped over the hinge. Above the clasp, a small silver plaque had been affixed cleanly, without flourish.

She read it.

HANNAH MARLOWE

She didn't reach for it right away.

Mary watched her, her expression careful. "It seemed right," she said. "To give you something that would keep."

Hannah placed her hand on the lid then, her palm resting flat against the wood. Cool to the touch, the grain fine beneath her skin.

"I didn't know if I should—" Mary began, then stopped herself. "But I remembered what it was to leave one house and enter another, and how much of yourself remains unspoken if you have no place to set it down."

Hannah nodded. Her throat tightened.

Mary reached into the pocket of her apron and withdrew a small book. It was unmarked, its cover plain, the pages thick enough to take ink or pencil without complaint.

"This is for writing," Mary said. "Not for instruction. Not for record. For yourself." She placed it inside the box. "You will have many voices around you. Good ones. Worth listening to. But you should not give them all of you. My mother gave me something similar when I married Christian. For the same reasons. I believe if your mother, Elizabeth, were here, she would have done the same."

Hannah gently closed the lid, then rested both hands on it. "I will keep it."

They stood there together, the space between them filled with things neither felt the need to name. Specifically, the how and why of Elizabeth Mehring's passing.

At last, Mary reached for Hannah's shoulders and turned her slightly toward the chair. "It's time."

Hannah sat.

Mary lifted the dress from where it had been laid across the bed. The fabric caught the light without reflecting it. It was plain, as all such things were meant to be; deep indigo, steady as river water in shadow, its seams careful and exact. No ornament. No excess. Only what was required.

As Mary helped her into it, Hannah noticed the sounds beyond the room—the murmur of voices, the measured tread of footsteps on the stairs, the shifting of chairs below. The house was full now, but the room remained still.

Mary fastened the last button and stepped back.

Hannah reached for the white covering and set it over her hair, her hands steady. She adjusted it once, then let them fall.

In the mirror, she looked as she always had, and not at all.

Mary met her gaze there. "You're ready, Hannah."

Hannah didn't smile. She lowered her head once, accepting the truth of it.

Mary lifted the box and placed it into Hannah's hands. "For later."

Hannah held it a moment longer, then set it back on the table. "Yes. Later."

Mary crossed the room and opened the door.

The sound of the house came in at once; voices rising and settling, the day moving forward without pause. Hannah took one last look at the room as it was now, stripped and waiting, then stepped across the threshold.

The door closed behind her.

XIV

When Hannah entered the front room, the house had settled into stillness.

Chairs had been drawn close, their legs aligned carefully along the floor. The larger table had been moved aside to clear space, its place taken by a simple stand where Elder Roop waited, his hands folded, his expression neither solemn nor warm. Light came through the windows unfiltered, falling across faces without preference.

George Mehring stood at Hannah's side.

He had placed himself there early, before anyone thought to question it, and no one had asked him to move. His posture was straight, his presence quiet, the authority of Myrtle Hill residing in him.

Josephus waited across from them.

He stood alone, his hands at his sides, his gaze steady but not searching. He had chosen his position deliberately. Not at the center of the room, but slightly back, as though leaving space for what had not yet been said.

His coat was dark and newly pressed, the wool falling clean along his shoulders. The waistcoat beneath lay smooth and unadorned, its buttons fastened without ornament. A white collar framed his throat, the black tie drawn neat and narrow. Nothing about him called attention. Everything about him was in order.

Christian and Mary stood together to one side. Mary's hands were folded at her waist. Christian's rested loosely before him, his shoulders squared, his attention fixed on nothing that might distract.

Elias Koontz stood near the wall, Emma beside him. They didn't speak. Their presence required no explanation.

Along the back of the room, near the door, Jacob Marlowe leaned against the frame.

He arrived early and placed himself there without asking; his coat neat, his posture correct. If anyone noticed the flask hidden at his side, they gave no sign. His gaze moved often—not restless, but watchful—taking measure of the room as though it were an unfamiliar machine.

Elder Roop cleared his throat. The sound was slight, but it carried. "We are gathered to witness a covenant. This is not a matter of haste. Nor of display. It is a binding, entered into freely, before God and this community."

Hannah stood without moving. The white covering rested evenly against her hair, the deep indigo of her dress steady beneath it. Her hands were folded before her, her posture neither rigid nor yielding.

Josephus listened, his attention fixed on the elder, though his awareness extended beyond the elder—the shift of weight, the sound of breath, the quiet pressure of time. His dark coat held its shape along his shoulders, unmoving.

The elder turned first to Josephus.

"Do you take this woman, Hannah Mehring, to be your wedded wife," he asked, "to live with her after God's ordinance, to love, honor, and keep her, in sickness and in health, as long as you both shall live?"

Josephus didn't answer at once. He lifted his eyes then, meeting Hannah's for the first time since she'd entered the room. There was no surprise in his expression, no relief. Only recognition. "I do."

The elder nodded and turned to Hannah. "Do you take this man, Josephus Marlowe, to be your wedded husband, to live with him after God's ordinance, to love, honor, and obey him, and to serve him faithfully, as long as you both shall live?"

The room drew inward. Hannah felt the weight of the words settle against her, familiar and unadorned. "I do."

There was no tremor in her voice.

The elder continued, his cadence unchanged, as though the words had always existed and waited to be spoken again. "You are asked now to pledge your troth," he said. "Your truth. Your loyalty."

Josephus stepped forward then, closing the distance between them. "I plight thee my troth," he said, his voice steady.

Hannah answered without pause. "I plight thee my troth."

The words fell into the room and held.

No one moved. No one spoke.

The elder raised his hand once, then lowered it. "By the authority entrusted to me and before God and this congregation, I declare you husband and wife."

There was no applause.

No music followed.

The room exhaled as one.

Josephus and Hannah stood together now, the space between them altered by something that couldn't be seen but was immediately felt.

The elder stepped back. George did the same. The gesture was small, but it carried the full weight of relinquishment. He didn't linger. He didn't look away.

Josephus offered his arm without looking. Hannah took it.

As they turned, she leaned close enough that only he could hear and said, "It's you. It's me. It's us."

He didn't answer. He didn't need to.

Christian bowed his head. Mary closed her eyes.

At the back of the room, Jacob straightened.

For a moment, just one, his expression faltered. Something like disbelief crossed his face, then calculation. He reached for his flask and took a brief swallow, careful not to draw attention.

The elder spoke again, briefly, offering a prayer that was more acknowledgment than blessing.

When it was finished, chairs shifted. Feet moved. Voices rose, restrained but present.

Josephus and Hannah didn't leave at once.

They stood where they were, together; the day having changed shape around them.

Outside, the yard waited. The meal waited. The road waited.

Inside, the covenant held.

XV

George's brother, Jacob Mehring, stood near the side window, his hat held loosely in both hands.

He'd watched the ceremony without speaking, his expression thoughtful. When the elder stepped back and the room breathed again, he turned to the woman beside him.

His wife, Mary Mehring, hadn't taken her eyes from Hannah. "She held herself well."

"She always has," Jacob replied.

They stood a moment, letting the room reassemble itself around them. Then Jacob nodded once, as though confirming something already settled. "I should speak to George."

Mary touched his sleeve. "You should."

George Mehring stood near the table where the meal would be set, accepting murmured congratulations with the same measured nod he offered most things. When he saw Jacob approaching, he straightened slightly.

"Brother," George said.

"Brother," Jacob returned.

They clasped hands briefly. Firm. Familiar. Not ceremonial.

"You raised her right," Jacob said.

George inclined his head. "She raised herself."

Mary stepped forward then. "She will make a fine household," she said. "Josephus is steady. Fairlight is well-regarded."

"Those matter," George said.

Jacob glanced around the room, taking in the careful order of it—the chairs, the light, the way people moved as though aware of one another's space.

"We're building as well," he said, almost casually. "In Westminster."

George's brows lifted. "Are you?"

"A good lot," Jacob went on. "Stone foundation and walls. Close to town, but not pressed in by it."

Mary smiled faintly. "It's taken time."

George nodded. "It always does." He hesitated, then added, as though confirming a detail already half known, "That land off Uniontown Turnpike?"

Jacob's mouth curved in a small, pleased smile. "Tis the one."

"I've passed it," George said. "Looks near finished."

"Just about," Jacob replied. "The roof is on. The rest will come."

George glanced once more across the room, to where Hannah stood with Josephus, her hand resting lightly on his arm.

"When it's done," Jacob said, "you and Hannah should come see it."

"I expect we will," George said.

Mary followed his gaze. "She won't forget where she came from."

"No," George said. "She won't."

The sound of voices rose then; someone calling for help with the tables. Mary turned to go, already reaching for her apron.

Jacob lingered. "You did right by her."

George met his eyes. "She did right by herself."

Jacob Mehring nodded, satisfied, and stepped away.

Across the room, Hannah laughed softly at something Josephus said; her voice carried just enough to be heard.

Mary Mehring paused, listening, then smiled to herself and went to work.

XVI

Saturday, May 25, 1997

"Wait, hold on a sec," Carrie said, her hand raised to pause. "I'm sorry, Ernest." She turned and looked at Ryan. "Jacob Mehring? Uniontown Pike? Is he talking about the guy who built our house on Uniontown Road?"

Ryan smiled. "I think so, Scout."

Todd's hand met Ryan's bicep with a firm slap. "I told you before the night was over, we'd know."

Carrie whirled around to face Ernest. "Is that true?" Ernest nodded once and smiled. "Oh, my God! That's totally cool!" Carrie offered a sheepish, apologetic smile. "Sorry for interrupting."

Ernest chuckled softly. "It's okay, Carrie. Continuing…"

XVII

Sunday, May 15, 1859

The tables were set in stages.

What couldn't fit in the front room was carried out to the side porch and the yard beyond, where boards were laid across barrels and crates brought for the purpose. Cloths were spread, weighed down at the corners with stones. Bread was cut thick and set in baskets. Dishes appeared without announcement and were taken up when emptied.

No one called it a reception.

It was simply what followed.

Hannah and Josephus moved through it together at first, answering quiet congratulations, accepting hands offered and released. They didn't linger in any one place. The rhythm of the meal guided them: pause, listen, move on.

Mary Marlowe directed the flow without raising her voice. She'd done this before, though never for this. A nod here, a hand there, a word passed low and brief. The room answered her.

Christian stood where he could see the door.

George sat at the head of one of the tables, speaking with an uncle Hannah hadn't seen in years. Johannes Mehring. Their conversation turned to crops and weather, then back again, the way such things did when neither man felt the need to impress.

Elias and Emma ate quietly, plates balanced in their laps. No one remarked on their presence, which was precisely the point.

Jacob Marlowe took his food near the back.

At first, he did as he'd been instructed. He spoke when spoken to. He ate enough to appear settled. If anyone noticed the flask passing briefly from his coat to his hand and back again, they gave no sign.

Children were served and sent away to play. Chairs scraped and were set right again. Someone laughed, then stopped themselves, as though remembering where they were.

Hannah took her place at the table beside Josephus and bowed her head when the elder offered thanks. The words were familiar. The cadence steady. When they lifted their heads, the day resumed its course.

Josephus cut bread and passed it without thinking. Hannah poured cider and did the same. Their movements had already begun to align.

Across the yard, Jacob leaned against the railing and drank again.

The liquor burned less now. The edge dulled, leaving warmth in its place. He watched how people moved around the couple; how easily they accommodated them, how little attention was paid to anything else.

He took another swallow.

Christian noticed. He didn't act on it yet.

Mary passed Jacob once on her way back from the kitchen, her eyes flicking briefly to his face, then away. She said nothing. The day didn't require her to.

Josephus felt Hannah's hand brush his sleeve and turned toward her. She leaned close, her voice low. "Are you all right?"

"Aye," he said, smiling and meeting her eyes. "Are you?"

She nodded and smiled, a slight flush in her cheeks. "I am."

They stood together for a moment longer, then separated again as someone called Hannah's name.

Jacob watched her go.

The flask was lighter now.

He smiled to himself—not broadly, not yet. It held the private assurance of someone who believed the evening hadn't finished revealing itself.

Above them, the light shifted. The sun moved westward, catching the edges of plates and glasses before sliding away.

The meal continued.

No one rushed it.

XVIII

The light thinned first at the edges.

Shadows lengthened across the yard, gathering beneath the tables, turning the white cloths gray, then dim. Lamps were brought out and set, their flames adjusted low. The air cooled enough that shawls were fetched and laid across shoulders without comment.

Some had left.

Goodbyes were spoken softly. Hands met and parted. Wagons rolled away down the lane, their wheels cutting shallow tracks into the dust. Children were called in and sent on ahead, their laughter fading as distance did the work adults would not.

Hannah stood near the doorway with Josephus, watching the day empty itself of noise. "It went well."

"Aye. It did," he replied.

They stood a moment longer, not needing to move.

Behind them, the house continued its work. Plates were gathered. A bench scraped and set right again. Someone hummed a line of a hymn, then stopped.

Christian remained near the edge of the yard, his posture

unchanged.

Jacob leaned against the porch rail, the flask now empty.

He turned it once, as though surprised by its lightness, then slipped it back into his coat. His face had flushed; the careful control he'd worn earlier loosening. He watched Hannah and Josephus with a narrowed gaze. Not angry yet, but sharpened.

He pushed himself upright.

The evening had reached its pause.

XIX

"You've done very well for yourselves," Jacob said, too loudly. "You've made it look easy." He gave Josephus a slight, humorless smile. "Is this how it's supposed to end?"

The words cut across the low murmur of the yard and landed hard.

Conversation stilled. Not all at once, but in stages, the way sound does when it realizes it has been challenged.

Josephus turned.

George Mehring, who'd been speaking with a cousin near the far table, also turned. He didn't move forward. He didn't need to.

The facade Jacob had maintained earlier crumbled as he stepped unsteadily from the porch's edge. He smiled as he spoke, but it was the smile of someone who'd already decided the outcome of a game. "A fine thing. Everyone gathered. Everyone agreeing. As though it all just…settled itself, as though Jos was always the one meant to end up standing there."

Christian shifted, placing himself where Jacob could see him. "Jacob."

"I'm speaking," Jacob said, waving him off.

That alone was enough to draw George's full attention.

"You always did like order," Jacob went on, his gaze returning to Josephus. "Consider Fairlight. You always thought if you built something carefully enough, it would stay put."

Josephus said nothing.

Hannah felt the change in Jacob's stare—the tightening, the focus. She didn't step back.

Jacob's laugh was a sharp, careless sound that cut through the air. "Look at you, *Hannah*. Standing there like this was inevitable."

"It was," Hannah said. The word carried farther than she intended.

George stepped forward then. Not quickly. Not with force. He placed himself beside Hannah, his presence steady and unmistakable. "Ja. It was."

Jacob turned to him, surprise flickering across his face. "You don't get to decide that."

"I already did," George said, never breaking his gaze from Jacob's.

The yard seemed to draw closer.

"You think this is about love?" Jacob said, turning back to Hannah, his voice rising. "You think that's what this is?"

"It is," she replied. "And also about respect."

Jacob scoffed. "Respect?" His laugh cracked. "It's about alignment. Possession. Fairlight is your home now. Not Myrtle Hill."

George didn't raise his voice. "You shan't speak to my daughter in such a manner."

Something broke fully then.

"You're all so eager to claim things," Jacob snapped. "Land. People." He gestured broadly, his balance slipping. "As if it were all yours by right."

Elias stiffened where he stood. Jacob's eyes caught on him. "You take in who you like. You run it your way. And the rest of us are supposed to fall in line."

"Leave," Christian said. "Now."

Jacob ignored him.

"You don't see it," Jacob continued, his voice turning almost plaintive now, the drink pulling him sideways. "You don't see what's coming. The change. The *shift!*"

Hannah stepped forward, her voice quiet but firm. "This is my family's home. You shan't speak here like this."

George didn't move, but his presence at her side made the words final.

"That's enough, Jacob," Josephus said.

Jacob rounded on him. "There it is! Big brother always stepping in. Big brother always correcting."

Christian reached for Jacob's arm. Jacob shook him off. "Don't touch me!"

"I will," Christian said evenly, "and I shall walk you out."

"You'll choose him?" Jacob spat, jerking his chin toward Josephus. "Again?"

"Aye," Christian said with no hesitation. The word landed cleanly.

For a moment, Jacob looked at George, then Hannah, then Josephus as if searching for a crack that no longer existed.

"Fairlight matters now," he said, the words slurred, but deliberate. "You hear me? It matters!"

Josephus met his gaze. "Not to you."

That was the end of it.

Jacob lunged forward, but Christian caught him then, his grip firm and practiced. George stepped up to assist.

"You will go. Now," Christian said low as he and George grabbed Jacob's arms and propelled him toward the lane.

Jacob shouted something incoherent as they dragged him away, the sound breaking apart as distance took it. Brimstone whinnied sharply, startled, then quieted.

The yard held its breath.

Christian and George returned without Jacob.

No one spoke.

Hannah exhaled slowly and leaned into Josephus. He wrapped an arm around her without looking.

The lamps flickered and were steadied.

Someone gathered the last plate. Someone else set a chair back where it belonged.

The house resumed its shape.

Outside, the creek kept its course, indifferent to names, vows, or men who mistook noise for consequence.

What had been built that day still stood.

XX

Josephus and Hannah didn't linger at Myrtle Hill.

Goodbyes were made carefully, without haste. George kissed Hannah's cheek once and stepped back. Mary pressed her hands together and nodded, her eyes bright but steady. No one followed them to the lane.

The carriage ride to Fairlight was quiet.

The night had settled by the time they reached it, the mill house dark except for the single lamp left burning in the front room. Josephus stepped down from the carriage first, then turned to help Hannah down. She took his hand without thinking.

Ash lifted his head from the porch as they approached, tail giving one brief wag before stilling again. He circled once, satisfied, then settled back near the door as Josephus unlatched it.

Inside, the house held its familiar order—clean, spare, purposeful. The day hadn't reached here yet.

Josephus lit another lamp and set it low. The glow gathered along the walls, catching the edge of the table, the back of the chair, the threshold worn smooth by use.

Hannah stood near the door a moment, listening. Ash remained where he was, just inside the frame, watching her without expectation. When she moved deeper into the room, he turned and padded back out onto the porch, the door closing softly behind him.

The creek ran steady beyond the walls, its voice constant, unbothered by vows or gatherings or the passage of hours. She let it settle her.

They went upstairs together.

The room prepared for them was simple. The bed had been turned down. A pitcher and basin stood ready. Nothing had been added beyond what belonged.

They moved without speaking.

Later, the house grew still around them, the mill quiet below, the night pressing close. Hannah rested her hand against Josephus's chest, feeling the steadiness of it beneath her palm.

"So," she whispered.

"So," he answered.

Hannah smiled, unseen. "We're here."

The word *here* held more than place.

"Aye," he said. "We're home."

Hannah smiled and considered that. "Home," she whispered with a slight smile. "Yes."

She lay quiet a moment, then spoke again, her voice unhurried, deliberate. "Jos?"

"Aye?"

"I love you."

The words were plain. They didn't reach.

He turned toward her. "I love you, Hannah."

Nothing followed. Nothing needed to.

The lamps burned low. The mill slept. The creek kept its course.

Fairlight held.

CHAPTER X

Saturday, May 25, 1997

I

Christian Marlowe—Journal
Undated, written the week following the wedding

The house at Fairlight has altered its posture.

It is not disorderly. Nothing is misplaced. Yet the rooms receive the day differently now, as though they have accepted purpose beyond labor.

Hannah moves through them with care, not deference. She does not ask permission of the space, nor attempt to master it. She attends to what requires tending and leaves the rest to time. I see no fault in this.

Josephus has changed less than I expected. He remains steady, deliberate, inclined to weigh consequence before motion. There is a difference in him now. A readiness that does not hurry. As though some internal question has settled and no longer demands reply.

Jacob was not mentioned again.

I do not know whether this is restraint or relief.

I have learned that order, once shared, is no longer singular. It must be trusted to another hand without oversight. This is not loss.

It is transfer.

If there is blessing in this season, it lies in continuity, not the absence of threat, but the presence of work worth doing.

II

Mary Marlowe—Journal
Sunday evening

The wedding passed as such things ought to. Without display, without indulgence, and without injury.

I am grateful for that.

Hannah bore herself well. She has always done so, but there is a steadiness that comes of being chosen and choosing in return. It does not announce itself. It holds.

Josephus listens to her. This is not common among men raised as he was. I do not mistake it for weakness. It is a skill learned early or not at all.

I gave her the box before the ceremony, as I had planned. She received it without tears, which pleased me. Some gifts are not meant to be cried over. They are meant to be kept.

Jacob troubles me still. Not for what he said, anger announces itself, but for what he no longer attempts to hide. There was a time when he wanted to be corrected. That time has passed.

I will pray for him. I will also set the table tomorrow.

The world is not improved by neglecting either duty.

III

Josephus Marlowe—Journal
May 16, 1859

We returned to Fairlight last night.

The house received us as it always has, without remark. I am grateful for that. It would trouble me if the place required reassurance.

Hannah has begun to notice things I had ceased to see: where the light settles in the afternoon, how the floor near the back door bears weight unevenly, how the creek's sound changes after rain. She does not speak of these observations as claims. She notes them, and they remain.

I believe this is how stewardship ought to be practiced.

The mill ran today as expected. Elias says nothing requires attention. I take this as good news.

I do not know yet what kind of husband I will be. I know only that I intend to remain worthy of the trust placed in me.

That, I have learned, is not a fixed condition.

IV

The fire had burned down to a steady bed of coals.

No one noticed this time until Ernest stopped, closed the last journal, and rested it on his knee. He didn't immediately lift his gaze. The surrounding woods seemed to have closed in, as if also listening to a tale the land had told them long ago.

No one spoke. Nor did anyone notice that the time had crossed into the three a.m. hour.

Carrie was the first to breathe out. Not a laugh. Not quite a sigh. She wiped tears from her eyes. "They were so happy."

Ernest nodded. "They were."

Ryan leaned forward, elbows on his knees. "I'm waiting for the other shoe to drop."

A sniffling sound escaped Carrie as an amused chuckle followed. "So negative, MacGyver."

"Realist, Scout," Ryan countered. He gestured to the overgrown, empty foundation of a house perched atop the hill, its stone basement walls peeking through the tangled weeds. "It did drop. The only question is how. And why?"

Ernest's head dipped in agreement, no words spoken.

Deborah folded her arms after stoking the fire and adding new kindling, then watched it. "That's worse. Waiting for the catch."

Todd nodded. He'd heard this story from Ernest before, but Ernest's telling tonight was far more elaborate and captivating than he remembered. "Yeah. Because it means what they had wasn't fragile. It wasn't doomed from the start."

Carrie looked down at her hands while Ryan rubbed her back. "It was totally real."

Ernest shifted, the leather of the journal creaking softly. "It was."

Ryan frowned. "So when people say—" He stopped and recalibrated. "When historians talk about inevitability—"

"They're lying," Ernest said gently. "Or they're making things less complicated." He glanced toward the dark beyond the firelight, where the land dipped away. "What came next wasn't written into the marriage. It was written into other choices. By other hands."

Carrie swallowed, recognizing the dark implication in his words. "But Ernest, they did everything right."

Ernest nodded. "As much as is humanly possible."

A sharp crack echoed through the trees, its sound traveling from far away. A splash in the creek followed.

Everyone turned their heads toward the house and mill that was.

With a smile, Ryan nudged Todd. "Your ghosts, brother?"

Carrie flicked her eyes at Ernest. He offered a slight smile and a nod of recognition. Carrie knew. She understood.

"It's not ghosts, Ryan. It's memory," she said, continuing to stare into the dark of the woods around them. "The land of Fairlight remembers. You can hear it if you listen." She turned to Ryan. "It hasn't forgotten them. It weeps."

CHAPTER XI

Wednesday, July 4, 1860

I

The year following Josephus and Hannah Marlowe's wedding arrived with no fanfare.

It passed in work and weather, in small decisions that held, in days that ended where they were meant to. Fairlight didn't grow larger. It grew steadier.

Inside, the house altered by degrees. Shelves that had once held little now bore books, jars, and the small necessities of settled living. A new clock marked the hours more faithfully than the old one had done. Hannah chose paper for the sitting room in a pattern sober enough to last, and Josephus mounted additional brackets so the lamps cast fuller light across the table in winter. A small, framed likeness of Josephus and Hannah standing before the Fairlight main house rested above the mantel, their figures held in stillness beneath the photographer's careful light. George Mehring commissioned it last spring. The glass plate itself remained secured in the basement below the stairs with deeds and ledgers in the Marlowe family safe, a wedding present from Christian and Mary, passed down from the first in their family to come to America, Hezekiah Marlowe. Josephus kept it in the basement, where the air stayed cool even in high summer.

Hannah learned the measure of the place by living in it. She marked stores in a hand that was already her own. She took to the garden early, setting rows with care and keeping them weeded even when the mill ran long. Ash followed her there at first, nosing along the fence line and settling in the shade where he could watch without interfering. In time, he learned which paths were not his to cross and kept to the others.

Josephus noticed afterward that meals had changed: more variety, less waste, nothing taken for granted. He didn't comment. He adjusted his habits to match.

The grain and corn they set aside for charity came from their own fields. Josephus had been firm on that point from the beginning. What others brought to the mill was milled and returned. What Fairlight gave had been grown on its land, tended by its hands, and accounted for without flourish.

Elias said the yields would hold if the weather stayed kind. Josephus told him to wait until the second cutting was in before promising anything further. Elias nodded. That was how decisions were made now: without hurry or argument.

The Koontz children were part of Fairlight, as children are when work is honest. The oldest boy, Samuel, ran messages, and he'd learned where not to stand near the raceway. Louisa, two years younger than Samuel, helped Emma with washing and knew which herbs Hannah preferred for cooking. The younger ones stayed underfoot or out of the way as instructed. Ash tolerated them in passing, moving off when the noise rose too high, returning when it settled again.

None of them belonged to Fairlight, and yet the place accounted for them.

Trevanion was not spoken of often.

Jacob was not spoken of at all.

When the Fourth of July approached, Hannah suggested they go into town. "But not Taneytown."

Josephus agreed, equally without comment.

They chose Westminster.

The grounds of Emerald Hill, the home of their host, Colonel John K. Longwell, were already full when they arrived. Wagons were already ringed by the grass, and people had gathered in loose, shifting clusters. Families spread blankets, men leaned together in talk that had no urgency, parents sent their children off.

A small platform had been raised near the trees. When the reading of the Declaration of Independence began, the crowd drew closer without instruction, voices settling into attention. Hannah listened closely, not just to the words, but to how they were received. Some phrases were met with nods, others with stillness.

When the staged debate turned to Britain's claims of order and restraint, one speaker lingered too fondly on the virtues of crown and hierarchy.

Hannah leaned toward Josephus. "They called it order. They always do when they mean obedience. Britain did. That word may ring familiar to you, Jos. Order."

Josephus laughed before he could stop himself. It surprised them both.

The drum band played. Flags were passed from hand to hand. Small rockets were set aside for later; their promise was more noise than light. Elias and Emma were there as well. Hannah saw them and nodded once. Emma returned it.

By evening, the bonfires were lit.

They weren't grand, nothing towering or reckless, but steady, tended. People gathered near them in small groups, conversation lowering as the light faded. Children were called back in and sent home. Wagons rolled away in ones and twos, the ground remembering their passage.

Hannah watched the crowd settle, the way a place empties itself gradually, not all at once. She felt no hurry to leave, and no reason to stay.

They didn't linger late. They didn't ride back to Fairlight.

Instead, they turned their horse toward town and took a room at Cockey's Tavern, the distance short enough to feel like a continuation of the evening rather than a departure.

The door closed behind them. The noise below softened and fell away.

The day had been full enough. The night didn't ask to be marked.

Later, much later, Westminster quieted. Drums fell silent. Fires burned down to embers. The world resumed its ordinary shape.

No one remarked on the night that followed.

II

Thursday, July 12, 1860
Eight days later

The springhouse lay just beyond the garden, its stone walls half-set into the slope, cool even in midsummer. Hannah had passed it countless times before, but this was the first morning she approached it without purpose assigned.

She carried the lockbox under one arm.

The path was narrow, worn by use rather than design. The ground held the night's dampness, and her shoes darkened at the edges as she walked. Ash followed at first, pacing her with easy familiarity, then slowed when the path narrowed, his steps hesitant as though sensing the change before she did.

Josephus passed her on his way back to the mill. His sleeves were already rolled up. "Hannah, I've changed the safe."

She glanced up. "To what?"

"Our day."

She held his gaze for a moment. "All of it?"

"Aye. All of it."

She nodded once. "Five. Fifteen. Fifty-nine."

He dipped his head. "So long as we keep it, it will open."

A hint of a smile touched Hannah's lips. "Then we shall keep it."

Josephus left her to her work.

When Ash drew close, Hannah stopped and looked down at him. He sat at once, tail resting still against the earth, waiting.

"Not here," she whispered. She didn't gesture. She didn't scold. Hannah only laid her hand briefly against the top of his head, then straightened.

Ash watched her a moment longer, ears flicking, then rose and turned back toward the garden, disappearing between the rows without protest.

The door opened with a familiar sound, wood swelling slightly against the iron latch. Inside, the air shifted at once—cooler, heavier, carrying the clean, mineral scent of water held to stone. Light filtered in through the small opening at the far wall and scattered across the shallow channel where the spring ran steady and clear.

Hannah stood just inside and listened.

The water didn't rush. It didn't hesitate. It moved at the pace it had chosen long ago, shaping nothing it didn't intend to pass.

She reached up to the higher shelf near the back wall, where the stone jutted unevenly, and set the box there, partly hidden among the jars already cooling in the shade. The wood was cool beneath her palm. She slipped the small key from the ribbon beneath her collar and turned it once, the sound barely more than a breath. With a soft click, she lifted the lid and withdrew the small book Mary had gifted her and a pencil she'd placed there later.

The pages were blank.

Hannah didn't sit at once. She walked the length of the room instead, noting the places where the stone had been worn smooth by hands setting jars, the faint marks where shelves had been moved and moved again. This was not a place for keeping things untouched. It was a place for tending.

She sat finally, not on the bench but on the low stone ledge near the water, her skirts gathered carefully beneath her. The sound of the spring filled the space without demanding attention.

She opened the book.

For a time, she did nothing more than rest her hand against the page, feeling the slight resistance of the paper beneath her fingers. The quiet held. Not empty, but expectant.

When Hannah wrote, it wasn't at the top of the page. She left space.

The words came slowly, not because she lacked them, but because she was choosing which ones were worth keeping. She wrote of the house as it was now, of the way the light fell across the table in the mornings, of the garden rows beginning to hold their shape. She wrote of the mill only in passing, as though it were a given rather than a concern.

She didn't write of the Fourth.

She didn't write of Jacob.

She paused once, listening to the water again, then continued.

The entry wasn't long.

When Hannah finished, she closed the book and set it and the pencil back inside the box, turning the key once before slipping it beneath her dress again. The box she pushed farther back on the shelf, out of sight unless one knew to look for it. The sound was slight, final enough to satisfy.

She stood and brushed the grit from her hands. Before leaving, she touched the stone beside the channel, just once, feeling the cold seep briefly into her skin.

Outside, the day had warmed. The garden waited. Ash lay in the shade at its edge, head lifting when he saw her.

Hannah closed the door behind her and didn't lock it. Ash settled again when she passed without stopping.

The springhouse returned to its work.

III

Friday, July 27, 1860
Fifteen days later

The sound reached them before the shape did.

John Dorsey, who kept the sluice true and the hands steady, heard it first: something between a cough and a call, caught and released by the bend. He stopped where he was, one hand still on the sluice lever, and listened.

It came again. Faint. Strained.

"Hold," he said without raising his voice.

The men paused. The mill was already awake, the wheel turning steady. Dorsey stepped away from the mechanism and followed the sound upstream, keeping to the bank where the grass lay pressed flat by use.

They saw him then. A man clung to the log chain strung across the creek, his arms wrapped tight around one of the larger timbers, his legs dragging uselessly in the current. The chain had done its work. It caught what didn't belong, but this was no debris. His head hung forward, chin pressed to his chest, breath coming in sharp, uneven pulls.

"Christ's blood," one of the hands muttered.

Dorsey was already moving. He waded in without hesitation; the water climbing fast around his thighs. Another man followed, then another. Together they worked the chain loose, pulling the log toward the bank, their boots sliding on stone, their grips sure.

When they hauled him out, the man collapsed at once, shaking so hard his teeth rattled. His clothes were soaked through; the fabric torn and slick with mud. His hands were raw where he had gripped the chain.

Elias Koontz arrived as they pulled the man clear of the water. He took in the scene at a glance and said nothing. Josephus came moments later, breath quickened from the walk, his eyes already searching for cause.

The man lifted his head slightly, enough to speak. "Please," he said. "Please."

Dorsey crouched beside him. "Isaac?"

Isaac blinked, squinting as though the world were too bright. "John? That you?"

Dorsey nodded once. "It is."

Isaac's shoulders sagged, the fight leaving him all at once.

IV

They settled Isaac in the shade near the barn, wrapping him in what dry cloth they could find. Water was brought. Someone stood watch without being told.

Ash lingered a little way off, nose low to the ground, circling once before stopping where he could see without being in the way. He didn't approach the man against the wall. He watched the hands instead.

Elias pulled Josephus aside. "You know what this is."

Josephus didn't answer at once. His eyes were still on Isaac, whose hands wrapped around the cup Dorsey held steady.

"Aye. I know," Josephus said finally.

Elias's voice didn't change. "He's a fugitive. Under the law, we are required to report him."

Josephus looked at him. "And if we don't?"

Elias held his gaze. "Then we are harboring stolen property.

That's what they'll call it."

Ash shifted his weight and sat, ears angled toward the road rather than the barn.

Hannah came to them then, her face pale but steady. She'd seen enough to understand. "He came from the creek."

"Aye," Josephus said.

She looked past them to where Isaac sat. "Where is he from?"

Josephus hesitated, finally meeting her eyes. "Trevanion."

The word landed hard.

Ash lifted his head at the sound of it, then lowered it again, resting his chin on his paws.

Hannah didn't speak for a moment. When she did, her voice was low. "They whip men who are caught."

Elias nodded. "Or worse, if they choose."

Josephus clenched his jaw, the muscles in his face tensing with resolve. "We can't send him back."

"That may not be our choice," Elias said. "Not if they come looking."

Hannah's eyes lifted. "Pennsylvania."

Elias considered it. "It's possible," he said. "But only just. And only if we move fast."

Josephus said nothing. He was already weighing distance, time, and consequence.

"Bixler, or even Dallas himself, will come here first," Elias added. "Creek or road. This place is the nearest."

Ash rose and took a few steps toward the barn door, then stopped, as if listening for something that hadn't yet arrived.

Hannah didn't look away. "Then we decide before they arrive."

V

Isaac sat upright now, his hands steadier, his breathing slowed.

When they entered, he rose, swaying only slightly.

Josephus raised a hand. "Stay."

Isaac obeyed, watching them.

Elias spoke plainly. He explained the law, the danger, and the narrowness of the window. He didn't soften it.

Isaac listened without interruption. “My wife be in North Carolina,” he said when Elias finished. “She there still.”

Josephus’s chest tightened. “If you go south—”

“I won’t make it,” Isaac said. Not bitter. Only certain.

Elias nodded. “Your best chance is north. Pennsylvania. Work. Save. Find a way back for her later.”

Isaac looked at Josephus then. “I won’t put your name to this,” he said. “If it come to it.”

Josephus met his gaze, a flicker of understanding passing between them. “We’ll try.”

They agreed after that. Too quickly to be brave.

Josephus would take the carriage. Hannah and Emma would keep the house as usual. Elias would manage the mill. No one would speak of it beyond those present.

Josephus turned to go.

He didn’t get far.

VI

The sound of hooves came sharp and sudden, too close to ignore.

Ash lifted his head at once and moved to Hannah’s side without being called, standing just ahead of her, angled outward, ears forward, tail low and still.

Jacob arrived first, Brimstone reined hard, his expression already set. Silas followed with two other men. Behind them came County Sheriff William Segafoose, mounted and calm.

Silas dismounted and nodded to Josephus. “We’re looking for a man,” he said civilly.

Jacob moved first. His eyes were already on the carriage. “Where you off to, brother? Business across the line?” Josephus didn’t answer him. Jacob turned to Segafoose. “You know my brother. Always doing the right thing. Helping where he shouldn’t.”

Segafoose’s expression didn’t change. “We shall see.”

They moved toward the barn.

Isaac stepped out before they reached the door. He fell to his knees in an act of surrender. “I’m here! I was hidin’ on my own!”

Ash stiffened but didn’t advance, his gaze fixed on the

movement, his weight settled back on his haunches as if holding himself in place.

Jacob laughed. "Liar!"

Dorsey came into view behind the crowd of mill hands, his posture straight, his face closed. The Koontz children also watched from a respectable distance.

Jacob spun toward him and pointed. "Him!" he shouted. "Ask that nigger there! They help their own!"

The word hung in the air, sharp and wrong.

Ash took one step forward before stopping himself, a low sound gathering in his chest and dying there without voice.

The silence held before Segafoose raised a hand. "That's enough, Mr. Marlowe."

Jacob didn't stop. He turned to point at Josephus. "Arrest him! Arrest my brother! He's an abolitionist!"

Segafoose looked at Josephus. Then at Isaac. Then back at Jacob. "I see no proof of that."

Silas's jaw clenched, his mouth forming a grim line.

Segafoose continued. "We have the slave. If Mr. Dallas wishes to pursue the matter further, that is his prerogative."

Jacob's face flushed. "This is how we stop him! This place!"

Segafoose shook his head once. "Not today, Mr. Marlowe."

They took Isaac, placed him in chains, and led him toward Silas's horse. Isaac would have to walk the distance to Trevanion while the others rode.

Ash watched until Isaac was out of sight, then turned his head away, choosing instead to press closer to Hannah's skirts, his flank touching her leg, steadying.

Jacob stayed, glaring at his brother. There were no more secrets. Jacob tipped his hand.

When the yard was empty again, Hannah spoke. "What will happen to him?"

Jacob turned his head without facing her, already walking away. "Belsnickel."

VII

Wednesday, August 1, 1860
Five days later

Hannah didn't go back to the springhouse straight away.

With Silas Bixler and Sheriff Segafoose having taken Isaac, the subsequent days were occupied by the usual routines: preparing food, balancing ledgers, tending the garden, no matter the readiness of those involved. The mill ran. The wheel turned.

Elias didn't alter the schedule. Josephus didn't suggest that he should. They didn't speak of what had happened. They spoke of weather. Of yields. Of whether the second cutting would come in clean. Hannah listened and answered when addressed. She didn't press. She didn't withdraw. Whatever shifted had done so beneath the surface, where it wouldn't show easily.

On the fifth morning, Josephus left early again.

Hannah waited until the house had settled into its quiet before she took the path toward the springhouse. Ash followed her as far as the edge of the garden, then stopped. He watched her a moment, ears lifting, then turned back on his own and lay down in the shade, the boundary already understood.

The air had cooled slightly overnight. The ground still held the impression of damp where shade lingered. Hannah walked more slowly than she had before, not from reluctance but attention. The world felt narrower, as though it required more exact placement of the body within it.

Inside, the springhouse was as she'd left it.

The water moved steadily along its channel, clear and untroubled. The stone walls held the cold without complaint. The space did not acknowledge what had passed beyond it.

Hannah stood for a moment, listening.

She reached up to the higher shelf near the back wall and drew the lockbox forward, setting it carefully where the light could reach it. The jars beside it were cool to the touch. She slipped the small key from the ribbon beneath her dress and turned it once.

The diary lay where she'd left it.

Hannah sat on the low stone ledge near the water, her skirts arranged with care. When she opened the book this time, she didn't hesitate.

She wrote of the morning Isaac arrived—only the facts. The sound from the creek. The men at work. The way the chain had held.

She wrote briefly of the law as Elias had explained it: that a man could be taken without trial, that help itself could be named a crime, that across the line in Pennsylvania the law did not reach as cleanly, though nothing there was guaranteed. She didn't elaborate. The words stood on their own.

She didn't write Jacob's name.

She wrote of choice instead. Of what it meant to decide and still be overruled. Of how care didn't always carry the authority one expected it to.

Her hand stilled once. She listened to the water again, as though it might answer.

It did not.

When she finished, she closed the book and returned it to the box. She turned the key and slipped it back beneath her collar; the weight settled against her skin. The box she pushed farther back on the shelf, out of sight.

Before leaving, she placed her hand briefly against the stone beside the channel. The cold seeped into her palm, sharp enough to ground her.

Outside, the day warmed. The garden waited. Ash lifted his head when she emerged and rose.

Hannah closed the door behind her. Ash fell into step beside her without comment.

The springhouse returned to its keeping.

VIII

From the Carroll County Democrat
Thursday, August 9, 1860

TO THE EDITOR OF THE CARROLL COUNTY DEMOCRAT

Mr. Joseph Shaw,

There comes a time when silence, mistaken for tolerance, must give way to plain speech. Recent events in our county compel such speech, however unpleasant the task.

It has come to my attention, through sources both credible and concerned, that a certain mill on Big Pipe Creek, long held up by some as a model of virtue, has engaged in conduct that cannot be reconciled with either the laws of this State or the duties of responsible citizenship.

I refer, plainly, to the unlawful harboring of a fugitive slave, in direct violation of the Fugitive Slave Act of 1850, a statute enacted by Congress and binding upon all who claim the protection of the Union. This was no act of momentary confusion or error. The individual in question was concealed upon the property while preparations were made to convey him across the Pennsylvania line, under the pretense of ordinary business. That Pennsylvania has seen fit to indulge in so-called "non-cooperation" does not absolve Marylanders of their obligations under federal law.

Let us be clear: to assist in the escape of property legally held is theft. To conceal such an act beneath a cloak of moral exhibitionism is worse.

That such conduct should emanate from a man of standing in the community is troubling enough. That it should be excused, or even praised, by those who mistake sentiment for virtue is more troubling still. Law does not exist to flatter individual conscience. It exists to preserve order. When men decide which laws bind them and which do not, they set themselves above the very society from which they profit.

Nor is this the first instance in which this establishment has seen fit to overstep its proper bounds. Readers will recall recent disruptions at the County Almshouse, an institution already burdened by expense and disorder. Into that fragile system, certain parties chose to inject unsolicited aid, distributing stores without oversight, thereby encouraging dependency and prolonging abuses that recent reforms were at last beginning to address. Charity that disregards structure is not benevolence; it is interference.

We are told such acts are humble. I find them conspicuous. We are told they are quiet. I find them loudly self-regarding.

Meanwhile, long-established enterprises, law-abiding, tax-paying, and accountable, are asked to suffer the consequences of competition distorted by moral grandstanding. One wonders how many local hands must go idle before the county asks whether righteousness, so selectively applied, has become a liability.

This is not a question of slavery or freedom, as some would have it. It is a question of order. Of whether we remain a county governed by law, or whether we permit individual actors to redraw its boundaries according to private conviction.

I trust that the good people of Carroll County are equal to this distinction.

Respectfully submitted,

William W. Dallas
Trevanion

IX

From the American Sentinel
Thursday, August 16, 1860

A QUESTION OF CHARACTER, NOT NOISE

Last week's issue of the *Democrat* devoted considerable space to an alarmed letter to the citizens of Carroll County that law itself is imperiled, this time, not by corruption, neglect, or misuse of public funds, but by a mill that minds its own business too carefully.

Readers will note the strategy. We are asked to look past a year of documented abuse at the County Almshouse and focus instead on a single, unnamed man, stripped of circumstance, history, and humanity, and transformed into an abstract violation. We are told this is order.

Order, however, is not preserved by shouting statutes while ignoring conduct.

The mill on Big Pipe Creek stands accused of two things: quiet charity and restraint. It did not advertise its gifts. It did not seek praise. It did not petition the county. It did not profit. It gave from its own stores and returned to its work.

That such behavior should be reframed as "interference" would be remarkable were it not so familiar.

We are further informed that obedience to federal law must be absolute, even when that law requires private citizens to act as agents of cruelty. This argument would carry more weight if it were not advanced by the same interests that recently protested public oversight of the Almshouse on grounds of inconvenience and expense. One is left to wonder whether the objection lies with disorder or with the loss of discretion.

As to competition: if honest labor is now to be faulted for the failure of others to retain their contracts, we have reached a curious understanding of commerce. Fairlight did not take business by force. It earned it. That some prefer mills that sell to the county rather than serve it quietly is not a moral principle. It is a preference.

The people of Carroll County are not children to be frightened by raised voices or Latin phrases. They know the difference between exhibition and example. They know which enterprises call attention to themselves, and which would rather be left alone.

Let us dispense, then, with insinuation. The issue before us is not lawlessness, nor rebellion, nor decay. It is whether this community will be guided by those who profit from disorder, or by those who work, give, and ask nothing in return.

On that question, the record speaks clearly.

William H. Grammer
Editor, *American Sentinel*

X

Sunday, August 19, 1860
Nineteen days later

Hannah went to the springhouse later than usual.

The path was familiar now, worn smooth by her passing, but she walked it more slowly, aware of how often she'd been stopped that week—how many hands had taken hers, how many voices had spoken her name with warmth she'd not invited.

Ash followed her as far as the bend where the garden fell away into shade, then stopped. He stood there a moment, watching her go, before turning back on his own and disappearing between the rows.

She didn't look back.

Hannah didn't begrudge the kindness. That wasn't the trouble.

The trouble was the attention.

It had followed her into town, into the market, into the spaces where work was meant to be done quietly. People thanked her for things she had not done alone. They praised Fairlight as though it were a performance rather than a place that held.

She opened the springhouse door and stepped inside, closing it behind her with more care than before.

The air was cool, the stone steady beneath her hand. The water ran as it always had, indifferent to reputation. That constancy eased something in her chest, even as it unsettled her.

She reached for the lockbox, drew it down from its shelf, and unlocked it without thought. The diary opened easily to the last page she'd written.

She didn't add much. Only a few lines. A question, half-formed. A note about the way sound carried differently now, as though the world had grown closer. She paused more than she wrote, listening to the water, pressing her fingers lightly against the page as if to keep herself from drifting too far.

Hannah felt tired in a way that sleep hadn't touched.

When she closed the book, her hands trembled slightly. She waited until they stilled before replacing it and turning the key. The ribbon settled again beneath her collar.

Before leaving, she stood with her back to the wall and let the cool stone press between her shoulders.

The water moved on.

She didn't stay long.

Outside, the garden lay quiet. Ash lifted his head when she emerged, rose, and fell in beside her without sound, as though he'd been there all along.

XI

The house was quiet when Hannah returned.

She set her things down and stood a moment longer than she meant to in the front room, listening for sounds that weren't there. The stillness felt heavier than it should have.

Ash settled and lay near the hearth, lifting his head as she passed, tail stirring once before settling again. He watched her enter the room and cross, then rested his chin back on his paws, content to let her pass without following.

She sat, then stood again.

When the tears came, they surprised her. Not for their strength, but for how quickly they arrived. She didn't sob. She pressed her hand to her mouth and turned away from the door, ashamed of the sound she might make.

She didn't hear Josephus come in.

He stopped short when he saw her, one hand still holding the garment he'd come to fetch. For a moment, he only watched, uncertain whether to intrude.

"Hannah," he whispered.

She turned at the sound of his voice, wiping at her face with the back of her hand.

"I'm sorry," she said, though she didn't know what she was apologizing for.

He crossed the room, set the garment aside, and took her hands in his without asking. His grip was firm, familiar, steadying.

"You needn't be," he said.

She shook her head. "I don't know why I feel this way. Everyone has been so kind. And I—" She stopped, frustrated by her own voice. "I feel as though I'm being watched. Measured."

Josephus said nothing. He drew her closer instead, resting his forehead against hers.

"You are not a thing to be displayed," he said. "You never were."

She closed her eyes. "I know."

His thumb brushed lightly across her knuckles. "Whatever comes, we meet it here."

Hannah breathed out slowly; the tension easing from her shoulders.

Josephus smiled then, just slightly. "It's you. It's me."

She looked up at him, the last of the tears drying on her cheeks. Her voice was steady when she answered, smiling softly. "It's us."

He nodded once, as if sealing something already decided, and held her until the quiet returned to its proper shape.

XII

Silas Bixler rode in alone.

It was late afternoon at Fairlight when he came up the lane, the sun already lowering toward the trees. The mill was running, the wheel turning at its usual pace. Nothing paused for his arrival.

Josephus saw him first from the doorway and felt the familiar tightening of recognition. He stepped down from the threshold and waited.

Silas dismounted carefully, dusting his hands on his trousers as though this were any other visit. He didn't look toward the mill right away. He nodded, polite and composed.

"Marlowe," he said. "I won't take much of your time."

"Bixler," Josephus said, dipping his head. "Speak."

Silas glanced around the yard, taking in the order of it—the stacked grain, the clean lines of the race, the absence of idleness. His mouth tightened briefly, then relaxed.

"There's been a lot of noise. More than is good for any of us," Silas said. Josephus said nothing. "The papers have had their say. Accounts have shifted. Feelings have been stirred." He shrugged slightly. "It happens."

"What is it you want?" Josephus asked.

Silas met his eyes. "To put an end to it."

Josephus folded his arms. "You've tried."

Silas didn't deny it. "And it hasn't gone as planned." He paused, choosing his words. "Which is precisely why I'm here."

He took a step closer, lowering his voice. Not conspiratorial, but practical. "Mr. Dallas believes there's no sense in continuing this back and forth. It serves no one. Certainly not the county."

Josephus's jaw tightened. "Then he's welcome to stop."

Silas nodded. "That's what we're proposing." The word hung between them. "A meeting. Neutral ground. Union Church in Taneytown. Just us. No papers. No witnesses. We clear the air and see if there's a way forward that doesn't leave everyone poorer for it."

Josephus studied him with a keen and appraising gaze. "You don't speak for Jacob."

Silas's expression flickered just once. "Jacob's…enthusiasms…are his own. This is business."

"And business requires that I leave my mill?"

"Briefly," Silas replied. "After services, perhaps. In view of the public. Respectable."

Josephus looked past him, toward the water, the steady turn of the wheel. "Why now?"

Silas hesitated. Not long enough to matter, but long enough to register. "Because matters have changed," he said. "And because we'd prefer not to see them change further."

Josephus turned back to him. "I shall consider it."

Silas nodded, satisfied with that much. "Good." He mounted his horse again without lingering. "Sunday, then. I'll expect you."

Josephus didn't correct him.

Silas rode out the way he'd come, leaving the yard unchanged.

The mill ran on.

Ash watched him go from the edge of the porch, standing still until horse and rider disappeared beyond the bend. Then he turned and stepped back inside.

Only when Silas was gone did Hannah step forward from where she'd been standing inside the doorway. "Do you trust him?"

Josephus took a moment before replying. "No."

XIII

Josephus and Hannah went to Marlowe Farm, as they often did on Sundays, without announcing it as a decision.

The light was already softening when they arrived; the fields holding the day's warmth. The house stood unchanged, its posture familiar enough to feel like a relief. Mary and Molly were in the kitchen when they entered, sleeves rolled, the smell of supper already settled into the rooms.

Christian rose from his chair by the window when he saw them and nodded once, taking in their expressions without comment.

"You'll stay," Mary said, not asking.

"Yes," Hannah said.

They ate together, as they always did. The meal was plain. The talk carried more weight. Christian listened more than he spoke, his attention moving between Josephus and Hannah with quiet precision.

It was only after the table had been cleared and Mary had stepped back into the kitchen that Josephus spoke. "Silas Bixler came to Fairlight."

Christian didn't react. "When?"

"This afternoon."

"And?"

"He proposed a meeting," Josephus said. "Neutral ground. After services at Union Church in town. To put an end to things."

Christian folded his hands loosely in his lap. "Did he say why now?"

"He said matters had changed."

"They have," Christian said, nodding once.

Hannah watched him closely. "You don't think the offer is sincere?"

Christian met her eyes. "No."

Josephus shifted. "You don't think there's any good to be had from it."

"I think," Christian said carefully, "they want you somewhere other than Fairlight, on a time and day of their choosing."

The words settled heavily.

Josephus frowned. "Why?"

Christian looked at him then, fully. "Because they have exhausted every other means of forcing your hand. Law failed. Reputation failed. Trade failed." He paused. "This is misdirection."

Hannah's breath caught slightly. "You think they mean harm."

"I think that men who feel themselves losing control will reach for what remains."

Josephus leaned forward. "If I don't go—"

"—they will be angered," Christian finished. "Aye."

"And if I do?"

Christian hesitated before answering. When he did, his voice was low. "Then you leave what you have built unattended."

The room stood quiet.

Mary reentered and stood near the doorway, her hands folded in her apron. She didn't speak, but her presence steadied the space.

Josephus exhaled slowly. "If I refuse, they will say I'm unreasonable."

"They already say worse," Christian replied.

Hannah turned to Josephus. "You don't owe them access."

He looked at her, searching her face. "No."

Christian nodded. "Standing them up will cost you their goodwill."

Josephus gave a short, humorless breath. "I cannot pay with currency I don't have, Father."

Christian's mouth curved, just barely. "Then you lose nothing by refusing."

Josephus sat back. The decision had already taken shape, but hearing it spoken made it real. "I shan't go."

Christian reached out then, resting his hand briefly over Josephus's. "You've made the right choice."

Hannah felt the words settle into her bones—not as comfort, but as certainty.

They stayed a while longer, speaking of small things: of the weather, the harvest, and work that needed doing. When they rose to leave, the night had deepened fully, the path ahead lit only by what they carried with them.

When they stepped out into the yard, Hannah glanced back once at the house.

Christian stood in the doorway, watching them go.

He didn't wave.

XIV

Sunday, August 26, 1860
A week later

Hannah went to the springhouse before the day had decided itself.

The air was close, the kind of late-summer morning that carried heat before it arrived.

Ash followed her as far as the garden's edge, then stopped. He stood there a moment, watching her cross the open ground, ears lifting once at a sound only he could hear. When she didn't turn back, he lay down in the shade and didn't rise again.

The path felt different under her feet, though nothing about it had changed. The grass bent where it usually did. The stones lay where they'd lain for over a year now. And yet she found herself counting her steps, as though distance might shift if she didn't pay attention.

Inside, the cool struck her at once.

She closed the door behind her and leaned back against it, pressing her shoulders into the wood until she felt its resistance. The spring ran on, clear and untroubled, its sound filling the small room without pause or question.

This place had never asked anything of her.

That was what had made it safe.

She crossed to the channel and knelt, resting her hands on the stone edge. The water moved past her fingers without acknowledgment. She let them stay there longer than she intended, the cold seeping upward until it steadied her breathing.

"I know," she said quietly.

She wasn't sure who she was speaking to. The water didn't answer. It didn't need to.

She reached for the lockbox then, drawing it down from its hiding place with care. The key lay warm beneath her collar. She held it a moment before using it, feeling the slight weight of it against her palm.

The diary opened easily.

She didn't write at once.

Instead, she listened. Not just to the water, but to the sounds beyond the walls: the distant turn of the wheel, the muted movement of the house, the world continuing as though nothing were amiss.

When she wrote, the words came unevenly.

She wrote of fear without naming it. Of the way kindness could draw attention. Of how order, once disrupted, didn't always return to its former shape. She wrote that there were places meant for keeping, and places meant for passing through, and that she was no longer certain which Fairlight had become.

Her hand pressed harder into the page than she'd planned. Hannah paused, breathing through it, then softened her grip.

She didn't write Josephus's name.

She didn't write Jacob's.

She wrote instead of holding. Of what it meant to build something not to be admired, but to be used. Of the danger of being seen too clearly by those who wished to unmake rather than understand.

At last, she stopped.

The entry was longer than the others. Not because it said more, but because it circled what it couldn't say directly.

She closed the book and returned it to the box. The key turned once, the sound small and final. She slipped it back beneath her dress and pushed the box farther into shadow than before, adjusting the jars around it until the shelf looked unchanged.

She stood then and rested her forehead briefly against the stone wall.

"Keep it," she said, though she didn't know what she meant by *it*.

The springhouse remained cool. The water ran on.

When Hannah opened the door, the light outside seemed sharper than it had been when she entered. She stepped into it slowly, closing the door behind her with deliberate care. The day brightened. The garden lay quiet. Ash was no longer where she'd left him.

She didn't look back.

XV

Sunday came and went without remark.

At Fairlight, the morning unfolded in its usual course. The mill didn't run. The wheel rested. The house kept its ordinary stillness, shaped by habit rather than expectation.

Josephus rose early. He didn't dress with unusual care. He didn't linger.

Hannah watched him from the doorway as he stepped outside, the light already gathering in the yard. He went about the small tasks that didn't announce themselves: checking the gate, walking the length of the fence, standing a moment longer than necessary near the race.

Nothing in his manner suggested avoidance.

Nothing suggested preparation.

By the hour Josephus would've left for Taneytown, he was still there.

Hannah said nothing.

They shared a midday meal, plain and unhurried. Josephus spoke once of the weather, once of the fields. Hannah answered when addressed. The house didn't hold its breath. It didn't release it either.

At the Union Church, the hour passed.

Silas Bixler waited.

He stood near the edge of the grounds after services ended, watching people disperse in small groups, their conversations turning toward suppers and afternoon rest. He checked the road once, then again, waiting longer than politeness allowed.

Josephus did not come.

By late afternoon, his absence was no longer a misunderstanding.

Silas mounted his horse without display and rode back the way he'd come, his face set, his posture unchanged. Those who noticed him didn't remark upon it. There was nothing to remark upon.

At Fairlight, the day closed as days do.

Josephus and Hannah walked the grounds together before dusk, speaking of nothing that mattered and everything that did. When night fell, the house settled around them.

The mill slept.

No message arrived. No word was sent.

The absence held.

XVI

The air at Trevanion had turned sour long before anyone named it.

Silas returned near dusk and dismounted without speaking. He didn't seek out Dallas. He didn't need to. He found Jacob instead, standing near the edge of the yard where the light faded first. "He didn't come."

Jacob's mouth twitched. "Of course he didn't."

"We offered him a way out," Silas said, exhaling slowly.

Jacob laughed once, sharp and humorless. "You offered him permission to survive."

Silas's gaze flicked toward the main house, then back. "That was more than we owed him."

"And he refused," Jacob said, stepping closer.

"Yes."

Jacob's smile faded. "Then he's made his choice."

Silas studied him, a flicker of curiosity in his expression. "This isn't how we discussed it."

"You discussed it," Jacob said, his voice dropping. "I listened."

Silas stilled. "You don't speak for Mr. Dallas."

"No," Jacob said. "But I know what he can't afford."

Silas didn't answer.

Jacob gestured toward the mill road, dark now, empty. "Fairlight's taken accounts we won't get back. The papers made sure of that. Hands are already whispering."

A muscle twitched in Silas's jaw as his anger built. He peered at Jacob. "We'll adjust."

"With what?" Jacob pressed. "You'll let men go. I'll be first. You know it." Silas's silence confirmed it. Jacob straightened. "It would be a shame if something happened to Fairlight."

Silas turned sharply. "You're out of line, Marlowe!"

Jacob met his eyes. "Am I?"

The night pressed closer around them. Somewhere beyond the yard, water moved.

Silas looked away first. "We didn't speak of this."

"No," Jacob said, nodding.

They stood there a moment longer, neither of them moving, neither of them retreating.

Then Silas turned toward the tenant house.

Jacob didn't follow. He remained where he was, watching the dark road that led back to Big Pipe Creek, his hands loose at his sides, his breath steady.

Permission didn't need to be spoken.

It had already been given.

XVII

Sunday, September 2, 1860
A week later

The night had settled into its second quiet.

Not the first sleep, when the body is still negotiating with the day, nor the last hour before dawn when the birds begin to stir and the mind starts its slow return. This was the middle space, the small, private interval some called the dorveille, when a man might wake and find himself wholly alone with the sound of his own breathing.

Hannah heard the sound after the dorveille began.

She was busy with her hands, with one of Josephus's trousers across her lap, the fabric worn thin at the knee where work and habit met. The lamp cast a steady circle of light over the stitches as she guided the needle through, careful not to pull the thread too tight. Ash lay at her feet, chin on his paws, the slow rise and fall of his breathing keeping time.

The sound came from the woods beyond the mill. A sharp crack, followed by the rush of breaking limbs. It traveled unevenly, as though something had given way and taken others with it.

Hannah paused, needle held still, one hand resting on the cloth.

Ash lifted his head but didn't rise. His ears angled toward the window, then settled again.

Josephus looked up from where he was setting aside his coat. “Old tree.”

She nodded.

The sound came again. Closer this time, then finished all at once.

Hannah waited, listening for what sometimes followed such noises: the hooting of an owl, the scattering of deer, even the howl of a surprised animal.

Nothing did.

The house held its shape around her. The lamp didn’t flicker. The mill wheel continued its measured turn, water answering stone as it always had.

Ash lowered his head and sighed; the slight sound of it oddly reassuring.

Hannah set the needle back to its work. The thread slid through cleanly. The patch would hold.

By morning, the fallen tree would be cleared or left where it lay.

Either way, the day would begin.

XVIII

At the tenant house, Elias Koontz sat at the table with a lamp turned low, the flame trimmed down to a narrow tongue of light.

Emma had gone back to bed. The children slept in the next room, their bodies in the careless angles of youth. The summer air pressed close even at night, and the windows had been left open to let what little breeze there was move through.

Elias had work he could do without making noise. Numbers didn’t require daylight.

He checked his own figures first—feed, flour, nails, a new hinge for the smokehouse door—then set them aside and stared for a time at the empty margin where Fairlight’s accounts would later sit. He could have waited until morning. He did not.

He rose, took his cap from the peg, and stepped out into the yard.

The air smelled of creek water and mown grass. The mill lay downhill, black against the darker line of trees. Above it, the main house, Fairlight, held its lights shuttered, some of its windows open for air.

Elias walked the short distance up to the door and knocked once, firm enough to be heard, not enough to alarm.

Footsteps came after a moment. The latch lifted.

Josephus stood there in shirtsleeves, hair slightly disordered, eyes clear despite the hour. He had the look of a man who slept lightly even when he slept.

"Elias," he said.

"Sorry to wake you," Elias replied. He didn't sound sorry; he sounded practical. "I wanted the ledger. I can make use of the hour."

Josephus glanced past him into the dark yard, then nodded. "Come in."

He didn't light more lamps. Instead, he moved by memory, crossing the room and reaching for the shelf where he kept what mattered. Josephus brought down the book, thick and plain, its cover worn at the corners.

Elias took it with both hands, not from reverence but from habit. A dropped ledger was a ruined week. "I shall have it back before morning."

Josephus's mouth curved slightly. "You always do."

Elias turned to go, then paused.

The house was quiet behind Josephus, the kind of quiet that held presence. Elias saw, in the dim, the edge of Hannah's sewing basket near the chair; the faint outline of fabric folded carefully. A domestic marker left where it belonged.

Josephus followed his glance, then looked back at Elias. "She's sleeping," he said quietly, not as apology, only as fact.

Elias nodded. "Good."

He stepped out again into the night, the ledger tucked under his arm.

Behind him, Josephus closed the door and returned upstairs to the bed without waking what he didn't need to wake.

Outside, the creek ran on.

XIX

Elias had just set the ledger on the table after checking on Emma and the kids when the smell reached him.

It came through the open window. A thin, sharp tang that didn't belong to summer air or lamp oil. At first, he thought it was Fairlight's hearth stirred too late, a stray ember. But Josephus had returned to bed. Then he recognized the smell for what it was.

Pitch.

Burning wood.

His body reacted before his mind finished naming it. He was on his feet, lamp forgotten, moving toward the door.

Outside, the night had shifted.

Downhill, at the line where the mill ought to have been a darker shadow, there was light—wrong light, living and restless. A flicker climbed and fell. Then another. And then, as his eyes adjusted, he saw it.

The wheel was burning.

The great wooden spokes that had turned so faithfully on Big Pipe Creek were lit from within, flame running along the rim as though it had been painted there. Pieces broke away and dropped into the water, hissing once before the creek swallowed them. The fire didn't care. It fed on what remained.

Elias stood frozen for only the length of a breath.

Then he turned sharply toward the hill.

Fairlight rose above the mill. The barn stood to one side of it, nearer the line of fields. And the barn—the barn was already caught.

It wasn't merely smoking. It was engulfed, flame licking up the sides and into the loft as if it had been waiting for permission. The roofline glowed red; the timbers showing through like ribs.

The stables, which were set apart from the barn, hadn't been lit. The sound of panicking horses filled the air, echoing across the property.

"Emma!" Elias shouted, his voice breaking the night open. "Emma, wake!"

He ran outside. Behind him, Emma's voice rose from the tenant house, sharp with fear, calling the children by name.

Elias turned to shout into the house. "Samuel, to the stables! Free the horses before it catches. They'll find their way back."

"Ja, Papa," Samuel called back.

Elias ran for Fairlight, boots pounding the packed earth, lungs filling with smoke as he climbed. He reached the yard and saw the worst of it at once: the lower level of the main house had begun to catch, not in one place, but along the line where flame could take and travel. The wraparound porch glowed in patches. The air thickened fast.

A bucket brigade from the springhouse would have been a gesture, not a rescue.

Elias cupped his hands and shouted toward the upper windows. "*JOSEPHUS!*"

Again: "*JOSEPHUS! WAKE!*"

The house didn't answer.

Seconds later, a window above shifted. A shadow moved behind it.

Elias felt something in his chest loosen, not relief—relief wasn't possible—but recognition that the moment of sleeping was over. Now there was only decision.

Emma appeared at the edge of the yard with the children in their shirts, hair wild, eyes wide. The younger ones clung to her skirts.

"Get the blanket!" Elias snapped, pointing without looking. "The wool one. Now!"

Louisa, old enough to obey without question, ran back inside, while Emma pulled the other children closer, her mouth moving in prayer or command. Elias didn't know which.

Above, the upstairs window opened wider. Smoke spilled out, thick as cloth.

XX

In the bedroom, Josephus woke as though dragged.

Heat reached him before the sound. It pressed against his skin in a steady wave, too constant to be a hearth, too close to be summer. The air in the room tasted wrong. He drew breath and felt the bite of smoke in his throat.

Josephus sat up sharply and saw the flicker of orange reflected not from a lamp but from the walls themselves.

"Hannah," he said, the word rough.

She stirred at the sound of his voice, blinking, confused, then coughing as the smoke found her lungs. The second cough was worse. It bent her.

Josephus swung his feet to the floor. The boards beneath his soles were already warming. He crossed the room to where her dress lay folded over the chair and thrust it toward her.

"Dress," he said, more command than gentleness. "As you can."

She didn't ask why. She saw Josephus's face and understood. "What is it?"

"Fire!" he said. "The house is on fire!"

Hannah's hands shook as she reached for the dress. Josephus pulled on his trousers, not bothering with boots. He moved to the door and put his hand to the latch.

The metal burned him instantly.

Josephus jerked back, breath catching.

The other side was already blazing. He could hear it now—the low roar of it, the crackle of it feeding on boards and air.

Smoke thickened in the room, sinking from the ceiling. Hannah coughed again, longer this time, eyes watering.

Josephus crossed to the nearest window, the one they kept open for air. His breath became shallow and useless as he shoved it higher and leaned out.

Below, Elias stood in the backyard, face upturned, shouting, arms raised in frantic instruction. Behind him, the barn was an inferno. The stables remained as horses began fleeing from them. Beyond that, at the bottom of the hill, the mill burned like a beacon.

Josephus didn't think of who. He didn't think of why.

He thought only: *Hannah.*

As he turned back into the room, his sight dimmed, the edges of his vision growing hazy. "Window," he said hoarsely. "We go by the window."

Hannah had managed to pull her dress on, not properly fastened. Her hair lay loose around her shoulders. She looked at him, eyes wide, and nodded once.

Josephus's gaze flicked to the back window, the one that would have taken them down toward the basement entrance. It was too far, too steep, a drop that would break bones even if the fire didn't take them first.

He looked to the front, toward the window that opened onto the porch roof. It was open, but too small for Hannah to escape quickly.

Josephus grabbed the blue velour curtains, pulled them down, and grabbed the desk chair beside the window.

The first strike splintered wood, not glass. The second found the pane and shattered it outward with a burst of sound that seemed obscene in the roar of fire. Shards scattered across the porch roof, catching the light.

Josephus leaned out and shouted into the smoke: "Front window!"

Below, Elias and Emma moved at once, dragging the wool blanket into place. Samuel met them. He and Louisa took the corners with them, arms straining, feet planted.

Hannah stepped closer to the broken window and hesitated as heat surged behind them like a living thing.

Josephus took one curtain and flung it over the sill, pressing it down over the jagged edge where broken glass remained.

"Here," he said, voice lower now. "Step on the cloth."

The smoke thickened again. Hannah's breathing turned ragged.

Josephus put his hands on her shoulders, steadying her and guiding her forward. The room swayed. Or perhaps it was his sight.

"Go," he said.

Hannah climbed into the window, her hands gripping the frame, her feet finding the cloth. She turned her head to look back at him.

Even in that moment, with fire behind and smoke between, her eyes held him.

Josephus swallowed, forcing breath into lungs that did not want it. "It's you. It's me."

"It's us," Hannah whispered.

Her face tightened, as if holding back something larger than fear.

"Hannah!" he said again, sharper now, snapping her out of her daze. "Now!"

She moved, stepping out onto the slanted porch roof, crouching instinctively as heat and wind pushed at her. The roof shingles were hot beneath her palms as she edged toward the eave.

Below, the blanket shifted as Elias called up to her.

Josephus leaned once more into the open frame. Smoke rolled low now, thick and pressing. The far wall behind him glowed in a way walls shouldn't.

"Hannah!"

She reached the edge, crouched, ready to drop.

He gripped the window frame to steady himself, feeling the heat bite through the wood. "The cellar," he said, forcing the words past the burn in his throat. "The safe."

She froze, looking up at him.

"Our day," he said. "Five. Fifteen. Fifty-nine."

Her mouth formed the numbers without sound.

"Say it."

"Five. Fifteen. Fifty-nine."

"Remember."

"I will."

"I love you, Hannah Marlowe." He nodded once. "Now."

Below, the blanket stretched wide in Elias's and Emma's hands, Samuel's arms locked, Louisa bit down on a cry as she held.

Hannah closed her eyes briefly—not long enough to linger, only long enough to gather herself—and then she let herself fall.

The blanket caught her with a heavy sag, pulling all four of them down in a single breath. Their knees buckled. The fabric bowed, and Hannah dropped through the center enough that her hips struck hard, not breaking, but jarring. She gasped, winded, then rolled to the side as hands steadied her and pulled her clear.

XXI

Josephus didn't see her land.

The angle of the porch roofline prevented it.

The room shifted. Or he had.

The floor tilted beneath him, heat rising through the boards as if the house itself were breathing.

Josephus stepped back from the window to follow. The smoke met him first. It moved low and thick, no longer drifting but pressing, filling the space he'd just occupied. His chest seized against it. He coughed once, a dry sound that cleared nothing.

The doorway to the hall was gone in the haze.

He tried to fix on the desk, the bedpost, the wall—something that would hold its shape.

But the air would not come.

He took one step and found nothing certain beneath it.

The roar deepened. Something above gave way with a crack like splitting timber.

He thought not of the fire, not of the safe, but of Hannah stepping out onto the roof and off without looking down.

That was enough.

He reached once more toward the open window. The frame felt farther away than it had been.

The smoke thickened again, dark and close.

The floor met him before Josephus understood he'd fallen.

XXII

Hannah didn't stay down.

She turned at once, scrambling upright, eyes to the window.

"Josephus!" she called, her voice still a summons and not yet a scream.

The window was empty. Smoke poured out of it in a solid sheet.

"Josephus!" she called again, louder.

Elias stepped closer to the house, squinting upward, shouting into the roar. "*Jos, come!*"

Nothing.

Hannah took a step forward, as if she could cross the yard and climb back through the fire to reach him.

Emma caught her arm, gripping hard. "No, Hannah," she said, the word raw. "No."

Hannah pulled against her, not in anger, but in refusal to accept what she was seeing.

"Josephus!" she cried again.

Still, no shape appeared in the window.

The porch roof cracked beneath the heat, the wood complaining in a long, dreadful groan.

Elias looked at Hannah, face gray with smoke, and shook his head once.

"I cannot go in," he said, as if answering a question she'd not yet spoken. "It's too hot. It's too far gone."

Hannah's breath hitched. Her eyes stayed on the window.

"Josephus," she said again, smaller now, as if calling him back from somewhere inside the room rather than outside it.

The house answered with a sharp crack as a beam gave way.

The window frame groaned as it shifted.

And still Josephus did not appear.

XXIII

Several hands were awake during the dorveille at Trevanion when the sky began to change.

The glow showed faint at first, low on the horizon, wrong for dawn, and too steady for lightning. One hand stepped out from the tenant house and stood, watching it thicken against the dark.

By the time voices rose and lanterns were fetched, hooves were already pounding the road. Jacob rode into Trevanion too fast.

Someone shouted at him to slow down. Another stepped back from the stables. A horse stamped in the yard, unsettled by the sudden charge.

Jacob hauled on the reins and swung down before Brimstone had fully stopped.

"Fire!" he shouted, and then louder, as heads turned, "Fairlight's on fire!"

The word moved faster than he had.

Men looked up from the yard. A woman appeared in the doorway of the tenant house, shawl pulled tight around her shoulders.

"What's burning?" one of them asked.

"Fairlight!" Jacob shouted again. He bent forward, hands braced on his knees, breath sawing in and out of his chest. "Josephus's place! It's gone!"

"Gone how?"

Jacob straightened. His face was streaked with sweat, a dark smear along one cheek that might've been dirt.

Or it might've been something else.

No one asked.

"It's burning," he said. "Full burn."

Silas came into view from the tenant house, already buttoning his coat. He took in Jacob, the horse lathered and restless, and the direction from which Jacob had ridden. "How do you know?"

The yard quieted around the question.

Jacob didn't hesitate. "I saw it!"

Silas held his gaze a fraction longer than he should have. He nodded once, not in agreement, but in conclusion.

That was enough. There was nothing more to say about it.

He turned to the men. "Someone ride to Christian Marlowe. Now!"

One of the younger hands was already moving, swinging up onto his horse.

Lanterns were lit. Voices rose. The night shifted, reorganizing itself around a new urgency. Jacob stepped back toward the rail and leaned against it, letting the wood take his weight. For a moment, he closed his eyes.

Fairlight.

The name moved through the yard again, no longer his to shape or control.

XXIV

Elias turned to his older son, Samuel, with a decision needing no explanation.

"Find a horse. Ride. Now. To Marlowe. Do *not* stop! Tell Christian…tell him—" His throat tightened, smoke and something else closing it. "Tell him Fairlight is burning."

Samuel didn't ask what else. He ran for the first horse he saw wandering near the tenant house.

Hannah dropped to her knees in the yard without seeming to choose it. The ground felt unreal beneath her hands. She stared at the window until her vision blurred.

Her mouth moved, saying his name again and again, each time louder, as though volume might build a bridge through smoke.

"Josephus?"

"Josephus!"

"*JOSEPHUS!*"

The last was a scream. Ragged, torn out of her, the sound of a body reaching past its own limits.

The house didn't answer. It only roared.

Behind them, at the other end of the yard, the barn collapsed in on itself with a shower of sparks that rose and scattered into the night like startled birds. The mill wheel, already broken, gave one final falling piece to the creek. The water hissed once and carried it away.

Elias held Hannah's shoulder, not gently, but firmly, keeping her from moving toward what would kill her.

Emma stood with her children pressed close, tears cutting clean lines down her face through the soot.

The roofline of Fairlight buckled.

The world narrowed to heat, smoke, and the refusal of a name to be answered.

XXV

Isaac had learned not to stop.

Stopping was how you got caught.

He'd been running since chains had been cut, since the yard had erupted, since the night decided for him.

The creek was behind him now, the cold still clinging to his legs, his breath burning sharp and thin in his chest. He'd reached higher ground where the trees thinned, and the road bent away toward nothing he knew.

That was when the sky changed.

At first, he thought it was lightning—heat without sound. Then the smell reached him.

Fire.

He slowed despite himself.

Across the fields, on the rise beyond the dark line of trees, something burned that wasn't brush, not refuse, not a farmer's clearing gone wrong. The light was too steady for an accident. It was too broad, holding its shape.

Isaac straightened, hands on his knees, and watched it climb.

He'd seen fire before. Fields burned to clear them. Slaughter pits. Punishment meant to be remembered.

This was different.

This was a house.

For a moment, only one, Isaac forgot to run.

The fire didn't roar. It breathed. The glow pulsed against the sky, deliberate as a signal. Whatever had begun there had been chosen.

Isaac felt it then; not hope, not fear, but recognition. This was what came of refusing to bend. Whatever had been set loose on that hill wouldn't stop for him, and it wouldn't stop because of him.

He turned away before the light could settle behind his eyes and ran harder than he had all night, carrying nothing with him but the knowledge that some fires were meant to be seen, and some survived only by looking away.

XXVI

When the upper floor gave way, it didn't fall in one clean moment.

It surrendered in stages. Timbers groaning, a sharp report of splitting timber, then the slow tilt of the structure as fire finally claimed what order had held. The window where Hannah had been only minutes before vanished in a cascade of flame and debris.

Hannah made a sound that wasn't a word.

Elias pulled her back as the heat surged outward, forcing them all to retreat into the yard where grass still held. They stood there, helpless, watching the house consume itself.

No one spoke Josephus's name again.

Not because they forgot. But because there was no place left for it to go.

The night filled with crack and roar, the sky above turning the color of iron under forge flame. Somewhere, far off, a dog barked once and then fell silent.

By the time Christian arrived—if he arrived before the last wall fell—there would be nothing to enter, nothing to pull apart with hands, nothing to save but those already standing outside.

And even that would not feel like saving.

Hannah remained upright only because Emma's hand stayed at her elbow, and Elias's arm didn't release her shoulder.

Her eyes never left the place where the window had been.

As the last of Fairlight's roofline folded inward, the creek kept moving below, steady enough that it could almost be mistaken for permanence.

It was not.

CHAPTER XII

Saturday, May 25, 1997

I

Again, the fire had burned down to a low bed of coals, forgotten in the pull of Ernest's storytelling.

He sat with the journal closed across his knees, his thumb resting along the worn edge of the cover as though he could feel where the words ended. The clearing had gone still. Even the creek beyond the trees seemed quieter now, its sound less certain.

Carrie hadn't moved.

She stood at the edge of the fire pit, a few steps beyond the others, staring past the fire toward the slope where Fairlight had once stood. The undergrowth thinned in places. In the dim wash of moonlight, stone showed through—low, broken lines where a porch had been. A darker rectangle where a basement had caved in and settled into the hill.

She covered her mouth with both hands, as though the sound might escape her if she didn't.

Ryan rose, then stopped, unsure whether touching her would help or undo her entirely.

"But they did everything right," Carrie whispered. Her voice broke on the word *right*. "Didn't they?" She turned back toward them, eyes bright and unguarded, furious in their grief, her hands clenched, shaking. “They worked. They helped people. They followed the rules. They didn’t take shortcuts.” No one answered. “Why? Who does that?” Her gaze flicked toward the dark again, toward the stones. “Was it Jacob?”

Ernest looked at her then. “Do you want me to spoil it? The truth is, Carrie, no matter what answer I give you, you won’t like it.”

Carrie glanced at Ryan for approval. He shrugged.

“Yes, I want to know,” she said. “It was either him or that Silas character.”

“The honest answer is, they never found out who started the fire.”

“What?” Carrie gasped. Deborah's jaw actually dropped slightly at that answer. “Did Sheriff…Pappensmoose, or whatever his name was, do any kind of investigation?”

She lowered her eyebrows as her stance became aggressive. “Or did he look the other way because of Trevanion?”

The misspoken name made Ernest grin despite himself. “Segafoose. He did investigate. As Grandpa Henry used to say, ‘Some questions don’t arrive until it’s too late to stop what answers they bring.’”

Carrie shook her head, a sharp, disbelieving motion. Her fingers brushed away the tears, leaving a slightly wet trail on her skin. “That’s not fair.”

“You’re right,” Ernest agreed. “It isn’t.”

The fire shifted, a coal collapsing inward with a faint hiss. Deborah stood and grabbed the remaining kindling they’d gathered for the night's tale to replenish the fire. When she finished, Deborah sat and folded her arms tighter across her chest. Todd stared into the flames, jaw set. Ryan finally stepped forward and placed a hand on Carrie’s shoulder. She leaned into him without looking away from the dark at the traces of the home that once stood there.

With a sigh, Carrie returned to her spot beside Deborah on the blanket, while Ryan took his place on the log behind them. She said, “Please tell me that evil son of a bitch got what was coming to him.”

“Evil is the wrong word, Scout,” Ryan said as Ernest opened his mouth to reply. Curiously tilting his head at Ryan's reply, Ernest gave him space to finish. “He was far worse than that. He was ordinary.”

The air thickened with Ryan's response, heavy and oppressive like a humid day, stealing the ease of breathing. Everyone looked at him.

"Evil knows it's evil," Ryan explained. "Jacob thought he was right. He was radicalized. He took his anger and let other people tell him what it meant. That made him far more dangerous than any mustache-twirling villain."

Ernest pointed at Ryan. "Exactly. I couldn't have said it better myself."

Todd nodded at Ryan. "Wow. You're right, dude. I didn't think of it that way."

"Me neither," Deborah added. She looked at Ernest. "Carrie has a point, though. Did Jacob get his comeuppance?"

Ernest looked at his watch. "It'll be four-thirty soon," he said, dropping his wrist and looking around the darkness surrounding them. "We'll be done by sunrise. Everything will be clearer then." He pulled one of the remaining cigarettes from the Marlboro box and lit it. "This is the final act. This…is the world that continues."

Behind them, beyond the circle of light, the land held what it had kept for more than a century.

Stone. Ash. Silence.

And the shape of something that had once been built to last.

ACT III

THE WORLD THAT CONTINUES

CHAPTER I

Sunday, September 2, 1860

I

Hannah Marlowe was screaming.

Not calling out, but screaming, the sound torn loose from her chest and spent against the night. It came again and again, breaking apart between breaths she couldn't pull in fast enough.

"*Josephus—*"

Then nothing but sound.

She surged forward. Elias and Emma caught her, their hands on her arms and shoulders, stopping her just short of the wreckage where the house had been. The heat still pressed outward from it as if it were alive. Smoke hung low and bitter, stinging her eyes, her throat, her skin.

"*No!*" she screamed, or tried to. It came out wrong. "*No! No! Let me—*"

She fought for space, for footing. Her feet slid on ash and broken earth. She clawed at the hands holding her.

"He's here," she sobbed. "He's here. He said…he said—"

Someone said her name. Someone else repeated it louder. It didn't reach her.

The front of the house was gone. Not burned away, but *collapsed.* The shape of it lay wrong against the ground, beams broken inward, stone dragged down where the upper floor had given way. The smell was unbearable now. Smoke and wet ash and something darker beneath it.

Hannah wrenched herself free and stumbled forward again.

Christian Marlowe and his foreman arrived with the sound of hooves and men moving fast, voices calling orders before they reached the clearing. He dismounted without looking back, already taking in the ruin, the angle of the fall, the places no one could safely stand.

"Hold her," he said.

Hands closed around Hannah again. Firmer this time.

She struck at them uselessly. "*He's inside!*" she cried. "*Jos is still inside!* He was at the window. He…he—"

Her voice broke entirely.

"No one goes in," Christian said. "The floor cannot take the weight. It will all collapse. Stay back."

Hannah heard him then. Not the words, but the *finality* of them. She turned toward him, eyes wild, face streaked black with soot and tears. "You don't know! You don't know! He got me out. He would come after. He would—"

Christian didn't answer her. He looked past her, toward what remained of Fairlight, and something in his face closed.

Men from Trevanion were arriving now, Silas Bixler among them, carrying buckets, shovels, anything that might be useful.

But it was too late. Too late for all of it.

Silas spoke quietly to Christian. Hannah caught only fragments.

"…rode in shouting…"

"…Fairlight's on fire…"

Christian turned. "Who?"

"Jacob," Silas said. "Came through like he'd seen the devil himself."

Christian said nothing. His eyes searched the clearing once, instinctively, then returned to the ruin. "Where is he now?"

Silas shook his head. "He was at Trevanion when we left. I couldn't say now."

Christian nodded once. The nod of a man setting something aside because there was no room for it yet. He turned to his foreman. "Ride to Myrtle Hill. Now. Tell George Mehring I am sending for him."

Hannah shook her head violently. "*No!* Don't send for Father! Don't—"

Christian stepped closer. His voice lowered, but it didn't soften. "Hannah, you cannot stay here."

She stared at him, disbelieving. "I am *not* leaving him!"

"There is nothing here for you now," he said. "And there will be worse before morning."

She sagged then. Her breath came in short, painful pulls. The world tilted.

Emma Koontz and Louisa were beside her suddenly, each taking an arm.

"Come," Emma said. "Just for now."

They led her toward the tenant house. Hannah resisted weakly, her feet dragging, her body heavy and uncooperative. Inside, the air was cooler, dimmer. Someone sat her down. A mug was pressed into her hands. Warm. She spilled it but didn't notice.

She was still crying. Quieter now. Broken.

Christian stood at the door long enough to be sure Hannah was contained, then turned back into the night.

"Elias," he said. "You take charge here. I must ride for Uniontown. To Segafoose's Inn."

He nodded.

Christian mounted again and rode hard to fetch Sheriff Segafoose, the road swallowing him up before the fire had fully died.

Behind him, Fairlight smoldered—unrecognizable, unfinished.

And Hannah, held between two women in a borrowed room, didn't yet know how thoroughly the night had taken her life apart.

II

As the sky lightened, the work had established a routine.

Men moved in lines between the creek and the field, passing buckets hand to hand. They threw water not at the remnants of the house or barn, but along the edge of the wheat where sparks had landed. The outbuildings were monitored, but not extinguished. What mattered now was containment—preventing the fire from spreading into the field and onto neighboring farms.

Trevanion's hands worked without complaint. So did the men from neighboring properties. Fire didn't respect boundary lines, and neither did obligation.

Elias stood where the drive met the clearing, issuing quiet instructions, his voice carrying just far enough. The house behind him was beyond saving. Everyone knew it. The work now was about what could still be kept.

A carriage came up the road from Myrtle Hill as the smoke thinned in the growing light.

Elias turned at the sound and stepped forward as Frederick Mehring climbed down, followed by Maggie. Behind them rode Christian's foreman, his horse blown and damp with sweat.

"George?" Elias asked at once.

Frederick shook his head. "He took ill in the night. He couldn't ride."

Elias nodded. "Then Hannah must go back with you. She cannot remain here."

Maggie's gaze drifted toward the blackened ground beyond the clearing, her face tightening before she looked away again.

Elias led them to the tenant house.

Hannah sat where Emma had placed her, wrapped in a borrowed shawl. Her hands were folded in her lap, fingers pressed together as though she were holding herself intact by force alone. She looked up as footsteps approached.

"Father?" she asked immediately.

Frederick crossed the room and knelt before her. "He's at Myrtle Hill," he said. "He's unwell. We've sent for the doctor. He'll be there by morning."

She absorbed this in silence. Then, softly, "I need to go to him."

"Yes," Frederick said. "That's why we've come."

Emma helped Hannah to her feet. For a moment, Hannah swayed, then steadied. Emma drew her into a brief embrace. Firm, practical, without words. Hannah didn't return it, but she didn't resist.

Outside, the light strengthened. The ruin looked smaller in it—diminished, not lessened.

Elias waited near the carriage. "You should go now. We shall see the rest settled."

Hannah nodded, her gaze fixed somewhere beyond him.

Frederick helped her into the carriage. Maggie climbed in beside her, taking Hannah's hand once the door was shut.

As the carriage turned back toward Myrtle Hill, Hannah looked once more toward the clearing, at the men, the buckets, the darkened earth where her home had stood.

Then the road curved, and Fairlight slipped from view.

Behind them, thc work continued. The fire was nearly out. Most of the wheat would be saved.

And the day, indifferent to all of it, had begun.

III

Later that morning, Sheriff William Segafoose arrived with Christian.

Segafoose didn't hurry. He walked the perimeter first, hat in hand, boots sinking slightly into the dampened ground where water had been thrown all night. Segafoose stopped often, crouching to study the remains with a practiced eye that knew what to ignore.

Christian walked with him.

"They didn't take naturally," Segafoose said at last, straightening. "House, barn, mill. Too far apart. Fire does not jump like that without help."

Christian nodded. "I thought the same. But I am not a lawman. It's why I came for you."

Segafoose grunted once. Not disagreement, just acknowledgment. His gaze drifted toward the tenant house, which still stood. "And yet that one remains untouched."

Christian said nothing.

They stood in silence before Silas Bixler's footsteps approached from behind.

"Sheriff, I hear you're taking statements," he said, not waiting to be invited. "I'd like to be on record."

Segafoose turned slowly. He knew Silas. Trevanion. The history. The Isaac incident ensured that. "Mr. Bixler. Go on."

"This wasn't Trevanion," Silas said plainly. "Dallas can account for every man we had on the grounds that night. Every one." Segafoose made a mark in his book. "Well, all except one." Silas paused, glancing once at Christian. "Jacob Marlowe."

Christian's head came up sharply.

Silas went on, unperturbed, nodding once at Christian. "He rode in as if he were running from the Shakers. Shouting that Fairlight was on fire before anyone else knew. That struck me as odd."

Segafoose wrote again. "You saw him?"

"I did," Silas said. "So did others."

Christian said nothing. But the shape of the night shifted inside him.

When Silas finished, Segafoose closed his book. "I'll want to speak to the others who were there."

"You're welcome to," Silas said. "We'd like this looked at properly."

Christian met Segafoose's eyes. "Would a fire investigator be appropriate?"

Segafoose considered it only a moment. "I think so. Baltimore would be the place."

Christian nodded once.

The matter was set in motion.

IV

Hannah reached Myrtle Hill as the light strengthened, the road sloping gently toward the house.

Nothing had been rearranged to meet them. The fence stood. The gate opened. Smoke from the kitchen chimney lifted straight into the air.

Hannah stepped down from the carriage without assistance.

Her legs felt heavy, as though the ground were resisting her. Still, she walked steadily to the door. Maggie moved ahead to open it, holding it wide as Frederick guided Hannah inside.

The house was quiet. Not sleeping quiet, but watchful quiet. The kind that held its breath around a sickbed.

George lay in the front room, propped with pillows, his chest rising unevenly beneath the blanket. His skin had taken on a gray cast, his features sharpened by effort rather than age. A small table stood at his side with a glass, a spoon, and a dark bottle stoppered tight.

His eyes opened when Hannah entered. "There you are."

She crossed to him and knelt, taking his hand carefully. It was warm and dry. He squeezed once, faint but deliberate.

"I'm sorry," he said. The words landed without force. Not apology, not explanation. Simply acknowledgment.

She bowed her head, pressing his hand to her cheek. "I'm here."

He studied her for a moment longer, then nodded, as though something he'd been holding himself upright for could finally be set down.

Frederick stood back, giving them space. Maggie moved quietly through the room, straightening what didn't need straightening, her movements practiced as though she'd already learned what the room required.

"The doctor will come again later in the morning," Frederick said. He gestured toward the bottle without touching it. "He left something to ease the breathing."

George didn't look at it. "Later, Frederick."

Hannah remained where she was.

When George's breathing grew rougher, she rose without being asked and adjusted the pillows. She learned the routine quickly: how to lift without pulling, how to keep him angled so the effort cost less. When he coughed, she waited, one hand steady at his shoulder, the other ready with the cloth Maggie passed her.

There was no discussion of arrangements. No naming of what was already known.

By evening, Hannah had been absorbed into the rhythm of the room. Water warmed, cloths rinsed, the lamp trimmed before dusk. When Maggie stepped away to tend the kitchen, Hannah stayed. When Frederick left to see to the factory and the mill, she didn't notice him go.

She sat beside her father's bed and listened to his breathing, counting the spaces between.

For two days, this would be her work.

And it would be enough.

V

Night settled early at Myrtle Hill.

The lamp had been turned low, its wick trimmed so the flame wouldn't smoke. The rest of the house had gone dark. Frederick and

Maggie took turns at the kitchen table.

Outside, the fields lay still. No wind. No sound but the insects and, from the front room, the uneven pull of George's breath.

Hannah sat beside the bed.

She'd learned the pattern now; the way his chest labored, the pause that followed, the shallow breath dragged back by force. When it worsened, she shifted the pillows, angling him just enough that the effort eased.

It helped. Not much. Enough.

The coughing came in spells. Hannah waited them out, one hand firm at his shoulder, the other ready with the cloth. She didn't speak unless he did.

Near midnight, Maggie came quietly into the room and stopped at Hannah's side.

"He's been holding off," Maggie murmured. "It might be time."

Hannah looked at the bottle on the table. Dark glass. Thick liquid inside.

George's eyes opened when Maggie touched his arm. "Is it that late?"

"Past," Maggie whispered.

He considered this, then nodded once. "All right."

Hannah watched Maggie carefully pour the laudanum, measuring by habit rather than sight. She held the spoon steady while George took it, grimacing faintly at the taste.

"There, Papa," Maggie said. "Just a little."

The effect wasn't immediate. Nothing dramatic changed. George's breathing didn't smooth all at once. Gradually, the tension in his shoulders eased. His eyes closed without effort.

Hannah remained where she was, her hand resting on his. She could feel the pulse there. Slower now, less urgent.

"You're doing well," George said suddenly.

She stiffened, then bent closer so he wouldn't have to raise his voice. "I'm here."

He nodded, satisfied with that answer. His eyes remained closed.

Maggie withdrew quietly, leaving them alone.

The night stretched.

Hannah didn't sleep. Instead, she counted breaths. She watched the lamp until its flame steadied into something constant and small. When her thoughts strayed, they returned without her willing them to. To Fairlight, to fire, to the moment when the house had ceased to be a house at all. Her screams echoed in her mind.

She didn't cry. Not yet. There would be time for that later, she told herself.

Just before dawn, George stirred again. His breathing roughened, the pause between draws lengthening. Hannah adjusted the pillows and called softly for Maggie.

They watched together as the first gray light crept along the floor.

George's eyes opened once more. He looked at Hannah, recognition clear, and something else beneath it—relief, perhaps. "I shan't trouble you much longer."

She swallowed hard. "You don't trouble me."

He nodded, accepting the correction.

When his breathing settled again, Hannah remained at the bedside, her hand steady, her body stiff with stillness.

Morning would come.

And with it, whatever was left to be done.

VI

Monday, September 3, 1860
The following day

The ruins of Fairlight had cooled enough by morning to be entered without danger.

Sheriff Segafoose and Christian Marlowe returned to Fairlight to walk the site, careful where they placed their feet. The stone had shifted in the night. Ash lay thick in the hollows, fine as flour, drifting at touch. He knelt near what had been the house and brushed a patch clear with his hand.

Christian stood back and let him work.

"They didn't take together," Segafoose said at last. "Not the way an accident would."

Christian nodded. "No."

"The mill burned hot and fast. The barn slower. The house collapsed inward." Segafoose straightened, wiping his hand on his trousers. "Separate starts."

"And the tenant house," Christian said.

Segafoose followed his gaze. The structure stood intact, its roof darkened by smoke but unburned. "Untouched," he agreed. "That has meaning."

They traced the ground where the barn had been, then the mill, measuring the distances between them. No clear path. No wind pattern that would have carried flame so far, so cleanly.

Segafoose made notes.

By midday, the men began the careful work of clearing the house. It was slow, deliberate labor—timbers levered aside, stone shifted only when it was safe to do so. No one spoke unless necessary.

Josephus Marlowe was found where Christian expected him to be.

Near the interior wall, beneath what had once been the upper floor. The remains were blackened, but the position was clear: Josephus turned back from the window. A chair leg lay charred nearby, as if the room had tried to open. He'd fallen where the smoke overtook him.

Segafoose observed, asked questions, and noted it. Afterward, he removed his hand and bowed his head, letting a moment of silence pass out of respect. "He tried to get out."

Christian closed his eyes once and reopened them. "Aye."

There was no sign of struggle. No indication of another hand. Only fire, collapse, and time.

In the afternoon, Segafoose began taking statements.

The questions were simple:

Who was present?
Who saw the fire first?
Who raised the alarm?
Who was on the road that night?

By evening, Segafoose closed his book. "This will be recorded as suspected arson. No finding yet."

Christian nodded. "Would you send for outside help?"

Segafoose considered it briefly. "Baltimore has men who've seen this sort of thing before."

"Then we should," Christian said.

"I will," Segafoose replied.

The decision carried no relief.

It took days to send word, and longer for a man to come—train schedules, duties, and the cost of leaving the city.

VII

Tuesday, September 4, 1860
The following day

George Mehring died just after dawn.

The light hadn't fully settled yet. It lay pale and undecided across the floor, touching the edge of the rug and the chair leg without warmth. The lamp had burned down to a low glow, its flame steady but diminished.

Hannah was awake when it happened.

She hadn't left the chair beside the bed. The strain of remaining still caused her body pain, but by morning, she'd discovered the night's cadence and how to be present without interfering.

George's breathing had changed. Not abruptly. There was no struggle, no final urgency. Just a thinning, each breath a little farther apart than the last, the pause stretching longer than before.

Hannah leaned forward and placed her hand against his wrist.

The pulse was there. Then faint. Then no longer.

She waited. A moment passed. Then another.

Hannah didn't call out right away.

She leaned in and listened, her ear near his chest, the way Maggie had shown her when the coughing grew bad. There was nothing. No movement beneath the skin. No return.

Hannah straightened slowly.

"Maggie," she said. Her voice sounded as if it belonged to someone else.

She came at once, crossing the room without hurry. She rested her fingers against George's neck, then nodded once. "That's it."

Frederick appeared in the doorway a moment later, already dressed. He stood there, taking it in, his face closing not with shock but with recognition.

Hannah remained seated as Maggie adjusted the sheet, drawing it up over George's chest with care. She smoothed the fabric once, then stepped back.

"He went easy," Hannah said.

Maggie nodded. She believed it.

Outside, the day had begun. A wagon passed on the Monocacy Road. Somewhere in the distance, a rooster called.

Frederick cleared his throat. "I'll send word. And for the doctor."

Neither of them moved to touch Hannah. She wasn't unsteady. She was simply still.

When they left the room, she remained where she was, her hand resting on the edge of the bed.

For a long while, she did nothing.

Then, with deliberate care, she reached up and closed George's eyes.

VIII

The Marlowes buried Josephus at Fairlight later that afternoon.

Not close to the house, not where the ground was scorched or broken, but beyond it, where the slope dipped and leveled again, where the grass had been trampled thin by work rather than fire. Christian chose the place with care, walking it once, then nodding to Elias.

Here, then, the nod said.

The coffin arrived at midmorning, plain and unadorned. Christian had selected pine. It smelled clean. Too clean. It had been carried by men who knew Josephus, set down gently as others gathered tools.

No one spoke much.

Christian and Elias took the first turns with the spades. The earth was cooperative, looser than expected, as though the ground itself had already made room. Fairlight's hands joined them in turn. Men who had worked beside Josephus, taken instruction without resentment. John Dorsey set his weight to the shovel and didn't look up again.

Mary and Emma stood with Hannah, apart from the work.

Hannah watched the hole deepen. The rhythm of the digging steadied her more than words could have.

Lift. Break. Set aside.

Each motion had a purpose. Each motion ended.

When the coffin was lowered, there was no ceremony. Just hands at the ropes, careful and deliberate. The box settled into the earth with a smaller sound than Hannah expected.

Christian spoke first. "Rest in peace, my son."

No sermon followed.

Mary reached for Christian's hand and whispered, "Godspeed, Josephus."

Someone else murmured agreement. Then silence again.

Christian stepped forward and placed the marker at the head of the grave. It was simple. Stone. His name. The dates.

JOSEPHUS MARLOWE
Born April 11, 1835
Died September 2, 1860

That was all.

Hannah stepped forward then.

She hadn't planned to speak. Words weren't required. But as she stood there, the air pressed inward, as though waiting.

"It's you," she said quietly, a single tear rolling down her face. No one moved. "It's me. It's us." Her voice didn't break. That surprised her. "I'll see you again, my love."

Hannah stepped back.

The men began to fill the grave. Earth returned to Earth. The sound of it landing was dull and final. Hannah watched until the shape of the coffin disappeared entirely, until only disturbed ground remained.

When it was done, Elias wiped his hands on his trousers and turned to Christian.

"I'm taking my family north," he said. "War is coming. Maryland is too divided. I want to be somewhere safe. Gettysburg first, probably. It's Union-friendly. Then farther, if I can find work."

Christian nodded. "Aye. You will do well."

Elias reached into his coat and drew out the journal. "Josephus gave me this the night of the fire. That's why it wasn't in the house." Christian took it carefully. "It belongs to your family. The hands and I dug the lock safe from the basement. We left it in the tenant house."

"Thank you," Christian replied.

They shook hands. Firm. Equal.

Elias gathered his family. The Fairlight hands followed him

down the slope, tools over shoulders, speaking softly again now that the work was done.

Hannah remained.

The grave had already begun to look ordinary. Earth smoothed. Stone upright. Grass pressed back into place.

She stood alone, looking toward the ruins, waiting longer than she needed to. Long enough for the others to disappear. Long enough for the creek to return.

Ash did not come. Perhaps he'd died in the fire. Perhaps he'd run and not returned. There was no way to know.

Hannah rested her hand briefly against her side.

A thought came, unbidden and unwelcome.

Perhaps she should have stayed.

Not because she wished for death—the thought wasn't that simple—but because survival now felt misaligned, as though she'd been preserved without instruction.

She didn't ask why. Why wasn't a useful question.

Hannah stood until the ground no longer looked newly turned, then turned away and walked toward what remained of Fairlight.

IX

Wednesday, September 5, 1860
The following day

Hannah rose with Maggie.

There was no discussion about it. The day had begun, and so had the work.

The water had already been set to warm. Hannah carried it carefully from the kitchen, mindful of the weight, the threshold, and the way the floor dipped near the front room. The house was awake now, not with voices, but with purpose.

George lay as he had been left. His face had settled into stillness, the lines eased in a way that did not belong to sleep. The sheet had been drawn up to his chest. His hands rested where Maggie had placed them.

Hannah wrung the cloth and began. She washed his face first, gently, the way she had when he'd been ill and restless. Then his hands. She worked steadily, neither lingering nor rushing. When the water cooled, she changed it without comment. Maggie handed her what was needed before Hannah asked.

They dressed him in the clothes Maggie had already laid out. Nothing new. Nothing chosen for display. Familiar things, worn into their proper shape.

Hannah smoothed the fabric once, then stepped back.

Frederick came mid-morning with paper and ink. Notices had to be sent—names to be written, distances to be considered. Hannah stood at the table with him as he spoke, listening, nodding when required.

"Have I forgotten anyone?" he asked.

"Uncle Johannes Mehring," Hannah said once. "And Aunt Mary's parents, Mr. Peter and Mrs. Elizabeth Royer."

Frederick wrote them down.

There was no list for grief. Only obligations.

By noon, the room had been set back into order. The bed was remade. The water thrown out. The cloths rinsed and hung to dry. The chair returned to its place near the window.

Hannah found herself wiping the table where nothing had spilled, her hand moving in a practiced circle.

Myrtle Hill looked like itself again. That unsettled her more than the sight of death had.

When Maggie touched her arm, Hannah stopped at once, as though she'd been waiting for permission to be still. "You should sit."

Hannah nodded and did so. She didn't feel weak. She didn't feel steady. She felt *present,* held in place by the sequence of things that had been done and those that remained.

Outside, the day moved on. The creek kept its course. The mill wheel turned.

Hannah folded her hands in her lap and waited for whatever would come next.

CHAPTER II

Thursday, September 6, 1860

I

Hannah woke before the house.

This had become common since the fire; sleep breaking into pieces she couldn't hold together. She lay still for a time, listening to the familiar sounds: the settling of the beams, the distant creek, the faint rustle of Maggie somewhere below.

Nothing hurt. That, too, was new.

She turned onto her side and felt it then. A faint, unmistakable resistance in her body. Not pain. Not illness. Not the dull ache of grief or exhaustion. Something else. A fullness that didn't belong to the night before.

Hannah closed her eyes.

She'd been taught not to rush to conclusions. Sensation wasn't certainty. Bodies often mislead. Fear amplifies small things. But this wasn't fear.

She pressed her hand flat against her abdomen and waited, as though whatever had changed might correct itself if given the chance.

It did not.

She lay there a long while, breathing carefully, counting nothing, letting the realization arrive without ceremony.

When she finally sat up, she didn't cry.

She dressed slowly, smoothing her skirt and straightening it with care, as though order might still be negotiated if she handled it gently enough.

II

Friday, September 7, 1860
The following day

The basin water was cold.

Hannah welcomed it.

She trusted the body more when it was uncomfortable. Pain clarified, warmth blurred. She washed her face and wrists, grounding herself in the shock of it, then standing still.

She counted anyway.

She didn't need to.

Her courses had not come since July. She had told herself there were reasons. Fairlight's charity openly named. People paying her attention she didn't seek. The stress of it rearranging the body's clock.

But stress did not do this. Nor did grief.

The last course ended days before the Fourth of July. She and Josephus had spent the night together at Cockey's Tavern on the fourth. That was the day.

Hannah reached for the towel and paused, her fingers tightening around the cloth.

Josephus loved order. Not control—order—things set in their proper places. Things accounted for.

She thought of Fairlight in the mornings. The way the light came in at the kitchen window, the way he set his tools down where his hand would reach for them again.

"This is yours," she said quietly, though no one was there to hear it.

The words surprised her.

Not mine.

Yours.

She folded the towel carefully and set it back where it belonged.

III

Monday, September 10, 1860
Three days later

The paper arrived folded tight.

Hannah didn't see who brought it. It came with the morning—milk, feed, news—set down as if it were no different. It was there on the table when she came down in the morning, as though it belonged among ordinary things of the house.

She noticed it because Maggie had turned it face down.

That, too, was new.

Hannah crossed the room and picked it up.

The headline was larger than necessary.

FATAL FIRE AT FAIRLIGHT
Prominent Mill Owner Perishes. Cause Undetermined.

She read it once without understanding. Then again, more carefully.

The words were wrong in small ways. The date was correct. The names were spelled properly. But the sentences leaned toward speculation, toward shape rather than truth.

...suspected arson...
...longstanding tensions with neighboring interests...
...questions remain...

She folded the paper back on itself and set it down.

Maggie watched her from the stove. "You don't have to read it."

"I do," she said, opening it again.

Josephus's name appeared three times. Once in full. Once abbreviated. Once, as *the deceased.*

There was a paragraph about the mill. Another about the loss to the county. A sentence about the barn. Nothing about the house as it had been lived in. Nothing about the work done there. Nothing about the charity grain or the careful books or the way the wheel had sounded when it ran true.

At the bottom of the column, her own name appeared.

...leaves behind a widow...

The word startled her more than the others.

She folded the paper carefully, aligning the edges, and set it back where she'd found it.

"Which one is this?" she asked.

Maggie hesitated. "The Sentinel."

Hannah nodded. "Another will come."

"Yes."

She didn't ask when.

By midday, the second paper arrived. This one was louder. The language sharper. The implication heavier. It named Trevanion, then stepped back just far enough to deny it.

Hannah didn't finish reading it.

Frederick took it from her hands and folded it away. "You don't need this, Hannah."

"I do," she said again. And then, after a pause, "But not today."

That afternoon, a man she didn't know came down the drive and stopped short of the door. He didn't knock. He lingered instead, hat in hand, as though weighing whether the story would improve if he crossed the threshold.

Frederick met him on the step. "No," he said quietly.

The man left without argument.

That night, Hannah lay awake, listening to the house.

It sounded the same as it had the night before. The same settling. The same distance between reminders. Nothing in the walls acknowledged what had been printed.

She pressed her hand flat against her abdomen, just long enough to steady herself.

This, too, would need to be accounted for.

But not yet.

IV

Tuesday, September 11, 1860
The following day

Maggie was at the table, trimming wicks, when Hannah came

into the kitchen.

The day had dulled its edges. The visitors had thinned. The house had settled into the low, steady noise of ordinary use; water poured, chairs moved, the clock marking time without comment.

Hannah stood for a moment with her hands resting on the back of the chair opposite Maggie. “I need to tell you something.”

Maggie didn’t look up at once. She finished what she was doing, set the scissors aside, then turned. “All right.”

Hannah drew a breath. “I think I am with child.”

Maggie’s face didn’t change. Not in the way Hannah braced herself for, at least. There was no surprise there—only attention.

“How long?” Maggie asked.

“Not long.”

Maggie nodded once. She stood and crossed to the stove, poured water into the kettle, and set it on. The movement was unhurried and deliberate.

“You’ve been eating little,” she said. “And sleeping less.”

Hannah didn’t answer. She hadn’t known that Maggie had been keeping count.

Maggie turned back. “You’re certain?”

“As much as one can,” Hannah said.

Maggie considered her for a moment longer, then reached out and took Hannah’s wrist gently, pressing her thumb just below the pulse. She released it again without comment. “All right.”

That was all.

Hannah felt something in her chest loosen. Not relief, exactly, but the easing of a weight held too carefully for too long.

“We won’t say anything,” Maggie continued, meeting Hannah’s eyes. “Not yet.”

“No,” Hannah said. “Not yet.”

Maggie nodded. “Then you’ll rest when you can. You’ll eat when I put food in front of you, whether you want it or not. And if anyone asks why you’re tired, I’ll answer them.”

Hannah looked at her. “Thank you.”

Maggie gave a brief, dismissive shake of her head. “You don’t thank people for doing what needs doing.”

The kettle began to sound on the stove.

Maggie turned back to it. Hannah remained where she was, her hands still on the chair, the room holding steady around them.

Nothing had been announced.
Nothing had been promised.
But something essential had been set in place.

V

Friday, September 14, 1860
Three days later

Hannah realized it in the doorway.

She'd paused there only to catch her breath. Not because she needed to—she told herself—but because the house was warm, the air outside thin. Maggie was behind her, speaking to someone in the yard, and Hannah had a moment alone with the light.

It was enough.

The dizziness passed quickly, but not before Maggie saw it.

"Sit," Maggie said at once.

"I'm fine," Hannah replied, even as she obeyed.

She took the chair by the wall, her hands folded carefully in her lap. She'd learned where to place them now, how to hold herself so the change wasn't immediately legible.

Maggie handed her a cup without comment. "Drink."

Hannah did.

From the yard came voices. A man's, then another's. Visitors again. Someone asking after arrangements. Someone who hadn't yet learned when to leave.

Hannah rose when she heard her name spoken.

Maggie's hand came out instinctively, stopping her.

"I'll answer," Maggie said.

Hannah hesitated. "They ask for me."

"They don't need you," Maggie replied.

The voices continued. Polite. Curious. Lingering.

Hannah sat back down. It was a small thing. But she understood then. This was no longer just a matter of silence. It was a matter of *timing*. Of how long Hannah could remain unseen before other people began to fill in the space she left open.

Later, alone in the front room, she caught sight of herself in the glass.

The change wasn't obvious. Not yet. But Hannah could see how it would be. The softening line, the way the fabric would begin to resist.

It wouldn't be long before someone else noticed.

Not Maggie. Not Frederick. Someone with no reason to keep quiet.

The thought settled heavily.

She pressed her hand briefly against her abdomen. Not to reassure herself, but to mark the boundary while it still existed.

Secrecy, she understood now, wasn't something she could keep indefinitely.

It was something that had to be placed.

And soon.

VI

Saturday, September 15, 1860
The following day

Frederick noticed the change at supper.

It wasn't anything Hannah did. It was what *others* did around her: the way Maggie placed a chair before Hannah reached for it, the way conversation curved away from certain subjects without explanation, the way decisions arrived already settled.

"You'll stay in tomorrow," Maggie said, setting the bowl in front of Hannah. "It's meant to be hot."

Hannah nodded. "All right."

Frederick looked from one to the other. "We were meant to go through the accounts."

Maggie didn't reply.

Hannah said, "Another day."

'Another day' had become a phrase that invited no response.

After the meal, Frederick carried the ledger to the front room and sat down to work. The numbers held his attention until he heard Hannah speaking quietly in the kitchen. Not to him, not to Maggie, but to someone else entirely. He couldn't make out the words, only the tone: practical, decisive.

When Hannah joined him a while later, she stood instead of

sitting. “Christian is coming by tomorrow.”

Frederick looked up sharply. “Christian…Marlowe?”

“Yes.”

“When did you speak to him?” he asked. She hesitated only a moment, and Frederick saw it.

“I didn’t,” she said. “Maggie did.”

The ledger lay open on his knee. He closed it. “To what purpose?”

Hannah met his eyes. She didn’t look evasive—she looked resolved. “To see how we are.”

Frederick let out a breath through his nose. “We are managing.”

“Yes,” Hannah agreed. “We are.”

The agreement unsettled him more than disagreement would have. “And what will you tell him?”

“That George is gone,” she said. “That the house is full. That the papers have begun to circle.”

Frederick waited. She didn’t continue.

“I should be part of that conversation,” he said.

Hannah nodded again. “I know.”

But she didn’t say, *of course*. The difference lodged sharply.

Later, Frederick stood alone in the yard, the air thick and unmoving, the sound of the creek steady and indifferent. Through the window, Hannah sat with Maggie, their heads inclined toward one another in a posture he recognized from years past—the posture of women deciding what must be done.

He understood then, not with resentment, but with a dull clarity.

The decisions had already begun.

And he was no longer the one they waited for.

VII

Sunday, September 16, 1860
The following day

Christian arrived at Myrtle Hill in the late afternoon.

He didn’t come alone. Mary was with him, seated quietly in the carriage, her hands folded in her lap. They brought no bags. No questions..

Hannah met them on the step.

Christian took her in with one look—the stillness, the careful way she stood, her hands remaining occupied even when there was nothing to hold.

"I shan't stay long," he said. "We came only to speak."

"That's all right," Hannah replied.

Maggie followed, but didn't sit. Frederick remained standing near the window, his posture formal, as though a meeting were already underway.

Christian didn't begin with condolences. That had been done. He didn't mention Fairlight. That couldn't be helped.

"The papers have started," he said instead. "And they won't stop."

Hannah nodded. "I know."

"They will grow less careful as they go," he continued. "They will speculate where they cannot confirm. They will fill space."

Mary's gaze remained fixed on Hannah, her expression composed but intent.

"This you do not need," Christian said. "Not now."

"No," Hannah agreed.

Christian folded his hands loosely in front of him. "You should come to our farm. At least for a while."

Frederick drew breath. Hannah spoke before he could. "For how long?"

"As long as it takes," Christian said. "Until things settle. Until the noise moves on."

"Yes," Maggie softly said. "Frederick is sending me to Mrs. Kleefisch's Academy soon. Papa made the plans before he died." She gently touched Hannah's shoulder. "You need someone else to care for you while I'm away. Frederick will be busy with the factory."

"And Myrtle Hill?" Hannah asked.

"It will be tended," Mary said gently. "Frederick has the factory and the mill. Your brother, William, is returning to Bruceville. Nothing here will be neglected."

Christian watched Hannah carefully. "This is *not* removal, Hannah," he said. "It's shelter."

Hannah considered it. "And if I don't wish to go?"

Christian didn't answer at once. When he did, his voice was even.

"Then you will remain where people feel free to come to your door. To watch. To ask."

Mary shifted slightly. "And you owe no one your grief."

Hannah looked at Frederick then. He met her gaze steadily. He didn't argue. He didn't insist. The decision had already passed the point where it belonged to him.

"When?" Hannah asked, turning to Christian.

"Tomorrow."

She nodded.

Mary stood and crossed the room, taking Hannah's hands briefly in hers. "We'll take care of you," she said, not as a promise, but as a statement of fact.

Hannah felt the truth of it settle. "I'll pack what I need."

Christian inclined his head. "We shall return in the morning."

When the Marlowes left, the room seemed to exhale.

Frederick remained where he was. Maggie moved at once, already thinking in lists. Hannah stood for a moment longer, then turned toward the stairs. Tomorrow, the shape of her days would change again.

She didn't resist it.

She'd learned by now the cost of standing still.

VIII

Maggie had been folding and refolding the same chemise when Hannah closed the trunk lid.

"It won't change its mind," Hannah said gently.

Maggie flushed. "I only want it right."

"It's neat." Hannah rested a hand on the trunk. "Come outside with me."

Maggie hesitated. "Should you—?"

"Yes."

They stepped out into the late light. The fields settled toward evening. A faint sweetness hung in the air where the grass had been cut earlier in the week.

"You'll miss this," Hannah said, not looking at her.

"I know."

"Then look at it properly."

They walked only as far as the edge of the Virginia pines. The trees rose thinner here than the oaks nearer the lane, their bark scaled, flaking, their needles murmuring overhead. The creek moved somewhere below them, unseen but constant.

Hannah bent, slower than before, and lifted one of the fallen cones.

"When you're away," she said, turning it in her hands, "you'll think you've forgotten the sound of this place. You won't."

A seed slipped loose from the cone's parted scales. It caught the breeze and spun.

Maggie laughed softly. "Like a little wing."

Hannah reached out and caught it mid-air.

She studied it—the narrow seed, the papery blade that carried it farther than its weight would allow.

From the house, her name was called.

Maggie stepped closer at once. "We should go back."

"In a moment."

Hannah brushed her fingers clean and slipped the seed into the pocket of her blue dress without ceremony.

Then she let Maggie take her arm.

IX

From the Carroll County Democrat

LET THE FACTS SPEAK
Joseph Shaw, Editor

It is in moments of public sorrow that rumor most readily disguises itself as concern, and speculation dresses itself in the garments of fact. The recent calamity at Fairlight has struck our county deeply, not only in the loss of a valued enterprise, but in the passing of a man long known among us.

It would be both improper and injurious to permit grief to be harnessed to conjecture, or to allow private suspicions, unspoken though they may remain, to outrun lawful inquiry. Let the proper authorities do their work, and let them do it without the clamor of accusation or the impatience of partisan tongues.

Carroll County has never lacked voices eager to speak before facts are settled. It has, at times, lacked patience. We urge the former to pause, and the latter to prevail.

X

From the American Sentinel

MORE THAN A MILL
William H. Grammer, Editor

The destruction of the Fairlight Mill by fire has deprived this county of one of its steadiest enterprises and one of its most respected citizens. Josephus Marlowe, whose name was long associated with honest labor and fair dealing, perished while attempting to save his home and livelihood.

The mill stood not merely as a place of trade, but as a gathering point for neighbors, farmers, and families whose daily lives were made easier by its operation. Its loss will be felt in ways that extend beyond account books.

We trust that the circumstances surrounding the fire will be examined with care and sobriety, and that whatever truths emerge will be worthy of the man who was lost.

XI

Sunday, September 17, 1860
The following day

Hannah woke to a different quiet that afternoon at the Marlowe farm.

Not the absence of sound, but a wider one, the kind that came from distance rather than emptiness. The Marlowe house held the morning loosely. Doors opened without haste. Footsteps moved with purpose, not urgency. No one watched her descend the stairs to see how she bore herself.

Mary was already in the kitchen. She glanced up once, smiled, and returned to her work. "You slept."

"Yes," Hannah replied.

"That's good."

Nothing more was required.

Christian came in a few minutes later with the paper folded under his arm. Not rolled. Not waved. Tucked close, as though it were something that might stain if mishandled.

The paper had been folded once, then again; the crease darkened where someone's thumb had held it too long.

Christian didn't read it right away. He set it beside his plate, finished his coffee, and let the silence stretch. Hannah watched him without asking.

Finally, he opened it. His eyes moved once, then again, then stopped.

"What do they say?" Hannah asked.

"They don't," he said. She waited. Christian tapped the page with one finger. "They speak of caution. About patience. About not letting rumor outrun inquiry."

"That sounds sensible," Hannah said.

"Aye," he replied. "It does."

He folded the paper back on itself, slower this time. "And here—" He turned it, smoothed it, pointed. "The Sentinel calls Josephus steady. Calls the mill a gathering place. Says we have lost more than lumber and grain."

She swallowed. "Have we not?"

Christian didn't answer at once. When he did, his voice was quieter. "They are telling two different stories about the same fire."

"Which one's true?"

He shook his head. "Therein lies the rub. One does not have to lie if one chooses the right tone."

Mary crossed the room then, setting a cup in front of Hannah without comment. She didn't look at the paper. She didn't ask.

Outside, the morning went on as it usually did. Chickens moved through the yard. A wagon passed on the road. Somewhere down the valley, the creek kept working its way around stone.

Hannah drank her tea and felt the house receive her without judgment. No one asked what she planned to do that day. No one asked how long she intended to stay.

The paper remained folded on the table.

But the words did not.

They had already moved elsewhere—into rooms she'd not yet entered, into conversations she wasn't part of, into a future that was already arranging itself around her.

She rose when the cup was empty.

Mary looked up again. "If you like, you can walk later. The air holds well this time of year."

Hannah nodded. "I would like that."

No one mentioned Fairlight. No one mentioned Myrtle Hill. No one mentioned what had not yet been said.

For the first time since the fire, Hannah understood what it meant to be kept.

Toward evening, the air shifted.

It wasn't a loud change—only the sort that settles over fields when the sun lowers and the heat releases its hold. Hannah had stepped out onto the porch, meaning only to feel the air Mary spoke of, when a sound carried up from the lower pasture.

Not thunder. Not wheels.

Hooves.

She didn't move at once.

Another soft strike against the fence—a low, uncertain nicker.

Christian, who'd been closing the barn for the night, paused and turned his head. He didn't look surprised. Only attentive.

Two shapes stood near the far gate.

They were leaner than before, their coats dulled with dust, burrs caught in their manes. They stood close together, flank to flank, ears turning toward the house.

Atlas shifted first.

Lark followed.

They'd not come in a panic. They'd come to the fence and stopped.

Mary stepped onto the porch behind Hannah, but said nothing.

Christian walked down the slope without haste and unlatched the gate. Atlas lowered his head as if in recognition. Lark breathed out long and slow.

Fifteen days had passed. The valley hadn't kept them.

Hannah descended the steps carefully. She didn't hurry. She didn't call their names. They didn't need calling.

The sun thinned along the horizon as Christian led them inside.

For the first time since the fire, something that had fled chose to stand.

XII

The safe sat against the far wall of the room that had once been Josephus's.

It did not belong there.

The metal was dulled, its surface blistered in places where the heat had caught it. The handle bore a faint bend, not enough to break it, only enough to remember.

Hannah stood in the doorway a long while before stepping inside.

Someone had wiped it clean. Not well, only enough to remove the ash that would stain clothing. It still smelled faintly of smoke when the lamp was brought close.

She set the lamp on the washstand. Then she knelt.

The dial was stiff beneath her fingers. She turned it once, then again, counting under her breath the way Josephus had taught her, though she'd never needed to use it herself.

Five. Fifteen. Fifty-nine.

The metal resisted at first, then yielded.

The door opened with a soft, reluctant sigh.

Inside, everything was as it had been. The deed lay in its leather pouch. A folded note, edges singed but legible. A small stack of bills bound with twine.

She touched none of them.

Her hand went instead to the wooden box at the back—plain, worn smooth at the corners. She lifted it carefully, as though it were something fragile and alive.

The lid creaked when she opened it. The wet-plate negative rested in its wrapping, untouched by flame. Hannah drew it out and held it toward the lamplight.

At first, there was only shadow. Then, slowly, as her eyes adjusted, the shapes resolved.

Two figures standing side by side. The porch behind them. The windows. The roofline whole and unbroken.

Fairlight as it had been.

She didn't gasp. She didn't break. Her shoulders lowered, as if something long held had at last been set down.

A tear slipped free and fell onto the back of her hand. She didn't wipe it away.

It was the first time Hannah allowed herself to see what was gone. And the first time she understood that what remained didn't require her to hold it upright any longer.

She wrapped the plate again, carefully, and returned it to the box.

The baby stirred.

Hannah rested her palm against her abdomen and bowed her head, not in prayer, not in despair, but in acknowledgment.

Then she closed the safe.

XIII

Jacob Marlowe didn't read the paper the way other men did.

He didn't skim. He didn't linger over the praise of Josephus or the lament for the mill. His eye went instead to the turns of phrase, the careful ones—the places where nothing was named and everything was meant.

Proximity, the article said.

Silence, it warned.

Selective caution.

He folded the paper once, then unfolded it again, as if the words might rearrange themselves.

They hadn't named him. That was the worst part. A name could be denied. A name could be challenged. This—this was suggestion—air itself. A fog laid gently enough that no one could swear where it began.

Jacob told himself it was Sentinel poison. Moral vanity. Northern smugness dressed as grief.

But when he left the room, he noticed who didn't meet his eyes.

That was new.

XIV

By the time the paper reached Trevanion's mill yard again, it wasn't the same paper.

"They're saying Shaw's people are hiding something," one man said, leaning against the post.

"That's not what it said," another replied.

"Close enough for me."

Another man laughed. "The Sentinel didn't need to say it. Everyone knows."

Jacob stood nearby, tying off a sack, listening without looking.

"What they said," the first man continued, "was that certain folks talk about patience when they ought to talk about facts."

"Facts like what?"

"Well," the man shrugged, "facts like who was around when the fire started."

No one answered that.

They didn't need to.

XV

Hannah didn't read the article.

She heard it the way most women did—through someone else's mouth, reshaped by concern.

Mary and Hannah were shelling peas when Mary mentioned it, almost carelessly, as if repeating a recipe half-forgotten.

"The Sentinel printed another one of those pieces," she said. "The Chronicles, they're called."

Hannah kept working. "About the fire?"

"Well, about…caution." Mary hesitated, then smiled. "About not rushing to conclusions."

It sounded reasonable enough.

"They didn't name anyone," Mary added quickly. Too quickly. "It was more about tone. About how people speak when they are close to a thing."

Hannah's fingers paused inside the bowl. "Close how?"

"Oh, close in town," Mary said. "You know how they mean. Meetings. Associations."

Hannah nodded, though she wasn't sure she did. She returned to the peas; the soft click of them against the bowl suddenly too loud.

Later, alone, she realized no one had said Josephus's name at all.

And yet she felt as if he'd been handled.

XVI

Tuesday, September 18, 1860
The following day

It took Hannah several days to understand what was happening.

No one argued in front of her. No one spoke sharply to her. And no one brought her the paper.

When she asked after the investigation, the answers were brief and carefully shaped, like stones set to fill a gap without showing what lay beneath.

"They're looking into it," Christian said.

"Everyone is being patient," Mary said.

"Best not to trouble yourself," Molly, the Marlowes' freedwoman, still kept on in the house, offered gently, setting a folded cloth aside.

One afternoon, Hannah found the paper by accident, folded beneath a ledger on the sideboard. She recognized it immediately by the weight of it, the way it resisted her fingers.

She didn't open it. She didn't need to. That was when she understood what was happening; they weren't keeping the news from her because she couldn't bear it. They were keeping the arguments from her—the *choosing* from her.

And for the first time since the fire, she felt something other than grief press against her chest.

Anger. Not loud, not sharp. Just steady.

Josephus had trusted her with hard truths.

She wondered when others had decided she no longer needed them.

XVII

Jacob learned Hannah wasn't at Myrtle Hill the way he learned most things lately.

Indirectly.

Someone mentioned it while discussing feed prices, as if it were incidental. "She's staying over with the Marlowes for now."

Jacob nodded. Too quickly. "Of course."

He told himself that it made sense. The house burned. The land unsettled. Too many eyes. Still, it settled badly.

The Marlowes.

Neutral ground. Quiet ground. A place where people read the Sentinel without comment. He wondered if she'd read the Chronicles yet, wondered what she'd been told, wondered what had been left unsaid.

He told himself she'd been advised to go there. That it wasn't her choice.

But the idea that she had chosen; chosen distance, silence, elsewhere…

That idea returned to him later, uninvited.

And with it came a thought he didn't like at all: that she was being kept safe.

And that whatever threatened her safety now wore a familiar face.

XVIII

Wednesday, September 19, 1860
The following day

It was days later when Hannah read the Chronicles section of the Sentinel herself.

Not because anyone brought it to her, but because she asked.

The request surprised Mary. She hesitated just long enough to give herself away before fetching it from the drawer. Hannah recognized the fold immediately. The same careful crease she'd seen on other tables. Other hands.

She read slowly. Not for names. Not for accusations. For tone.

She saw it then, the way the sentences leaned without falling. The way caution was praised not as virtue, but as necessity. The way certain silences felt placed.

Josephus was there, but only as memory. As steadiness. As something finished.

The fire was there, but only as event.

What wasn't there, what was carefully circled and avoided, was people.

Hannah folded the paper and rested her hand against her abdomen, waiting for the familiar ache to pass.

They were not writing to her.

They were writing around her.

And she understood, suddenly and clearly, that by the time she'd asked to read it, the paper had already done its work.

XIX

From the American Sentinel
(written by Know-Nothing, Charles W. Webster, to satirize Joseph Shaw)

IV CHRONICLES
Chapter III

There is a peculiar species of caution which arises not from prudence, but from proximity. It presents itself as restraint, counsels patience, warns loudly against rumor, yet always in tones that suggest it knows precisely which rumors require warning.

In recent days, our esteemed Brother Shaw has rediscovered the virtue of silence. The language of delay is fashionable once more. The wisdom of waiting is again held forth as the highest public good. One might be forgiven for thinking that time itself were on trial, rather than circumstance.

We have no quarrel with lawful inquiry. We object to none. But we note, with interest, that inquiry is most often praised when it promises stillness, and most often discouraged when it threatens motion.

Calls for calm are admirable things. They are less admirable when raised not in service of truth, but in fear of where truth may wander if left unattended.

Communities are not injured by facts. They are injured by the careful avoidance of them. And history, which is patient beyond any editor's counsel, has a way of recording who urged quiet, and who urged clarity.

XX

Excerpt from "Early History of Carroll County." Published in 1980 by the Historical Society of Carroll County

In the years that followed the Fairlight fire, arguments hardened where evidence did not. Editorials were reread, phrases underlined, silences examined more closely than statements themselves.

The American Sentinel would later be praised for its restraint, the Carroll County Democrat criticized for its caution, though both claimed, with some justification, to have acted responsibly. What lingered was not certainty, but posture. One paper mourned. The other warned.

And in a county where memory outlasted proof, those differences proved decisive.

XXI

A historian's handwritten and underlined note in the margin beside the excerpt.

The author got it wrong.

Later accounts often describe the Fairlight fire as a moment when partisan divisions sharpened suddenly, as though suspicion had arrived fully formed. This misunderstands the period.

Distrust didn't erupt; it accumulated. Editorials didn't accuse; they implied. Readers didn't decide; they absorbed.

By the time names were spoken aloud, they'd already been rehearsed silently for weeks.

CHAPTER III

Wednesday, September 19, 1860

I

Jacob came to the Marlowe farm only once.

He stood at the edge of the yard, hat in his hands, and said the right things in the right order. He asked after her health. He mentioned the weather. He spoke of Josephus without pause or stumble.

But he didn't meet her eyes.

That's when Hannah knew.

Jacob believed Hannah chose this place to get away from him.

Not from Fairlight. Not from the ashes. From him.

She considered correcting it. Considered saying that she came because she was tired, because the nights were long, because people spoke too freely where her house had been.

But the words required more strength than she had. So she let the misunderstanding stand.

Jacob left with his version intact, and Hannah watched him go with a quiet, unfamiliar sorrow. Not for herself, but for how easily absence became meaning when left alone.

II

Sheriff Segafoose arrived at the Marlowe farm just before noon.

He came alone, riding up the lane without haste, his horse steady, his posture unremarkable. There was no urgency in him now. Whatever had driven the investigation forward had already spent itself.

Christian met him at the gate.

"Morning," Segafoose said. "I won't take much of it."

"That would be kind," Christian replied.

They went inside. Mary set a cup on the table without asking. Segafoose nodded his thanks and removed his hat, resting it on his knee.

Then he saw Hannah.

He didn't react at once. He simply registered her presence—the stillness, the careful way she sat, the way the room seemed to hold her differently than it held the rest of them.

"I hadn't realized Mrs. Marlowe was staying here," he said at last.

Christian answered. "For now."

Segafoose inclined his head. "I see."

He took the folded paper from his coat and set it on the table between them. It wasn't dramatic. It wasn't a verdict.

"We've finished," he said. "The investigation, I mean." Christian waited. "The fire was set. More than one point of origin. Far enough apart that it wasn't an accident. The barn, the mill, the house. No pattern that could be explained by spread."

Mary's hands stilled in her lap.

Hannah said nothing.

"The Baltimore man agrees," Segafoose went on. "He's put his name to it. That's what this is." He touched the paper lightly once.

"Arson," Christian said.

"Ja," Segafoose replied. "But not chargeable." He didn't soften it. There was no point. "No witnesses. No physical evidence that points cleanly. Plenty of conjecture. None of it usable."

Christian nodded slowly. "And Brick Mills?"

"Cleared," Segafoose said. "Trevanion's hands were accounted for. Their men, too."

Segafoose paused.

"There is," he added, "one name that does not settle as neatly." Christian didn't ask. "Jacob Marlowe. He was seen riding hard that night by many witnesses. Declaring the fire before it was widely visible. That has been noted."

Mary looked at Christian.

"But it's not proof," Segafoose said at once. "Not of setting the fire. Not of intent. It makes him…unresolved."

Hannah's fingers tightened briefly against the arm of the chair.

Segafoose noticed. He didn't comment. "I shall continue to speak with him," he said. "For a while. This is all I can do."

Christian leaned back slightly. "And after that?"

Segafoose exhaled. "After that, the law is finished."

The words settled heavily.

"I'm sorry," he said then. Not to Christian, but to Hannah.

She met his eyes. "Thank you for telling us plainly."

He dipped his head again. "Ma'am. It seemed owed."

Segafoose stood, replaced his hat, and paused at the door. "For what it's worth," he said to Christian, "if anything further comes of it, I shall notify you immediately."

"I understand," Christian replied.

Segafoose left the way he'd come; without hurry, without spectacle.

The sound of his horse faded. The house remained quiet.

Mary reached for Hannah's cup and refilled it, though it wasn't empty.

Christian folded the report once, then again. "That's that."

No one contradicted him. But Hannah understood what he meant. The law had spoken. Everything else would be said without it.

And the fire at Fairlight passed into record—unresolved, uncontained, and finished only in ink.

III

Saturday, September 22, 1860
Three days later

Mary noticed without looking.

It wasn't the way Hannah moved—that had changed days ago—

but the way she stopped. The pause before rising. The slight bracing of a hand against the table that lingered a breath too long to be habit.

Mary said nothing.

At supper, she passed the salt and watched Hannah hesitate before reaching for it, then decline with a small shake of her head.

Later, she poured tea and set Hannah's cup down a little farther from the edge than before. No comment. No question.

The noticing continued. Incremental. Practical. Mary placed a cushion on the chair Hannah favored. She served smaller portions more often. She opened windows before the room grew warm.

Hannah accepted each change without remark.

It was only when Mary reached to lift a basin that Hannah spoke. "I can manage."

Mary paused, then set it down anyway. "I know."

They stood there together for a moment, the space between them unoccupied.

Mary wiped her hands on her apron. "How long have you known?"

Hannah took a moment to reply. When she did, her voice was even. "Not long."

Mary nodded. She didn't ask how. She didn't ask why. "And Christian?"

"No."

Another nod. Slower this time.

Mary reached out then—not to Hannah's shoulders, not to her face—but to her hands, folding them gently together as though returning something set down improperly. "All right."

That was it. No blessing. No warning. No prayer spoken aloud.

Mary turned back to the stove and adjusted the kettle. "You shall rest this afternoon," she said. "The air is heavy."

"Yes," Hannah replied.

Mary didn't ask what Hannah intended to do.

She already knew.

IV

Thursday, October 4, 1860
Twelve days later

Christian found Jacob at Trevanion near dusk.

The day's work had thinned. Wagons stood idle. A few men lingered at the edge of the yard, talking low. Jacob stood near the stable, sleeves rolled, hands dark with dust and grain. He looked up as Christian and Elder approached and didn't smile.

"Father," he said.

Christian stopped a few paces away and dismounted his horse. He didn't remove his hat. "We need to speak."

Tension pulled visibly at Jacob's jaw. "Here?"

"Aye."

Jacob glanced once toward the men, then back. "You've chosen your moment."

"I've waited long enough."

That earned a short laugh. "Have you?"

"The fire at Fairlight was set," Christian said, holding his gaze. Jacob's expression didn't change. "The law is finished with it. No charges. No names on paper. But that does not end the matter."

Jacob wiped his hands on a rag. Slowly. Deliberately. "You didn't ride all this way to tell me what I already know."

"No," Christian said. "I came to ask you why you didn't."

Jacob stilled. "Why I didn't what?"

"Come home. Speak plainly. Tell me where you were, and why."

"You already have your answers," Jacob said, his mouth twitching.

"I have suspicions," Christian said. "That's different."

Jacob stepped closer. "From whom?" Christian didn't answer. "That's what I thought. Bixler. Dallas. Men you've never trusted—until it suited you."

Christian's voice remained even. "This is *not* about Trevanion."

"It never is with you," Jacob snapped. "It's always about me."

Christian's eyes sharpened. "It's about Josephus."

Something dark flickered across Jacob's face. "You don't get to use him."

"I'm not," Christian replied. "I'm naming what was done to him. And what you did afterward."

Jacob laughed then—too loud, too sudden. "You think because I spoke first, I lit the match?"

"I think," Christian said carefully, "that you rode hard with knowledge you had not earned. And that since then, you have let silence do your work for you."

Jacob leaned in. "And I think you came here to condemn me because it's easier than admitting you never knew how to raise me."

That landed.

Christian didn't retreat. "I taught you restraint. I taught you that anger does *not* absolve you of consequence."

"You taught me to wait," Jacob said. "And watch other men take what they wanted."

Christian's voice dropped. "I taught you not to take what was not given."

Jacob's breath came harder now. "Josephus had everything handed to him!"

"That's a lie, Jacob," Christian said.

Jacob's eyes burned. "It's the only truth that ever made sense."

For a moment, neither spoke.

Then Christian said quietly, "If you have done this thing, Jacob. If you have stood near it, you are in danger of your soul." Jacob glared at him. "That…is why I came. Not for the law. For you."

The silence stretched.

Jacob's face hardened into something final. "You don't get to claim my soul now. Not after all this." Christian waited. "I don't answer to you. I don't answer to Josephus's ghost. And I sure as hell don't answer to whatever story you've decided to believe."

Christian spoke once more. "I am still your father."

Jacob laughed again, short and bitter. "No. You were."

Christian inhaled slowly. "Jacob—"

"You speak of the danger to my soul, sir?" Jacob asked, the last word careless. "Then tend to your own, for I damn yours to hell! I wash my hands of you!"

The words fell heavy and unmistakable. Not shouted. Not theatrical. Chosen.

The men nearby went quiet.

Jacob straightened. "You don't get to disown me. I disown you.

I want nothing from you. I will take nothing you offer. You are *not* my father."

Christian looked at him for a long moment. Then he said, very calmly, "That is not a thing you can undo."

Jacob shrugged. "I don't care."

Christian turned, mounted Elder, and rode away.

Jacob didn't follow.

CHAPTER IV

Saturday, May 25, 1997

I

Ernest Marlowe didn't read from a journal this time.

He sat with his hands folded loosely over his knees; the fire had reduced again to coals. The night had dissipated, giving way to the approaching dawn. Someone's watch chimed softly and was silenced at once—5:00 a.m.

Shock sat on every face.

Todd spoke first. "What should be appreciated here is that Jacob broke one of the Ten Commandments. Honor thy father. Such a thing wasn't taken lightly back then."

"Or now," Deborah added.

"In addition to murder?" Carrie asked, her eyes flicking to Todd from the corner of her vision.

"That was never proven," Ernest said.

Carrie angled her head, her gaze meeting Ernest's with a distinct expression of skepticism. "But we know. The evidence is all there. If they'd had modern-day forensics, they'd have totally busted his ass, but good!"

Ernest shrugged. "You're probably right."

"Did Christian ever see Jacob again?" Carrie asked.

Ernest shook his head. "Not after that day."

Ryan leaned forward. "Jacob worked at Trevanion, a few miles away from Christian's farm, and never ran into Christian anywhere?"

"Jacob left Carroll County, but not right away," Ernest replied. "The questions didn't stop. Sheriff Segafoose went back to Trevanion more than once. Not with charges, but with more questions."

Deborah frowned. "And Trevanion?"

"They tolerated him," Ernest replied. "Until they didn't need to anymore."

Carrie hugged her knees tighter. "What happened?"

Ernest glanced once toward the dark beyond the firelight, where the slope rose toward the ruins.

"Jacob left Trevanion in November, a little over a month after he disowned Christian," he said. "There was no notice or farewell. He took what he could carry and rode south. Virginia or the Carolinas, most likely. No one in the family knows."

"And he was never arrested?" Carrie asked.

"No," Ernest replied. "The law was finished with him. The people weren't. Sheriff Segafoose certainly wasn't. He knew, but he couldn't prove it. If I had to guess? He was hoping Jacob would slip up, change his story, or give Segafoose something to move against him. If Trevanion didn't ask him to leave, then Jacob fled to escape all the scrutiny."

Ryan nodded slowly. "He erased himself."

Ernest considered that. "Jacob Marlowe was never seen or heard from again by anyone in Carroll. So…yes."

The group sat with that.

"And Hannah?" Carrie asked quietly.

Ernest looked back at the fire. "Hannah stayed." After a moment, he added, "Everything else that mattered came after."

The fire shifted; a coal collapsed inward with a faint hiss. "Daylight's almost here. I don't think we'll need to stoke the fire again." He pulled the journals from his backpack and prepared to read. "Christian and Mary's reaction to Jacob's decision is important. You should hear them before we skip to the birth of Hannah's child."

Beyond the campfire, the land held.

II

Christian Marlowe—Journal
Undated, written following the visit to Trevanion

I have buried another son. One who yet lives.

This is a harder thing than death, for death closes its accounts. This does not.

Jacob spoke words to me today that cannot be recalled. I do not write them here. It is enough that they were chosen, and that they were meant to sever. He believes separation to be power. I believe it to be hunger.

I have searched my own instruction for the place where I failed him. I find many places where I was insufficient. I do not find a place where I taught him cruelty.

He says I no longer have claim upon him. This may be true in law, or in pride. It is not true in flesh. A father does not unmake himself by consent.

I fear not for my name, nor for the story he tells of me. I fear for the narrowing of his world, which now admits no counsel but his own.

I have commended him to God, because I have no other authority.

If I am wrong, I pray I will be corrected.

If I am right, I pray mercy will find him anyway.

III

Mary Marlowe—Journal
Undated, written the same week

Christian does not sleep.

When he does, he wakes as though called back sharply, as though something has been left unfinished and cannot be laid down. I do not ask what Jacob said. I do not need to know the words to know the damage.

A mother learns early the difference between harm and danger. Harm can be tended. Danger resists care.

Jacob has chosen danger.

I grieve not only for the son I may never see again, but for the man he refuses to become. This is a quieter, lonelier grief. It has no rites.

Christian speaks of duty and of prayer. I speak of neither. I keep watch.

There are things a mother cannot repair. There are things she can still hold open.

I will hold what remains open, as long as I am able.

IV

Hannah Marlowe—Journal
Undated, written at the Marlowe Farm

I have been among the Marlowes long enough now to see the shape of their care.

They speak more than we would. They name their fears and then set them down, as though the saying itself were part of the work. This is not wrong. It is not my way. I listen, and I learn where the walls are, and what they choose to leave open.

Christian bears his sorrow outward. Mary bears hers by watching. Between them, the house holds.

They have taken me in without asking me to become other than I am. I note this with gratitude.

I do not know yet what will be asked of me.

What I do know is this: the child moves when I am still.

It is not constant. It does not call for attention. It is simply there. A quiet assurance that something has been placed into my keeping without instruction.

Josephus would have liked that. He believed that what was given honestly required no embellishment.

I have not spoken of names. It is too early for that. But there is one that returns to me, unbidden, in the pauses between thought.

God with us.

Not as promise. Not as protection from what must be borne.

As fact.

If the child is a son, that name will stand.

If a daughter, its meaning will still be held.

I do not say this aloud. I write it only here, where words are not required to be proven.

God has not removed what was taken.

But He has not left me without company.

This, I believe, is enough.

CHAPTER V

Friday, April 5, 1861

I

Hannah Marlowe's labor began before dawn.

Not sharply. Not all at once. It announced itself the way so many things had lately: as pressure first, then insistence. She woke with her hand already pressed to her abdomen, breath shallow, the room dim and undecided.

Mary Marlowe was with her within minutes. "That's it," she said, not asking.

Hannah nodded.

Christian Marlowe sent the carriage for Mrs. Sarah Englar before dusk the night before, a midwife in her mid-fifties, whom they'd decided upon months earlier. By the time the pain gathered itself into something that could no longer be mistaken, the house was already arranged around waiting.

Molly moved quietly through the lower rooms, setting water to heat, laying cloths aside to be boiled. She didn't ask where she was needed. She knew.

By the time the carriage returned, the night thinned toward morning.

Mrs. Englar arrived without comment, her black leather bag held close against her side, the handle worn soft with use. She removed her cloak, washed her hands thoroughly, then again, and nodded once to Mary.

"How long?" she asked.

"Since before first light," Mary replied.

Mrs. Englar nodded her head once. "All right."

She went to Hannah and took her wrist gently, fingers firm and practiced. "Slow work," she said. "That's not a bad thing."

Hannah closed her eyes and nodded.

The hours passed without shape.

Pain rose and receded. Rose again. Each time it left her more emptied than before. Mrs. Englar spoke rarely, but when she did, it was with authority that didn't require explanation.

"Breathe with me now," she said.

Hannah complied in measured cadence. Her face flushed, sweat breaking and running freely.

Molly knelt when needed, braced Hannah's back, and pressed a cool cloth against her neck. Her hands were steady. Her voice was low.

"That's right. Let it come," Molly said, not as encouragement, but as statement. "You doin' it."

Mary remained close, silent except when asked. She offered water. She wiped Hannah's brow. She watched the midwife's face more closely than Hannah did.

Outside the room, Christian waited.

He didn't pace. He didn't pray aloud. He sat where he could hear if called and nowhere else.

When the labor lengthened, Mrs. Englar's mouth tightened slightly. She said nothing of it. "Stay with it, Hannah. Don't hurry what won't be hurried."

Hannah nodded. "I can't feel my hands," she whispered between labored breaths.

"That's normal," Mrs. Englar said. "Feeling shall return after your body has rested."

When the child finally came, it didn't come easily.

Hannah cried out then. Not from fear, but from the sheer demand of it.

Mrs. Englar's eyes darted from Hannah's face to the work before her. Her voice cut through the sound, calm and immovable. "Now!" she said firmly. "Now, Hannah!"

The room narrowed to breath and pressure, and heat. And

then…release.

A sound followed. Small. Wet. Alive.

Molly laughed softly before she could stop herself, one hand covering her mouth.

Mrs. Englar worked quickly and efficiently. She lifted the child, cleared him, and wrapped him. Her movements were practiced and economical. "It's a boy."

Mary closed her eyes, her lips moving in silent prayer.

Mrs. Englar placed the child against Hannah's chest. For a moment, Hannah struggled to lift her arms. When she saw the child's face, she found the strength.

He was warm. He was real. He rooted instinctively, as though he'd been waiting.

Hannah pressed her cheek to his head and breathed him in. "Emmanuel," she whispered.

The name came not as announcement, but as recognition.

Mrs. Englar noted the name but didn't comment.

The child quieted. Hannah did not. Her bleeding didn't stop as it should have.

Mrs. Englar moved at once, issuing instructions without raising her voice. Molly responded instantly. Mary's hands trembled only once before steadying.

"More cloths," Mrs. Englar said. Molly placed them on the table.

"Should I send for Christian?" Mary asked.

"Not yet," Mrs. Englar said without looking at her.

Hannah's vision dimmed and returned, then dimmed again. "What's happening? I feel faint."

"Flooding," Mrs. Englar replied, massaging Hannah's lower abdomen. She glanced once at Molly. "Help keep Emmanuel steady. The rooting will help contract the uterus. Mary, there are dried ergot spurs in my kit. Crush half a teaspoon and add it to boiling water. If you have honey, mix some to remove the bitterness. Hurry."

Mrs. Englar worked with all the skill she had. Molly held Emmanuel in place as Hannah struggled to stay with them. Mary brought Hannah the ergot tea, helping her drink as much as she could.

At last, the bleeding slowed. When Mrs. Englar leaned back, the lines at the corners of her mouth had deepened. "She's held. But she's paid dearly for it."

Mary heard what wasn't said and frowned.

Hannah opened her eyes, holding Emmanuel tighter now. "He's all right?"

"Yes," Mrs. Englar said. "He is."

That was enough.

Hannah closed her eyes again, Emmanuel still against her chest, his breath shallow and sure.

Outside, the morning had fully arrived.

Inside, the house rearranged itself around what had been given—and what had been taken.

II

Monday, April 8, 1861
Three days later

Hannah didn't rise from the bed for three days.

No one asked her to.

The room stayed dim, curtains drawn against the worst of the afternoon light. Emmanuel slept beside her in a shallow basket lined with folded cloth, close enough that she could reach him without shifting her weight. When he stirred, she didn't hurry. She'd learned already the difference between need and restlessness.

He rooted against her with determination, small mouth searching, hands opening and closing as though grasping for something he already knew belonged to him.

"There," she murmured, guiding him. "I know."

The word *know* surprised her. But it was true.

He fed slowly. Persistently. When he finished, he slept with his cheek against her skin, breath warming the hollow at her collarbone. Hannah watched the rise and fall of his chest until her own breathing matched it.

Mary came and went without comment.

She brought broth and bread, soaked until it would yield without chewing. She changed the linens herself. When Hannah slept, Mary sat nearby and read without turning pages, simply holding the book open as though that, too, were watchfulness.

Molly bathed Emmanuel each morning, humming under her

breath. She didn't ask Hannah's permission. She handed the child back, warm and wrapped, as though returning something borrowed.

"He strong," she said once. "Got a good grip."

Hannah smiled faintly. "He does."

Christian came only when invited.

When he did, he stood at the foot of the bed and looked down at the child without reaching for him. Hannah noticed the restraint and understood it for what it was. Reverence.

"You named him," Christian said quietly.

"Yes."

She didn't explain.

On the fourth day, Hannah sat up.

The effort left her lightheaded, but she held Emmanuel steady against her chest and waited for the room to settle. When it did, she smiled to herself. Not triumphantly, but with relief.

Mary noticed anyway. "You needn't prove anything."

"I'm not," Hannah replied. "I just wanted to see him from here."

She didn't sit up again that day.

III

Monday, April 15, 1861
A week later

In the week that followed, Hannah learned the shape of Emmanuel's wakefulness. The way his eyes searched before finding her. The sound he made just before sleep claimed him again. She spoke to him softly. Not stories. Observations.

"That's the window," she told him once. "That's the sound of the creek. That's your hand."

She didn't tell him about Fairlight.

Her strength didn't return as it should have.

Hannah tired easily. Feeding left her shaking. There were mornings when Mary helped her sit, and Hannah had to pause, breath shallow, waiting for her heart to remember its work.

Mrs. Englar came once more, unannounced.

She stood at the foot of the bed and studied Hannah with the same steady eye she'd used during the labor. "You're not mending as I'd like."

Hannah nodded. "I know."

Mrs. Englar didn't soften it. "You're holding because you must."

"Yes."

"That will not last forever."

"No."

Mrs. Englar pressed her lips together. "You'll need a doctor."

Mary inhaled sharply.

"Not yet," Hannah said. "Let him grow a little more."

Mrs. Englar considered her, then inclined her head. "Soon, then."

After she left, Hannah lay back against the pillows and held Emmanuel close. He slept, mouth slack, one hand curled against her skin.

She traced his ear with one finger, smiled softly, and whispered, "I'm here."

Outside, spring deepened. Fields greened. The world continued, unremarkable and insistent.

Inside, the house learned a new rhythm. Shorter days, quieter movements, careful hands.

By the time Christian sent for the doctor, no one was surprised.

Only afraid.

IV

Wednesday, April 17, 1861
Two days later

Dr. Myers came from Westminster on a gray morning.

He wasn't young, nor especially old. He spoke plainly and didn't waste motion. After washing his hands, he examined Hannah with care, asking questions she answered without embarrassment. Mary remained nearby. Molly stood at the window, listening without turning.

When the examination was done, Dr. Myers stepped back and folded his hands. "There is infection. Likely from the labor."

Mary's throat tightened. "Can it be treated?"

The doctor hesitated—not long enough to lie. "I can ease it. I can slow the pain. But the body has already been injured."

Hannah's eyes held his, steady and unblinking. "Will I recover?"

His lips tightened into a thin line before he answered. "No."

Silence followed. Not shocked, not panicked. Just present.

"I shall leave you laudanum," he continued. "In careful measure, it will dull the pain and steady your strength for a time. You must rest. You mustn't exert yourself."

Hannah closed her eyes and nodded. "How long?"

He considered. "Days. Perhaps weeks."

"That will be enough," she said.

Dr. Myers paused. "You should not ride."

Hannah didn't argue. She simply said, "I will."

He glanced at Mary, then back at Hannah. He'd seen this before. This wasn't defiance; it was decision.

Dr. Myers reached into his bag and set a small, corked glass bottle of laudanum on the table beside Hannah's bed. "I shall return if summoned."

When he was gone, Mary sat beside the bed. "You needn't be brave, Hannah."

Hannah smiled faintly. "I'm not. I've just finished waiting."

V

Friday, April 19, 1861
Two days later

The laudanum helped.

It softened the edges of the pain and allowed Hannah to sit, to stand briefly, to walk the length of the room with Emmanuel held close against her chest. It didn't make her strong; it made her *capable.*

She used that capability carefully.

Hannah watched Emmanuel wake and sleep. She learned the sound of his hunger and the quieter sound of his comfort. She memorized the weight of him, the exact curve of his head beneath her palm.

Some nights, when the pain receded far enough to leave room for thought, she let herself look ahead.

Not far. Just enough.

Mary looked up from the table where the newspaper lay. She looked pale and ill.

"What does the newspaper say?" Hannah asked.

Mary tilted the paper to show Hannah. The headline of the *American Sentinel* was large and bold in its announcement.

WAR! THE BLOW STRUCK!

"The Confederates attacked Fort Sumter in South Carolina," Mary softly said, setting the paper down. "Union troops stationed there surrendered. Lincoln called for 75,000 volunteers to suppress the rebellion."

Hannah closed her eyes and nodded in resignation. The news was inevitable. It did not concern her. She looked out the window into the yard and the fields her husband once tended. "It doesn't seem real. It's all so far away from here."

Mary folded the paper once and set it aside. "There are ripples. William Dallas of Trevanion has left to fight alongside the Confederates. His mill has closed temporarily. So they say."

Hannah didn't reply. She turned to Mary and spoke plainly. "I need to go back."

Mary didn't ask where.

"Soon," Hannah said. "Before I can't."

Mary closed her eyes. When she opened them again, she nodded.

Christian was told afterward.

He didn't argue. He only said, "I will make the arrangements."

Hannah thanked him.

CHAPTER VI

Saturday, April 20, 1861

I

Hannah spoke to Emmanuel that morning.

Not stories. Not prayers. Only truths.

"Your father was a good man," she told him when the room was quiet, and her breath came easier. "He believed in doing things properly, even when no one was watching." She rested her cheek against his head. "He loved you before he knew you." Hannah paused. "That's a thing you should keep."

She didn't tell Emmanuel about Fairlight. Instead, she told him about hands that built. About water that turned a wheel. About order that came from care, not force.

When she grew tired, she stopped.

When the pain returned, she waited.

It was that morning that Hannah knew she wouldn't see another sunrise. She asked Mary to ready her horse, Lark, and a carriage. "It's nearly time."

Mary nodded and left to tell Christian.

Hannah kissed Emmanuel's brow and held him longer than usual, breathing him in as though fixing him in memory. "I'm here," she whispered again. "That's what matters."

Outside, the carriage was being readied.

II

Hannah rose in the late afternoon from a nap she didn't know she needed.

She stood carefully but not quietly, as though the evening itself were something that might bruise if handled too roughly. There was no need. The laudanum steadied her enough to dress, to move without the room tilting away from her. She chose the blue dress, the one Josephus liked because it didn't pretend to be anything else. Mary helped her fasten it without comment.

The carriage stood ready in the yard. Lark was already harnessed, head lowered, patient in the familiar way of a horse that had learned through years of service.

The afternoon was cool and bright, the air clear enough to make distance feel negotiable.

Hannah paused beside Emmanuel's cradle. He slept, one small hand fisted against the blanket, breath soft and regular. She lifted him gently and held him against her chest, feeling the warmth of him, the undeniable weight.

"I love you," she said quietly.

She didn't say more than that. Love didn't require instruction.

She kissed his brow once, then again, and handed him to Molly, who took him without ceremony, as though this were an ordinary exchange, not something that would be remembered forever.

"You'll mind him," Hannah said.

Molly nodded. "I will."

Mary stood near the door, hands folded, watching Hannah with an attention that had nothing to do with fear. When Hannah reached her, Mary embraced her fully, without restraint, as though holding her might be the only honest response left.

"Take your time," Mary said, her voice steady.

Hannah nodded. "I will." She paused, considering her following words. "If I'm not back by dusk, have someone ride to Fairlight. Just to see."

Mary's mouth tightened for a moment before she mastered it. "All right."

At the threshold, Hannah stopped. She turned then, slowly, and looked at each of them in turn. Mary. Molly. The house that had held her when she could no longer hold herself.

"Thank you," she whispered.

It was enough. It had to be.

Christian waited by the carriage. He helped her up without haste, his hands careful, practiced, as though this were simply another kindness in a long line of them. For a moment, he stood close enough that she could feel his warmth, the familiar steadiness.

"You've always known what was right," Hannah whispered. "Josephus did, too. I never doubted where he learned it."

Christian swallowed. "I loved him."

"I know," Hannah replied.

He took Hannah's hand as a tear slipped down his cheek. "And I loved you as if you were my blood."

She nodded once, laying her other hand on top of his. "Goodbye, Christian."

He stepped back.

The carriage rolled forward, wheels turning slowly over the packed earth, Lark setting an easy pace.

Hannah didn't look back. Behind her, the yard settled. Emmanuel stirred, then slept again. The house resumed its quiet keeping.

Ahead of her, Fairlight waited.

III

The road to Fairlight hadn't changed.

That was the first thing Hannah noticed.

It bent where it always had, dipped toward the creek, rose again through the stand of trees where the light thinned and cooled. Lark kept a steady pace, hooves finding the familiar ruts without guidance, as though the way were still written into her.

Hannah sat back against the seat and let the carriage carry her.

The laudanum dulled her pain, but not the knowing. Each breath arrived shallow, then steadied. She focused on the rhythm of the wheels, the soft creak of leather, the sound of water moving somewhere just out of sight.

Fields passed. Then fences. A stretch of land where the grain had already begun to lift green and tentative. Life, unbothered by memory.

As the trees closed in, the air changed. It was cooler now. Heavier.

The creek came into view, its surface broken by light and shadow, stones showing through the clear water the way she'd remembered. She recalled standing there with Josephus once, his sleeves rolled, trousers damp at the cuff, both of them watching the wheel turn as if it were a thing alive.

"You can tell when it's right," he'd said. "It sounds different."

The memory arrived without warning and left just as quickly. Hannah didn't reach for it.

The road narrowed, and the carriage slowed of its own accord as the ground grew uneven, ash still worked into the soil in places where grass hadn't yet reclaimed it. Hannah felt the faint resistance beneath the wheels, the way the earth no longer yielded smoothly.

Then the clearing opened.

Fairlight didn't rise to meet her. It lay where it had fallen.

Stone showed through the undergrowth—low lines where walls had been, the suggestion of a porch, the darker hollow of the basement settled back into the hill. The millrace remained, water moving obediently through its channel, answering a purpose that no longer stood.

Hannah asked Lark to stop. The horse complied.

For a moment, Hannah remained seated, taking in what was left without judgment. The land was quiet. It didn't wait. It didn't grieve. It was simply present.

A sound came from the woods then—a crack, sharp and sudden, followed by the tearing rush of a limb giving way.

Hannah stopped, one hand pressed lightly against her side, and closed her eyes.

Nothing followed it. No answering call. No movement meant to be read.

She waited anyway.

The sound came once more, farther off this time, and then the woods settled back into themselves.

She exhaled. *Old tree*, she thought, not with relief, but recognition.

Hannah carefully stepped down from the carriage, one hand braced against the wheel until the ground steadied beneath her feet. The air smelled of damp earth and leaf mold, spring asserting itself even here.

By morning, the fallen tree would still be there, or it would not.

Either way, Josephus would not come back.

Fairlight didn't ask her to hurry.

It had time.

IV

Hannah took the path on foot.

It began where it had worn shallow by years of use, stones set by habit rather than plan. She moved slowly, not from hesitation, but from attention. Each step asked for its due now, and she paid it.

This was the way she'd walked in the early days, when Fairlight still stood whole, and the future had felt proportioned correctly; wide enough to live inside without fear of collision. She remembered the sound of her skirts brushing the grass, Josephus ahead of her, turning now and then to say something small and practical, as though the world could be kept in order by noticing it properly.

The basement ruins came into view first.

Stone steps rose from the earth and went nowhere, their upper end broken, purpose unfinished. She paused there, resting one hand against the cool surface. This had once been the heart of the house—cellar shelves, stores kept through winter, the steady logic of preservation.

Now it was only a shape the land had not yet erased.

Beyond it, the tenant house stood empty.

Its door hung closed, unlatched, a window left open just enough to admit light and no one else. It hadn't been disturbed. Seven months had changed little. A chair still leaned where it had last been set. The hearth was clean. The silence inside it felt provisional, as though someone had stepped out and not yet returned.

Hannah continued her walk without going in.

The ground dipped where the old privy pit had been covered, the soil darker there, settled unevenly. She stopped and looked down at it for a long moment, her breath shallow but steady.

From her pocket, she took the laudanum bottle. It was nearly empty. Enough remained to dull what lay ahead, to blur the edges, to shorten the distance between pain and rest.

She held it once more, then shook her head, almost smiling. "Not this," she said quietly. "Not anymore."

She knelt with care and pressed the bottle into the softened earth, covering it with her hands, packing the soil back down as though correcting a wrong.

The springhouse waited beyond the trees. Its stone walls stood firm, moss darkened by shade and damp, the doorway cool even in the lengthening light. The sound of water reached her before she crossed the threshold—steady, patient, unchanged.

Inside, the air bore a familiar smell: clean stone, cold water, leaf rot carried in on shoes. Hannah sat on the low ledge and drew the lockbox into her lap.

This was the journal she'd kept when she could no longer speak freely. The one she'd hidden here, believing, correctly, that the springhouse remembered what the house couldn't.

She wrote slowly.

Not everything. Just what mattered.

When she finished, she closed the book and returned it to the box.

She'd just settled the lid when she felt it. Not sound, but presence.

Hannah looked up.

Ash stood in the doorway.

For a moment, she couldn't move.

He was thinner now, his ribs faintly visible beneath his coat, his muzzle grayer, his eyes wary in a way they'd never been before. One ear bore a small tear she didn't recognize. He stood half in light, half in shadow, as though unsure whether he was welcome in a world that had burned without him.

"Oh," she breathed. Ash took one careful step forward, then another. He stopped again, waiting. "I thought you were dead."

The words surprised her with their steadiness.

Ash's tail moved once, tentative. He crossed the threshold and pressed his head gently against her knee, as if testing whether she were real.

Hannah rested her hand against his neck. "So did I," she whispered.

They stayed like that for a long moment, the sound of the spring steady beneath them, two survivors who hadn't known they were still counted.

At last, Hannah drew a breath and stood. "Come on."

Ash followed without question.

Outside, the light warmed, thinning toward gold.

Josephus waited.

V

The path rose gently at first.

Hannah took the steps slowly, one at a time, the lockbox held tight against her chest. The hill had never been steep. It had never asked much of her before.

Halfway up, it changed.

The ground tilted more sharply, and the effort required to place each foot became deliberate, then painful. Her breath shortened. The world narrowed to the space immediately ahead of her, to the simple work of lifting, setting down, lifting again.

She stumbled. Not far. Just enough to break the rhythm. Hannah caught herself, palms scraping the earth, then pushed back to her feet.

Ash stopped at once. He turned and watched her, head lowered, body angled as if he might place himself beneath her weight if she fell again. Ash didn't bark. He didn't move until she did.

"I'm all right," she said, though the words came thin.

She took another step. Then another.

The second stumble came harder. Her knee struck stone. Pain flared white and sudden, stealing her breath. She knelt there, one hand braced against the ground, the other still wrapped around the lockbox.

Ash moved closer, close enough that she could feel his warmth.

"I'm almost there," she whispered.

The third time, she didn't try to rise at once.

Hannah knelt with her head bowed, breath shallow, the world pulsing in and out at the edges. For a moment, she was unsure if she could stand again.

Then something brushed against her wrist.

She looked down.

A small shape lay against the dirt near her knee—narrow, winged, its thin blade dulled with dust. It must have slipped from her pocket when she fell.

She stared at it as though trying to remember where it belonged.

Carefully, she reached for the seed. The wing trembled between her fingers. The soil beneath her was loose, ash returning to earth paces from where the basement once stood.

With the side of her hand, she pressed a shallow hollow into the ground.

Not deep. Just enough.

She placed the seed there and covered it with her palm. "For you."

The words barely carried.

Then she drew her hand away, wiped it once against her skirt, and gathered herself to stand.

The clearing was just ahead.

Josephus's grave lay where Christian had placed it, set slightly apart from the ruins, the fence he'd built surrounding it with careful, loving precision. Grass had grown over the earth now, softening the lines. The headstone stood clean and legible in the lowering light.

Hannah pushed herself up.

The last steps were not walked so much as endured. Her vision blurred. The edges of the world dimmed and returned, then dimmed again. She stepped over the fence and made it only as far as the stone before her strength gave way.

She fell to her knees beside him.

The lockbox slipped from her grasp and landed softly in the grass. Ash whined once, low and uncertain, as Hannah's hands pressed into the earth, fingers curling as though to hold fast to something solid.

She knew, then. There was no more time to be careful.

Hannah turned and lowered herself onto her side beside Josephus's grave, drawing the lockbox back into her arms. She curled around it instinctively, protecting it as she had protected everything else she loved. This must be found. This must remain.

She faced the stone, her forehead nearly touching the carved letters. Hannah didn't speak them aloud. She'd already said his name enough for a lifetime.

Fairlight was gone, but the ground beneath it was still hers.

Ash approached slowly and lay down beside her, his body curving to match hers. He rested his muzzle gently against her neck, breathing with her, steady and warm.

"Good boy," she whispered, smiling.

The sun hovered just above the horizon now, the sky burning orange and red, color deepening as light thinned. Hannah loved sunsets. She loved watching them with Josephus from the porch of Fairlight. She stared at it now, tears slipping free without effort, trailing into her hair and the grass beneath her cheek.

"It's you…" she murmured.

Her breath shuddered, then steadied once more.

"It's me…"

The sun dipped lower, the light breaking and spreading, the world holding still as if it knew.

Hannah closed her eyes.

"It's us."

The light slipped away.

The land went still.

Ash did not move.

CHAPTER VII

Saturday, May 25, 1997

I

Ernest Marlowe finished speaking just as the sun broke the horizon.

It came up slowly, a pale line at first, then a spill of light that broke through the trees and touched the clearing where Fairlight had once stood. The ruins, so indistinct in the dark, resolved themselves all at once—stone edges sharpened, the slope revealed, the ground made legible again.

Carrie looked back at the fully grown Virginia pine standing sentinel behind the crumbling foundation of what was once Fairlight.

She drew a breath.

Ernest watched as she slowly pivoted to look at him. With a gentle smile, he let her know that he understood. An extended explanation was entirely superfluous.

Carrie folded forward, elbows on her knees, her face buried in her hands. The sound she made was small, restrained, as though she were trying not to let the grief outrun her body. Tears slipped through her fingers anyway.

Ryan moved first. He crouched beside her, one hand settling between her shoulder blades. Deborah followed, kneeling on the other side, murmuring something too low to be heard.

Even Todd had gone quiet. He stared out at the light with his jaw set, eyes wet despite himself.

No one hurried Carrie.

Eventually, her breathing slowed. She wiped her face with the heel of her hand, then looked up, eyes red but steadying. "Did they ride out to Fairlight to look for her?"

Ernest nodded. "Yes."

"Beside Josephus?"

Ernest nodded again.

Carrie closed her eyes, nodding as though the answer had been the only one that could have made sense.

"Christian and his foreman rode out when Hannah didn't return," Ernest said. "They found her after the sun had set. Ash was with her."

Deborah pressed her lips together. They trembled slightly as the surrounding light grew brighter through the trees.

"And the journal?" Carrie asked. "Did they recover it?"

Ernest was already reaching for his pack. He set the other journals aside first, carefully, reverently, as though clearing space. Then he dug deeper and withdrew an object wrapped in cloth and twine. The fabric was old but clean, folded with intention.

He untied it slowly.

Hannah's lockbox emerged into the morning light.

It was smaller than Carrie had imagined. Worn at the edges, softened by use. The plaque on its lid caught the sun as it rose, light flashing across the engraved name:

HANNAH MARLOWE

For a moment, no one spoke.

As Carrie studied the lockbox, she felt not just the wood and age, but the presence of hands long gone.

Ernest held it as if it were still warm. "Yes, they did," he said quietly. "They found it before they brought Hannah's body back to the farm. Mary read it later that night."

He turned the small key, the click sharp in the stillness, and lifted the lid. Inside, the journal lay exactly as it had been placed, a mid-sized A.W. Faber pencil lying beside it.

When Ernest removed it, even Todd leaned forward. The pages

were thick, and the pencil marks unfaded. It was an antebellum relic, yet it felt unmistakably personal.

This wasn't just history. This was something tangible. It was Hannah's touch.

Ernest opened it near the back, where the last entry barely filled the page. A faint smile appeared on his lips. "I think Hannah would want you to read it, Carrie."

Carrie straightened her posture. "Me?"

"You," Ernest confirmed, holding out the journal to her.

She hesitated for a moment, but then took it with both hands.

As the sunrise crested over the trees of the woods, the land listened as Carrie spoke.

II

Hannah Marlowe—Journal
Last entry

I have little strength left, so I will be plain.

I came back because this is the only place my life ever fit.

I loved him. I was happy.

If I am remembered, let it be for that.

I ask that Christian and Mary Marlowe raise my son, Emmanuel. I trust them to do so with care and truth. They raised Josephus well, and he was a good man. I ask only that my son be taught to love what is right and to keep his word.

I ask to be buried beside my husband, Josephus Marlowe.

I ask that my horse, Lark, be cared for.

I ask that Emmanuel receive stewardship of the land when he comes of age.

I ask that Fairlight not be rebuilt.

Do not raise another house there. Let it remain as it is. The work meant for it is complete. What remains belongs to memory and to the keeping of the earth.

Please speak of Josephus and me to our son often, and with love. When he is of age, bring him to Fairlight and tell him what his father hoped for there. Not the loss, but the intention.

Tell him that he was loved before he was known.

Tell him that his father believed order was mercy, and that he lived accordingly.

When the time comes, tell him that we will meet him again in God's kingdom.

This is my last will and testament.

Hannah Marlowe

III

Carrie handed the journal back to Ernest with both hands.

"Fairlight is where Hannah learned to stand," she whispered, drawing a breath as she stood. "I need a minute."

No one stopped her.

She walked past the place where Fairlight had once stood, the outline now unmistakable in the whole morning light. Seeing it more clearly didn't steady her. It only sharpened what had been taken.

The slope fell away toward where the stone steps had once climbed down from the basement. Carrie stopped there and looked around.

The tenant house foundation was plain now—low stone lines half-swallowed by green, more absence than structure. Beyond that, through the trees lining Big Pipe Creek, she could see the darker suggestion of the mill's foundation, water still moving where it had always moved.

Most of this land had once been open.

That realization struck her suddenly. The forest had not always been here. It had returned, inch by inch, year by year, filling the spaces people had abandoned. That was why Fairlight had been so difficult to see at night. The land had taken it back carefully.

Before moving past the remains of the house's foundation, Carrie turned her head without turning her body and reached out to the old pine, her fingers brushing the rough bark. A thin layer of weathered scale loosened beneath her touch and fell quietly to the leaf-and-needle-strewn ground.

She glanced upward. The trunk rose straight and unbroken,

narrowing as it climbed, its branches beginning only well above her reach. The sky beyond it was pale and clear.

Her hand hesitated slightly, staying in place for an extra beat.

A tear slipped down her cheek.

She let her fingers fall away. A faint smile crossed her face—not wide, not triumphant—just certain. She gave the smallest nod and turned back to the path.

Carrie continued her slow descent down the slope when the ground gave slightly beneath her foot. She startled, then knelt. When she brushed the leaves and soil away, a small bottle lay exposed, its glass clouded with age, its cork long sealed.

She recognized it. Laudanum.

Carrie picked it up, turning it slowly in her hands. This, too, had been touched, chosen, and set aside.

A thought came then—not fully formed, but steady. Not sadness, not fear, but something steadier.

She placed the bottle back into the hollow her foot had made and covered it again, smoothing the earth as Hannah must have done.

Lower on the slope, where the stone steps had once ended, a dense cluster of honeysuckle and witch hazel grew thickly together. Carrie thought she heard something and paused.

Carefully, she made her way down and tried to part the branches. They didn't yield. The bushes pressed back gently, firmly, as though holding a boundary.

Carrie stopped and listened. The sound of water reached her then—the springhouse, still flowing, unchanged.

She stepped back. A small smile found its way to her mouth as she wiped the last of the tears from her face.

"Hello, Hannah," she whispered.

She stood there a moment longer, listening.

Then she turned and walked back toward the others.

IV

Ernest waved her over.

They were no longer near the fire pit but farther east along the rise, where the land fell gently. A hundred and forty years ago, this part of Fairlight would have been open space. Fields stretching out along a road that no longer existed. They were now in the heart of an old-growth forest.

Drawn by Ernest's bearing more than any visible sign, the others trailed behind him with minimal deliberation. “One more thing,” he said. “Before we go.”

Carrie joined them and only then saw what the darkness and the surrounding trees had concealed the night before.

Two stones stood slightly apart from the crumbling foundation, enclosed by the remains of a low fence. The wood had silvered and bowed with time; one rail had come loose and leaned inward, half swallowed by fallen leaves from autumns past.

The grave markers themselves were still legible.

Not newly tended, nor forgotten, just left.

“Grandpa Henry used to say Emmanuel came out every Sunday after services,” Ernest explained. “He would talk to them.”

He glanced at the stones. “Christian and Mary kept it up first. Then Emmanuel. Then the rest of us, when we remembered. Pa comes out in the summer to clear the leaves since there isn’t much grass anymore. Ephraim and I usually tag along.”

Carrie approached Hannah's grave marker from the side, her fingertips brushing lightly over the cool, rough stone at the top.

Ryan observed her with a close eye, anticipating that Carrie might break down in tears once more. She did not.

Ernest removed a laminated photograph from his pack and handed it to her.

Carrie turned from Hannah’s grave and stared.

Josephus and Hannah Marlowe stood together, young and composed, Fairlight rising behind them—the house whole, the wraparound porch embracing it, the land open and clear.

"Emmanuel had a new photo made from the wet-plate negative," Ernest explained. "Pa had this photo laminated so it wouldn't get any more damaged than it already was."

Ryan seemed intrigued. "Does he still have the wet-plate?"

Ernest grinned. "In fact, he does. It's in the same safe Grandpa Hezekiah brought over from England. The same one that Christian gave Josephus. Pa keeps it in the basement. We don't take the wet-plate out of its wooden box because it's so old. Light would hurt it." Ernest paused and chuckled. "And just between us, the combination is still the same."

Carrie's eyes went wide. "Five. Fifteen. Fifty-nine," she whispered. "Wow."

Taking a step back, Ernest carefully guided Carrie's hand, lifting the photo into clearer view. "You can see the slope."

She stepped back a pace and lifted the photograph toward the slope. The others gathered behind her.

Where Fairlight had once stood, the land now rose uneven and green. The porch in the image hovered over brush and shadow. The windows looked out over nothing at all.

She adjusted the angle once, then again.

For a moment, the past and present held the same horizon.

The porch in the photograph rested against nothing but air. Trees stood where walls once had.

No one spoke as the sun climbed higher, and the illusion dissolved.

Carrie exhaled slowly and returned the photograph to Ernest. He took the photo and carefully slid it into his backpack.

"Whatever happened to the Almshouse?" Carrie asked. "I'm guessing it's not around anymore."

Ryan glanced down at Carrie. "You don't know?"

"Know what?"

"It's the Carroll County Farm Museum."

Carrie's eyes widened in disbelief, as if she'd seen an actual ghost. "Really? The big red brick building was the Almshouse?"

Ryan smiled and nodded. Ernest finished the answer. "It closed in 1965. A year later, it opened as the museum we all know. Which reminds me, I have one last thing to show you." With a hint of a smile, Ernest pulled out another laminated photo. "Emmanuel commissioned this photo in 1888. Actually, this is a photo of the original wet plate, which is also locked up at Pa's house."

He handed it to Carrie, who held it up for the group behind her to see. It was a black-and-white photo, worn around the edges, of a cast-iron plate at the base of a small tree. It read:

Ernest continued, "The next time any of you visit the Farm Museum, stop at the Landon C. Burns Park. At the end of the parking lot near South Center, you'll find Potter's Field and a single white oak tree. That's where this is."

Carrie, still smiling softly at the photo, whispered, "She wouldn't have liked that. Hannah didn't like the attention."

Ernest nodded. "That was her German Brethren upbringing. Christian mentioned in one of his journal entries that he and Mary weren't keen on going to the dedication. They only went because Emmanuel was eight, and it was important to them for him to see his mother remembered."

She handed the photo back to Ernest, who carefully tucked it away into his backpack.

"We are *so* going to see that tree, MacGyver!" Carrie said, playfully bumping Ryan with her hip.

"It's almost 6 a.m., Scout," he said, his grin widening as he nudged her in return. "Maybe we can catch a nap first?"

With a chuckle, Todd's gaze landed on his watch. "Thank God I don't have to work today."

Carrie turned to Todd. "Last night I said that I'd keep an open mind about ghosts. Show me a ghost, and I'd believe. You showed me one. Just not the way you thought." Todd waited. "The afterimage of Fairlight. That's the ghost, isn't it? And this place *is* haunted—not by anger, but by memory."

She gestured around them.

"Places aren't haunted because people suffered there. They're haunted because people were happy there once."

Todd nodded. He didn't argue.

Ryan slipped an arm around her shoulders and whispered, "You're right, Scout."

They began to gather their things, stamping out the last of the fire, leaving the clearing as they'd found it.

Ernest shook his head when Ryan leaned over to help move the stones. "I'll take care of that. It's my responsibility."

The others watched as he carried the stones back down the slope, returning them to the basement ruins of Fairlight, where he'd gathered them.

The land accepted them without sound.

Fairlight never needed to be rebuilt. It had already been remembered.

Fire may have destroyed the house, but it didn't destroy the name.

EPILOGUE

Friday, August 12, 1870

The lane that had once been the road to Fairlight was nearly gone.

Grass and saplings had claimed most of it; the ruts softened into suggestion rather than direction. A drifter rode slowly along what remained, his posture uneven in the saddle, his clothes stiff with dirt and long neglect. His hair hung past his shoulders in a tangled fall, his beard thick and matted, as though it hadn't known a blade in years.

He dismounted carefully.

The horse—old, ribbed, impatient—shifted and snorted as the man pulled a crutch from the sidesaddle. The leather there had once held a rifle. Now it held something simpler. Necessary.

He leaned on the crutch and walked, the pants of his left leg folded and pinned above the knee.

The small, fenced plots came into view first.

The grass around it was trimmed. Not recently, perhaps, but consistently. Someone still came. Someone still remembered. He stopped at the edge and looked down at the markers.

Josephus Marlowe
Born April 11, 1839
Died September 2, 1860

Hannah Marlowe
Born March 14, 1840
Died April 20, 1861

He read the dates twice. The second time, he didn't move.

She'd died within the same year, seven months after him.

The knowledge landed with no ceremony. His mouth opened slightly, then closed again.

He looked away.

The slope beyond the graves fell toward where the house had once stood. Nothing rose to meet him now. Ten years of undisturbed growth had done its work thoroughly. Trees stood where walls had been. Brush filled the spaces where windows once caught the light.

He stepped forward.

Halfway down the rise, he slowed.

The hardwoods crowded the clearing unevenly—maple, sycamore, young oak—their trunks narrow but certain. And among them, nearer the center of what had been the foundation, stood a single pine.

It rose straight and tall, its bark dark against the thinning sun, its needles stirring high above the rest. It didn't match the others. It didn't belong to their pattern. Yet there it stood, fixed where the house had anchored itself to the earth.

The drifter stopped.

The light caught behind the crown of it, breaking along the edges of the needles. He stood at the crest long enough that the shadow of the pine stretched toward him—then past him—then gathered around his boots as the sun lowered.

He descended the remainder of the slope without haste.

Up close, the tree was taller than he'd first measured. Its trunk was thick enough that his hand didn't quite span it. The lower branches had begun to die back, the living growth reaching higher, always higher.

He looked up.

The sky narrowed above him, framed in dark green.

The wind moved through the needles with a low, steady sound.

He stood there longer than he intended, the shade of the pine settling over his shoulders.

Then he lowered his gaze and continued toward the tenant house.

It remained, but only barely. Its roof sagged. One wall leaned outward, its bones showing through the rot. He made his way down, slow and uneven, and stepped inside. The floor dipped beneath his weight but held.

He rested the crutch against the wall. From his belt, he drew a knife.

The letters he carved were uneven, cut deeper in some places than others, the work of a hand that shook.

I'M SORRY

He stared at the words for a moment after he finished, as though waiting for something to follow. Nothing did.

The drifter turned and climbed back toward the clearing, the effort showing now. The horse waited where he'd left it, head lowered.

He'd gone only a short distance when he heard it.

A sharp crack—then the longer tearing sound of wood giving way, branches splitting as weight finally won.

He stopped.

It came again, farther off, the noise traveling more than it should have, the echo bending it into something larger.

He knew it at once.

A dead tree, hollowed through. Rain loosening the ground. Gravity doing the rest. He waited anyway.

No footsteps followed. No voice. No second sound meant for him.

Only the creek, steady and unconcerned.

He shook his head, faintly irritated at himself, and stepped sharply over a fallen limb.

People would say things about this place someday. They would need the sound to mean something.

Jacob Farrell did not.

He'd not answered to Marlowe in years. The name was no longer his. He did not want it.

He reached the clearing, mounted Brimstone, and rode away.

The woods closed behind him, unchanged.

January 15, 2026 – February 01, 2026
Summerville, South Carolina

WESTMINSTER HOLDS MORE STORIES FROM THE NINETEENTH CENTURY.

NEXT: COLLEGE HILL

AUTHOR NOTES

I

Where, oh where, do I begin?

I was never supposed to write this book. I was supposed to finish *Black Widow* first, the follow-up to 2024's *Scorpion* in the Ryan Thomas series. Life got in the way in early 2025. Specifically, a condition called vestibular hypofunction (VH) that completely undid me.

Basically, damage to the balance sensors in my inner ear disrupted my sense of orientation. Busy places became difficult. Screen time made it worse.

How I got it? Who knows. The likely causes could include a past viral infection, aging, or certain medications; it doesn't really matter. I got it, and it changed everything.

Since my day job involves extended screen time, which exacerbated my symptoms, I had to limit it. Shorter bursts, longer breaks, and then recovery time. Oh, and physical therapy twice a week to retrain my brain how to live like a normal person again.

PT began in late October 2025 and continues as of this February 2026 writing, although it's slowly improving, measured in quarter baby steps. It's frustrating as all hell, is what it is. Never take your balance for granted. When you lose it, it changes your life in ways you never imagined.

In early January, my PT cleared me to write again, as long as I did it in measured sessions with breaks when my eyes started to glitch.

Jumping back into *Black Widow* after a nine-month absence seems like a daunting task. It's difficult to pick up a scene where I left off, after what is, more or less, the time to be pregnant and give birth. Certainly, there must be something else I could work on to warm up, so to speak, to ease back into it.

Then it occurred to me: I've always wanted to write a period piece. Something before or during the Civil War, one era in American history that has consistently held my attention.

II

Before the VH, or at its beginning back in March 2025, I'd recently finished a documentary about an old house in Westminster, Maryland.

The Mehring house, or the old house on Uniontown Road with the wraparound porch.

Without a long dissertation about why, it's a house that has fascinated me since I first saw it in 1988. But I also needed to identify the man who built that house, since it appears in *Black Widow*. Jacob Mehring. That research took months of digging through deeds and wills.

In 1999, when that house was abandoned and falling apart, I took a walkthrough video of it. The company representing the deceased owner wanted to tear it down to build a new neighborhood on the ninety-six acres it sat upon.

I took that video because I feared that if the house were torn down, it would be forgotten.

I thought I'd take that footage of the house and make a documentary about it, complete with more history than you'd ever want to know. *Road to Resurrection: The Jacob Mehring House.* It's on my YouTube page. The link is in my biography at the front of this book.

The amount of history and stories from that era I'd compiled was more than I could use in the film. I figured there had to be enough leftover to craft a piece of fiction that would be historically accurate for Carroll County, Maryland.

There was.

But there was another story from my past, or previous life, should such things suit ya fine, that was begging to be told.

Fairlight.

III

When I was a young boy, perhaps six or seven, I would have recurring dreams about a fire and dying in it.

I'd wake up in a panic. Until I got used to it and didn't.

As I grew older, the dream evolved—or I remembered more of it.

By the time I was a teenager, I could recite chapter and verse the ending of that dream.

I was living in a nineteenth-century home. The bedroom was modest, with cream-floral wallpaper. A bowl and pitcher on a washstand. Thick, heavy blue curtains.

In the dream, I wake up and realize the house is on fire. A woman is lying beside me (presumably my wife, since unmarried people in that era could not stay overnight). I wake her and tell her to get dressed. I stand and toss her a dress while putting on trousers with suspenders. It's difficult to breathe.

I grab a desk chair, and after a couple of tries, bust out the nearest window. Glass flies every which way. Below, one story down, are several people, barely dressed in white shirts and black trousers, stretching out a huge wool blanket so my wife can jump and land safely. I throw a blanket over the windowsill and guide her up. She jumps and lands hard but safely. I turn back to step into the window, but do not make it.

Everything goes bright with fire.

Then I wake up.

The name of that house?

Fairlight Manor.

I've always known this in each iteration of that dream when it became more than just dying in a fire and waking up in a sweat.

The dream came less and less as I entered my twenties. Now, I barely have it at all. I think the last time was in 2016 or 2017.

Was it past-life regression, which often occurs in youth and then thins out over time as we age?

Who can say?

What I can say is that it's stuck with me all these fifty-plus years, and I've never forgotten it.

Much the same way, I didn't want the Mehring house forgotten.

Much the same way the Marlowes never forgot Fairlight.

When the internet became a way of life, I searched for that name, looking for clues that it might once have existed. Nothing ever turned up. I suspect if it were real, it disappeared into the mists of time, undocumented and forgotten. Because the reality is that unless there is documentation of a thing, a place, or people, time forgets us after two or three generations.

That thought frightens me more than death. It's also one of the many reasons I write and self-publish. My voice and my stories will continue long after I've shuffled off this mortal coil.

I don't want to be forgotten.

I want my life to have meant something more than survival.

Like Fairlight.

IV

The haunted house in the woods.

Where, if one approached, something unseen would come crashing through the trees to drive them back was a Carroll County legend before "urban legend" was a term anyone I knew used.

At least it was when I was in high school in the mid-to-late eighties.

The story was much the same as the one in this novel: woods somewhere in the county, a house no one could quite locate, and something that didn't permit visitors. In reality, the setting was said to be off Route 97, between Sykesville and Westminster, nowhere near Taneytown.

I heard it often enough during lunch period that the details fixed themselves, even as the location never did. No one could ever tell exactly where to go. Only that it was there.

As Ryan says, "Teenagers make most hauntings happen anyways."

That, I believe.

The closest location I was ever given was Bartholow Road. A friend and I went looking more than once. The only place we found was the Morgan Run Natural Environment Area—a broad stretch of Carroll County woodland, running roughly north to south for a mile and spanning several more east to west.

We didn't find a house. We found nothing that came crashing through the trees to turn us back.

To be fair, we didn't walk all of it. Not even close.

Still, the idea stayed with me. Not as something proven, but as something persistent; half memory, half invention, shaped by repetition more than fact.

I'll tell you what I think is closer to the truth: There's a private road out there, which I shan't name, that runs about a mile into those woods. Much of it isn't paved. Perhaps some curious kids wandered where they weren't supposed to, irritating some homeowners.

A cool haunted house story is far more enticing than being run off for trespassing.

Either way, it seemed, even then, like the beginning of a story.

This is that story.

V

I wrote this book in sixteen days and in fewer than 100,000 words.

Both are personal records.

For those nine months I couldn't write, when that's all I wanted to do, I had to believe this story, even in an unconscious form, was bursting to get out. I was sorely depressed for many of those months. I'm sure some folks would love nothing more than to lie on the couch and watch old movies and shows.

Not me.

Well, not anymore.

As I said, lose your basic sense of balance, and you'll take nothing so simple for granted again. I swear it.

All I wanted to do was write, but I couldn't.

I love this story more than I can explain. I love Jos and Hannah in equal measure.

I've never written anything like this. Putting aside the nineteenth-century cadence, which was challenging, most of my stories are verbose, with everything explained, including the ending, even if it's a cliffhanger.

Fairlight taught me trust. In you, the reader. That you'll understand enough of the subtext, of which there is plenty, to take something away from this story.

I've also never written an ambiguous ending that may have left you wondering to whom and what exactly Jacob was sorry for.

I don't know. That's for you to decide.

I trust you.

VI

Now for the historical bits.

The Mehring family was real. George was indeed the postmaster of Bruceville in the mid-to-late 1850s and died on September 4, 1860.

His wife, Elizabeth, did, in fact, hang herself in 1853 after losing three children to cholera.

Margaret (Maggie) kept a diary about the Civil War during her time at the Kleefisch Academy for Girls. It's one of the things she's best remembered for. The other was her deep involvement in the women's suffrage movement, which eventually led her to represent Carroll County at the Maryland state conventions in the 1910s. She lived to see the ratification of the 18th and 19th Amendments. Maggie died at Myrtle Hill in Bruceville in 1923, before the repeal of the 18th Amendment. Her life ended with her dream realized and intact.

Frederick founded the Mehring Phosphate Manufactory on Big Pipe Creek in Bruceville, processing phosphate for modern fertilizers. He, too, died at Myrtle Hill in 1923.

Hannah Mehring is a fictional character loosely based on Johanna Mehring in age and residence at Myrtle Hill. There isn't much information about Johanna except that she existed and died in 1908. It's why I created Hannah to replace her.

Joseph Shaw changed the *Carroll County Democrat's* name to the *Western Maryland Democrat* in 1863, making it a more aggressive, anti-Lincoln, pro-Confederate voice at a time when

Carroll County was sharply divided between Union and Confederate sympathizers. Shortly before President Abraham Lincoln's assassination, Shaw had published a sharply worded article condemning Lincoln and, according to contemporary accounts, suggesting that his death would be providential. A meeting was held at the Carroll County Courthouse on the night of Lincoln's assassination. At this meeting, attendees voted to run Shaw out of town because of his pro-Confederate editorials. A smaller group of five men broke into Shaw's room at the Anchor Hotel on April 24, 1865. They shot and stabbed him before dragging him into the lobby, where he bled to death. Those men were tried and found not guilty by a jury of mostly Know-Nothing sympathizers. After Shaw's death, Democrat William H. Davis formed an alternative newspaper, *The Democratic Advocate.*

William H. Grammer, the editor of the *American Sentinel*, died in 1878. His family and widow, Mary, continued the paper until it ceased in 1928.

Charles W. Webster, leader of the Carroll County Know-Nothing (American) Party, was the author of *Chronicles* in the *American Sentinel* that satirized Shaw. He was also one of the men who played a role in the public meeting that led to the mob that killed Shaw. Webster was also responsible for the structure that assured the mob's acquittal. He died in 1888.

William W. Dallas was an out-of-town farmer who bought the farm known as Brick Mills and renamed it Trevanion, a Dallas family name meaning "the meeting of streams" in Welsh. Dallas brought modern architectural trends to rural Maryland. At the outbreak of the Civil War, Dallas's sympathies lay with the South. He deeded Trevanion to his wife before leaving to join the Confederate Army. The war caused Dallas to suffer significant financial setbacks, forcing him to sell Trevanion in 1867. He and his wife, Louise, settled in Westminster in 1869 and built a new home called Graceland. He died in 1873.

William Segafoose was elected as the eleventh Sheriff of Carroll County, serving between 1859 and 1861. He was a registered Democrat and was often in conflict with the rising Unionists and Know-Nothings. He and his family also maintained a hotel in the Uniontown area of Westminster, and was described as "the most popular hotelkeeper who ever resided in the village." Segafoose died in 1891.

VII

I'd like to thank the following:

The Historical Society of Carroll County (HSCC) for its stewardship of the history where I grew up. The Box Lunch talks they do every month, as far as I'm concerned, are invaluable. I've perused their website enough not only to cobble together enough history for my documentary but also for this novel.

Laura Bankard, the Outreach and Events Director of the HSCC, for helping me get a copy of *Carroll County Newspaper Wars*. That book helped shape much of the history in this novel, including the animosity between the *American Sentinel* and *the Carroll County Democrat,* as well as the Carroll County Almshouse Scandal of 1858.

Yes, all of that is actual history from my hometown.

Jesse Glass Jr., the author of *Carroll County Newspaper Wars (Know-Nothings, Almshouse Scandals, and the Death of a Civil War Editor).* The information in his book was comprehensive and utterly fascinating. Mr. Glass clearly knew his material and loved it enough to document it. He, too, keeps the world that holds.

One of my favorite Facebook groups, *Friends of History in Carroll County, MD*, and its admins, Doris Hull and Wendy Raith. While compiling ideas for this novel, I posted there a few times to see if members had any stories they knew or remembered. I got way more than I could use. And thanks also to Paul Ledbetter for suggesting *Carroll County Newspaper Wars.*

Finally, thank you for taking the time to read *Fairlight.* If you enjoyed it, please consider leaving a review.

It helps stories like this endure.

The world that held, that burned, that continued.

It matters.

K.P.

PRISONER OF THE GAME

Beware of sounds that go "click" in the night.

In 1992, the case of Carter Frye went mostly unnoticed—just another quiet tragedy lost to time. Seven people were dead, and the man responsible claimed they'd all broken the rules of *the game.*

Told largely through Frye's own chilling perspective, Prisoner of the Game drags readers into the fractured corridors of a killer's mind—where reality and delusion blur, and every choice carries a price. Frye believes everyone must play. Those who refuse must pay the penalty. But even he doesn't realize he's trapped inside the very rules he created.

As the boundaries between sanity and madness collapse, one question remains:

What happens when he breaks his own rules?

This haunting, character-driven thriller blends psychological horror and dark suspense with a twist you'll never forget. Fans of *The Silence of the Lambs, American Psycho,* and *Seven* will find themselves compelled to keep turning the pages—long after the lights go out.

EXCERPT

We crossed the state line into Maryland in the early morning when the sky was still a crisp, deep blue. A mere few hours separated me from the town I'd left a year ago. I was getting nervous, almost scared. Before the day ended, I'd see her and my family again. I still didn't know what I'd say to any of them.

"Are you okay?" Julie asked.

I must have been fidgeting. I looked over at her and smiled a bit. "Yeah. There must be a thousand butterflies in my stomach."

"It'll be okay," she said with assurance as she sped the car up. I glanced out the windshield. A dusty white Chevy Caprice sat on the traffic island separating east-and westbound lanes. An undercover Law Enforcement officer watched us as we drove by. We were passing cars in the adjoining lanes, clearly over the speed limit—a tight knot formed in my gut.

"Slow down!" I snapped. "I don't want that undercover pig to stop us."

"Nobody's going to stop us. We're not really speeding." She smiled, totally laid-back. I turned around to watch the unmarked car pull out into traffic and speed up.

"Shit!"

Julie glanced into the rearview mirror with big, open eyes. "Whoops."

The cruiser caught up with us. Red and blue flashing lights on its dashboard lit up.

"*NO!*" I screamed. "I didn't come this far to get caught now!"

"Caught?" Julie asked as I watched a second state police cruiser approach from behind. This one had a distinctive Maryland State Police emblem painted on its side, its lights and siren going full force. "What do you mean '*caught*'?"

I was in trouble. It was over. They had me.

Maybe.

"Speed up," I said.

Julie panicked. "Carter, I can't outrun a cop in this car! I don't want to get caught, either. Let's just see what they want."

I looked around again. Two cruisers somehow turned into four.

"What the fuck is going on here?" I shouted to myself. This wasn't possible. How could they possibly have known I was coming? It made little sense. I glanced at Julie, her face pale and her forehead beaded with sweat. "Look. It's me they want. I'm wanted for murder." Julie looked at me with wide, shocked eyes. "I'm sorry. I wish you weren't involved."

"I'm not!" She declared, her voice low and menacing. "And I don't want you in my car anymore!" She slowed down. "I want you out of here and out of my life!"

I reached out and smashed her head into the door window without thinking. It shattered with the force of the impact, sending safety glass scattering across the front seat and onto the dashboard. The car swerved across the middle lane as Julie fell unconscious. I pulled her out of the driver's seat and into the passenger side. I looked at Julie once I was in control of the car to ensure she was still alive. She moaned. Blood dripped from an unseen cut on her head. I sighed, clicked the seatbelt into place, and stared at the highway before us. Other cars were pulling over at the coming melee.

Behind me, six or seven state Law Enforcement cruisers were screaming at me with sirens and blinding me with their lights. An assortment of red and blue flashes filled the rearview mirror as the white, blinding bursts of the cruiser's high beams added to the visual mash. I sped up, hoping to outrun them.

"Pull over!" a booming voice over a loudspeaker said. "If you pull over now, no one will be hurt."

"Bullshit!"

I drove faster, weaving in and out of thinning traffic. Other drivers caught in the middle pulled over and out of the way. I had the gas pedal of Julie's car on the floor. Still, there wasn't any measurable difference between Law Enforcement and me. This pitiful little car wouldn't outrun a pack of state police cruisers. I also suspected somewhere down the road, a roadblock awaited, probably the bridge spanning the Patapsco River. That's where I'd set one up if I were chasing myself.

Several more minutes of pursuit proved me right. I could see the expected roadblock in the distance. Law Enforcement set one up on the opposite end of the approaching bridge. I couldn't stop or turn in another direction. In a few seconds, I'd cross the bridge and collide with a barricade of police cruisers. I glanced at Julie, who was now semi-conscious. The car's tires double-thumped as I crossed onto the bridge. It was maybe a mile across. A microsecond glance in the rearview mirror informed me that the pursuing cruisers had backed off. I glanced at the speedometer and barked out a shrill laugh in response. Ninety miles and change per hour, it read. Hitting the roadblock at this speed meant certain death.

Therefore, I did what any sane person would do.

I entered the far-left lane of the bridge and twisted the wheel to the right. The barriers on the right side of the bridge were low, perhaps low enough to jump over. The car smashed into the wall. I could hear the car's front end crumple as the force of the impact with the guardrail sent us ass-end over the bridge. My stomach rose into my throat as the car flipped over during the descent to the river below. The G-force pushed my face into a prune as I failed to calculate the distance of the fall, except to say it happened in slow motion. I watched the river water race up to meet me through the broken windshield, anticipating the collision.

The car engine topping out was the last thing I heard before we crashed into the cold, rushing water. The seatbelt didn't prevent my head from meeting the oversized steering wheel.

"DADDY...STOP!"

>SLAM<

"This is what you get—"

>SLAM<

Into the wall.

"—For not—"

>SLAM<

"—playing the game!"

>SLAM<

Thrown to the ground.

"I love you, son."

Daddy kicks me.

Blackness.

SCARECROW

One sin. Ten people. Twenty-five years later, the bill comes due.

In the quiet college town of Westminster, Maryland, the past refuses to stay dead.

When student journalist Ryan Thomas and his roommate Jarrod Mayfield stumble upon the brutal murder of a beloved professor, they're thrust into a nightmare that stretches far beyond campus. The killer leaves behind two cryptic clues—a crow branded into the victim's forehead, and a note reading only: *Ring me a Porter.*

As Ryan and his friends chase the story for the school paper, they begin uncovering a web of secrets buried for decades—sins committed by the very people they trusted most. Each revelation peels away another layer of safety until Ryan realizes the truth is closer than he thinks...and far deadlier.

Now, hunted by a killer who sees the murders as art, Ryan must face the shadows of his past and decide how far he'll go to stop the next masterpiece.

Dark, relentless, and unforgettable, Scarecrow is a psychological thriller about guilt, vengeance, and the price of silence.

EXCERPT

Ryan ran straight for Tiffany's room. The sound of a struggle emanated from behind the closed door. Ryan didn't bother calling out Tiffany's name this time. Instead, he kicked open the flimsy door.

Tiffany lay spread-eagled on her bed, bound up with duct tape like he'd discovered her in the art supply room. She wasn't wearing pants or underwear. Ryan saw them strewn across the floor.

Her eyes met his. They pleaded for help.

Ryan realized with sickening disgust that he'd interrupted, just as the killer promised for non-compliance.

An individual in black clothing stood at the rear of the bed in a defensive posture. He wore black gloves and a black ski mask with the mouth and nose sewn shut. Behind the mask were black sunglasses that concealed his eyes.

Was this the killer? Was Ryan now confronting the person causing so much trouble in their lives?

Ryan began studying this man for signs of identity. He found no way of identifying this person based on physical features. Ryan determined him to be a male based on the lack of identifiable breasts or feminine curves.

The scene froze as the man in black pulled a gun and aimed it at Ryan. Tiffany attempted to whine beneath her duct-tape gag. He pointed the pistol at her and then swiftly back at Ryan. The intruder studied Ryan and cocked his head in curiosity.

Eeriness crept over Ryan. It overshadowed his fear.

Nothing happened. Ryan and the intruder stood facing each other without saying or doing anything.

"Who are you?" Ryan whispered. The trespasser approached Ryan aggressively, sticking the gun barrel to Ryan's forehead. "Oh, shit!"

Tiffany tried to scream. Ryan felt his knees wobble as if he might faint. He stared into the man's sunglasses. Light reflected off the pupils beneath. Ryan couldn't see color or shape. However, he saw anger and rage within them. "Do it," he whispered, breathing fast. "Just do it!"

The perp backed off instead and walked backward toward the window. He pointed the gun at Ryan as he opened the window, quickly glancing toward the black Honda at the hill's bottom. Ryan realized he meant to jump two stories to the cold, hard ground below. The perp returned his gaze to Ryan. He could feel the hate there even if he couldn't see it. The perp pushed the bug screen out of the window frame. It landed on the ground below with a soft whoosh.

"Hey!" Ryan snapped. The intruder stiffened his arm, holding the gun in Ryan's direction as a warning. "Is it you? Are you Scarecrow?"

The perp cocked his head in curiosity again and lowered the gun. He opened his arms and leaned slightly forward as if to say, 'At your service.' He then climbed out of the window. Ryan rushed the killer without thought for his own safety. The killer raised the gun in response and fired.

Ryan felt the bullet strike his right shoulder. The hit stopped

Ryan's forward momentum. Even though he felt no pain, he screamed and clutched at the wound. Heavy blood flowed from it and through his fingers.

The killer sat halfway out the window and prepared to jump. Ryan found the strength to finish his rush. He screamed at the top of his lungs as he sprinted toward the killer sitting halfway out the window. The killer looked back in surprise. He didn't have time to raise the gun for another shot. Ryan tackled him. They both crashed through the window and fell two stories to the ground.

The impact knocked the wind out of Ryan. His head exploded in millions of white twinkles, each delivering a spear of pain. He writhed around on the cold ground and in the broken glass. Blood flowed out of him in several places as he tried to scream. It came out in gasps and moans.

Ryan rolled onto his front to see the killer. He was already on his feet and hobbling down the hill toward the road. Ryan attempted to stand and give chase. He fell again as vertigo overtook his consciousness. Ryan could see the killer's gun lying on the ground to the right from his vantage point. He struggled to reach it while suffering from cuts from the shards of broken glass beneath him. Ryan threw his arm toward the gun and grabbed it with one finger. He grasped it, lifted it, and rolled to his other side. Gunfire and blinding flashes of white light filled the air as Ryan fired in the road's direction and the car parked there. Ryan couldn't see the killer anymore. His world faded into darkness.

"No," he whispered as he disappeared into a spiraling pool of black.

Tiffany's parents returned ten minutes later.

SCORPION

One man tried to repay a substantial debt. The cost was too steep. Now, everyone must pay the price.

Six months have passed since the Scarecrow killer terrorized Westminster, Maryland—and investigative journalist Ryan Thomas wants nothing more than normalcy.

But when a frightened woman confronts him in a grocery store, claiming to know his late father, Ryan's world shatters once again. Moments later, she's abducted by men posing as government agents.

Ryan's instincts tell him something far darker is at play. His search for answers uncovers a web of corruption, murder, and betrayal stretching back decades—one that ties his father and his father's business partner, Milton Donner, to a West Coast cartel known as the Scorpion Syndicate.

The deeper Ryan digs, the closer he gets to a truth he isn't ready to face. Every revelation threatens to destroy what's left of his family's legacy—and the people closest to him.

When the venom spreads to Westminster, Ryan must make an impossible choice: expose the Syndicate and lose everything…or protect those he loves and become complicit in the cover-up.

Fans of *Michael Connelly*, *Harlan Coben*, and *Linwood Barclay* will be riveted by this page-turning thriller packed with shocking twists, deep emotion, and a finale that will leave you breathless.

EXCERPT

Ryan led Carrie away from the monitor bank in time for one of the upstairs bedrooms, Ryan's old bedroom, to burst into flame. The thought that everything he'd ever owned was in that room danced around the corners of his mind, and it'd all be lost forever.

"What little I know about panic rooms is that the phone, electricity, and air all work on separate systems in case intruders cut the main lines. I'm not sure if those lines are buried or run on different wires in the house."

"It's getting really hot in here," Carrie whispered as sweat trickled down her forehead.

Ryan entered the shower room and turned on the cold water, letting it run with the shower curtain open. Carrie followed, feeling the chill from the water waft from the shower stall. "Does that help?"

"A little," Carrie said, her voice cracking. A massive thud crashed down above them. Startled, Ryan and Carrie snapped their heads up toward the ceiling. "Is that what I think it is?"

Ryan nodded. "The house is coming down."

"Is it getting hotter in here?" Carrie asked, her voice filled with a sadness Ryan had never heard.

"I think so," Ryan whispered. He reached out and stuck his hand into the water stream. "It's still cold. The pipes must run underneath." He reached up to the showerhead and shifted it as far forward as it would go. Carrie watched with interest as Ryan led her into the shower's rear. They sat, letting the water stream over their bodies from chest to feet. "How's that?"

"Better," she whispered. "The heat makes it hard to breathe."

"I know. I feel it too, but listen to me," Ryan said, staring down into her wide, innocent eyes. "We are going to make it. You hear me?" Carrie nodded, avoiding direct contact, revealing her lack of conviction. "As long as the water stays cold, we'll breathe as best we can."

"What if it doesn't?" She asked, her eyes barely lifting from the stall floor.

Ryan encircled her with his arm. She laid her head on his shoulder. "It will."

"Okay," Carrie said listlessly.

Another thunderous crash came bearing down on top of the panic room, hard enough to shake the bunker. "Think about it this way, Carrie. After everything that's happened over the past few days, it can only get better."

Carrie replied with a weak giggle. "I don't remember where I heard it, but relationships that start under intense circumstances never last." She grinned, peeking at Ryan. "I guess we're totally boned, huh, MacGyver?"

Ryan chuckled. "No. Not at all. We'll just base it on sex."

Carrie laughed. "Why did I know you were going to say that?"

"It's from the movie 'Speed.'" Ryan said, pulling Carrie closer. "It's the witty banter between Annie and Jack after they survive the bus exploding."

Carrie nodded vigorously. "That's it. 'Speed.' What a totally awesome movie that was."

"I'll be sure to rent it for you once we're out of here."

Not appearing convinced, Carrie looked down and nodded, though her eyes held doubt. "I love you, Ryan," she whispered. "I thought we'd have all the time in the world together. I didn't want to waste a single second of it."

"I love you, Carrie," Ryan replied. "Why would you say that? We're going to live through this." Another section of the roof fell, crashing down into the bunker. Carrie winced, a small gasp escaping her lips. "Don't give up on me, Scout."

"It's been such a long day," she whispered. "I can't remember the last time I slept."

"Hang on a little longer, baby," he said, feeling the hoarseness in his voice. He wondered if smoke was getting in somewhere. "Okay?"

Carrie smiled and sighed. "Would you have married me, Ryan?"

Ryan stared down at her while she watched the water splash off the tiled shower floor. "Yes," he said, kissing her head. "Waking up to you and staring into your amazing blue eyes is more than I could ever have asked for. Baby, let's not play 'what if' like we're saying goodbye. We're going to live."

"I'd have married you in a heartbeat," Carrie said, tears forming under her eyes. "I'd have totally given you the most amazing reasons to come home to me. I'd have rocked your world every night, staring into your eyes and showing you how much I loved you through them."

"Carrie—"

"We could've bought the beautiful old house on Uniontown Road. You know? The one across Route 31 with the wraparound porch?"

"I know the house," Ryan whispered. "It's a gorgeous old home that needs a lot of work."

"We could've done it together," Carrie whispered. "Fixed it up. Made it ours. Put recessed lighting in the ceiling of that wraparound porch. We'd light it up at night for everyone driving down Uniontown to see. And that huge front yard. We could've planted some new Kentucky bluegrass to make it pop during the summer."

Carrie struggled to meet Ryan's gaze, her eyes red with emotion and silent crying. The tears cascaded down her face. "Our children could've played in that yard—a boy named after your father and a girl named after Tiffany. We'd have bar-b-ques and invite all our friends over—Alan, Elizabeth, Susannah, Ian, and my parents. We could've sat on that porch in rocking chairs, watching the cars pass by and staring into the valley. We could've watched the sun set over Westminster after another amazing day of our lives, Ryan." Carrie sniffled back her sobs, wiping tears from her eyes. "Always thankful I found you, that we found each other. Thankful that we live in such a beautiful small town, I love so much." She glanced up at Ryan. "But no more than I love you. I wouldn't have let you go to sleep without telling you, hitting my knees, and thanking God every day for you and the life we'd have built together."

Carrie's words were bringing Ryan to tears. "I regret bringing you into this, Carrie."

She jerked her head from side to side. "After Lauren and Tiffany, I couldn't have taken another death. No, I don't understand how or why you brought me back to life only after a few days. But you did. Where you go, I go. For better or worse. 'Til death do us part."

Ryan kissed her wet hair. "We're not going to die, Carrie," he said, struggling to take the breath that followed. He wasn't sure he believed his own words.

Carrie buried her face in Ryan's wet shirt and released the sobs she'd held back. "It's okay, Ryan. I'm at peace being with you. Just...hold me. Please?" Ryan pulled Carrie tighter. She held onto Ryan's midsection and wept. "I only wish we could've had more time together. There were so many things I wanted to do with you. And I'm really sorry we won't be able to get to know Susannah better."

Another crash from above struck the panic room near the stairwell. The lights flickered, dimming, and the air filtration motor hesitated.

"Hold on, Carrie," Ryan said, forcing himself to breathe as deeply as possible.

"I can barely breathe anymore," she whispered.

The lights grew dimmer with each flicker until they went out completely, enveloping Ryan and Carrie in unsettling darkness. After gradually slowing down, the motor of the air filtration system came to a halt. The only thing keeping them from slowly baking to death was the cold shower water, which continued to run under its own pressure.

"I love you, Ryan."

Carrie closed her eyes.

ABOUT THE AUTHOR

Kevin Provance was born in Carroll County, Maryland, and grew up surrounded by back roads, ghost stories, and quiet fields that would later become the settings of his fiction.

A lifelong technologist and storyteller, Kevin has worked as a technician, consultant, and WordPress developer, specializing in plugin design and code security. But when the screen goes dark, he builds other worlds—places where time folds, truth bends, and redemption always comes at a cost.

He is the author of the interconnected *Displaced* saga, the Ryan Thomas thrillers (*Scarecrow* and *Scorpion*), and the haunting standalone novels *Prisoner of the Game* and *Fairlight*. Each work unfolds within a shared universe that blurs the line between science fiction, mystery, and human frailty.

Kevin's stories are known for their cinematic pacing, emotional depth, and a touch of darkness that lingers long after the final page.

When he's not writing, he's behind a camera, producing or photographing life under the banners of *Furious Conundrum Productions* and *SVL Studios*.

He currently lives in Summerville, South Carolina.

For updates, release dates, and exclusive content, visit:
www.kevinprovance.com

www.ingramcontent.com/pod-product-compliance
Lightning Source LLC
LaVergne TN
LVHW100507110826
845146LV00002B/544

9798995160212